Masquerade

BOOK ONE

ARIA WYATT

This one's for Krystal Dixon.

You licked Garrett first. That makes him yours.
But remember, sharing is caring and all that jazz.
Thank you for your enthusiastic support.
XO

CONTENT WARNING

Masquerade contains several heavy topics that may be upsetting to readers.

My goal with this novel was to unite two survivors and show the healing powers of love. I won't lie, Garrett and Ella's **backstories** are tough, but I did my best to handle them with care.

That said, only you can determine what is right for you. Before reading, please review the following list carefully.

Feel free to reach out to me via email with any questions that arise. Aria@ AriaWyatt.com

- Adoption
- Alcoholism
- Anxiety
- Childhood abuse
- Cutting
- Depression
- Rape
- Suicide

Masquerade

One

Pineapples, black cats, and a change of plans

Garrett Casey

I'm no dessert connoisseur, but it doesn't take a genius to know he made the wrong decision. Hands down, it should've been a cake. Or maybe an ice cream cone. Hell, even a fucking oatmeal raisin cookie would do. Any of those would've been better options for my client's new logo and web banner. What did he choose? A lame-ass fruit.

Nothing against healthy options, but I'm not a fan of pineapple. It makes the roof of my mouth tingle. Also, since it has absolutely *nothing* to do with the guy's dance studio business, giving his logo some relevance is going to be a challenge. I glare across the counter at the prickly offender, increasingly annoyed by its lack of human characteristics.

How the hell am I supposed to give it realistic limbs?

I hate that it's been like this lately—my creative juices a slow trickle instead of the gush I strive for. With all the hurdles life has thrown in my path, my art shouldn't be complicated. I deserve an easy jump for once.

Yet I'm stumbling.

Obviously, I intend for my client's project to be a unique design, but I need a frame of reference to get me started. A few ideas to percolate in my brain. Sipping my coffee, I envision the talking pineapple from *Téléfrançais*, the TV show we watched ad nauseam in sixth-grade French class. While that was animation, my peers from many moons ago nailed the living fruit concept.

If memory serves me, that bastard's arms were midway down—

A woman's scream from overhead makes me drop my cup. Dark liquid floods the countertop, saturating the design I've been working on. And lucky me, the scalding java I just re-microwaved for the twelfth time spatters onto my lap.

"Son of a motherfucker!" I leap from the stool and peel off my soaked khakis. My inner thigh stings like a bitch, so I shed the boxers to do a quick check of my reddened skin. Luck was on my side for once. Another inch higher, and I would've had boiled chestnuts and a poached kielbasa.

Relieved my naughty bits are unscathed, I shuffle bare-assed to the sink and plunk my empty mug into the basin. It's no tragedy—the coffee was mud after that many nuke sessions. I should've switched to water hours ago.

Better yet, I should've gone to the office.

Today's change of scenery was meant to spark my creativity, or at the very least, recharge my batteries. That didn't happen.

I snatch a nearly empty roll of paper towels and mop up the spill, grateful I was working on a predesign instead of the real thing. I'm the only one in my office who needs a paper sketch to get started, a game plan before I dig out my computer. The inherent lack of efficiency used to piss me off, but this time it spared my expensive equipment from a countertop flood. That's a win in my book.

She screams again, even louder this time, raising the hairs on my arms and the back of my neck.

"Are you fucking kidding me? Don't you people get tired?" I sneer at my ceiling fan as it rattles like some punk kid cranked the bass in his car stereo. Loud music, I could deal with. Hell, I'd even welcome it. This? Not so much.

After I finish mopping up the puddle, I stomp down the hall to put on fresh clothes, muttering to myself the whole way.

My decision to work from home was a soggy, stinging bust. There are few things I hate more than wasted time and energy. Given the chaos awaiting me next week, it's no secret I'm in desperate need of a mental health day. Or seven. Today proves my subconscious would never allow a break, even if I gave it the old college try.

Responsibilities don't go away when you ignore them. The guilt got to me before ten o'clock. Nine fifty-two to be exact.

It's no mystery why I can't concentrate. My upstairs neighbors have been going at it nonstop for days, damn near fucking their furniture through the ceiling. This isn't the first time they've had sex today, and I doubt it'll be the last. I was stupid to think I'd accomplish anything worth merit while listening to their bedroom antics. Of course, my kitchen is beneath their living room, so there's no bed involved—he's probably got her bent over a couch. Either way, I'm over it. I'd call the cops if she weren't my landlord.

Nah, that's not true. Loud fuckery notwithstanding, it would be a dick move to call the cops on my best friend, regardless of property ownership.

Lena Hamilton is my chosen family. I've lived on her building's bottom two floors for the past nine years. She's the light to my darkness. Calm to my chaos. The one person who has never turned her back on me. She's also the only reason I'm alive.

That doesn't mean I want to listen to her having make-up sex—or *any* sex—especially when it affects my focus. It's not that I'm a workaholic. At least, I don't think I am. I just despise lulls in productivity. Time is money, and I'm not in business to lose profit. My quest for perfection has lined my pockets well, so I'm not about to change tactics. If it ain't broke, don't fix it.

My process may have a few cracks, but it isn't broken. I'll keep pushing myself harder, diving deeper into my work, and reaching beyond my limits until I achieve the level of excellence I expect from myself.

Why? Because I don't know any other way to function. Burning the candle at both ends is my standard mode of operation, and until I burn off the tenacity fueling my fire, that's the way it's going to be. Award-winning designs don't create themselves.

Too bad my brain didn't get the memo.

Once in my bedroom, I scavenge the laundry basket full of clean clothes for something to wear. I haven't gotten around to putting them away yet, but it's on my list for today, along with about eleven thousand other tasks. It's fine. I'll get it all done. Eventually.

Sighing, I yank on new boxers and jeans before heading back to the kitchen, armed with a fresh roll of paper towels from the hall closet.

The light fixtures are still vibrating. It's times like these when I kick myself for converting the basement into a gym instead of setting up a home office.

I peel my sopping-wet sketch off the granite and toss it into the trash with the others. They're all shit. Sometimes I question whether I own a design firm or a preschool art center. When I opened Hudson Graphics a few years back, I went from starving artist to successful entrepreneur in no time. But now, I can't draw a pineapple playing the violin to save my life. I've morphed into an amateur who doesn't grasp the color wheel. Forget graphic design and web banners, someone ought to dig out the fingerpaints and my smock. Better yet, give me some macaroni and a glue stick.

One thing's for damn sure: I'm going to need noise-canceling headphones if the coital marathon upstairs continues. Or maybe I'll buy a desk and put it next to my weight bench.

Even if I weren't attempting to work, I'm in the middle of an epic dry spell, so I'd still find their mating calls unnerving. Although I suppose I deserve it. Lena has put up with her share of *my* loud extracurriculars over the years.

Everyone has their preferred coping mechanisms. I can't help that sex dominates my wheelhouse. Maybe it's my all-consuming drive to succeed at everything, but I love making my women scream. So loud, Lena calls my preferred phone-a-fuck "Yowling Yolanda," even though her name is Anya.

Guess what, Leens. Pot, meet kettle.

Another wail rings out, followed by a male bellow.

The fucking dude seriously just roared.

"I've gotta get out of here." I snatch my keys and phone and take off, bounding down the shared front stoop.

With no destination in mind, I scuff through leaves and brambles on the sidewalk. The brisk November wind blasts my back, pushing me along. I make it halfway down the block before a sleek, black cat darts out from behind a trash can.

I sidestep the animal, gripping a spindly tree for leverage. "Whoa, dude. I almost trampled you."

He squints and weaves through my legs, purring softly, like he's thrilled to have my attention. I've seen this cat on our stoop before. He basks in the sun, waiting for the old lady across the street to leave out a can of tuna. Joan is reliable, which is likely why he hangs around. Glancing up and down the block, I wonder if he has a home. Chances are, he belongs to one of our neighbors. He's super friendly, and his fur is too shiny for him to be a stray.

Leaning down, I scratch his head. "Weird day, am I right?" He chirps and rubs his jaw on my hand in agreement. "Must be a full moon or something."

I'm sure talking to animals about moon phases is a sign of insanity. So is wearing a T-shirt in twenty-degree weather, but I always run hot. The fuckfest upstairs certainly hasn't cooled me down, and I've been semihard all morning. Dundee needs to slow his roll before I pop a blow dart into his ass cheek.

My phone rings, startling my feline buddy who scurries beneath a parked car.

"Stay out of the road, okay? Go warm up somewhere." I yank the device from my back pocket and glance at the screen. I don't usually answer unknown callers, but it could be pineapple violin client calling from a different number. If he adds a French horn to the mix, I'm going to lose my shit. "Hello?"

"Garrett. It's Jake Bennett."

The multiplatinum singer-songwriter is a close friend of Lena's new famous actor boyfriend, Wes Emerson, a.k.a. Dundee. She introduced me to Jake at the airport last month, after returning from her forsaken Alaska odyssey.

"Hey, man. What's going on?" I resume my walk at a more relaxed pace.

"Nada. I called to see what you're doing." His rich baritone rumbles through the phone.

I know I saved his contact info, so I'm not sure why it says unknown caller. "Did you get a new number?"

"No. My cell battery's dead. I'm calling from my landline. You working?"

"Not today. Why? What's up?"

"I know we talked about meeting up at my studio on Wednesday, but unfortunately Ella has a scheduling conflict."

Damn.

Today's Tuesday. I've been fantasizing about Ella Sammons since Friday night, when I first laid eyes on the photojournalist at Jake's benefit gala. It's no exaggeration to say she knocked me senseless when I watched her move through the gala attendees, snapping photographs, and rubbing elbows with celebrities and industry moguls alike.

The brunette brought hourglass to a new level, and I swear she painted on her fiery red dress. Forget the plunging neckline, it was the way the material showcased her ass, hips, and thighs that destroyed me. When we finally made eye contact, those vivid turquoise orbs stole my ability to breathe. Ella looked at me—inside me—like she knew all my darkest secrets.

And suddenly, I wanted her to.

"Can she reschedule?" I ask, hoping I don't sound as desperate as I feel.

"That's why I'm calling. What does your week look like?"

"My schedule's kinda insane. I've got work stuff on Thursday. On Friday, I have the official cast meet and greet at our director's place. Next week, rehearsals start."

I recently snagged the lead role in a controversial new Broadway production. Landing the part of Xavier Crane fulfills a lifelong dream of mine, but damn if I'm not disappointed to miss a chance to mingle with Lady Caribbean Sea Eyes.

"I know you're busy, but Ella would *really* like to meet you. It's great publicity for *Prodigy*, and I want her to score the first interview with the dark professor. It's a win-win in my book."

The many ways I'd like for that win-win arrangement to go down flash through my mind. No joke, the woman is sex personified. She can score anything she wants with me.

I tighten my grip on the phone. "Let's make it happen."

"Was hoping you'd say that."

"Is she available next weekend?"

He clears his throat. "I was thinking more like tonight."

I stop in my tracks and glance at my watch. It's noon. "Tonight?"

"Yeah, she's finishing her gala article for the *Tribune* and has some questions for me. She's swinging by the studio at six. Are you free?"

Fuck yes, I'm free.

"Yeah," I say, as nonchalantly as I can manage. "I don't think I have anything going on. I'll double-check when I get home, but it should be fine. I can always shuffle things around if necessary."

"Great. With all the shit that went down at the gala, I never had the chance to formally introduce you. How's that going, by the way? I mean, with Lena and Wes," he clarifies. "Everything seemed copasetic at dinner."

Last night, as part of her "please bond with my boyfriend" campaign, Lena cooked dinner for Wes, Jake, and me. I won't lie, the bonding potential is there—even though it'll be a while before I admit that to Lena.

"Still picture perfect."

"I detect a hint of sarcasm, my friend," he murmurs.

"Dundee's up there deep dicking her right now, if that's what you're asking."

"Sweet Jesus." Jake snorts a laugh. "You really don't mince words, do you?"

"Nope. Like I told you, I'm not Willy Wonka. I see no reason to candy-coat things. Waste of time."

"Then you'll like Ella's style."

"Tell me more."

"As Wes and I mentioned to you last night, Ella can be a little . . . intense."

Intensity is my drug of choice. One might even say I have a zeal for life's crescendos. After spending years beneath the numbing blanket of alcoholism, I've got no use for a muted version of life. My days of apathy are over. Been there, done that.

I toy with the tattered leather band on my wrist. Symbolic of my hard-won sobriety, it's a reminder of the life I left behind and the milestones I struggled to reach. I can't believe it's been nine years. Garrett the alcoholic is still in there, but I beat that fucker back anytime he tries to claw his way out.

I live my life full throttle now, drawn to extremes. I don't have a choice—I need the distraction to keep the cravings at bay. When I can't exorcise my demons with exercise, I turn to sex and fuck them out. If Ella wants high octane, I'll give it to her.

"I'll see her intensity and raise her mine."

Jake's low chuckle tells me he knows something I don't. "Just remember you asked for it."

Two

A breakup, a tormented professor, and the unexpected

Ella Sammons

Damn, it's cold.

I lean against the smooth concrete entrance to NorthStar Studios, pivoting away from the blustery wind with a body-racking shiver. I should be inside, bullshitting with my friend Jake Bennett, but one of my girlfriends called, begging for an emergency vent session. I excused myself for a few minutes to see what was going on.

Alessia Benicasa is the closest thing I have to a sister, and one of the few women I trust. She, on the other hand, has once again proven she's far too trusting. Sadly, her frantic call to inform me about her cheating boyfriend wasn't a surprise. I knew he was bad news the moment I met him, but she couldn't resist the hot Brazilian doctor's charms.

Pressing the phone closer to my ear with chilled fingertips, I struggle to make out what she's saying over her tears and the sirens blaring in the distance.

"I can't," sniff, sniff, "believe I fell for his lies. I'm *such* a fucking idiot."

I shake my head. "Hey. None of that. His dishonesty is a reflection of him, not you. Now is not the time to put yourself down."

"Why do I keep going for the same types of guys?"

"Uh, do you really want me to answer that?" I am the *last* person who should be giving relationship advice—mainly because I've never been in one—but Alessia does have a habit of attracting cocky assholes who use her as arm candy.

"No, don't. I already know what you're going to say. That means my stupid brothers were right. Again."

As the youngest of eight children, and the only girl, there's never a shortage of opinions on her love life.

"It's a good thing they can't hear you saying that," I tease, knowing full well at least three of said brothers would gleefully punch Dr. Dickhead out.

"Good point. Listen, do me a favor. Please don't say anything to Paolo. I know how you guys talk."

"I won't tell him." I shudder against the wind and tug my collar closer to my neck, wondering how I'll keep the breakup news from her eldest brother, a.k.a. my best friend and fuck buddy. "But you may want to let your family know *before* Thanksgiving, so you don't have to deal with everyone's questions about why Alejandro isn't there." *And so I don't slip up.*

She groans loudly. "Maybe I'll just skip Thanksgiving this year."

"Don't you dare. Your mother would be devastated. Plus, you need to help us cook." The Benicasa family adopted me as one of their own when I was a teenager, so my presence—and kitchen help—during holidays is expected.

"Okay, okay. I'll be there. I'm sorry for blubbering. I know I'm interrupting your important interview."

"You're not. The guy isn't due to arrive for another hour. I'm hanging out with my friend Jake."

"The singer?"

"Yes."

"Is he single?"

I laugh. "I think so, but I'm not setting you up with him."

"Why not?" she whines.

"Because you need to focus on yourself for a bit and stop man hopping."

"I guess you're right. I'm quite the springy bitch," she concedes with a giggle. "Anyway, I'll let you go. Thanks for listening."

"Anytime. No more tears tonight, okay?"

"No promises. Ciao."

"Ciao." I end the call and stuff my phone into my pocket before rushing back inside.

The tension eases out of my body as soon as the building's warmth cloaks me. Hurrying upstairs, I reenter the studio and toss my coat onto a hook.

Jake's lair doesn't seem like the appropriate place for tonight's interview. For one, it's too quiet. While I understand the need for acoustics in a recording studio, I hate silence. The stillness reminds me of myself, hollow and lonely.

I'd feel more comfortable on my turf, so I'll suggest we relocate to Paolo's restaurant once my interviewee arrives. A shiver races down my spine at the mere thought of said subject.

I'm accustomed to being around people who are out of my league. As the entertainment photojournalist for the *Tribune*, I spend my time in theaters, backstage at concert halls and arenas, and mingling with celebrities at events for the arts. My ability to work a room, schmoozing and networking with the best of them, has earned me a reputation among New York's rich and famous. Good thing I'm a fake-it-till-you-make-it kind of woman, because it's difficult to develop a rapport with someone when you've got nothing in common. While I'm no Lois Lane, I'm slowly making a name for myself in a cutthroat, male-dominated industry.

Jake is busy reading my article about the benefit gala he hosted on Friday night. The event had an incredible turnout, raising more than enough money to fund the construction of the Phoenix, a Manhattan community center for the arts he has his heart set on.

"This is outstanding, El. Your talent never ceases to amaze me."

"Is there anything you'd like me to add?"

He shakes his head. "No. You hit all the key points and mentioned everyone worth mentioning. *And* you made me look good."

"That's hardly a challenge, dear." I hold up a picture. "You should wear a suit more often. You clean up nice."

His cheeks and ears flush pink. "Thank you."

"It's my pleasure. I'm ridiculously proud of you."

"Means a lot, El." He squeezes my hand. "I appreciate your support."

Jake is a kind, beautiful soul. We met in college, where he starred in many school productions. A budding journalism apprentice at the time, I was there to document his rise to stardom and made it my goal to highlight the best parts of him. We formed a solid friendship and have stayed close over the years. Despite his success, he hasn't forgotten his roots, sending stories and opportunities my way any chance he gets. That's the main reason he wants to introduce me to Garrett Casey, the lead in a revolutionary Broadway production slated to open next year.

Prodigy.

The show's evocative title intrigued me before I even had a clue about the plot. What is a prodigy? I first envisioned a young pianist holding audiences rapt with their music. But I was wrong.

This show is much darker.

The producers have cast Garrett as the brilliant, tormented Xavier Crane, a drug-addicted musical theater professor. Haunted by his past, Crane uses sex and drugs to escape, yet somehow manages to feign an image of normalcy.

My relationship with sex is tumultuous at best. While I've never used drugs, I can relate to hiding behind a veneer—I've done it for over a decade.

Something tells me *Prodigy* is one of those shows destined for greatness, unapologetic in its portrayal of a deeply flawed man seeking salvation. Would I feel this way if someone else scored the male lead? Possibly. Although I have a hunch the casting is what will make or break this production.

Case in point, the female lead provides exactly the strong-woman catnip I crave. Starring opposite Garrett is rising Broadway legend Tess McPherson, who landed the role of one of Xavier Crane's vocal students.

Phantom of the Opera has been my favorite musical since childhood, so *Prodigy's* dark professor theme is up my alley. Admittedly, my enthusiasm for tonight's meeting is a wee bit selfish: scoring the first interview with the up-and-coming male lead will add a few notches to my journalist career belt. Given the depth of the show's subject matter, this may be my opportunity to prove I'm more than tits and ass.

Hopefully.

Objectification notwithstanding, my job has its perks. For one, I was able to get a sneak peek at *Prodigy's* script, and the exposure of the entertainment industry's underbelly floored me. The themes of sex, drugs, and rock and roll have been around for decades, but never has a production attempted to delve into the issues of addiction and mental health in the way this show does.

I don't think people realize the extent of the opioid pandemic's reach. The darkness isn't limited to grungy rock stars and their groupies. *Prodigy* proves musical theater is not immune to the troubles that plague the rest of the industry. I'm excited to see how audiences receive it.

I love storylines which beg a question. In this case, will Xavier Crane's infatuation with his student draw him out of the darkness, or will his desire lead them both down the path to destruction?

I understand the concept all too well. I'm no stranger to rock bottom.

There's something to be said for trauma's impact on a person during their formative years. Our suffering translates into the tapestry we become. My love-hate relationship with power vacillates from titillating to terrifying fast enough to make my head spin. I shouldn't gravitate toward the demons that haunt me, but I do. It's a comfort zone thing. Or maybe I need an intervention. Either way, I'm drawn to *Prodigy's* premise—and male lead—like a moth to a flame.

Something tells me the flutter in my belly has nothing to do with pre-interview jitters. Because I don't get them. My interviews are known to make people squirm, but right now, seated on Jake's piano bench to await Garrett's arrival, I'm the one squirming.

"You okay?" Jake asks.

"I'm fine. A bit nervous maybe."

"Why?" Amusement dances in his warm brown eyes. "Because you think he's sexy?"

My face heats. "Um, excuse me, but I never said that."

"You didn't have to. I saw how you watched him at the gala."

"I don't know what you're talking about."

Forget sexy—Garrett is brutally gorgeous. Jake first mentioned him a few days before the gala, and when I scanned the ballroom full of guests, I knew him instantly. The man filled out his suit like it was made for his body. Glossy black hair, a shadowed jawline, and plush lips didn't hurt. What struck me most were his golden, lionlike eyes and the way he watched me. Intense, unabashed lust mixed with something I couldn't put my finger on. Whatever it was, it pulled me in. As I drew closer, I saw in his eyes elements I recognized from inside myself—yearning and loneliness.

No matter how hard I tried, I couldn't look away.

It disappointed me to see his arm wrapped around the waist of a beautiful woman. I later learned they're only friends. Lena is actor Wes Emerson's girlfriend, and her sudden departure was the reason I didn't acquaint myself with Garrett at the gala.

"Well? *Do* you think he's sexy?" Jake waggles his brows.

"That's neither here nor there." I sit straighter on the bench. "Besides, I'm not interested in anything more than an interview."

"Uh-huh. Keep telling yourself that. Not for nothing, but you're a shitty liar." His phone buzzes from where it's plugged in across the room. He moseys over and looks at the screen. "Oh, wow. He's already here."

My eyes dart to my watch. "Seriously? I didn't expect him to be forty-five minutes early."

"El, with Garrett, you'd better learn to expect the unexpected."

"What does that mean?"

He grins. "You'll see."

I stand and smooth my dress. "Do I look all right?"

"Thought you weren't interested in more than an interview?"

"I'm not." Heat crawls up my cheeks. "Is it a crime to want to look presentable?"

"You always look presentable."

I roll my eyes. "You're not helping matters."

"There's a mirror in my office. Go see for yourself while I let him in," he says with a chuckle.

I hurry across the studio to check my appearance, my stilettos clicking on the hardwood like the rapid tick of my heart.

Or a bomb.

Three

Tulips, a sex fairy, and a femme fatale

Garrett

Patience is a virtue, my ass.

I found a parking spot down the block from Jake's studio, and I've already paced the sidewalk for twenty minutes. This was *after* sitting in my parked Jeep for close to an hour. There's nothing like steering wheel percussion to help you chill the fuck out, and the drum solo in Rush's "Tom Sawyer" is one of my all-time favorites.

The alcohol cravings have been bad lately. I can't fuck my way through them since Anya is away on business. Boxing has been a godsend. Hours spent pummeling my heavy bag have kept the whiskey out of my mouth, but even that's not enough anymore. With the chaos at work, and prep for *Prodigy*, my sobriety hangs on a dangerously thin filament.

Lately it seems everyone's got scissors.

I came so close to cracking open a bottle when Lena was lost in the wilderness. Boxing didn't cut it that time—my bruised knuckles lingered for weeks. Thankfully, Anya was home, or nine years would've gone down the drain. The sickening close call made it abundantly clear I need another weapon to fight the cravings.

I flex my aching hands and rap on the door, then glare at my watch like it's insulting me. Forty-five minutes ahead of schedule doesn't seem too desperate. Maybe.

While I pride myself on punctuality, I prefer to arrive early. It gives me the surveillance advantage, like a military scout on a recon mission, looking for clues. Intel on *what*, I couldn't tell you, but my inner watchtower makes me feel better. At the very least, *I* can be the one who catches someone off guard, rather than the other way around.

I don't do surprises. Spontaneity breeds danger, so I like to know what I'm getting myself into. Preparation is critical in all areas of life. I've learned the hard way that exit strategies and escape plans take time to formulate. One wrong move or misinterpretation and you're fucked.

Literally and figuratively.

My back muscles seize up at the thought. One day I'll slay those demons. Today is not that day.

The studio door swings open, and Jake appears, dressed in dark jeans and a black blazer over a charcoal collared shirt. His messy chestnut waves and stubbled jawline complete the relaxed look.

He grins. "Hey."

"Howdy." I clap him on the shoulder. "Sorry I'm early."

"It's all good. Come in. We're just finishing up."

I follow him into the soundproofed studio, which was designed for stellar acoustics. The eclectic lighting and abstract pieces gracing the walls lend the space an artsy feel. I marvel at the grand piano in the center of the room.

Jake caresses the gleaming instrument as we pass it. "This is my girlfriend, Mona."

"I see she has you all keyed up."

"Well played, my friend. Well played."

"That's what *Moan*-a said."

Jake's laugh echoes through the studio. "It's no wonder Lena spends so much time with you—you're hilarious."

"The psychosis is real."

"Indeed."

"Wanna hear a dirty joke?"

He eyes me. "Is that a serious question? Of *course* I do."

I point to the piano. "What's better than a rose on your piano?"

He rubs his jaw as he mulls it over. "Uh, I dunno, a puppy? Pizza? Cake?"

"Nope." I flash him a grin. "Tulips on your organ."

Jake blinks. "Huh?"

"Stumped you, didn't I?"

"Yeah, man. I don't get it."

"Think about it." I point to my lips, then thrust my tongue against the inside of my cheek.

He doubles over in laughter the moment my blow job simulation registers. "Two lips. My *organ*. Oh, my fuck."

I squeeze his shoulder. "You're welcome."

He continues to laugh as we meander down a short hallway and enter a room that houses recording equipment. Ella leans against a wall, jotting something on a notepad.

She lifts an eyebrow at Jake. "Something funny?"

He points to me. "This guy's a riot."

"Oh? I could use a laugh." Her eyes lock with mine, the Caribbean-blue orbs peering at me with intrigue. A fringe of dark lashes flutters as she blinks. "Do tell."

My lungs keep the air inside them captive. All I can do is stare as the punch line to every joke—and all logical thought—flies out the window. I'd attempt to mime my way through a funny anecdote if I didn't think I'd fall on my ass.

She props her hands on her hips. "Not gonna share the wealth, huh?"

"Nope." I clear my throat. "I'm a greedy fuck."

She smirks and tucks her pen inside her notebook's spiral. "Seems that way."

"Ella, this is my friend Garrett Casey."

She approaches, her gaze never leaving my face. "We didn't get a chance to connect at the gala, Garrett Casey." Her velvety voice caresses the syllables of my name. "It's nice to officially meet you."

I've never seen a woman this enticing, so I take a moment to appreciate the view. She's tied her mahogany-colored hair back in a loose bun, leaving several face-framing tendrils free. A pair of diamond stud earrings sparkle up at me, like winks from a tiny sex fairy ready to enchant the brain right out of my head. Sheathed in a luxe satiny dress, her curves are just as mouthwatering as they were at the gala.

"The pleasure's all mine," I murmur, taking her hand. Electricity courses through my body when we touch. "Red is your color."

Ella strokes her other hand over her hip, then rests it on her thigh, drawing my attention to shapely legs—bare from the knee down to a pair of black patent stilettos. My mind conjures images of her ankles thrown over my shoulders, those sexy shoes near my ears. Cue my *immediate* hard-on. I release her hand and take a step back. Good thing it's dimly lit in Jake's studio.

"I know it's my color." Her full red lips curve into a coy smile and satisfaction lights her eyes, telling me she also knows what she's doing to me. "But I appreciate the compliment."

I want to say something, but the inferno of lust threatening to engulf the room has rendered me mute. My heart's racing and my lungs aren't working. At this point, I can't think because all my blood is pooling in my cock.

I'm so fucked.

This femme fatale will destroy me, shred my defenses, and burn me alive.

And I welcome that destruction.

Four

Vampires, stilettos, and a scarf

Ella

My God, he's pure sex.

Carnality seeps from Garrett's pores and washes over me, tugging me beneath the surface of a lust-filled whirlpool. As the seconds in his presence tick by, it becomes clear I have no hope of resurfacing.

His body is a study of muscles and hard ridges. Power and virility. My appreciative gaze fixates on how his chest and shoulders fill out his white collared shirt, stretching the fabric. He's rolled his sleeves to his elbows, exposing corded forearms I ache to trace my fingertips over. And if that wasn't enough, olive skin and a smattering of dark hair peek from beneath the few buttons he's left undone. Some hedonistic part of me wants to kiss and lick his throat, latch on to him like a fucking vampire.

Oh, yeah, this is dangerous territory.

My eyes travel lower, despite my attempt to control them, and I don't need X-ray vision to know he's got chiseled abs. His waist tapers to lean hips I want to wrap my legs around. The thought unleashes a flood of heat between my thighs.

Now, the preinterview jitters I never get are in full force.

I draw my shoulders back and suck air into my lungs. I try to stand straighter, counting on my trademark stilettos to give me a boost. I wear them because they make me taller. Empowered. Safe. My own pointy security blankets.

But right now? I might as well be barefoot because Garrett towers over me. Even with stilettos, I'm five foot seven at best. He's got to be at least six-three. Big men freak me out, so I'm anything but empowered.

"We haven't eaten yet," Jake informs him. "Are you hungry?"

"I'm always hungry."

"I mean for sustenance. Like, *actual* food," Jake clarifies with a chuckle.

Garrett's pillowy lips curve into a smile, showcasing a set of perfect teeth. "Like I said, I'm always hungry."

Pieces of glossy black hair fall over his forehead, begging my fingers to tangle in them. His jawline is that place between clean-shaven and stubbled. Shadowed, just like his eyes—those amber orbs that drink me in like whiskey.

"There's an Italian place down the block." Jake mentions the restaurant before I have a chance to breathe, let alone think.

"I was about to suggest La Bussola," I say, grateful he's on my wavelength.

Jake turns to Garrett. "Have you been there?"

"No, but I've heard the food's excellent."

"Best Italian food in the city," I blurt out, feeling the need to defend my haven. "I suppose you'd call me a 'regular.' I've been going there for years, and the owner's a close friend of mine."

Garrett tilts his head to the side, eyeing me with an intensity that makes it hard to focus. "Must be an interesting guy."

"What makes you think it's a man?"

"Just a guess."

"Paolo helps me keep my Italian fluent, and yes, he's *very* interesting."

His expression darkens. "All right, then let's pay Paolo a visit."

Jake grabs his wool coat from the back of a chair and shrugs it on. "Sweet. Let's go."

I force my fumbling fingers to button my fitted black peacoat to my throat. This proves a challenging task with Garrett watching my every move. Hell, breathing right now is a struggle.

His scrutiny doesn't falter as he closes the distance between us and touches the end of my teal scarf. "Matches your eyes."

"I know it does. That's why I bought it."

He smirks. "You have good taste."

"I know."

Great. Now I sound like a snooty bitch.

I could have simply thanked him, but I'm not wired to react to his statement with grace. History trained me to be wary of seemingly nice men, so I'm often a little stiff. While I don't know Garrett's motives, I've learned most pleasantries are a vehicle to butter me up before tossing me into the flames. God knows I'm tired of double-entendres masquerading as praise. People who try to disarm me for the sole purpose of crossing my boundaries. Sure, not everyone has bad intentions, but I don't trust myself to know the difference.

I want to be a normal woman around Garrett, but politeness escapes me. Besides, all I can think about is tasting him, kissing his neck. All the impolite things I want to do to him.

Jake gestures to Garrett. "No coat?"

"Nope. I rarely wear one. Too hot."

Goddamn right, you are.

I follow Jake out of the studio. Garrett trails behind me, his shadowed gaze no doubt locked on to my ass. While the attention raises my hackles, I can't help but sway my hips as I walk. Should I be baiting him? No, probably not. Too bad his sharp inhale eggs me on.

And just like that, I flow into the mold everyone's cast for me.

Five

An interview, innuendo, and stormy seas

Garrett

La Bussola is one of those hidden gems, the kind of place that doesn't look like much from the curb. Inside? There's no denying the restaurant's authenticity. Delicious aromas waft from the kitchen, making my mouth water. I can almost taste the herbed breads, garlic, tomatoes, and cheeses that await. Pavarotti serenades us with "Nessun Dorma," the tenor's intoxicating voice caressing the aria as it pours from hidden speakers. I visited the Amalfi Coast during college and everything about this place transports me back to Italy.

"Wow," I murmur, taking in the oil paintings on the walls.

Ella smiles. "Beautiful, aren't they? Paolo's father bought them in Rome."

"They're amazing."

She nudges me. "Wait until you taste the food."

I'd rather taste you.

The maître d' greets us and asks our seating preference. Since Jake wants to avoid any possible fan attention, we opt for a private table in the far corner of the restaurant, passing the bar on our way over there. Like always, I force my attention to the people seated on barstools rather than the glass devils lurking behind. But this time it isn't the booze that captures my attention, it's the bartender. Likely in his midthirties, he's tall and muscular, with thick, black hair and olive skin. His grin transforms his face when he spots Ella.

Must be Paolo.

He makes his way out from behind the bar and kisses both her cheeks. *"Ciao, bella."*

"Buona notte, caro," she replies smoothly, her smile a bit too sweet for my comfort. *"Come stai?"*

"Non c'è male." He hungrily sweeps his gaze over her, then juts his chin at me. *"Un amico?"*

"Sì."

Yes, I'm a friend, motherfucker. Not that it's any of your business.

Lena insisted we take French class in school, and it's been a decade since my Amalfi trip, so my Italian comprehension is mediocre. Funny how this asshole's smug expression and territorial stance translate every word of their exchange. And when he leans in to whisper something in her ear, I hate him even more.

"Enjoy your meals." He's speaking to all of us, but his dark gaze lingers on mine like he's trying to assert his dominance. Little does he know—I've looked into the eyes of a monster—I'm not easily intimidated. My unblinking stare earns me a scowl before he returns to his post behind the bar.

"This way, please." The maître d' ushers us across the dining room to our table, where I settle into a chair with my back to the wall.

My refusal to put myself in a position of vulnerability means I need a clear view of my surroundings, no matter the circumstances. Lena understands my paranoia and always gives me first dibs on seating. I like to consider myself observant, rather than hypervigilant, but history's given me a damn good reason for vigilance. I'm not about to let anyone else attack me from behind. Jake and Ella don't seem to notice, which works for me. I hate explaining my patterns.

The waiter arrives with the wine list and menus. Pointing to the mini chalkboard he's holding, he describes the evening's specials, but I don't hear a word he says.

Ella consumes me.

Candlelight flickers on the contours of her cheekbones as she studies her menu. Dark lashes flutter like a butterfly's wings with every blink. Then she looks up at me with those Caribbean-blue eyes and I can't fucking breathe.

"Garrett?" Jake's voice jolts me from my thoughts.

"I'm sorry, what?"

He flashes a knowing smirk. "I asked if you were getting a drink. They have nonalcoholic beer options here."

"No, thank you."

Water and seltzer are my go-to cold beverages. I don't fuck around with nonalcoholic drinks. They're too close to the real thing; I've got enough temptation in my life.

He nods and peruses the wine list. Jake and I have discussed my alcoholism before, and if anyone understands forbidden fruit, it's him.

After a few minutes, the waiter reappears for our beverage order. Ella and Jake order glasses of prosecco, and I request a water.

"Be back in a few." He heads toward the bar.

Ella eyes me. "So, you don't drink?"

"Nope." Holding up my wrist, I motion to the leather band. "Nine years now."

She nods her approval. "Good for you."

"Thanks. I drank enough for a lifetime. Worked that vice out of my system."

"Have you ever fallen off the wagon?"

"Not yet."

She smiles. "That's admirable."

"It really is," Jake adds. "You should be fucking proud."

"Well, my early twenties were less than admirable, but I'd like to think I'm better for it."

Ella tilts her head to the side. "Is that what drew you to Xavier Crane's character?"

"Is this off the record? I'd prefer to keep my issues with sobriety private."

She makes a lip-zipping gesture. "Of course."

"Yes, there are many aspects of Crane's character I can relate to. His addictive personality tops the list. All of us have some darkness inside, it's simply a question of whether we can keep it at bay."

The waiter returns with our drinks, and Jake requests more time for the food order.

"You make a good point, Garrett," he says. "I've read the script and I think audiences will find Crane's character relatable, even if they don't battle addiction."

"Exactly. We all have our struggles. We all have our vices. Some, we can conquer, while others threaten to destroy us. Xavier Crane showcases the extreme end of the spectrum, which may be hard to witness. Possibly triggering for some." I pause to sip my water, the cool liquid soothing my throat. "But I think if people focus on the bigger picture, they'll find his redemption."

Ella withdraws her notebook. "What got you into theater? Has it always been part of your life?"

"Wait, should we choose our food first?" Jake points to his menu. "I know how immersed you get when you're in interview mode."

"I already know what I want," she tells him. "I don't know why I bothered looking at the menu because I get the same thing every time."

I peruse my options. "Ella, what do you suggest?"

"Chicken piccata, hands down." She frowns and taps the menu. "But it's made with white wine, so you should probably get something different. Their fettuccine Alfredo is also excellent."

"Then I'll have that." I'm not sure if I'm annoyed or embarrassed my alcoholism dictates my food choices, but I appreciate her concern, nonetheless. I jut my chin at Jake. "What are you having?"

"I'm copying Ella." He places his menu on the table, then rearranges his silverware in size order.

"Honestly, you guys could order anything on this menu and be guaranteed to love it. The food here is that good. I consider myself a foodie, and Maria Benicasa is the only person who comes anywhere close to my grandmother's cooking talent." Ella's smile lights up her face. "She's Paolo's mother."

Some petty part of me wants to change my mind, but I don't have any beef with the guy's mother. Besides, I can respect a family business that thrives in the city's cutthroat restaurant scene.

Ella waves the waiter over and places our order in Italian.

I watch him disappear into the kitchen. "Wow. So, you're fluent beyond greetings and such?"

"Yes. Since I was a kid. As I mentioned before, Paolo helped me practice."

I envision the other man teaching her the intricacies of the language and wonder what else he's taught her. Images of bedposts and tangled sheets come to mind, making me clench my jaw.

Focus on the interview, Garrett.

I shake my head to clear it. "To answer your earlier question, I started acting in high school. I had a minor role in *Fiddler on the Roof* and one of the leads in *West Side Story*. I sort of dabbled here and there as I got older."

We chat for a bit about *Prodigy's* plot and how I plan to portray Crane's character. Ella asks thoughtful, informed questions, telling me this isn't her first Broadway rodeo.

"Is acting your passion?" she asks.

"You could say that, yes. It's an escape from reality."

"What is your reality? What do you do for a living?"

"I own Hudson Graphics, a design firm in Manhattan."

"Tell me more about your company."

"I started it about eight years ago. After I sobered up, obviously. We have seven designers, including myself. My buddy Nate is the only other man in the office, and I'm considering making him partner."

"Why?" Ella cocks a brow. "Because he's a *man?*"

Easy there, tiger.

"No." I'm picking up on some hard-core feminist vibes, so I choose my next words carefully. "It has nothing to do with his gender. It's about trust. Nate is damn good at what he does. I know I can count on him to uphold my vision for the company. Besides, he's more organized than me, and his tech aptitude far exceeds mine."

"But you're a graphic designer. Doesn't that imply some degree of tech savviness?"

"Yeah." I chuckle at her attempt to trip me up. She may think she has the upper hand in this conversation, but she's wrong. "I have some techy abilities, yes. But *my* tech skills are limited to design software and a couple of website platforms. Overall, I'm not great with finances and analytics. That's Nate's jam. I'm also a shitty delegator. I'd much rather focus on the hands-on design work and let someone else handle the numbers and administrative aspect."

"So, he's your secretary?"

"No. Nate's a graphic designer who specializes in websites. He also happens to be a numbers guy. Juliana is my secretary. She runs my life and the whole damn office." I smile and sip my water, thinking of the quirky spitfire I employ. "Jules is an angel. I just show up with my crayons."

"And sign the paychecks," Ella reminds me.

"That too. I find the boss role challenging, which makes zero sense."

"Why?"

"Because I enjoy having control in all other facets of life. By enjoy, I mean, *need*. My comfort zone is at the helm."

Jake refolds his napkin. "I understand that better than you think."

"Seems to be a theme at this table," Ella says on a sigh.

"Yeah, control's a huge thing for me. But it's different at work. I guess that's because I'm an artist first. My art itself is a vehicle for control."

"How so?" she asks.

"We all hold some things sacred, right?" I motion to Jake. "He's got the songs he writes. The way he arranges lyrics and melodies. How he commands the piano like it's an extension of his body. Music *defines* him. When people think of Jake Bennett, that's the word that comes to mind."

"Thanks, man."

"Well, it's true." I meet Ella's gaze. "From what I've seen of your work, I think it's fair to say the same concept can be applied to you and the way you tell a story. People equate Ella Sammons with photojournalism."

Some unnamed emotion flickers across her face. She sits taller in her seat and draws her shoulders back.

"I'd say that's an accurate assessment," Jake chimes in. "You've certainly done right by me. I've always loved your writing style." When she doesn't reply, he briefly makes eye contact with me. The look on his face tells me I'm not the only one who notices her discomfort. He gives her elbow a gentle nudge. "Let's not forget your darkroom and digital prowess, my dear."

"Thanks." She flushes and clears her throat, dismissing his compliments like they're gnats buzzing around her head. "Garrett, can you please explain what you mean by your art being a vehicle for control?"

She doesn't like to talk about herself. Interesting.

"Sure. Bottom line, *I* control the quality of what I put out. No one else can do that for me. Not to sound arrogant, but I take a lot of pride in my talent. I refuse to settle for less than perfection." I rub my jaw, hoping I make sense. Although, hearing the words leave my lips makes me wonder if I really am a pompous bastard. "I want my designs—my artistry—to embody those ideals. I want my quality to define me. Also, since my name is attached to anything that leaves the studio, I like to give every client my personal attention."

"Is that even possible?" Ella asks.

No, and that's the problem.

I release a heavy sigh. "It's getting harder as our client list grows. I can't give them my focus if I'm worried about bookkeeping shit, who's on vacation what week, how many sticky notes to order, what pods we need for the coffee maker, or where we're having the holiday party. Especially now. Once *Prodigy* rehearsals are in full swing, I'll really be stretched thin. My team and my clients deserve my best. Taking Nate on as partner will help me give it to them."

"Sounds like a solid plan." Jake straightens the vase of flowers, lining it up with the tablecloth's stripes. "How does Nate feel about all this? Is he on board?"

Chuckling, I lean back in my seat. "He doesn't know it yet. I'm propositioning him tomorrow."

"Sounds kinky," Ella murmurs, watching me over the rim of her glass. "How about your personal life? What do you do for fun?"

Her unexpected transition amuses me. I ponder an appropriate response, since my idea of recreation might be considered unorthodox. Then again, can coping mechanisms really be classified as fun?

My father used to say, "Once an addict, always an addict," and his words ring true. While years of therapy have helped me understand the neural pathways of addiction, those habits never went away. I've simply replaced booze with endorphins, swapping headaches and hangovers for orgasms and an eight-pack.

No one understands the energy I burn trying to stay sober. Or how easy it would be to slip back into my old patterns. I've learned you can't escape the blood you're born with. There isn't a magic cleanse. I've seen the reaper waiting for me in the wings. My dad drank himself to death. Gene pool bloodletting isn't possible, so sex and workouts are my lifeline. I cling to their high like my survival depends on it.

Because it does.

"That's not a hard question, Mr. Casey."

"Maybe in your eyes it isn't."

"We're going to have one hell of an interview, because I'm just getting started," she teases, picking up her pen. "So, tell me, what does Garrett Casey do in his downtime?"

"Physical exertion."

"Like sex?" She scrawls something in her notepad.

"*Not* what I said."

"You didn't have to say it."

"I was referring to boxing and running, but you can draw whatever conclusions you'd like."

"Thank you. I will." Her eyes burn into mine. Jake shifts in his seat, and Ella turns toward him. "I'm sorry, Jake. Am I making you uncomfortable?"

"Who, me? Nope. Not at all," he says unconvincingly. He folds his napkin into a tidy triangle, then rearranges his silverware once more. "Sexual frustration is my jam."

I feel for Jake. According to what I've heard from Lena, his love life is nonexistent because he's spent years pining for a woman he can't have—Wes Emerson's little sister, Isla. Of course, Wes doesn't know that yet, but I have a feeling the shit's going to hit the fan when Isla moves to Brooklyn in December.

The waiter arrives with our meals and more prosecco for Jake and Ella. Refills they didn't request.

She tilts her head to the side, brows furrowing. "What's this?"

"Paolo sends his regards," he explains, setting their glasses in front of them.

"Oh." Ella smiles and waves to the bartender. "Please tell Paolo '*Grazie*' on our behalf."

"Yes, thank you," Jake agrees.

Glancing at the bar, I meet Paolo's espresso-colored gaze. I'm not a violent dude, but when his lips curve into a smirk, I have the overwhelming desire to punch it off his face. Then, the fucker has the balls to wink. I clench my jaw to keep from sneering.

Ella eyes me. "Garrett, are you all right?"

"Oh, I'm wonderful," I mutter.

"All right, Mr. Wonderful, shall we continue then?"

"Yep. Fire away." I stuff some pasta into my mouth. She's right—it's delicious.

"Are you married?"

I finish chewing and shake my head. "Nope."

"Tell me about your childhood."

Jake wasn't kidding when he called her intense. Direct, and without a hint of reserve, her questions aren't questions; they're commands. My need for control wars with my desire to obey, confusing the fuck out of me.

I cross my arms. "Let's skip over that part."

"Why?"

I clamp my lips shut because I'm not going there with her. I've already got enough demons to battle. The last thing I need is my fucked-up child-hood being broadcast to her readers.

She arches a brow. "Are you the strong, silent type?"

"Hardly."

"Interesting. So, you won't discuss your sobriety or your childhood, which I'm assuming must play a factor in why you drank in the first place. What *can* you tell me? Is your favorite color off-limits too?"

"You're quite persistent."

"You have no idea."

Jake elbows me. "Don't say I didn't warn you. I believe you said you could handle it."

"What?" Ella feigns innocence. "I'm behaving."

My gaze finds her mouth, and those plump lips ignite me. She catches me staring and licks them.

And just like that, my cock hardens. Rock hard in a fucking millisecond.

I stare into her eyes. "My new favorite color is teal." My voice is gravelly, deeper than I expect. "And for the record, no one asked you to behave."

"I'll keep that in mind. Especial—"

"My manager thinks I should cover this song," Jake blurts, his voice cutting through the sexual tension like a warm knife in butter. Clearly, there's a reason Wes calls him Cockblock Bennett. He rubs his jaw, then turns his attention to the capers he's lined up on his plate. "You know, broaden my horizons with some foreign language tracks."

A waitress clears a nearby table. I strain to listen over the clatter of plates. "What song?"

Jake moves his fork around, spearing the capers so there's one on each prong. "It's 'Caruso.' This is Bocelli's version, but Dave thinks Austin and I should record it for our album. Austin mentioned maybe switching it up and doing something acoustic."

Austin Pines, the pop star who rounds out the entertainment industry's Three Musketeers, is best friends with Jake and Wes. Lena met the famous trio in a twist of fate that landed her on a retreat at a remote Alaskan lodge—a vacation that nearly cost them their lives. She's been back home for over a month now, but I still can't fathom that I nearly lost her. At least she got a man and some new friends out of the ordeal.

"I say go for it. You said your album's gonna be eclectic, so why the fuck not?"

Jake nods. "Yeah. Maybe."

"Did you ask Emerson for his thoughts?"

"Wes thinks we should take some risks with this album. You know, step outside the box."

Ella nods her agreement. "If anyone can make it work, it's you and Austin. Let me know if you need any help with the Italian."

"Thanks." He stares at the green spheres on the end of his fork, then eats them one by one. "These kinda remind me of olives. I don't like olives. Well, that's not entirely true. I like them better than pickles, but I hate when they have pits. Talk about a choking hazard. That's the same reason I never buy cherries."

"You okay, Jake?" Ella asks.

"Oh, I'm great. Just trying to figure out how the fuck I'm gonna handle Isla living across the street from me." He barks out a laugh. "Without being murdered, that is."

"Wait, who's Isla? Is she someone in the industry?" Ella eyes him. "You haven't mentioned her before."

"That's because she's his forbidden fruit," I murmur, watching him twist his napkin again. I swear, the man's nervous energy could be bottled and sold.

She glances between us. "Can I get some clarification, please?"

"No, she's not in the industry. She keeps a low profile because she's Wes's little sister," he mumbles. "As in, completely off-limits."

Her eyes widen. "Oh boy."

"Right." Jake runs a hand over his face and peers at us from between his fingers. "Oh boy is a fucking understatement."

"Just keep your distance, man. Everything will be all right."

"Let's hope so." Frowning, he pulls his vibrating phone from his pocket. "Excuse me, but I need to take this call." He rises and walks out of earshot.

I turn my attention to Ella, thrilled to have a few minutes of alone time. She's watching me as she sips her prosecco, and the gleam in her eyes tells me she knows she's got me under her spell.

"Now, it's *my* turn." I lean forward in my seat. "Tell me about yourself."

"There's nothing to tell." Her coy smile says otherwise.

"Ah, you're a woman of mystery. I can respect that."

"Most people don't."

"I don't need your life story, but at least give me the basics. Where are you from?"

"California."

"It's a large state. Wanna be more specific?"

"Santa Barbara."

"Wine country. Nice. Does your family still live out there?"

"No. I don't have any family." She studies her red nail polish. "Just close friends."

"That's something we have in common."

She glances at me. "You're an only child?"

"Yep."

"What about your parents? Do they live around here?"

"Nope. Both dead." My statement comes out like I'm announcing something as simple as the weather.

She sighs. "I'm sorry to hear that. Mine are gone as well."

Looks like we have more in common than I thought.

"What happened to them?"

"Uh . . ." She chews her lip and pierces a caper with her fork, mirroring Jake's move from before. "They died in a car crash."

"How old were you?"

"Seventeen." She stares at her plate. "What happened to your parents?"

"Suicide. First my father, then my mother. I was only seven."

"Oh my God." Her gaze snaps to mine and widens in shock. She snags my hand and gently squeezes. "I'm so sorry."

"Don't be." I return the squeeze, reveling in the feel of her silken skin. "It was a long time ago. I've put it behind me."

Liar.

Ella stiffens and releases my hand when Jake returns with a perturbed expression on his face.

He reaches for his coat, shrugging it on. "I'm sorry to do this to you guys, but I have to run. The construction company's owner called about a potential issue with the community center. We need to change some stuff to meet a recent code update. I took care of the check. Again, I apologize for running out."

"No worries, man. Thanks for dinner, you didn't have to do that. Let's touch base next week. I need your opinion on some stuff with the script."

"Absolutely. Also, I need your help with the Phoenix's logo design." Jake smiles and presses a kiss to Ella's cheek. "It's always a pleasure, my dear."

"Likewise, Jake. Thank you for dinner. I'll call you."

We wave our goodbyes to Jake and watch him leave the restaurant, then sit in silence for a few minutes. Every movement is slow and deliberate as Ella eats her meal. It's clear she prefers to savor her food. I like that about her. Haste dulls far too many of life's experiences.

She meets my gaze, her glass pausing midway to her mouth. "Why are you watching me?"

"You're easy to watch. You belong in the spotlight."

"That's coming from a man who's used to being on a stage."

"Maybe I know what I'm talking about."

She smiles and sips her prosecco. "Flattery won't get you anywhere with me."

I lean forward in my seat. "Then tell me what will."

Ella shakes her head. "Let's keep this professional."

"Am I being unprofessional?"

"You're toeing the line."

"Oh?" I cock a brow at her statement. "Funny, I seem to remember *you* drawing some conclusions earlier. Suddenly those don't apply?"

I'm not trying to be a dick by calling her out, but I need to know where I'm going wrong. Maybe it's my relationship with Lena, but I like to think I understand women better than most men. I can usually read them like books, which is why I know she's feeding me a line of bullshit.

She shifts in her seat, toying with a strand of hair. "That's not what I mean."

I've got her flustered now. Good. I like a level playing field.

"All right, then tell me what you mean."

"You ask too many questions." Eyes narrowing, she crosses her arms, and the defensive pose somehow makes her sexier.

"You spend a lot of time deflecting them."

"No, I don't." Fear and vulnerability dance in her eyes, and her faint whisper tightens my chest. "But you said you'd respect me by not asking for my life story."

I lean back in my chair, placing some distance between us. "Sorry. I'll stop interrogating you."

Her posture immediately softens, the tension dissipating as quickly as it came. Level playing fields are great, but I prefer her relaxed because I don't want the night to end. I need more time to learn her secrets.

I take a moment to memorize her curves, from the contours of her cheekbones to her slender neck, and the way it hollows where it meets her collarbone. I ache to trail kisses from the dip in the center to each graceful shoulder, then lick and nibble my way down to her pussy. I could spend hours that way, my face buried between her legs, tasting and teasing her until she screams my name.

"You're staring, again," she murmurs, winged lashes fluttering.

"I'm an artist. Works of art intrigue me." She rolls her eyes, so I add, "It's not my fault you're gorgeous, Ella."

"Don't judge a book by its cover. Believe me, I've got chapters even the devil runs from."

I lean forward once more because I can't help my desire to be close to her. "All the more reason to turn the page."

"You don't want to read these pages." Her chair scrapes the floor as she shoves it back and lurches to her feet.

"Whoa. Where are you going?"

"Home." She slides her arms into her coat, pulling the wool tightly around her. "It was nice meeting you, Garrett."

Fuck, I came on too strong.

I shuffle to a stand, awkwardly stuffing my hands into my pockets. "Uh, let me walk you to your car."

She waves me off. "That's not necessary."

"I insist." We walked to the restaurant from Jake's studio, but she'd mentioned parking a few blocks away. Since my idea of a few blocks means twenty, and I don't like the idea of her walking alone in the dark, it's only right I accompany her. This is one of those times I get to prove chivalry's not dead. Besides, I hate the vibe we're ending our night with. "It's cold out, so there may be ice. I'll feel better knowing you've made it safely to your vehicle."

Ella shrugs. "Suit yourself."

I follow her out of the restaurant, and we walk several blocks in heavy silence, my plan to lighten the mood a total bust.

I consider myself good with words. It may be my hypervigilance, but I can usually read an encounter's emotional barometer with ease. Tonight, I'm flying blind. I have no clue why my questions set her off so abruptly. I didn't anticipate the flip, and I'm pissed at myself for pushing her too hard. I want to say or do something to disarm her, but I'm at a loss. It's rare to meet a woman whose code I can't decipher.

Her heels click on the sidewalk, drawing my focus to the stilettos. How the hell does she walk in them? As we navigate cracks, metal grates, and protruding roots, she moves gracefully, like the impractical footwear is a pair of ballet flats. All too quickly, we reach her car, a red BMW.

She unlocks the door, tosses her purse onto the seat, and peers up at me from beneath her lashes. "Thank you for allowing me to interview you."

The streetlight overhead illuminates flecks of gray in swirling blue-green irises. Her eyes take me to the Wild Atlantic Way on the Western coast of Ireland. Not the color, but what's inside. Turmoil. Like waves crashing on rocky cliffs.

"My pleasure. We should do this again."

"I don't date."

No surprise there.

"Neither do I. It wouldn't have to be a date. Call it what you like . . . or call it nothing."

She pulls her phone from a pocket and unlocks the screen. "Give me your number. Perhaps I can pencil you in sometime."

"I'd prefer ink."

"Your preferences don't concern me."

Ouch. Despite my inner cringe, I rattle off my number, watching her fingertips glide over the screen as she saves me in her phone as "Prodigy." Maybe she knows other Garretts, or maybe she needs a clue to jog her memory about my identity. Neither sits well with me.

"My last name is Casey."

"I know your name."

"Do you plan to remember it?"

"I'm a busy woman, so I can't make any guarantees. We'll have to see where the universe takes us."

"So, uh, I'm gonna be in Manhattan a lot during the next few weeks. Let's align some planets or something." It's corny as fuck, but I don't care. I don't want her to leave without knowing whether I'll see her again. Being close to her has become a sudden necessity.

"Perhaps." Ella surges up to her tiptoes and presses a kiss to my neck. Her warm, soft lips on my skin steal my breath, but she's in the driver's seat before I can react.

Door slamming, she cracks the window and studies me from behind the safety of the glass. "I'll call you . . . if I feel the need to swing into your orbit."

Then, she closes the window and speeds off, leaving me alone on the sidewalk.

I stare after the car, reeling from her abrupt departure. We went from a kiss to squealing tires in a matter of seconds. She crashed into me—just like a wave—and her retreat swept me away.

Yeah, I'd like to paint, draw, and sculpt her. But most of all, I want to calm her stormy seas.

Or drown in them.

Six

Truth serum, a proposal, and a lie

Ella

I pride myself on my ability to function with detached professionalism. The arm's length approach has never failed me.

Until tonight.

I chance a peek in my rearview mirror as I speed away. Garrett is cemented to the sidewalk, staring after my car like I slapped him. I can't see his eyes, but I know the confusion in those golden depths. I saw it at dinner, each time I deflected him.

I'm the one with a journalism degree. I don't know who he thought he was, trying to interview me like that. A little voice inside reminds me he was only asking for basic demographics, but even that felt like the third degree. I'm aloof for a reason. Perhaps a little frosty at times, but I never claimed to be an extrovert. I can mingle with the best of them when an encounter is work related. Real-world interactions? It's no secret my conversation skills leave a lot to be desired.

Still, leaving him in the dust was by no means appropriate. Forget socially awkward, my behavior tonight was erratic. Abnormal even for me. I'm sure Jake—my predictable, innocuous friend—noticed I wasn't able to hold my own, even with him as a buffer.

Garrett charged the evening with uncertainty. Especially once we were alone. I don't know how to act around a man whose presence feels like truth serum.

What I find most unsettling is the force of my attraction. The man's aura is a fucking aphrodisiac. His energy makes me want to throw myself headlong into his orbit. Cosmic bedroom encounters included. Of course, I'm so far out of my element, there's no guarantee I'd be capable of handling the physical connection I crave. Closeness leads to vulnerability, and I've made it my life's mission to avoid that at all costs.

So why do I want to turn this car around?

How can I *want* to be vulnerable with a man I don't know?

Because you're not normal.

My fucked-up relationship with intimacy has proven the reciprocity of normal emotional bonds escapes me. I stopped trying years ago.

Trauma has a sneaky way of thieving normalcy. Some wounds never heal, they simply fester, leaching their poison into your soul. Mine is steeped in a boggy wasteland of bitterness, regret, and shame. My anger flares with every slight—real or imagined—because the pain of my loss is never too far from the surface. Sometimes, the loneliness makes it hard to breathe. Other times, the self-disgust takes over. If I could peel off layers of my flesh, it would be in a pile at my feet. No one should have to go through what I endured. Or cope with the aftermath.

Maybe it's because I get the feeling he's just as fucked up as me, but Garrett is an enticing change of pace.

There's something magnetic about him, some element that draws me in, no matter how hard I fight it. Something that tells me to take a step closer. Is it his eyes, the golden orbs that see right through me? Or is it the way he carries himself with such fluid potency? I swear, the man infuses his every move with a smooth confidence that promises sex.

Despite my uneasiness, my attraction has only intensified since our conversation this evening. It goes beyond the physical. He's vulnerable too. His eyes reflect a kindred pain. Like there's a broken, haunted part of him reaching out to my soul. Whatever it is, I can't deny him, and that terrifies me.

My phone rings, and I pull it from my purse. "Hello?"

"Bella . . ." Paolo murmurs, drawing out the nickname. "You didn't warn me you had a date."

"It was an interview."

"Looked cozy once Jake left. Who was that guy?"

"His name's Garrett Casey. He's the lead in the Broadway show I told you about." There's a crash, then muttered curses in Italian. "You all right, caro?"

"Yeah. Angelina dropped a tray of glasses. Let me go so I can help her clean it up."

Angelina is the only one of his employees I don't like—and not just because she wants him. There's something about her that rubs me the wrong way. I don't trust her. I've been telling him for years, but he doesn't listen. Paolo has a soft spot for young Italian women with troubled pasts.

"Be careful with the glass," I warn.

"Will do, bella. Be careful with Grady."

"It's *Garrett*."

"Whatever. I don't like him."

"I'd expect nothing less from you."

Another crash. "Jesus Christ!"

"She drop something else?"

He sighs. "No, it was Gio this time. He *thinks* he's helping. I'm losing my goddamned mind. Please marry me and help me run the place."

La Bussola is Paolo's livelihood and his pride and joy. His parents have been visiting family in Italy for a few weeks, leaving him to play bartender, host, chef, and waiter. Thankfully, they're due back home before Thanksgiving. His brother Giovanni is there tonight, but it doesn't sound like he's much assistance.

"We've been over this. For the twentieth time, no. I'm not marrying anyone."

"Was worth a shot."

I change the subject before he lectures me about the tax benefits associated with marriage. "Have you talked to Alessia today?" I know it's dangerous territory, but I need to know what he knows about his sister's breakup, if anything.

"No. Why?"

"Oh, uh . . ." Feeling slightly flustered about having to keep a secret from him, I scramble for a good excuse. "Just wondering if she mentioned helping out at the restaurant until your parents return?"

There. That's believable.

"Are you kidding? My mother would *kill* me if I distracted the Benicasa family's future doctor from her studies. She already grilled me when I suggested the idea before they left for Calabria. 'School comes first, Paolo. She's under a lot of pressure.' Like I'm fucking *not*? Whatever," he mumbles. "Besides, it wouldn't work. My sister is too bossy to be in the kitchen with me."

"And Gio isn't?" I ask with a laugh, knowing how much the boisterous firefighter loves being in charge.

He snorts. "Oh, he's bossy all right. And he's about as helpful as tits on a bull."

"Thanks for the visual."

Paolo's deep laugh makes me smile. "Anytime. Now, let me go. Pretty sure something's burning. Ciao, bella."

"Ciao." I hang up and sigh, wishing I could embrace the idea of marrying him.

Our relationship is complicated due to my hang-ups, yet simple because he accepts and understands them.

Paolo is my closest friend, my refuge. He and his family helped me get on my feet after my tumultuous first few years in this country. He's also a frequent bed partner—the only one for years. He knows my past and understands my limitations, even if he's not thrilled with my conditional approach to sex. I keep telling myself we should stop sleeping together, but he's the only closeness I get. It's hard to surrender tried-and-true comfort, so I cling to him—and our bond—for dear life. Still, my gut tells me my selfish habits are unfair to him. He deserves a nice woman to settle down with, not a broken shell like me.

I pull into the lot outside my Manhattan apartment building. I've lived here since I was seventeen, when I moved into Paolo's great-aunt's apartment after she was transferred to a nursing home.

Snatching my purse and notebook, I head inside, determined to finish this article before bedtime.

My paper's theater column is the city's go-to for information on Broadway shows and off-Broadway productions alike. Lately, the theater scene has become stagnant. It aches for some broken barriers and ruffled feathers. *Prodigy*

is exactly the shake-up people don't know they need. I have no doubt Garrett will command the audience's attention, just as he did mine.

The piece on *Prodigy* was surprisingly easy to write, but now I need a visual aid. Thankfully, I snapped dozens of pictures at Jake's gala. Settling on my couch, I scroll through the images on my computer, seeking one that captures the essence of Garrett.

My gaze lands on a photo of him with Lena at a cocktail table. *Perfect.* I zoom in and crop the image, leaving him as the sole subject. This one highlights his eyes. A striking gold, like those of a lion, they possess and unravel me with just a glance. Beyond their beauty, Garrett's eyes are a window to the immeasurable pain churning within.

Whereas I'm an orphan by choice, his parents *chose* to orphan him when they committed suicide. My heart clenches at the thought of him as a lost, broken little boy. Tears brimming in his eyes as he ached for the two people who were always supposed to be there. How could they do that to him?

The guilt squeezing my chest is a stinging reminder of my hypocrisy. When it comes down to it, I'm no better than them. I also left my child behind.

The usual wave of pain crests, threatening to spill over as memories float to the surface. I wrap my arms around my abdomen in a futile attempt at comfort. It didn't have to be this way. I chose my hollow existence. Rather, four years without agency decided my path. I know I chose the right direction, but sometimes, when the phantom flutters keep me awake at night, I wonder about what could've been.

It was for the best.

The unbearable ache tells me otherwise, but I cling to notions of selflessness like they can erase what happened. Who am I kidding? My truth still haunts me, even after thirteen years. I feel it every time I shower, my soap-covered hands gliding over my scar and the stripes on my softened belly. Each glimpse of my naked body reminds me of my loss.

My parents drift through my mind again. I hate that I lied to Garrett about their deaths, but it was easier than explaining my reality. My mother may still be breathing, but she's been dead to me for years. As a person who *lost* his mother so tragically, I doubt he'd understand my decision.

Paolo knows my reasons, and claims to understand my pain, but I have my doubts. How can he fathom what I went through when his childhood was perfect? He has a big, beautiful, loving family, full of warmth and security.

Despite their occasional good-natured bickering, everyone works together and supports each other. His only trauma is that he has no trauma.

In an ideal world, we'd be great together. We both know it, which is why he's constantly proposing to me. Yes, I love Paolo. The problem is I'm not *in* love with him. I've tried to deepen my feelings, but I can't move beyond what we share in the bedroom. You can't force what you don't feel. Great sex is not the same as true love. No matter how hard I wish it were a reality for us, I won't disrespect him by faking it. A piece of the puzzle is missing for me. It's fucking tragic when I think about how lucky I am to have his attention.

Even if I could summon those feelings, his family dynamic is so far from what I've experienced, the differences are insurmountable.

He has seven siblings, while I'm an only child.

His father is the family's steadfast patriarch. My father died in a Rome car crash when I was two. Mr. Benicasa is known for his hilarious anecdotes. Everything I know of my dad came from my mother's stories.

Paolo's mother is a spitfire, known for how deeply she loves her family. My mother is a shell of a woman, destroyed by her husband's death. Mamma allowed her heartache to infuse every part of our lives.

That all changed when we moved to America after I turned eleven. My mother's fresh start was only the beginning of my nightmare.

Seven

Constellations, nachos, and a marionette

Garrett

Alcohol cravings have nothing on this.

I lean against my Jeep's cool leather interior and toy with the keys in my lap. My neck still tingles from Ella's kiss, even after sitting here for an hour.

I can't believe she left me on the curb. I've always rolled my eyes at the idiom of someone stealing one's breath, but when I stood on that sidewalk struggling to breathe, it gave the words new meaning.

Staring through the moon roof at the night sky, I trace constellations with my eyes. Like Orion, I'm on the prowl. Ella awakened something inside me, some primal lust that heats my blood. I want to take her to bed and make her scream in ecstasy. I moan aloud at the image of her writhing beneath me, absorbing my thrusts. Clawing my skin and giving it back as good as she takes it. My dick's already hard with the fantasy.

One night in her presence tells me she's no ordinary woman. I know damn well she'll elude me. Her coy response to my suggestion of a second meeting made it clear she has no intentions of making it easy between us.

That's all right, I like the chase.

The hunt.

Who am I kidding? I'm the hunted, not the other way around. If my recollection of the myth is accurate, the huntress Artemis far surpasses Orion's prowess. Ella will bring me to my knees.

I haven't fallen since Carissa. I entrusted my ex-girlfriend with my heart and soul and genuinely believed she was meant to be my wife. She was everything I ever wanted. Or so I thought. Carissa's abandonment was the ultimate betrayal. I thought I knew her. Turns out, I didn't just have the wool over my eyes, I had the whole fucking sheep on my head.

I beat back the memories of our fallout, suppressing my torment like always. No matter how deeply I bury it, my pain won't go away. In the past, I learned to self-medicate. Now that alcohol's out of the picture, strenuous exercise and casual sex are my drugs of choice.

Right now, neither appeal to me.

I don't have the energy for boxing, nor do I want to "phone-a-fuck" as Lena calls it. She's not a fan of my *sexcapades* or the *harem* I keep in the wings. That's the only aspect of my life she doesn't understand. She envisions me as a man slut, when in actuality, I have a couple of trusted friends with a mutual need for unattached sex.

I've known Anya and Lisa for years and see them whenever one of us needs some connection. The ladies reach out from time to time, but thanks to my insatiable appetite for sex, I'm usually the one making the booty calls. However, Lisa's new boyfriend and Anya's work schedule have landed me in a bit of a dry spell.

Anya only lives a few blocks away. She's my favorite bed partner. I've known her longest and she's been a critical part of my recovery. She's also my AA sponsor, so our sexual relationship is highly unethical. Maybe I'd have a firmer grasp on ethics if my parents stuck around. But they didn't. So, here I am, unscrupulous personified. Fucked up and horny.

When the alcohol cravings hit—and sometimes they hit hard—Anya's my go-to girl. She knows how I like it and gives me the high-octane release I need. *You feel the urge to drink, you call me, and I'll work it out of your system. Don't let yourself go down that rabbit hole. I'll give you what you need.*

Her body has saved me from alcohol on countless vulnerable nights. Like me, Anya doesn't do emotional connection. She likes to fuck, hard and dirty, and she has what it takes to soothe the beast inside.

But right now, it's not Anya or Lisa on my mind. The woman I desire left me in the dust.

I clench my hands on the steering wheel to keep from texting Jake for Ella's contact info. I'm not *that* desperate. She has my number. I'll have to wait to see if she reaches out. Too bad I hate waiting as much as I hate to *feel*.

I shove my keys into the ignition and head back to Brooklyn. I don't bother with the radio this time because I'm not in the mood for steering wheel percussion. There's enough noise in my head.

After making the trip on autopilot, I'm mildly surprised to pull up in front of the brownstone. It thrills me to find a close parking spot because that shit never happens.

A lamp illuminates Lena's living room. I glance at my watch. It's nearly eleven—she's never up this late. With heavy limbs, I trudge up the stoop, pausing when a soft mew alerts me of my cat friend's approach.

I glance over my shoulder, spotting him on the sidewalk. "You, again. Twice in a day, huh?" He perches himself on the bottom step and stares up at me like he's wondering where I've been all night. Oddly, I feel the urge to explain. "It wasn't technically a date, but it could've been. *If* I were the kind of guy who went on dates. But I'm not. So, it really doesn't matter. Anyway, she's . . . interesting."

Moonlight glints off his eyes. He slow blinks, and if I were one of those animal whisperers, I'd swear he could understand me.

I shake my head to clear the thought. I'm not *that* crazy.

Yet.

"See ya later, dude. Go catch some mice or something." Unlocking the door, I wave at the cat and let myself in. My phone vibrates in my pocket the moment I cross the threshold.

I yank it free in hopes it's Ella. No such luck.

Lena: You're home early.

Me: You're up late.

Lena: Just finished a movie. So?????????

I chuckle and make my way into the kitchen, stuffing the phone back into my pocket. I know it comes from a place of love, but my best friend is relentless with her quest for details. Lena wants me to open my heart again and settle down, but my reality doesn't breed happily ever afters, and I have no intention of settling down. Thanks to my parents and Carissa, the walls I've built around my heart are impenetrable.

Am I lonely? Not really. I keep myself too busy to be plagued with loneliness. No one can hurt me if I don't let them in.

And I'll die before I let someone do what *he* did.

Every muscle in my body tenses on instinct, as searing pain travels down my back, nearly bringing me to my knees. My past closes in on me, and I sag against the fridge and force myself to breathe.

That's the thing about suppressing your trauma. History is never too far behind us. You can't predict when it will seep through the cracks.

Don't go there.

It's over.

They locked him up.

I repeat the mantra in my head, drawing from my deepest self-preservation reserves.

I'm safe.

He can't hurt me.

My phone buzzes in the distance. It takes a few minutes before I'm able to drag the thing from my pocket and unlock the screen.

Lena: Don't leave me hanging.

Me: I'll be over in a few minutes.

I plop the phone on the counter and grab a seltzer from my fridge, then head upstairs to Lena's place, forcing a calm I don't feel. I refuse to put a damper on her night with my mood. I'm Garrett, the rock. I'm supposed to be strong. Unbreakable. I may crack, but I don't crumble anymore.

I let myself in using the key she made me years ago. "Honey, I'm home."

"You hungry?" she calls from the kitchen.

"Not really, thanks." I make my way toward the living room.

"Too bad. I made a boatload of nachos and you're gonna help eat them."

Giving a salute she can't see, I greet Wes, who's lounging on the couch. After watching so many of his movies on the big screen, it's surreal having him in my best friend's living room, dressed in a white T-shirt and pajama pants like an ordinary guy. With messy, sun-kissed hair, bronzed skin, and a laid-back vibe, Wes is your typical surfer dude.

Except when he's not.

I've been up close and personal with his hotheaded alpha side too. Nearly kicked his ass after the gala. In truth, he may have kicked mine, but I'll never admit that aloud. At six-five and two-forty, the guy is shredded. His weight training surpasses mine, but I've got boxing and an MMA background in my corner. He'd be a worthy opponent in the ring.

Lena keeps him in check though. She doesn't take his—or anyone else's—shit, which is one of the things I love most about her.

"Bossy, isn't she?" Wes says with a smile.

I shrug and plop onto the couch. "Eh, I'm used to it."

"Heard that," Lena informs us.

He smirks. "And she's got ears like a bat."

I nod. "Unless it's something she doesn't wanna hear."

"A valid point."

She enters the room with a steaming plate of nachos. "Heard that too. And bats use echolocation, thank you very much."

My mouth waters at the sight of the meat and cheese she's piled on the chips. "Jesus, that's beautiful."

Lena doesn't fuck around when it comes to nachos. Make that, *any* food. As one of those women who gets stabby when she's hungry, she takes nourishment seriously. I'm talking quality ingredients and skilled cooking. There's never a bland dish, or a recipe with corners cut. Over the years I've learned the secret to making her happy is keeping her fed and killing spiders. Hopefully Emerson gets the memo.

She sets the plate on the coffee table and settles in her favored couch spot, the epitome of cozy with her yoga pants and woolen socks. Her long, caramel-colored hair is tied back in a loose braid. She draws her knees up, tucking them beneath the oversized T-shirt she's wearing. It's Wes's shirt. Despite a closetful of clothes upstairs, I know she wears it to be closer to him. It's a sweet reminder of their bond.

Yet, as much as I love seeing her happy, I can't help the pangs of jealousy ricocheting in my chest. I've never experienced the kind of affection where you want to wrap yourself in the other person.

She watches me closely, her jade eyes flashing. "Okay, spill it."

I play the idiot. "Spill what?"

"Oh, c'mon, Gar, don't hold out on me. I've been waiting to hear about your dinner for *hours*."

"It's true," Wes says. "She kept peeking through the blinds every time she heard a car pull up."

I grin and nudge her. "I'm glad you're so invested in my life."

"Someone needs to be. Now, gimme some deets."

Wes laughs and drapes his arm over her shoulder. "Give the bloke a break. He just walked in."

"And your point? Pretty sure I've been waiting all night." She slaps my knee. "Speak unto me, child."

"Yes, your queenship." I give her a mock bow, then make her wait a little longer because she's fun to fuck with.

Wes flashes me a broad grin. "C'mon, you'd better tell us before she loses her bloody mind."

He gets a kick out of our dynamic. Mainly because he also enjoys fucking with her. And fucking her, apparently.

"She can wait while I gather my thoughts."

"Not gonna lie, I'm *also* curious to hear what you think of Ella Sammons."

Where to begin? Shaking my head, I shove a fistful of nachos in my mouth, eyeing him while I chew.

"Yep, I'd say that's a typical response to her."

I swallow my oversized bite. "What do you mean by that?"

"Austin calls her 'Ella the enigma,' and it's so true. She's a walking, talking mystery." He bites into a nacho and holds up a finger telling me to wait.

Austin Pines is based out of Memphis. I don't know him well, but he seems cool. Lena speaks highly of him. If given a choice of which celebrity I prefer, Jake wins. Hands down. He's a fellow theater guy—and Brooklyn resident—so we hit it off right away.

Then there's *this* dude who fucks my light fixtures off the ceiling. Yeah, jury's still out on him.

Wes finishes chewing and clears his throat. "It's fair to say anyone in the entertainment industry who's attended events in New York, knows who Ella is. At the same time, no one really *knows* her. Not even Jake, and they've been mates since college."

"How well do *you* know her?" I probe, not entirely sure I want the answer.

"I met Ella eight years ago, around the time the first *Olympus Fire* movie released. I've seen her at dozens of events, both work related and recreational, but still know little about her. I've tried to engage her in conversations, ask questions about her life, but she always deflects the attention back onto me. Once, I told her, 'Ella, stop interviewing and *talk* to me' but she shut me down," he answers, reaching for a water bottle. He swallows a gulp. "She's the queen of deflection."

"Yeah, I noticed that tonight. She answered most of my questions with one word and zero elaboration. All I know is she's an only child and her parents died in a car crash."

"That's more than she's ever told me, so that's a good sign for you. Like I said, she's pleasant, but not forthcoming. She keeps everyone at arm's length. She never appears in any photographs, and I've never seen her with a man, other than when Austin's cousin made an unsuccessful attempt to date her."

"Oh?" I say, around a bite of nachos.

"Lance works for a film company that contracts with her newspaper. He's engaged to someone else now, so I'm assuming he lost interest. Anyway, he followed her around like a lost puppy for months, but she barely gave him the time of day. She didn't lay a finger on him, not even a peck on the cheek, which is odd, given the way she carries herself."

"How does she carry herself, Wesley?" Lena chimes in with a dangerous arch to her brow. Wes grins but doesn't speak. She sighs. "I've met her, so I already know the answer to that. Ella's sex on legs."

"Leens, chill. He's on *your* couch right now." I turn to Wes. "If you haven't noticed, someone has a jealous side. Tread carefully."

Wes laughs. "Oh, I've noticed."

Lena sticks out her tongue at us. "Gimme back those nachos."

"Not a chance. Wes, tell me more."

"I wish I could give you more, but she's a mystery to me. I've noticed men seem to freak her out though. Or maybe it's just me who makes her nervous."

Lena snorts. "Because you're loud and like eight feet tall. You've gotta admit, you're a tad on the intimidating side, Ace."

"Please. Everyone knows I'm harmless. *Unless* there's a threat to my loved ones."

I gesture to Lena. "I can relate. Hence my hypervigilance."

"Right." Wes straightens. "I consider myself a people watcher. I've seen Ella flinch on more than one occasion when a bloke raised his voice or got too close to her."

Now that he mentions it, I remember her change in demeanor when we questioned her at the gala.

"From what I gathered, she had a terrible childhood, which makes sense now that I know about the car crash. Jake would be a better source. He's known her longest."

"Yeah, I figured. But I didn't want to come across as desperate."

"Did you get her number?" Lena asks.

"No, but she took mine."

Wes drums his fingertips on Lena's knee. "That'll be the true test. If she calls you, she's interested."

"We'll see," I mutter.

"Just be careful with her, mate. She's nice, but I sense a darkness in her. Like I told ya the other night, she's a master puppeteer when it comes to men. I'd hate to see you tangled up in that. Don't allow her bedroom eyes to steal your wits."

I meet his gaze. "It's a little too late for that."

Eight

A liaison, donuts, and a mission

Ella

"So, what you're saying is, you think he's fuckable?" Alessia asks, and I can only imagine the mischievous gleam in her eyes.

I called to see how her pharmacology exam went, and we've been chatting for about ten minutes. During that time, I briefly filled her in on last night's interview.

"Extremely fuckable." I press my knees together and clutch the edge of my desk at the mere thought of sex with Garrett. "In fact, he's the *definition* of fuckworthy. Seriously, he was so gorgeous, I couldn't think straight."

She laughs. "Good. Don't think. You do too much of that."

I look up at the sound of my boss's knock, and heat crawls up my cheeks. *Busted.* "Shit. Gotta go. I'll call you later." I hang up and straighten, praying he didn't hear what I said about Garrett. "Hey, Harvey."

"Hi, Ella. Do you have a minute?" He leans against the doorframe with a smile. "Or if you're busy, I can stop back later."

Harvey Watson is easy to work for because the man is always cheerful. He's got eye crinkles and laugh lines permanently etched into his features. Beyond that, he's considerate and respectful of his employees' time and boundaries. That's a big deal for me, after years of having my boundaries exploited.

My photojournalism gig allows me to nurture my creative side, while still preserving my veneer. I can experience—on my terms—the social interaction I so desperately crave. When it gets to be too much, I retreat behind the barrier of professionalism. There's safety in my position behind the lens. The *Tribune* is my haven in the industry. Mostly. Too bad my paper's upper echelon doesn't share my immediate boss's level of respect.

"Now is totally fine." I point to the phone. "Sorry about that. I was just chatting with a girlfriend."

"No worries. You're entitled to a break."

"Thanks. What's up?"

Warm brown eyes peer at me from behind his wire-rimmed glasses. "For starters, I wanted to compliment you on your article on Jake Bennett's gala. Superb reporting, as always."

I feel myself flush again. "Thank you. Jake is a good friend of mine. I was happy to be there."

"With all the money he raised, he'll have the Phoenix up and running in no time."

"That's what he's hoping for."

The community center is Jake's passion project. I'm incredibly proud of his vision.

"So, I wanted to see if you'd be interested in doing a series of stories tracking its progress? Maybe a column every few weeks or so?" He rubs his salt and pepper goatee as he speaks. "I know it's not technically entertainment, but since the center will be a haven for the arts, I think your readers would embrace it. I'd really like for the *Tribune* to do our part to raise awareness of a worthy cause."

"I'd love that."

He smiles. "I figured you would. Also, Jake approached me about making you the Phoenix's official press liaison. He'd love for you to interview some of the staff, as well as the kids who earn membership grants and sponsorships. And, well, you *know* how much I love seeing kids involved with the arts, so I may or may not have already agreed to your participation on this one. I hope that's okay?"

I couldn't stop my smile if I tried. "Tell me when and where."

The thought of authoring a meaningful story, instead of the superficial crap I'm used to, infuses me with giddiness. Not to mention, the assignment involves hanging out with Jake, whom I adore. I'm sure he'll pack the Phoenix to the brim with talented mentors and mentees alike.

"I'll let you coordinate directly with Jake, if that works for you."

"That's perfect. Thank you, Harvey."

"You got it. Hey, I meant to ask, how was your interview with *Prodigy's* lead?" He points to the camera bag on my desk. "Did you get any pictures?"

The mention of Garrett has my heart rate accelerating. I still haven't recovered from last night.

"No, I didn't. We just talked."

"What's his story?"

Good question.

I clear my throat. "Mr. Casey seems like a passionate man. He has some theater background, but his career is in graphic design. He owns Hudson Graphics in Manhattan."

Harvey chuckles. "No kidding. They maintain the *Tribune's* website. They've got a guy over there who's a real whiz with that kind of thing. He's helping to digitize us."

"Small world," I say, fiddling with my necklace. I wonder if he's the guy Garrett mentioned, and whether he offered the partnership yet. Then I wonder why I care. "I'll send you the article when I'm finished."

"Sounds good. Enjoy your afternoon. Oh!" He flashes a devious grin and rubs his hands together. "Someone brought donuts. They're in the break room if you're interested."

I raise a brow at him. "I certainly hope you abstained, Harvey Watson."

The man has a sweet tooth that rivals mine. Sadly, he was diagnosed with Type II diabetes last month. I've been on his case about adhering to his new low-carb diet. My missive is clearly a lost cause.

Harvey pats his plump tummy. "No comment."

"You won't be saying that when I tell your wife."

"I can't hear you," he singsongs, scampering from my office, likely back to the break room for another treat.

I love that man. I'm fortunate to finally have a direct boss who appreciates my work, instead of reducing me to tits and ass like my previous employer. And every other man out there.

Curling my lip at the thought, I reach for the *World's #1 Reporter* mug Paolo's mother gave me. I sip my coffee, welcoming the caffeine fix.

It's midafternoon now, and I've got a long day ahead. I'm heading to the Brooklyn Brewery after work for their open mic night. I don't sing but discovering new talent to photograph is a hobby of mine. Especially, new *female* talent. I've made it my mission to lift others up and be the woman I so desperately needed during my youth.

Unlike the one who birthed me.

Nine

Bar fruit, Goldilocks, and a proposition

Garrett

The best place for a recovered alcoholic is at a bar.

Yeah, *nope*.

I'm technically tonight's designated driver, but that won't make being there any easier. I twist my sobriety bracelet in circles, brushing my thumb over the tattered leather. Since beer was never my drink of choice to begin with, I should be fine at a brewery. Besides, I'm going for the live music and parmesan truffle oil fries, *not* the alcohol.

My stomach growls for the third time since I pulled up outside my friend Nate Stark's brownstone. The original DD backed out at the last minute, which is the only reason I agreed to go watch his cousin sing at an open mic.

"C'mon, dude, what's the holdup?" It's been a long day, and I'm hungry as fuck, so my impatience has gotten the better of me.

Knowing Nate, the delay is his hair. I'm sure he'll be a while. I crank the radio, craving some steering wheel percussion to help pass the time. "Power Over Me" by Dubliner Dermot Kennedy pours from the speakers.

I appreciate the dude's stellar lyrics and soulful, raspy voice. Plus, he's Irish like me—an automatic win in my book.

Nate bounds down the stoop as Kennedy's song finishes and yanks the door open.

"Took you long enough." I crack my knuckles. "You missed my drum solo."

"I'm not late. You're early." He grins and climbs into the passenger seat, sporting khakis and a charcoal blazer. He's clean-shaven with his chestnut curls gelled to perfection. The bastard even smells good.

"Why are you all dressed up?"

A flush creeps over his cheeks. "Daria might be there."

Daria Barnes is another of my employees, a gifted graphic designer whose spontaneity and attention to detail make her an asset to the company. Nate has been crushing on her for ages but doesn't have the balls to do anything about it.

I lift a brow. "You actually gonna make a move?"

"Nah, I'll probably do my usual awkward stare and jumble my words, but a man can hope."

"That's the spirit."

We ride the short distance to the brewery while discussing a new client. I value Nate's perspective and plan to mention my partnership proposal this evening. I hope he's receptive.

We enter the riverfront brewery after parking in the designated lot. I came here over the summer with Lena. I can't recall the occasion, but I remember the food was fucking fabulous. As a food memory kind of guy, my mouth waters the moment we set foot inside. The place boasts the best parmesan truffle oil fries I've ever eaten, and a wide variety of artisanal brews for the selective palate. As in, *not* mine. We decline the hostess's offer of a table and make our way to the bar instead.

Nate waves his cousin over and introduces us. Zara is an attractive brunette with piercing green eyes like him. She's working the bohemian rocker chick vibes with delicate feminine accessories alongside tattooed flesh. The three of us chat for a few minutes. Zara reminds me of Nate, animated with a quick wit. He claims her vocals are a cross between Adele and Florence Welch of Florence + The Machine. Zara has gathered quite the following. I look forward to hearing her sing.

I order a seltzer with lime and lean against the bar, taking in my surroundings. The brewery is a lofty structure with an eclectic mix of modern and rustic decor. My gaze lands on a series of framed prints on the far wall. In addition to hosting aspiring musicians, the brewery showcases the talent of local artists. As an artist myself, I respect that.

Nate orders a pale ale and a platter of the infamous truffle fries to share. We chat about assorted topics while waiting for Zara to begin her set.

Daria enters the brewery with a trio of women and waves at us before taking a seat at a high-top table in the corner.

Ladies' night.

Nate stiffens and pauses midsentence, then fixates on the orange wedge from his beer. He's not even within thirty feet of the woman and he's already a mess.

"You need to relax. Women can sense fear."

He sighs heavily, peeling the fruit from its rind. "It's not fear. I just really like her and don't know how to act."

"Be yourself."

Sure, it's cliché, but I know the caliber of man Nate is. Good-natured, genuine, and sensitive, he's what women would call "husband material."

"This is coming from Mr. Confidence himself." Nate rolls his eyes. "Sadly, not all of us can possess your swagger."

I bark out a laugh. "I don't have swagger."

"Really? That blonde in the corner would probably argue the opposite."

I follow his gaze to the far side of the bar. Sure enough, an incredibly attractive woman flanked by a couple of girlfriends is staring. She quickly looks away when we make eye contact. Petite, with long, flaxen hair and a curvaceous frame, she's the picture of Barbie meets girl next door.

I shrug. "She's cute."

"She's more than cute, G. She's fucking stunning."

"So, why don't you go talk to her?"

"Nah, man. Goldilocks has been undressing you with her eyes for the last twenty minutes."

"And she's probably like *twenty* years old."

"She's gotta be at least twenty-one," he corrects me. "We're in a bar, remember?"

"Trust me, Nate, I'm well aware we're in a bar."

"Fuck." He grimaces and touches my arm. "Sorry. That was insensitive."

"It's all good." I sip my seltzer and glance at Goldilocks again.

Our eyes meet, and she allows her sapphire gaze to linger for a few beats before shyly averting it. Not going to lie, the woman is gorgeous.

Nate chuckles. "See what I'm referring to?"

"Yep." I nudge him. "Incoming."

"Oh, shit." He sucks in a sharp breath, then stuffs the orange into his mouth.

"You're fine, man. Don't forget to chew."

Daria approaches, wearing a fitted, olive-green sweater and skinny jeans, paired with knee-high brown boots. Her auburn curls cascade to the middle of her back. She always wears her hair in a bun at the office, so the loose tresses are a rare sight.

She smiles. "Didn't I just see you guys two hours ago?"

I rub my jaw. "Has it been that long?"

"Feels like an eternity. How's it going, boss man?"

"Oh, you know, living the dream." I mean it as a joke, but my statement holds truth. I *am* living out my dream.

"Better than a nightmare." Turning to our coworker, she smiles sweetly and touches his shoulder. "Hi, Nate."

"Hi." Nate barely manages the weak greeting, sounding like a cross between a parrot with laryngitis and a dying antelope.

"Ladies' night?" I ask.

"Yes. Those are my college roomies. We try to get together at least once a month," she explains, turning to Nate once more. "Hey, isn't Zara related to you?"

"Yeah," he answers, with zero elaboration. Then the poor bastard shifts his weight and fumbles with a cocktail napkin, eyeing the lime on my glass like it's his next victim.

Oh, for fuck's sake.

"Excuse me, but nature calls." Panic flares in Nate's gaze as I rise from my stool. Ignoring the pleading look on his face, I retreat to the restroom.

I don't really have to go, but I can't bear to witness any more of the awkward exchange. One as shy as Nate doesn't need an audience to watch him attempt to flirt. Hell, the poor guy can't even make complete sentences right now.

Once inside the restroom, I linger for a few minutes and give my reflection a once-over, then wash my hands before emerging. Daria and Nate are still engrossed in conversation, so I wander along the brewery's perimeter, studying the artwork on display. A former client recognizes me, and we make small talk for a few minutes until it's time for Zara's set to begin.

I meander through the crowd and rejoin Nate at the bar, smirking at the enormous grin plastered on his face. "Nice chat?"

"She invited me to go with her to a gallery opening in Queens tomorrow night."

"Sweet. Are you picking her up or meeting her there?"

"I'm picking her up at six."

"Even better." I clap him on the shoulder. "See? I told you it'd be fine."

Soon, Zara's sultry, intoxicating voice fills the air. She's seated on a stool, playing the acoustic guitar for her cover of Bonnie Raitt's "I Can't Make You Love Me." Her talent blows me away. I think I'll mention her name to Jake. He's notorious for paving the way for aspiring actors and musicians.

We devour our fries while watching the performance. I order a second seltzer. Nate's enjoying the brewery's trademark lager, his posture newly infused with confidence. Daria keeps casting furtive glances in his direction, but he's oblivious. Hopefully, now that she's invited him to the gallery opening, he'll relax and let things happen.

I peer across the bar and lock eyes with Goldilocks again. She's been watching me the whole time but made no move to approach. That's fine—I don't have the energy to engage in conversation. Pivoting my body in her direction, I return her unabashed stare, allowing my gaze to roam her curves. I lay it on thick, even adding a sly wink because I can't help myself. I've been told I'm a master at eye fuckery. It's clear this time is no exception when she flushes and looks away.

Ah, you can dish it out, but you can't take it?

"Looking mighty self-satisfied there, G." Nate's voice brings me out of my mini gloat. "Why don't you get her number and add her to your collection?"

"I don't have a collection, dude. It's literally two friends with benefits. And Lisa has a man now, so it's just Anya. I'm not a player."

Yes, it's well known I enjoy casual sex and avoid relationships like the plague, but I hate when people assume I'm a Casanova.

"Not calling you a player. I'm just saying you get more action than anyone I know."

"Yeah, that's what happens when you use sex like a drug."

He doesn't have a response for that, so he sips his beer and stares at his feet. Now I feel like a dick.

Sighing, I roll up my sleeves. "Besides, I don't have time for all that dating bullshit."

His eyes lift to mine once more. "Tell that to Goldilocks over there."

"No, really, between work and prep for *Prodigy*, I'm stretched pretty thin."

"I get it," Nate concedes. "Sorry, man. I was just fucking with you. Believe me, I know how much you have on your plate. It makes sense your extracurriculars need to sit on the back burner for a bit."

"Hopefully, not for long." He raises a brow, and I continue. "I have a proposition for you."

If all goes as planned, he'll accept my offer and help shoulder some of the weight of running Hudson Graphics. I'd cross my fingers if I believed in that kind of shit.

He leans against the bar. "I'm listening."

"I need your help with something near and dear to me." I poke my straw at the lime in the bottom of my seltzer glass. "You're the only one I'd ever ask this of."

Curiosity lights his green eyes. "C'mon, man. The suspense is killing me."

"I know, but this is important. You're gonna have to deal with my dramatic pauses and shit." I need to choose my words wisely, so he understands how much added responsibility he'd be agreeing to. "As you know, I've been stressed lately, and I think you're my solution to that."

He laughs. "For once I'm the solution instead of the problem? That's fucking refreshing."

"Well, prepare to be freshened the fuck up," I say, unable to stop my grin.

Nate is top quality, and I have a good feeling about this. Who knows, if I get some free time out of the deal, maybe I'll even try the whole dating thing. As in, pursue a sexual relationship with someone other than my AA sponsor.

After all, I deserve regular orgasms as much as any other guy.

"I want you to be my partner."

"Your partner? What do you mean?" He tilts his head to the side, eyes widening. "Wait. I know I said you have swagger, and I'm capable of admitting I think you're an attractive dude." He gestures between us. "But I don't wanna fuck you, bro. I'm not into you like that."

My laugh startles the woman behind him. "Not *that* kind of partner, jackass. I'm talking about Hudson Graphics."

"Ohhhh." Comprehension floods his face. "Sorry. You confused the hell out of me with the whole, 'You're the only one I'd ever ask this of.' It felt kinda intimate and shit."

"Clearly." I poke him in the chest. "For the record, I don't wanna fuck you either, but thanks for saying I'm attractive."

Nate laughs. "Don't let it go to your head, you cocky fuck."

"No guarantees." I flash him a grin. "So, what do you say? Do you wanna help me run the company?"

Ten

Pheromones, a bromance, and an apology

Ella

The brewery is packed. A young man plays the saxophone while his partner croons a song about heartbreak. The talented pair holds the audience rapt as I navigate through the crowd toward the bar.

I nudge my way closer, stopping short when I spot Garrett Casey. Eyes trained on the duo's performance, he's leaning against the sprawling steel and maple fixture, holding a glass of clear liquid. His hair is tousled to perfection and a layer of black scruff coats his jaw. Although he's dressed casually, he couldn't be sexier. I love how he's rolled up the sleeves of his white button-down shirt, exposing muscled forearms. I can only imagine how big his biceps must be.

He sips from his glass, and my pulse quickens, watching his throat move on a swallow. The man standing beside him leans over and says something. Garrett's responding smile sets my body on fire.

It's not fair he can do this to me. I practically grew up around Paolo and his six gorgeous brothers, so I'm not one to lose my cool around attractive men. Call it desensitization, but I've always considered myself immune. What I'm feeling right now doesn't make sense. My insides don't flutter. Nor do my panties dampen with a simple facial expression. Yet here I am, ready to rub up against him like a feline in heat. *He's probably an animal in bed.* The hollow ache between my thighs intensifies with the thought.

Then, like my pheromones are calling out to him, his head swivels in my direction. Our eyes meet. His lips curve into a wicked smile, and I have to bite my lip to suppress a moan.

When I don't move, he lifts a dark brow in challenge.

My days of backing down from a challenge are over. My legs and feet carry me forward before my brain catches up, and I close the distance between us, stopping directly in front of him.

"Ella, it's a pleasure to see you." His voice is a rumbled invitation, a promise of sin and sex.

"Good evening, Garrett." I motion to the gleaming bar. "Never expected to find you in a place like this."

He holds up his glass. "It's only seltzer."

"That's a relief. I would've confiscated it if you said vodka."

He chuckles. "Nah, I was always a whiskey man."

"I'll keep that in mind."

I smile and hold out my hand to his friend who's eyeing me curiously. "Hello, I'm Ella Sammons."

"Nate, Ella is the photojournalist who interviewed me for *Prodigy*."

The guy grins as we shake hands. "Nice to meet you, Ella. I'm Nate Stark, Garrett's new business partner."

I glance at Garrett. "Ah, I see he was receptive?"

"Yeah." He squeezes Nate's shoulder. "And thank fuck for that."

I motion to Nate. "I hear you're the web design guru at Hudson Graphics?"

He flushes. "That might be a stretch."

Garrett elbows him. "Nope. Stop being modest. You know you're fucking stellar."

"My boss informed me you manage the *Tribune's* site."

Nate stands taller and smiles. "Yes, I manage several media accounts. I wanted to be a journalist, but I can't write for shit. I learned early on it was better for everyone if I focused on the visual aspect."

"Congratulations on your new partnership. I'm sure it's interesting to work with Garrett."

"That's an understatement." Nate laughs. "We have a good time. He's one of my best friends. We've got the whole bromance balance thing going on."

Garrett snorts. "Yeah, something along those lines. Take out the balance part because we all know how well I manage that."

An attractive redhead makes her way over to them and flutters her lashes at Nate. "Since boss man is your chauffeur, can I buy you another beer?"

Nate turns tomato red and shifts his weight, shyly meeting her gaze. "Thanks, Daria. I'd love that."

Garrett's fingertips brush my arm, sending a flare of heat to my core. "Take a walk with me."

I follow him across the brewery to the back hallway that leads to the restrooms. It's much quieter here. And we're alone. I'm not a woman who willingly accompanies men to secluded places, but after our interview's intimacy, I don't feel threatened by Garrett. The fact shocks even me.

He stops midway down the hall. "Sorry. Nate gets really shy around Daria and I didn't wanna make him more nervous. Plus, I wanted to speak with you privately."

"What's up?"

"I wanted to apologize for coming on too strong last night. I'm sorry if I made you uncomfortable." His lionlike eyes seek mine. "I promise that wasn't my goal."

My pulse quickens. "What *was* your goal?"

"Just to know you better." He stuffs his hands into his pockets and shrugs. "You're an interesting woman. I want to know everything about you."

I stiffen my spine. "No one knows me, Garrett. And that's how I like it."

He tilts his head to the side. "Why?"

Staring up at his towering frame, I'm tempted to tell him my reasons are none of his business. But I can't form those words. "We'll call it self-preservation."

His gaze burns into mine. "I understand that concept better than you think."

And as a child orphaned by suicide, he would. A man clinging to his sobriety would also be well versed in the garrisons of self-preservation. This poor man has fought so many battles.

I touch his forearm, brushing my fingertips over corded muscles, textured skin, and crisp hairs. "I'm sorry you've seen such darkness."

"Thank you." His voice is gruff, deeper than usual.

His chest rises and falls faster from my touch. He doesn't reach for me, or even remove his hands from his pockets, just stares into my eyes like they hold the answer to every question.

Little does he know, *I* don't even have the answers. Maybe I should stop caressing his skin, take a few steps back, place some distance between us.

Instead, I move closer.

Eleven

A request, a mistake, and a reunion

Garrett

My every muscle is tensed in anticipation, like an Olympic swimmer poised on the edge of the starting block waiting for the signal to dive. Forget gunshots, I'm so turned on I wouldn't be able to distinguish a mouse fart from an air-raid siren. I force my lungs to expand, drawing in the oxygen that eludes me.

Ella's perfume, a sultry mix of jasmine and vanilla, drifts to my nose. I keep my gaze pinned to hers as she slides her hands over the scarring on my forearms, then grips my biceps like they're the only force tethering her to the planet.

I spooked her last night, so I'm not about to make the same mistake twice. As much as I want to kiss her—or better yet, fuck her up against this wall—I'm not moving. She is one hundred percent in control of the situation.

Cupping my jaw, she brushes her thumb over my lower lip. "You're a beautiful man, Garrett."

I've been semihard since I spotted her near the bar. I barely resist the urge to suck her fingertips into my mouth. "Thanks. Now, fucking kiss me already."

When she fists my shirt and pulls me closer, it's clear my self-control doesn't stand a chance. My eyes dart to the plush, beautiful lips I want wrapped around my cock. I clench my jaw to keep from begging her to suck me.

Her touch travels upward as she threads her fingers into my hair, then lightly drags her nails over my scalp. "Ask nicely."

"*Please*, kiss me."

She rises to her tiptoes and presses her lips to my throat. Unlike last night, she lingers, kissing her way to my ear. Wet, open-mouthed kisses that have my balls tightening. Her lower body rubs against my cock, making it hard to breathe.

"I want your mouth."

"Patience." Her whisper goes straight to my dick, snapping my last filament of control.

"Fuck patience," I growl, hauling her up against me.

A startled gasp escapes her when my lips crash down over hers. Only a second passes before her body goes rigid, making me break the kiss. Her wide, panic-filled eyes freeze my chest.

"Ella?"

"Let go of me."

Releasing her, I step back, and hold my hands up in surrender. "What's wrong?"

"Nothing. Everything." She wraps her arms around herself. "It's fine."

"I'm sorry. I, uh—"

"No. *I'm* sorry." She disappears into the women's restroom without another word.

I knot my hands in my hair and pace the hallway. What the ever-loving fuck just happened? One moment she was all in, practically licking my neck. And the next? She repelled me like I'm a goddamn leper.

Nate appears at the end of the corridor. "What are you doing, G? Ready to head out?"

No, I'm ready for a drink.

"I, uh . . ." My throat goes dry as the all too familiar cravings bubble to the surface.

As much as I want to figure out why Ella is upset and apologize for my part in making her that way, I need to get the hell out of this bar. Besides, I doubt she'd appreciate me lurking out here like a creepy fuck.

Nate approaches, his brow furrowing in concern. "You okay, man?"

No.

When I don't answer, he touches my arm. "Talk to me, G."

"Yeah, I'm fine. Let's go."

The half-finished logo on my computer screen taunts me. It worked when I sketched it on paper, but now, the colors are all off, and I can't pinpoint what I don't like about the design. Besides the concept's stupidity, of course. I still can't understand why my client wants a violinist pineapple for his dance studio. It makes no fucking sense. I shove the laptop across my desk, then rub my temples.

I haven't accomplished a damn thing in the last three hours. Or two days. Wes hit the nail on the head. Ella's bedroom eyes stole my wits, and there's nothing I can do about it.

I stretch and lean back in my leather desk chair, then glance at my phone for the umpteenth time. Nothing. Not that I expected anything after Wednesday night's shit show, but a man can hope.

I should've stayed to apologize. No. I should've kept my fucking hands to myself and let her take the lead. Instead, I ruined things between us before they had a chance to start. So, here I sit, unable to work, staring out the window at the surrounding skyscrapers, wishing for the peace that won't come.

My stomach growls in the distance. I haven't eaten anything today because nothing appeals to me. I miss my lunch break dates with Lena. We'd hang between the giant lion sculptures, on the steps of the New York Public Library, sharing a sub and a bag of chips. She's on a leave of absence from work until January so she can fully recover from the Alaska ordeal. I hope to jump back into our routine when she returns.

If she has time for me now that Wes is in her life.

A pang of sadness takes my breath away. Emerson is the first man truly worthy of Lena. While I'm happy she found him, their bond means I won't have her all to myself anymore. She's my only source of stability. The thought of losing her is more than I can handle. Tensing, I beat back my emotions and focus on the big picture: her happiness is all that matters.

Nate pops his head into my office, his broad grin a perfect distraction from my depressing thoughts. "You want pizza? We're ordering from Donatello's."

"Yeah." Pizza always works for me, and Donatello's makes the best garlic knots in the city. "Order some knots too. Put it on the firm's credit card."

"Cool, man. Thanks." He smiles and points to my desk. "Whatcha working on?"

"Just a stupid fucking logo for the guy who owns Swing Sultans."

"You sound so enthused." He enters my office and comes to stand beside me. "What's bothering you about it?"

"It doesn't make sense. I mean, I can understand the violin because they do a shitload of swing dance classes, obviously. But the pineapple? What the fuck?"

Nate eyes the design and chuckles. "I think it's fucking clever."

I raise a brow at him. "Please enlighten me."

"Pineapples are a commonly known symbol of hospitality, right?"

"Yeah."

"But you probably didn't know they can also symbolize swingers."

I blink. "As in, couples who fuck other couples?"

"Exactly. Now, it may or may not be intentional on the business owner's part, but since Swing Sultans is a *swing* dance studio, the pineapple is a funny and clever play on words and symbolism. Although, you never know what else goes on there outside of dance lessons. Maybe it's a front for a sex club or something. You know, like, lemme rub your wife's viola strings with my cello bow. And you can put your lips on my tuba."

I stare at the logo in progress with a new appreciation for the design. And my business partner. "You're smart as fuck, Nate-Dawg. You know that, right?"

He pats himself on the back. "My bizarre trivia obsession comes in handy sometimes."

"I'll keep that in mind the next time I can't figure shit out."

"Sounds good. I'm starving. Let me go order our food." He leaves the office.

I filled him in on my unsettling Ella encounter on the way home from the brewery. He didn't have any real insight, but it was helpful to vent. He's the only person at the office who knows about my alcohol battle, so he understood why I needed to leave so abruptly. Still, I felt like a dick for interrupting his time with Daria. At least they'd already made their plans. Last night's date was a success, and they're going out again this weekend. I'm happy they connected. They're a great match.

Nate is ecstatic about my partnership offer. He clearly has no concept of his worth because he thought I was joking at first. He claims he never imagined himself at the helm, but I'll show him he's got what it takes to help run Hudson Graphics. I couldn't be happier to have someone like him in my corner. The man's a brilliant designer and a damn good friend. And as the logo interpretation just proved, he's the kind of guy who thinks outside the box. I know I made the right decision. We just need to wait for my attorney to draw up the contracts so we can move forward.

A weight has been lifted from my shoulders. Despite my best efforts, I can't run my business on my own anymore. Stress and sleep deprivation exponentially increase my risk of falling off the wagon.

My phone rings.

I snatch it and sigh when I spot Lena's name. "Hello?"

"You sound thrilled to be alive. Sorry I'm not Ella."

"What's up, Leens?"

"Where are you?"

"At work. You know, the place where most of us need to go five days a week."

"Shut up and open the *Tribune* to page D-1."

"I don't get it delivered to the office."

"Then go online. Duh."

I type the newspaper's web address into the browser and locate the entertainment section, then click on the link in the page's menu. My breath catches at the sight of my face. The picture is from Jake's gala. I don't remember Ella taking the shot, but my pensive stare captures the essence of Xavier Crane. The column's title is "From Casey to Crane: Catching Up with the Lead in *Prodigy*, Broadway's Anticipated New Show."

"Your jawline looks sexy in that pic, Gar. Or should I call you Professor Crane?" Lena's voice makes me jump and nearly drop my phone.

"Thanks, Leens. I'm almost afraid to read it," I admit, thinking of Ella's line of questioning and the hallway fiasco.

"Don't be. It appears you made quite the impression on someone. Call me later. Love you."

"Love you too. Bye."

I hang up, take a deep breath, and start reading.

```
Recently, I had the opportunity to sit down with
Mr. Garrett Casey, who has been cast as Professor
```

Xavier Crane, the male lead in *Prodigy*. If you haven't heard of the show, or Garrett, allow me to enlighten you.

Prodigy is the forthcoming Broadway production slated to open at the Compass Theater next year. Loosely based on Elias Hawke's bestselling novel, *Prodigy Undone,* the show is unapologetic with its dive into the trappings of addiction. *Prodigy* follows Xavier Crane's struggle with alcohol and painkillers.

After a shoulder injury leaves Crane addicted to opiates, he's plagued by the turmoil of his past and his inability to cope with the present. He spirals out of control until the ethereal Annaca Collins walks into his classroom. The student's beauty and prodigal vocal talent consumes Crane. Could she be the beacon of light in his darkness, or will his infatuation destroy them both?

Garrett Casey is tasked with the embodiment of the tormented professor and his vices. Handsome, charming, and intense, Casey's presence commands one's attention. He is the owner of Hudson Graphics, a design firm in Manhattan. When the self-made man is not involved with the business of visual artistry, the talented actor and vocalist immerses himself in theater.

Garrett and I discussed the challenges associated with the controversial plot and his portrayal of Crane over some delicious Italian food, courtesy of Manhattan's La Bussola.

"We all have our vices, our demons, so I think we can all relate to Xavier Crane on some level. Yes, he deals with the extreme, which may be unfathomable for some, but let's face it, no one's immune to hardship. Everyone's fighting a battle, some are just better at hiding it," Casey explained.

A deeply private man, he made no comment when my line of questioning touched on his vices, nor did he wish to discuss his childhood. He called himself "a man of the present" and instead drew my focus to current day.

ES: "What kind of 'present' do you wish to attain?"

GC: "I don't have any use for altered reality. I

want the real deal, good and bad alike. If it hurts,
bring it. If it feels good, I want it without en-
hancement. I refuse to live a fabled version of life.
I demand truth, clarity, and authenticity. I'll settle for nothing less."
    [For full interview click here]
    Audiences, trust me, once you catch a glimpse of
Garrett Casey, you won't look away.
    Keep watch for *Prodigy* next year.
    —Ella Sammons

I read the article's extended version, then stare at the screen in stunned silence. I don't know what I expected, but it certainly wasn't *that*. I check my phone again.

Still nothing.

Hindsight is twenty-twenty, right?

The next time I have an event scheduled for after work, I'll skip my afternoon coffee run. I needed a pick-me-up. Instead, I collided with a man on the sidewalk and spilled it all over myself. Never even got a sip. My ruined shirt forced me to make a field trip home to shower and change.

I make a mental note to keep spare clothes at the office. Or use the damn coffee machine I bought for the break room, instead of taking my daily stroll to Compass Roasters.

Now, I'm fighting traffic on my way back into Manhattan for *Prodigy's* cast meet and greet. Everyone important to the production is gathering at the director's posh apartment overlooking Central Park.

And I'm going to be late.

Way to make a first impression, dickwad.

"C'mon, man. Some of us have places to be." Trapped behind some idiot who can't follow the speed limit, my muttered epithets increase as the minutes tick by, my blood pressure rising accordingly. "This isn't Sunday afternoon in the country."

I pass him the first opportunity I get. While I highly doubt my sideways glare affects him, it makes me feel better.

Tonight proves I need to figure out my game plan for when rehearsals are in full swing. I'll need to grab dinner and hang out at the office longer, rather than doing the back-and-forth shit every day. It's a waste of time, gas, and money. While I understand why Lena prefers public transportation, access to my own vehicle is critical. I won't allow myself to wind up stranded someplace. Escape routes and getaway cars are part of the Garrett Casey survival kit.

Even though I'm not on time, at least I look presentable. Clean-shaven with damp hair, I'm wearing my go-to outfit—dark jeans and a crisp, white, collared shirt. Hopefully, I didn't miss a memo about the party being black tie. *That* would be almost as awkward as showing up late. Sighing, I crank the radio. The station is playing some older alternative songs, and soon enough, I'm drumming to the beat of Incubus's "The Warmth."

I arrive at Tom's address after what feels like an eternity. As I step into the foyer, I'm greeted by an older gentleman, who introduces himself as simply "the butler."

Seriously? Tom has a butler?

My brain runs down a list of butler-appropriate monikers, settling on Edwin. I beat back a few dumb jokes that want to break free, instead following in silence as he leads me into the living room. Scanning the unfamiliar people milling about, I spot Tom and give a sheepish wave.

He approaches with a grin. "Ah, it's the man of the hour."

"Tom, I apologize for being late. Traffic got the better of me," I mumble, rolling up my sleeves.

"Don't worry about it. You're here now, and that's what matters." He pats my shoulder, then turns to the butler. "Jason, this is the last guest to arrive, so please make sure you fix yourself a plate of food."

"Thank you, sir."

Jason? He doesn't look like a Jason.

Tom tugs me along, stopping beside a stately older woman. "I'd like you to meet my wife, Helen." He caresses her cheek. "Darling, this is Garrett Casey, the young man who so perfectly fits our vision for Xavier Crane."

"It's a pleasure to meet you, Mrs. Berkley." I shake her hand.

She has a warm smile, the kind that instantly puts you at ease. "The pleasure's all mine, and please call me Helen. We're theater family now. No need for formalities."

"Thank you, Helen. I'll keep that in mind."

"I've heard a lot about you, Garrett. Tom and Elias were thrilled to pieces with your performance."

"Oh?" I frown, thinking of the reclusive author who didn't show for my audition. I think I read somewhere he's agoraphobic, but I found it strange he wouldn't want to screen the people who'd potentially play his characters. I assumed authors were particular about that kind of shit. I know *I'd* want a say in performance fundamentals like casting. "He must've seen the video. Tom was the only one at the theater that day."

"Au contraire mon frère." Tom chuckles. "Hawke was most definitely watching."

My eyebrows fly upward. "Really?"

"Yep. He was in one of the private boxes."

"Holy shit." I'm floored he liked my audition, and more than a little bummed I didn't get to meet him. Tom based *Prodigy's* stage adaptation on Elias Hawke's novel, *Prodigy Undone*. I hoped to pick his brain about certain aspects of Crane's character.

"Elias was so impressed with your singing voice," Helen gushes. "He said so when we had dinner at his place last week." She shakes her head sadly. "It's a shame he's always cooped up there. He rarely leaves the house since—"

"*Helen.*" Tom grips her wrist. "Remember what we discussed earlier."

She flushes. "Oh, yes. Sorry, dear. You know how my mouth gets going."

His face softens. "It's all right, darling. Perhaps you should see if Sydney needs anything."

"Good thinking." She touches my shoulder. "I'm going to check in with the caterer. Enjoy the party, Garrett."

"Thank you." I watch her retreating form as she flits toward where I assume is the kitchen.

"Come with me." Tom ushers me into the dining room. "You'll have to forgive my wife. Helen *loves* to gossip." He sighs heavily. "And some things . . . shouldn't be talked about."

"Makes sense."

"Hawke is a deeply private man. I doubt you—or anyone else involved with the production—will meet him, so I wouldn't waste energy getting your hopes up. I'm not sure if you had the opportunity to read his novel, but he approved some key changes for our stage adaptation. As such, I will be fielding all character and plot questions."

"Gotcha." I nod my understanding, but now I'm even more intrigued by the mysterious Elias Hawke who seems content to hide in the shadows.

"C'mon. I want you to meet everyone else."

We pause at a cluster of people, who he introduces as the stage crew. I smile and make small talk for a few minutes. Some actors tend to turn up their nose at the crew, but that's not my style. I appreciate their vital behind-the-scenes wizardry.

Tom leads me deeper into the room. "Let's get you acquainted with your leading lady, shall we?"

I know embarrassingly little about my costar, Tess McPherson. Other than her name and powerhouse vocals, she's a complete mystery to me. Maybe if my best friend hadn't been lost in the Alaskan wilderness, I would've put some effort into researching the people I'll be sharing the stage with.

Since Tess and I are supposed to play convincing lovers on stage, I'm eager to get to know her.

We approach some people near the row of windows overlooking Central Park.

Tom addresses a pair of women engaged in conversation with their backs to us. "Sorry ladies, I don't mean to interrupt," he lightly touches one woman's arm, "but I need to steal Tess away for a moment. Tess, this is Garrett Casey, your Xavier."

She turns to face us, and a pair of shocked sapphire eyes lock with mine.

Recognition slams me in the solar plexus. It's Goldilocks from the brewery.

Fuck.

Fucker.

Fuckity-fuck.

I open my mouth to speak but choke on my tongue, coughing and sputtering like a drunkard with his head in a wishing well. Too bad I can't wish Wednesday's encounter away.

Tess gapes as I thump my chest a few times, desperately trying to regain my composure.

"Sorry," I wheeze, holding out my hand. "I swear I'm not sick."

She blinks up at me in silence.

"*That* was one hell of a bizarre introduction."

Tom's voice makes me jump. I'm all kinds of fucked up right now because I forgot he was standing there.

He eyes me. "Do you two know each other?"

I clear my throat. "Uh . . . no, not officially. Just by sight."

When Tess doesn't reach for my palm, I awkwardly stuff both hands into my pockets. Maybe I can crawl in there and hang out with some lint.

Tess still stares, lips parted, lungs expanding on shaky breaths. The woman is even more beautiful up close. She's wearing a formfitting navy-blue dress, and her thick, blond mane cascades over her shoulders and down her back. She's got on spike heels, but I still tower over her.

Tom chuckles. "Well, I'll let you two get acquainted. You're going to be *seeing* a lot of each other." He turns and rejoins his wife across the room, leaving Tess and me to stare at one another.

I'm fucking mortified by how I acted on Wednesday. Nate tells me I have swagger. This is the polar opposite. Someone should make me the poster child for awkwardness. I need to get my shit together if I want a productive working relationship with this woman.

I make a second attempt at a handshake. "Hi. We meet after all."

This time, she clasps my outstretched palm. "Life's funny like that, isn't it?" Barely above a whisper, her southern accent flows like honey.

The woman she'd been speaking with announces she's getting a drink, and Tess nods.

"Where are you from?" I ask.

"Savannah, Georgia. And you?"

"Lancaster, Pennsylvania, but I spent most of my childhood in upstate New York."

"Do you live in Manhattan now?"

"No, Brooklyn. My office is in Manhattan though."

She nods, thoughtfully sipping her wine.

Silence stretches between us.

Determined to push past any awkwardness, I clear my throat again. "Listen, I . . . uh, I'm sorry I acted like an idiot at the brewery."

There. Straight to the point.

She watches me over the rim of her glass for a moment. "Sorry for staring. Rest assured, Mister Garrett, I wasn't trying to flirt. I thought I recognized you from your audition photo, but the lighting in there wasn't great. By the end of the night, I assumed I was wrong."

I had to go and fucking wink at her like a prepubescent punk.

She lifts a brow. "Didn't you know it was me? Tom emailed everyone's bio and pictures last month."

I remember the email. I moved it to my inbox's "Prodigy" folder with plans to familiarize myself with everyone later. I also had every intention of reading *Prodigy Undone*. Yep. Didn't happen.

"Yeah, uh, here's the thing. I've kinda had a lot on my plate. My best friend was missing in the Alaskan wilderness for a while, so my focus was shot. I'll be honest with you, Tess, I didn't read the email yet."

"Oh, my goodness! Is he all right?"

"*She*, actually. My best friend is a woman. And yes, Lena is home safe now. *I'm* still shaken but getting better each day."

Sort of.

"Holy sugar-honey iced tea!" Her eyes widen. "Your friend is the woman who's seeing Wes Emerson?"

"That'd be her." I snort at the reverent way she said Wes's name. Sometimes I forget the muscled behemoth's effect on millions of women. "Lena has been my best friend since elementary school."

"That's amazing. I'm glad everyone is safe and sound. I wouldn't know what the heck to do with myself if one of my friends was missing. I'd be worried sick."

"Yeah, it was rough. I was in a bad place for a while." I stare out the window for a moment as echoes of my nightmare taunt me. I beat back the rising wave of panic and refocus on Tess. "So, I take it you don't swear?"

"I try my darndest not to. My mama would wash my mouth out with soap."

"You've read the script, right? *Prodigy* features some colorful language for a Broadway show. Should I be worried your mom will show up here with a bar of Ivory?"

Tess giggles. "No, silly. She doesn't pay my acting any mind. She knows darn well I only say fuck when I'm being paid to."

I bark out a laugh. And just like that, the tension between us dissipates.

"Where'd you go to college?" I ask.

"I graduated from NYU this past May."

"Sweet. I'm a fellow NYU alum. I did my undergrad work there." I chuckle and rub my jaw, feeling suddenly old. "But *I* just had my ten-year reunion."

"What did you study?"

"I received my bachelor's in graphic design from NYU and then got my MBA from Columbia. How about you?"

"I have a bachelor's in English and creative writing, but I minored in theater."

"Nice, so you're really a pro. I don't have any formal stage schooling. All I'm bringing to the table is my experience with some musicals in college and an off-Broadway production a couple of years ago." I smile, thinking of all the talented people I've met. Many of whom I still keep in touch with. Tess's sweet demeanor reminds me of the costume designer from my *Fiddler on the Roof* days. "I'm curious. Do you have a day job, or is theater your focus right now?"

Tess stands taller, tipping her chin up. "I'm a part-time romance editor at Cooper Press."

Uh-oh.

My friend Lincoln works at Cooper, so I've heard of the small publishing house. I'm also well-acquainted with their biggest threat, publishing mogul Elinora Iverson. Elinora is the force of nature whose company has single-handedly put dozens of tiny presses out of business. She's positioned Iverson Press among New York's "Big Five" publishing houses, taking the industry by storm. I'm not about to mention this to Tess, but Elinora currently has her sights set on buying out Cooper Press.

Not only does Hudson Graphics share an office building with Iverson headquarters, but Elinora is my personal client. My firm takes care of her company's book cover design, web management, and marketing materials. I get all the juicy inside scoop.

"Why are you making that face? Are you judging me?"

"No. Not at all. Why do you think I'd judge?"

A sigh deflates her chest. "Sorry. My mama gives me trouble for working on 'smut books' instead of quality literature. I assume everyone shares her viewpoint."

"Romance is a billion-dollar industry. Fuck the haters."

"I couldn't agree more. I like to tell her sex sells."

"Yes, it fucking does. My friend Lena is an avid romance reader. She spends enough money on books to keep the industry afloat. I'm not ashamed to say I've read quite a few of them myself. I kinda like picking up a book and knowing it will have a happy ending."

After all the shit I've dealt with, deep down there's a sad little part of me hoping for my own happy ending.

"That's exactly why I love romance," Tess gushes. "Nice to know we're on the same wavelength."

"Yup. All the cool kids read romance. Speaking of cool kids, you must know my buddy Lincoln Kennedy. He works at Cooper too."

"Sure do. Linc is a doll." She makes a circle with her finger. "Small world, huh?"

"True story."

She sips her wine. "Do you work for a design company?"

"No, I own one called Hudson Graphics."

Her eyes widen. "Oh, my goodness! That's *your* company? Wow, Mister Garrett, I'm impressed. How do you find time to do the acting thing?"

"It's always been my passion, so I make time."

"Good for you."

"How about you? What brought you to the city for college? Savannah's a long way off."

"I needed a change of pace. My parents wanted me to go to Georgia State, but I applied to several schools up north. When my acceptance letter from NYU arrived, I jumped at the opportunity," she explains, chewing her lip. "They weren't too thrilled about it. And they *really* weren't happy when I decided to stay after graduation."

"They must be pretty excited about you being cast as Annaca Collins?"

Sighing, she shakes her head sadly. "No, not exactly. They don't approve of the subject matter." Her eyes convey a gut-punch wistfulness, but it's the bitterness in her tone that screams her frustrations. "I grew up singing in our church choir. My mama wanted me to be a gospel singer or a Sunday school teacher, so, like my *smut books*, the *taboo plot* doesn't sit well with her."

I nod in understanding even though I can't relate. The concept of parental disapproval is foreign to me because, oh yeah, mine weren't around. My parents obviously didn't give two fucks about my future. If they had, they'd both still be alive.

"Hopefully you can prove them wrong."

"I intend to." After a sip of wine, she asks, "How about your family? Are they supportive?"

My definition of family differs greatly from the picture she's painted of her life. As a rule, I don't share details of my childhood with anyone other than Lena, and I certainly don't want to cloak this sweet woman in my darkness.

"Let's just say, the people I consider my family have been extremely supportive."

And it's true. Lena and my work friends have been cheering me on from the start. In an ideal world, my aunt, uncle, and more than only *one* of the cousins I lived with, would be proud of me as well. But my reality shattered the confines of idealism when I was only a child.

"Have you been reading the script?" I ask, changing the subject.

"Yes, but I've spent more time memorizing lyrics and practicing arias. I figure the script will be easier to learn when I'm not talking to myself."

"Good point. It's a little challenging to be emotive alone. I'm free most evenings to rehearse, you just let me know."

"Oh, I'll be sure to, Mister Garrett."

Twelve

An urge, tortellini, and a realization

Ella

I fold the flyer for the event I'm covering tomorrow night and stuff it back inside my purse. It's now the third time I've done it, but this was the closest I've come to inviting Garrett. My fingers practically twitched to dial his number. So far, I resisted.

Taking a long sip of my wine, I ponder all the reasons I can't go there.

For one, the setting is hardly a dating environment. Not that I would consider it a date because, well, I don't date. More importantly, I'll be working, and if I have any hopes of growing my freelance photography side hustle to include *more* than events hosted by my friends, I need to preserve my professional facade.

Never mix business and pleasure. My grandmother's words echo in my mind as I feather my fingertips over the castle tattoo on my ankle. Her memory and motto—*stand strong, even when the rest of the world crumbles*—lives on in the ornate fortress inked into my skin.

Giada Castiglione knew the way to a man's heart and wallet was through his stomach. Her restaurant became Rome's thriving culinary epicenter because she let nothing distract from her passion. She taught me everything I know about focus, cooking, quality ingredients, and creating meals with love. My grandfather died young, and even though her beauty knew no match, my grandmother never let another man in. She succumbed to her breast cancer battle when I was seventeen. I miss her fiercely.

My life would be so different if I'd gone to live with her, instead of letting my mother drag me to America. I'd give anything to go back in time and follow a different path. I could've helped at the restaurant, taken over the place after Gigi passed. Instead, my greedy uncle sold it the moment we laid her to rest. God, I wish I had more time with my grandmother. More stories and songs. More gnocchi and tagliatelle carbonara. Tiramisu and cannoli.

Here I am, alone and empty, yet filled to the brim with regrets. All because of my loyalty to the woman who birthed me. I brush my hand over my abdomen as the phantom ache nearly brings me to my knees. There's still no room in my reality for happiness and pleasure.

Unless it involves food.

As if on cue, Paolo pushes through the kitchen door and makes his way to my corner table at La Bussola.

He sets a small bowl of tortellini in front of me. "I know you said you already ate dinner, but I'm working on some new specials for the month and need your opinion on this sauce."

"What kind of sauce is it?" I point to the orangey-red mixture. "It looks like an a la vodka."

He grins and hands me a fork. "Taste it and tell me what you think the ingredients are."

"Oh, I love this game." I spear a few tortellini and bring them to my lips, pausing for dramatic effect. I nearly moan aloud when the creamy decadence coats my tongue. It's rich and cheesy, with a hint of something else.

Paolo watches me chew, gauging my reaction to his recipe. "Your eyes are fluttering. That's usually a good thing."

"This is incredible. Do I taste nutmeg?" I take another bite, chewing slowly, so I can decipher what I'm tasting. "And mascarpone?"

"Yup. It's a pumpkin Alfredo sauce."

"It's sweet and savory."

"I can't decide which I'd rather lean into." He rubs his scruff-covered jaw. "I wasn't planning on a dessert pasta."

"Maybe add more cheese and garlic then."

He nods. "Should I do ravioli instead?"

"Well, ravioli have more filling than tortellini, so if you want it savory, you should switch from mascarpone to ricotta."

"If I make one of each, will you taste test them?"

"Caro, you know I'll never turn down food from you."

A fleeting look of sadness crosses his face, but he quickly recovers. "Thanks for your help, bella."

"Anytime." My chest tightens knowing I hurt his feelings last night when I turned him down for sex.

He squeezes my shoulder and retreats to the kitchen.

Guilt unfurls in the pit of my stomach. I don't allow myself satisfaction outside of my occasional romp with Paolo. He's given me the only taste of physical comfort I've ever known, but our sexual encounters need to stop. I can't give him what he needs, and he deserves better than my mind games.

Garrett, on the other hand, shares my relationship dysfunction. I have a hunch his fucked-up meter registers close to mine, which is oddly soothing. Too bad that doesn't translate into us being a good idea.

All week I told myself to forget about him, tried to force those soul-stealing eyes from my mind. But I can't. Especially, not after Wednesday night. I hate how I reacted to his embrace, and the confusion written on his features when I told him to let me go. He must think I'm a complete and utter lunatic.

I hoped to find him in the hallway when I finally exited the restroom, but he'd already left the brewery. I wanted to call him to explain, apologize for my reaction, ask him out for coffee. But I didn't. Which, if I'm being honest with myself, is for the better. I *should* keep my distance.

Trouble is, I want him closer.

I'm not used to focusing on something other than loneliness. Daydreaming, wishing, and hoping for change don't change a damn thing. It doesn't ease the ache or make me forget. I learned a long time ago life's no fantasy.

Garrett Casey is my *every* fantasy. He's the man I can't stop thinking about whether I'm awake or asleep. He stole my focus, and no matter how hard I try, I can't fight the magnitude of my attraction.

I wonder what he thought of my article. I'm sure he's used to women finding him appealing. Once *Prodigy* opens, everyone will know his name. His face. Those eyes. On second thought, maybe I *will* invite him to tomorrow's event. It will give me a chance to make an impression before I'm lost in a sea of beautiful women.

God knows there are plenty on Broadway. Especially his costar, Tess McPherson, a Southern belle with gold-spun hair and sapphire eyes. He's probably already enamored with her after the cast meet and greet.

As much as I hope *Prodigy* is successful, the idea of him rising to fame and falling for the talented, beautiful actress sparks an intense jealousy. As that flame burns deep inside, my body thrums with knowledge of what I must do to make Garrett mine.

Even if it ruins me.

Thirteen

Insomnia, sweat, and a missed call

Garrett

I throw the covers off with a groan. It's time to accept that after tossing and turning for several hours, my insomnia wins. Sitting up, I scrub a fist over my eyes and wait for the room to come into focus. It's not that I'm not tired. I'm exhausted, yet my mind refuses to allow me the solace of slumber.

I climb from my bed, shrug into a thermal shirt, and pull on boxers and pajama pants. Even though it's counterintuitive to my hypervigilance policy, I always sleep naked. I hate the confinement and constriction of clothes. Hell, I'd parade my naughty bits around here all day if Lena didn't have a key. I'm not completely reckless, though. I keep clothes on my nightstand and shoes at my bedside in case I need to escape during the night.

Two things I've learned the hard way, watch your back, and always have an escape plan.

I glance at the thermostat on my way to the kitchen. Fifty-eight degrees. It's three weeks into November, and I've yet to turn on the heat. Shivering makes me feel alive, but I don't have time for frozen or burst pipes. I also don't have time to listen to Lena's shit, so I push the temperature up to sixty-two.

I pour a generous amount of dark roast into the coffee maker and stare out the window as it brews. I need to head to the office later for a meeting with a potential client referred to me by Elinora Iverson. It's a large account with a steep price tag and no room for error. The guy is still on the fence about the project, so I'm hoping to solidify the deal this afternoon.

The coffeepot beeps, and I fill the "Black Like My Soul" mug Lena picked up for me last year. Its caption fits my current vibe. Even the microwave's boxy red numbers mock me. Most normal thirtysomethings would still be sound asleep at four a.m. on a Saturday. I hate the restless energy that plagues me. The constant yearning, the intangible quest for peace. I've done well for myself. I own a successful business, and I scored a dream role on Broadway.

So why is it never enough?

The truth is, I don't know what my soul aches for.

I sip my coffee and sift through the stack of mail on the counter. The colorful grocery store flyers remind me Thanksgiving is just around the corner. Lena planned a surprise get-together next weekend for Wes's thirty-fifth birthday. She's calling it Friendsgiving. Naturally, I'm expected to attend.

As a rule, I don't do holidays. I don't need another opportunity for disappointment and loneliness to creep in. Christmas is the only exception, and that's solely because of my friendship with Lena. Her birthday is Christmas Eve. She relishes the entire month of December, which means I have no choice but to celebrate the holiday.

How will things differ this year now that she has Wes in her life?

Tensing, I beat back the twinge of sadness that surfaces. Lena is the only one who has consistently given a damn about me. What will happen when she no longer has time for me?

After my parents chose the abandonment route, my aunt and uncle followed it up with a hefty dose of dismissal. Wendy barely looked at me. I served as a constant reminder of her sister's suicide, courtesy of my resemblance to my mom. There were no warm embraces, no kind words of encouragement. Just a fucking cold shoulder.

I get it. She had her own four boys to look after, so she didn't have time for me. I wasn't her beloved nephew; I was an obligation she "dealt with" in memory of her sister. Fuck that. I would've been better off in foster care.

Aside from my youngest cousin, Connor, my "family" hasn't even called to congratulate me for landing the role of Xavier Crane. It's no surprise, but I'm tired of being dismissed.

Suddenly annoyed at the universe, I down the contents of my mug and plunk it into the sink. I head to the living room, settle on the couch, and immerse myself in a mind-numbing steam mop infomercial.

"Not this year, Leens. I'm sorry." I politely decline the offer to join Lena and Wes on their journey to a Christmas tree farm upstate.

She's one of those lunatics who puts her tree up before Thanksgiving. This year she's even more excited because her goal is to have all her decorations out before next week's Friendsgiving party. While I'm always her tree selection partner, I'm not feeling it this year. No offense to Wes, but the last thing I need is to be the third wheel on a Hallmark Channel Christmas outing.

"Plus, I've got my big meeting today with that CEO Elinora put me in touch with."

"Okay, fine."

Her heavy sigh makes me cringe. I *hate* disappointing her. "Look, if it makes you happy, I'll help you throw a few ornaments on when you set it up."

"I'd love that. Also, don't think you're off the hook for gingerbread cookies. You're gonna have to suck it up and deal because you're doing it."

Picturing the bossy look she gets when she wants something, I grin. "Yes, Your Highness."

I won't admit it to Lena, but I look forward to baking our annual gingerbread cookies because it symbolizes the birth of our friendship.

It's been a quarter century since my first Christmas in the Catskills when she invited me over to play outside after a huge snowstorm. We spent hours building forts and securing an arsenal of snowballs until her mom called us inside for cocoa. Adele fed us chicken noodle soup, we decorated gingerbread cookies, and I felt included for the first time since I moved up there. I'll never forget that Christmas. Lena and I have been inseparable ever since. She's more than my best friend—she's family.

"You love it, and you know it," she says with a laugh. "Ooh! I found some new cookie cutters online. They're like those drama theater masks or whatever they're called. You know, the masks with the funny expressions? Anyway, I bought them with you in mind so we can eat Prodigy-themed cookies."

"They're called comedy and tragedy. And that's why I love you." No one else shows the same level of support and enthusiasm for my accomplishments. "When are we making them?"

"Does tomorrow afternoon work?"

"Sure."

"Gar," she begins, and I already know where she's going. "Wes will be here too . . ."

Of course he will. "Yeah, I kinda figured. That's fine."

"You sure?"

Guilt nudges me at her hopeful tone. I get it—she wants us to be friends. And I'm *trying*. Deep down, I know Emerson is the one for her, but I'm afraid of the inevitable. It's only a matter of time before he whisks her off to Australia and I lose her forever.

Since the last thing I want is for my insecurities to put a damper on our tradition, I mentally put on my big boy pants. "Yes, I'm sure. It'll be fun. What would you like me to bring?"

"Just yourself, Gar."

"Sounds good. Lemme go, I'm gonna get a workout in before my meeting."

"Okay, bye. Good luck with that account. Love you."

"Love you too, Leens."

I yawn and stretch, flicking off the TV. It progressed from steam mops to headlight cleaner and I'm over it. I don't feel like lifting weights or running on the treadmill, but I need to do something other than lying around like a slab of rotting meat.

I jog downstairs to my home gym. My eyes land on the boxing gloves. I snatch them, suddenly in the mood to punch something. I'm not overly aggressive by nature, but there's something to be said for pummeling a heavy bag.

I strip my thermal off and toss it onto the weight bench, then bend into a few stretches. Warm-up complete, I wrap my hands, pull on the gloves, and strike the bag, channeling my frustration into the bunch and flex of my muscles. The intensity of my punches mirrors my soul's restlessness. Sweat pours into my eyes, but I keep going, determined to funnel off the mental anguish and replace it with pure exhaustion.

Boxing is liberating. I'm not a man with these gloves on—I'm a machine. I need that disconnect right now. It provides me the opportunity to release my pent-up anxiety without confronting it. Call it a welcome catharsis for my tormented soul.

My doctor insists my "bury the past and move on" approach is unhealthy, but with a history like mine, it's safer—and less painful—to leave the damage behind me. Besides, I'm not known for healthy decisions.

When I'm finally spent, I plop onto the weight bench. I toss the gloves aside and unwrap my hands, stretching them out and flexing my fingers. Then I mop sweat from my face and chug some water. It was a vigorous boxing session—exactly what I needed today. I trudge back upstairs after allowing my breathing and heart rate to normalize.

I pad across the cool tile of the kitchen and grab a banana, then glance at my phone as I peel it. One missed call from an unknown number twenty minutes ago. Hopefully, McAllister isn't canceling.

Whoever it was, they didn't leave a message, and it goes to voice mail when I call back.

"Leave a message and I'll consider returning it."

Ella's voice makes me clench the phone. I shake my head to focus enough to leave a message. "I'm sorry I missed your call. I'll be in Manhattan this evening. I hope we can connect."

That's it. Nothing witty or pithy. The lackluster message is all I can manage.

Cranking the ringer volume, I carry the phone with me into the bathroom. If the fucker rings, I'll leap naked from the shower, soap covered or not.

Fourteen

Ear porn, a rain forest, and an invitation

Ella

I dump fish food into the tank in my living room, watching Mario and Luigi gobble it up. I've had the pair of angelfish for over a year now. I enjoy watching them swim between the water wisteria and hornwort plants I bought for them. Flakes settle on the miniature Leaning Tower of Pisa nestled in the smooth pebbles on the bottom, and I make a mental note to change their water this weekend. As far as pets go, Mario and Luigi are low maintenance. Not that I have anything to compare it to. These guys are my first pets. They're a quiet, colorful distraction when I need to escape the memories of my past.

I glare at my phone on the coffee table. I don't know why I let Garrett's call go to voice mail. I called *him* for God's sake, the least I could do is answer. Instead, I panicked and stared at his name on my screen, fingers hovering over the green icon, until I abandoned the device and darted across the room like a scared chipmunk. If fish could talk, mine would tell me I'm a coward.

I watch them swim for a few minutes, transfixed by their graceful beauty. Sighing, I set down the container of food and finally head for the couch, fueled by Mario and Luigi's imaginary pep talk.

I listen to Garrett's message twice, reveling in the rumble of his words. I love a man with a deep voice—especially one who can sing—and his baritone doesn't disappoint. His voice mail is close enough to ear porn, so I save it. I'll listen again later, maybe use it as a soundtrack for when I reconsider my decision to call.

Just call him.

I take a deep breath and dial.

He answers on the second ring. "Ella, hi. Sorry I missed your call."

His breathless greeting makes me smile. "Hello, Garrett."

"I was hoping to hear back from you."

Frowning, I press the phone to my ear. "It sounds like you're in a rain forest."

There's a loud squeak, then the water stops. "Sorry. I was showering."

"With your phone?" My pulse quickens, imagining soapsuds flowing over hard musculature.

He chuckles. "No, I jumped out to answer it. Didn't want to miss your call again."

"What are you doing tonight?" I blurt out.

"Seeing you."

He sounds so self-assured, the confidence a stark contrast to the winged battalion fluttering through my insides. These aren't butterflies, though. I'm imagining a flock of hummingbirds. Or seagulls.

"I'm working a private event at the Wayfarer this evening until close. I have a spare VIP pass if you're interested in joining—"

"I'll be there."

"Excellent. Show them photo ID at the door and they'll let you in. Then, come find me."

The beauty of having a side hustle means the freedom to pick and choose which jobs I want to accept. The *Tribune* is my bread and butter, loaded with garlic and cheese. My freelance business is the palate cleanser that keeps my creative juices flowing. The passion project where *I'm* in control of all aspects. Whatever money I make is a bonus, tucked aside for a rainy day. Or an emergency. I won't allow myself to become destitute, dependent on others for my survival. Been there, done that. No, I'll make damn sure I thrive in the face of adversity, no matter what it takes. Even when that means stepping beyond my comfort zone.

The Wayfarer is the exclusive nightclub affiliated with Hotel Polaris, an opulent five-star hotel. It's located in a ritzy area, flanked by a historic waterfront park and several gourmet restaurants. Tonight's event, a benefit for survivors of domestic and sexual abuse, holds tremendous personal significance, despite its unconventional premise.

No—forget unconventional—it's downright bizarre.

I don't know who masterminded the concept of Burlesquerade, but they hit the nail on the head. Sex sells, regardless of the circumstances.

I consider giving Garrett a warning but decide against it. I'd rather watch his reaction. It's a surefire way to gauge his ability to comply with my restrictions. It will be interesting to see whether he can accommodate me, or if he'll decide I'm not worth the trouble.

"Where will I find you?" he asks.

"Look for the woman with the camera."

He snorts a laugh. "Thanks for the tip. When do you want me there?"

"Arrive at six sharp, and I suggest you dress to impress."

"Black tie?"

"Uh, something like that," I murmur, glancing at my fish for reassurance.

"I can't wait to see you."

"Likewise, Garrett." I square my shoulders. "But so we're clear, this isn't a date."

"Goes without saying since neither of us date. But let me know when you change your mind; I'm easily swayed."

Hopefully you're this smooth under pressure. My stomach twists into a knot, knowing he may not be able to give me what I need. Rather, what I *think* I might need, venturing into this uncharted territory. The plan I formulated this morning seems ironclad, but I can't predict how he'll receive it. Who am I kidding? I don't know if *I* can handle what's in store for us. But at this point, it doesn't make sense to dwell on my fears because I've already invited him.

"See you tonight. Don't forget your ID—security's tight for this event." My words race past my lips. I collect myself and add, "I'd hate for them to detain you in a back room somewhere."

"Yeah, that'd be a shame. Although it might not be so bad if you're the one doing the detention."

"I'll be working," I remind him. "You'll be my assistant if you choose to join me."

"Oh, there will be a *joining* if I have anything to do with it." His deep voice strokes down my spine, making me press my knees together.

"This isn't your show to run."

Garrett's low chuckle releases an answering throb between my legs. "You clearly don't know me very well, Cupcake. I always run the show."

"Six o'clock." The words leave my lips in a breathless rush, and I can't expand my lungs enough to say anything else, so I hang up. I stare at the phone in my hand and wait until the backlight dims.

My lust is incandescent, and unlike the pixels, it won't fade to black. The moment the screen goes dark, it lights up again.

Prodigy: I'll be there.

His text sends the hummingbirds in my stomach into flight. All at once, wings are flapping, everyone's colliding and changing course in a frenzied cluster of energy. If he's got me this unsettled with a fucking text message, I can't fathom what he'll do to my body.

But first, I need to see if he can handle my limitations.

Fifteen

A mask, a throne, and nipple tassels

Garrett

For a dude who's always early, I'm not sure where this sudden late trend is coming from, but I don't like it. The last thing I need is tarnish on my reputation for punctuality. It's not entirely my fault this time. My meeting with McAllister ran longer than expected. Now, I'm cutting it close for mine and Ella's nondate. I lock my Jeep and hustle to the venue with less than fifteen minutes to spare.

To make matters worse, I parked in West Bumfuck. Yes, Hotel Polaris offers valet parking, but surrendering my keys to a stranger goes against my whole escape plan principle, so that's a no-go.

My brisk stride carries me the few blocks to the nightclub. Rounding the corner, I collide with the line of people outside the door. I know the place is exclusive, so it should've occurred to me there'd be a line. I sidestep the crowd and approach the enormous bouncer guarding the door.

"There's a line, dude," says some hipster punk with blue hair. The fucker is literally wearing a cape.

"I'm with the press," I tell him, stopping in front of the bouncer.

The guy is busy turning away a group of drunk women, barely listening to their whined protests. "Sorry ladies, but this is a private, invitation-only event."

Meanwhile, I'm over here wondering how blue-haired Dracula made the list.

The bouncer juts his chin in my direction. "Name?"

"Garrett Casey." I hold up my driver's license.

He glances at my ID and scans a page on his clipboard. "Sorry, you're not on the list."

"There should be a press pass for me—"

"There's no press at this event."

I blink, wondering if I showed up at the wrong location. No. That's not possible. There's only one Hotel Polaris. "Maybe it's just a ticket then? General admission or whatever."

He curls his lip and points behind me. "First of all, you cut the line." His derisive tone raises my hackles as he crosses his huge arms over his chest. "And now you're wasting my time."

This motherfucker needs a personality transplant.

"Listen, man. I know you're just doing your job, but you don't need to be an asshole. Evidently, there was some miscommunication." He narrows his eyes like he's about to tell me to fuck off, but I hold my ground and square my shoulders to match his territorial stance. "I was told to show the bouncer my ID and there'd be a pass for me, courtesy of Ella Sammons."

Something registers on his face, and it dawns on me I was an idiot for not mentioning her name from the jump. The anticipation of tonight is throwing me off my game. I guess that's what happens when your brain cells are hardwired to your dick.

"Hold on." He dials his phone. "Yeah, I have a Garrett Casey here. Said he's a guest of Ella's?" He listens for a moment before scowling. "Don't you think it would make sense for someone to give the dude guarding the door the newest list? I've been turning people away all night." He rubs the back of his neck and sighs. "Yeah. Whatever. Thanks." He stuffs the phone into his pocket before sheepishly meeting my gaze and stepping aside. "Mr. Casey, it seems my colleagues forgot to give me an updated version of the guest list. I'm sorry about that."

"No worries."

He motions to the door. "You can go on in. Please take the left staircase at the end of the hall. Jenna will meet you at the top with your pass."

"Thanks, man. Hope your night gets better."

"Me too."

I enter the hotel and make my way down a long, dimly lit hallway. The house music coming from upstairs vibrates my chest, reminding me of my booze-filled clubbing days. Taking the steps two at a time, I pause on the landing, where a strikingly beautiful woman with dark eyes and skin greets me with a smile. She's wearing a royal-blue minidress with teal stilettos, but what most intrigues me is her elaborate, peacock-feather headdress.

I raise a brow at her. "Jenna?"

"That's me." She hands me a lanyard. "Here's your VIP pass. Please keep it with you at all times."

"Thanks." I loop it over my neck.

She motions for me to follow as we stride down another hallway, the subversive music growing louder with each step.

Jenna smiles over her shoulder at me. "Oh, I almost forgot. You'll be needing *this* as well." Without slowing her pace, she places a simple black masquerade mask in my hand.

I stare at it in confusion. When Ella said "dress to impress" I assumed that meant black tie. Now I'm wondering if Dracula knows something I don't.

"Is this a costume party?"

She flashes a wicked grin. "Something like that."

Brain-dick connection aside, it occurs to me I neglected to do my research. A big no-no in the hypervigilance playbook.

"What's the nature of this event?"

Jenna stops in her tracks outside a heavy steel door. "Put on the mask, Mr. Casey."

I slide it down over my face while searching her eyes for clues. "Is it an organized game of cops and robbers?"

"If that's what you'd like it to be, we can arrange that . . . but only if I get to be a cop." Her gaze travels the length of my body, satisfaction infusing her features. "Because I have a few sets of cuffs I'd love to try out."

"Oh, now I get it. It's a sex toy party, isn't it?"

"Close, but not quite." Jenna pushes through the door into the nightclub. *Holy. Fucking. Shit.*

Trailing behind her, I enter the realm of fishnets and nipple tassels. It's a middle schooler's wet dream, with breasts and asses in every direction. It wouldn't be far from the truth to call it my fantasy too.

The dance floor surges with a gyrating mass of limbs as primarily female guests move their bodies to the hypnotic music. A long catwalk extends the length of the club. On stage, burlesque dancers give a scandalous display of bare flesh, feathers, sequins, and lace. Everyone in the room is wearing some variation of a costume, headdress, or masquerade mask.

"What the actual fuck have I gotten myself into?" The flash of lights on sequins stupefies me. Here I am, in my suit and tie, surrounded by tits and ass like a fucking penguin caught in the headlights.

She trails a fingertip down my chest. "Welcome to Burlesquerade, where fantasies come to life."

Astonishment wars with intrigue as Jenna leads me farther into the room. I've never seen anything like this. I can't believe Ella didn't give me a heads-up.

She smirks. "Not quite what you expected, is it?"

"You think?" I loosen my tie. "I'm assuming there's a compelling reason for this gathering?"

"It's a benefit for victims of domestic or sexual abuse. They funnel all proceeds into a selection of charities. This is the second annual Burlesquerade. Last year, we raised almost one hundred thousand."

Despite my bewilderment, assisting abuse victims is certainly a cause I can get behind. Hell, it's been two decades, and the shit I went through still keeps me up at night, curling into a ball on my side. I still look over my shoulder and sit with my back to a wall. So, yeah, if a roomful of tits and ass is going to help someone else cope, I'm on board.

"That's impressive. How can I help?"

"There will be several silent auctions with opportunities to bid on private performances. Or, if you prefer, you can visit Stefania at the reception desk and write a check. The main show will begin shortly, and trust me, you're in for a treat."

"Where can I find Ella?"

"She's out there somewhere. I'm sure you'll cross paths, but I'll give you a hint. She looks purrrrfect tonight."

"I imagine that's every night, but I'll keep the tip in mind."

"See ya." Jenna sashays toward the bar.

I edge along the club's perimeter, carefully navigating through the crowd. Scanning the partially concealed faces around me, I'm Orion again—a man on the hunt. My prey eludes me, and the problem is, I don't know whether I should be on the lookout for a catsuit or leopard print, and there's plenty of both.

"Good evening, lovelies," croons a female voice. "Is everyone having a good time?" A burlesque dancer saunters onstage with her microphone. She's wearing stilettos, a black thong, and little else. Like a sultry raven, the buxom blonde has an ornate feather headdress and a pair of obsidian wings. She shimmies her shoulders in a potent dance of seduction, rhinestone-encrusted nipple tassels in full force. The audience erupts in cheers. "My name's Lady Raven and I'll be your hostess tonight."

Lingering near a group of nearly naked bird women, I listen to her spiel and continue scanning the room for Ella. I can't believe she kept me in the dark about the nature of this event.

A shudder courses down my spine. Forcing a deep breath, I unfasten my shirt's first two buttons.

Lady Raven struts along the catwalk. "I'm looking for a volunteer to come onstage and help me out. I promise it'll be worth your while. Any takers?"

I narrow my eyes on a group of people near the bar, hoping to glimpse Ella. There's a woman in a little red dress with a similar hair color, but she's the wrong height.

"Hey, tall, dark, and handsome over there, get up here."

A bird woman nudges me, and I glance at the stage. I'm met with a beckoning, come-hither stare.

Huh? Wait, what?

My head darts from side to side. I'm the only man in the vicinity.

"Yes, I'm talking to you, baby," she drawls, and a spotlight finds me in the crowd. "Get up here."

Oh, hell no.

Shaking my head, I hold a hand up to decline. Suddenly, I'm flanked by a set of bluebird women who tug me toward the stage. Since I'm already wildly off my game, I relent and follow them up the steps at the end of the catwalk. The last thing I need is to look like chickenshit if Ella is watching. I stop in front of Lady Raven, who awaits with her hands on her hips.

"Look at *you*. What's your name?" She holds the microphone out to me.

"Garrett."

"Welcome, and thank you for volunteering," she says with a wink.

"I didn't, but that's okay."

"Well, are you open minded enough to brave the spotlight for a few minutes?" Her syrupy sweet voice dares me to back down. "It's for a worthy cause."

"What do I have to do?"

"Just relax, baby. We'll take care of the rest. And if at any point you wanna tap out, all you've gotta do is say the word."

"Wait. You're telling me I need a safe word?"

"That's up to you." Her smirk is laced with a challenge. "Do you like animals, Garrett?"

"Yeah, but what does that have to do with safe words?"

"You'll see. What about cats? Do you like them?"

"Cats are fine," I say, shrugging. My experience is limited to Lena's two, and the black one who hangs around, but I've never minded the animals.

"Good to know, because I have some kitties who wanna play . . ."

The blue harpies reappear, leading me to a red leather throne positioned at center stage.

Lady Raven pushes me into the chair with her palm on the middle of my chest. "Have a seat, Garrett."

Like Mafia enforcers, the bluebirds shackle my wrists to the throne before I can even react. My mouth drops open, but no sound comes out.

Knots aren't new to me. Anya loves being tied up when we fuck. I don't have an issue with restraints, as long as *I'm* the one in the position of dominance. We've never done a role reversal. Willful submission is new territory for me.

Never mind the fucking audience.

Lady Raven covers her mic and leans in close, speaking so only I can hear, "There are buttons on the arms of the chair. One on each side. Feel them?"

My fingertips locate the buttons and I nod.

"Press and hold both simultaneously for ten seconds and everything stops."

"Got it."

"This is meant to be fun, but if you're uncomfortable, let us know and we'll cut you loose. I mean it, Garrett." Her tone is earnest and kind, without a hint of her sultry Lady Raven persona, making me wonder about who she is in real life. She touches my hand and smiles. "No questions asked, and no one's the wiser. Okay?"

"Yeah."

"Good." She lifts the microphone to her lips as she slowly backs away, reverting to performance mode. "Don't look so nervous, baby. These kitties don't bite too hard."

A strangled shout escapes my throat when an iron cage slams down around me. If it weren't for the shackles, I would've gone through the roof.

"Are you ready for a little game of cat and mouse?" Lady Raven laughs wickedly as the first few notes of Ariana Grande's "God is a Woman" spill from the speaker. "Audience, what do you think? Is Garrett gonna make some kitties purr tonight?"

A troupe of six feline burlesque dancers prowl onto the stage and position themselves outside the enclosure. The music grows louder, and the women climb the iron bars, arching their sinewy bodies. It's a decadent display of fluid sexuality.

Meanwhile, I'm in a cage—shackled to a chair—pondering the irony of the event. But hey, at least they didn't blindfold or ball gag me. I would've lost my ever-loving shit. My fingertips glide over the safe buttons and I relax a little, knowing if I need to take control of the situation, I can.

Not going to lie, I'm enjoying the show. Although I'd much rather see Ella. My cock twitches in agreement.

After a few minutes, the dancers untangle their bodies, and the cage slowly lifts. I breathe a sigh of relief as my enclosure is raised by a set of heavy steel cables and vanishes somewhere overhead.

Now, the dancers advance on me, prowling closer and closer. The crowd goes nuts.

Lady Raven sashays into the scene. "Shall we crank this up a notch?"

The audience cheers, and I shift in my seat, unable to adjust myself.

She traces her fingertips along my jawline. "What do you think, lovelies? Can Garrett get any hotter?"

Equal parts mildly disturbed and more than a little aroused, I shake my head in protest.

"He doesn't seem to think so. How about we prove him wrong?"

The audience goes wild, and the song changes to Christina Aguilera's "Nasty Naughty Boy." As the dancers sexily crawl their way to the throne, I know I'm fucked.

They pounce in a blur of bare flesh, nipple tassels, and leather. One woman trails her tail up my arm and across my neck. I clench my jaw as a different one drags her nails down my chest and gives me a lap dance.

I channel every ounce of energy into my composure. I never realized how hard it is to think your way out of a hard-on.

Oh, the irony.

Sweat collects on my brow, and my scalp prickles as I imagine some extremely unsexy scenarios involving sandpaper condoms. I grip the chair and force my lungs to expand on shallow breaths, my heart hammering in my chest. The last thing I need is to come in my pants in front of a roomful of people.

Then, I spot Ella's vivid blue-green gaze watching me from the audience.

Camera in hand, she's standing stage left, wearing a platinum, sequined minidress. Mocha waves cascade over her shoulders and down her back. A silver feline mask partially obscures her face, but when we make eye contact, her red lips curve into a smile. She tilts her head at me in a sultry nod, and just like that, she tips the balance.

Everything around me fades, and my vision tunnels, focusing on the contours of her face. Those plush lips. Her hypnotic eyes. In this moment, she's the only woman in the room. Arousal steals the spotlight, making me forget my discomfort and the sordid irony of the event. I imagine *her* hands on me, her body moving on top of mine. My cock painfully strains against my zipper, giving the dancer grinding in my lap way more than she bargained for.

When Ella bites down on her lower lip and winks, I damn near implode with lust. Nostrils flaring, a low growl leaves my throat. In all my life, I've never been so horned up that my nostrils flared. Yet here I am, like a motherfucking bull in a corral, waiting for some asshole to blow his trumpet.

Ella's gaze is lit with lust and amusement. She licks her lips, and my thoughts wander south.

My matador awaits. And I'm ready to fuck her senseless.

Go ahead, baby, wave your red flag.

Sixteen

A setup, foreplay, and a test

Ella

Garrett saw me when I was ready to be seen, and not a moment sooner. Now, my gaze roves over him as he struggles to contain himself. I take a few steps closer to the stage, watching the rapid rise and fall of his chest like a sinful voyeur. Everything about him screams barely leashed, from the clench of his jaw to the way he white-knuckles the throne, his muscular frame flexing and tensing against his arousal.

His eyes smolder with dark promise, a carnal heat that steals my breath and sets me afire. When I lick my lips, his expression morphs into a picture of pure, unfettered lust, effectively melting my panties.

I don't look away.

And neither does he.

The song ends, and Lady Raven saunters to the throne. "Once again, thank you for volunteering, Garrett." She unlocks the shackles that bind him. "She gave me a *fabulous* description, so it was super easy to spot you in the crowd."

Realization of his setup dawns in his sexy head, making his eyes darken. Those piercing orbs narrow on my face.

She gestures to the audience. "Wasn't he a great sport?"

Everyone cheers when Garrett rises to his full height. My gaze drifts to his prominent erection. He doesn't adjust himself or try to hide it, just prowls across the stage, slowly shaking his head as he descends the steps.

My insides flutter when he closes the distance between us, his molten gold eyes pinned to mine.

As a rule, I don't do well with tall men. If he were any other man looming over me, I'd have to take a step back. Garrett is different. Like Paolo, he doesn't use his height as a weapon. His towering frame doesn't make me shrink or cower. I stand taller.

"Hello," I purr the greeting. "Enjoying yourself?"

"You tell me." His gaze darts below his belt before meeting mine once more. "Was that your idea of foreplay?"

"I'm not sure what you're referring to," I say with feigned innocence.

"I'm curious what you were hoping to achieve with that little arrangement." His rumbled words are as silken as they are rough.

"So quick with the accusations, Mr. Casey. Haven't you heard of giving someone the benefit of the doubt?"

The hint of a smirk plays at the corners of his lips. He rubs his jaw as his gaze leaves mine to wander the curves of my body. "Did you enjoy the show, Ella?"

"More than you can imagine." Eyeing his bulge, I fight off the urge to take him into my hands and stroke him. Instead, I hand over my camera bag. "Thanks for being my assistant this evening."

"My pleasure." He shoulders the equipment like it's featherlight.

My aching body knows otherwise. I've never had a massage, but now is one of those times I'd consider trying one.

I rub at the tender spots where the straps dug into my skin. "You ready?"

"Born ready, Cupcake."

Without the weight of my collection of lenses, I can flit about and do my thing.

I motion for him to follow, and we position ourselves near the end of the catwalk. A furry-masked, male burlesque dancer prowls onstage to Bruno Mars's "Gorilla."

"This event's a bit sexually charged." Garrett tilts his head to the side, his gaze searching mine. "Seems ironic and potentially triggering as a benefit for sex abuse victims."

"Are you triggered?"

"Not what I said."

"Sex sells," I tell him with a shrug. "All attendees are given full disclosure, so they can opt to avoid triggers, as necessary. Burlesquerade is about taking back power. Repairing your relationship with sex and pleasure. Regaining control after it's been taken from you by an intimate partner, be it someone you trust or a stranger."

"I get it."

"Besides, no one is forced to come here. It's all spelled out on the invitation. Everyone knows what to expect before they arrive."

"Everyone except me," he murmurs.

I stare up at his face. "Were you not given the option to stop?"

He crosses his arms over his chest but doesn't answer.

"And in my defense, I didn't know you'd be getting a lap dance," I add, hoping he's not truly pissed.

"What did you *think* would happen when they shackled me to a chair?"

Good question.

"I guess I didn't give it much thought." I turn my attention to the stage and photograph the dancer, pausing to swap out a lens. The guy notices and struts down the catwalk, performing a series of erotic hip gyrations for my benefit.

Garrett's turbulent expression intensifies, his brows meeting when the dancer blows me a kiss. "Enjoying *his* show?"

"Not as much as yours. This is just a performance." I snap a few more pictures before turning to face him. "Yours was a test. Albeit, it went a bit further than I anticipated."

"Oh? What kind of test?"

It was a test of limits and restraint, but I don't dare tell him. Deeper than that, it was a test of his ability to relinquish control. I need to know if he's capable of giving me what I need.

"You're not gonna elaborate?"

"I wasn't planning on it, no," I say coyly.

He steps closer and lowers his lips to my ear. "Did I pass?"

"With flying colors."

Seventeen

Burgers, mixed signals, and hard limits

Garrett

I stare at Ella's face, floored by her enigmatic comments. She said it was a test. Maybe she's a dominatrix, or she gets off on watching other people have sex. Then again, she claims she didn't expect the lap dance, so voyeurism doesn't really track. Whatever her story, I'd be lying if I said I didn't want to know more.

I ponder her motives while watching a leather-clad female shoulder-shimmy her way on stage, armed with a riding crop and cat-o'-nine-tails. Rihanna's "S&M" is the soundtrack for this performance.

Eventually, the event winds down. We linger by the stage as Ella scrolls through her pictures on the camera's LCD screen. Her smirk tells me she's pleased with herself. As if sensing my thoughts, she holds the camera out for me. Sure enough, it's a close-up of my face contorted with a mixture of shock and amusement.

"I better not see any of these in the entertainment section of the *Tribune.*"

"This isn't a *Tribune* assignment."

I tilt my head to the side. "So, you're saying *this* is how you spend your free time?"

"No. Like I mentioned when I invited you, I'm working."

"But you said—"

"Yes, the *Tribune* is my main employer, but I also moonlight as a free-lance photographer. I guess you could call it my passion project. My typical clients hire me for private events like this, or the occasional boudoir shoot. You know, sensitive situations and subjects where discretion is imperative. I love it because I get to be choosy about my workload. I only commit when something fits into my schedule"—she gestures to the room around us—"or aligns with my beliefs."

"Makes sense."

She purses her lips. "Although, sometimes, I step outside my comfort zone when the money is too good to refuse."

"Like weddings?"

"Exactly. I'm not big on divas. I don't have the energy to deal with brides on a regular basis, so I rarely agree to shoot weddings. That said, I've pho-tographed a handful of celebrity marriages—and handled *extreme* bridezil-las—because the clients were willing to pay top dollar."

Carissa would've been a bridezilla. Of that, I'm fucking certain.

"Oh, I can only imagine the entitlement. I've encountered some real as-sholes in my line of work too."

"Yeah. They suck." She rolls her eyes. "I call them silver platter people."

I chuckle. "My description is usually much more colorful." I shift gears, intrigued by her side gig, and more than a little impressed with her work ethic. "What's your company called?"

"It's not really a company." A rueful smile curves her lips. "Yet." She tucks the camera away and glances up at me. "But I hope it develops into a sustainable income source one day." Shrugging, she releases a wistful sigh. "Anyway, are you hungry?"

I smirk because she's a professional subject changer. "I'm always hungry."

"You've mentioned that." Her eyes sweep the length of my body. "I'm currently starving. Let's get something to eat."

We head to the restaurant affiliated with Hotel Polaris and settle into a private corner booth. I choose the bench that allows me a full view of the room. It's nearly the kitchen's closing time, so we opt for something quick, ordering burgers and a platter of fries to share.

Ella sips her water and smiles. "Thank you for coming tonight."

"Thanks for surrendering to my gravitational pull."

She gnaws her lower lip. "I hoped to explore that notion this evening." Her voice is soft, uncertain. At odds with the desire in her eyes.

"What are we waiting for?"

"First, there are things about me you need to understand."

I lean forward in my seat. "I'm listening."

"I'm not your typical woman."

"Oh, I'm well aware of that, Ella."

"I'm not a missionary kind of girl. And I don't make love."

This woman is a fucking dream come true.

I barely hold back my grin. "Works for me. I don't fall into the slow and gentle category."

She shifts position, crossing and uncrossing her legs. "I don't think you understand where I'm going with this."

Uh, I think I do. "You're asking me to come home with you?"

"I don't bring men to my home."

"All right, then come back to my place."

She shakes her head. "I don't go home with men."

I study her face, the indecision warring on her features. She prearranged for me to be shackled to a chair and watched me get publicly dry humped. I supposedly passed her test, whatever it may be, but she shuts me down when I try to have an open conversation about our expectations for the night?

I release a heavy sigh. "I think maybe I'm misinterpreting the signals you're sending."

She stares at her plate. "You're not."

"You sure?"

Keeping her eyes averted, she feverishly twirls a lock of hair. Her nervous energy is driving me crazy, so I grip her wrist to still it. She flinches, yanking from my grasp.

What the fuck is going on here?

"Whoa." I hold my hands up in surrender. "I didn't mean to freak you out. I'm sorry."

"No, I'm sorry." She reaches for her purse. "This was a mistake," she whispers, rising from her seat.

"Ella, look at me." She meets my gaze, and I make a show of sitting on my hands. "I won't touch you again. Please sit back down and talk to me."

"You seem like a nice guy. You don't want to get involved with a woman like me."

"You don't know me well enough to make that assumption."

"I know myself well enough to know I'm not good for you."

"I'll be the judge of what's good for me. Don't tell me what I want."

What I want is *her*.

I want to uncover her secrets; vanquish the demons she's hiding. My desire eclipses any doubts, any second-guesses my mind tries to conjure. Right now, I don't give a flying flamingo fuck whether we're good for each other. I'll deal with the fallout.

"Please sit back down."

She slowly sinks onto the bench. "I don't like being touched."

"Got it."

"In any capacity."

"What *do* you like?" I ask, determined to understand what's behind her skittishness.

"Feeling safe."

"How do you feel safe?"

Her gaze, wide with vulnerability, finds mine. "I need to have total control of the situation."

"Define control. Are we talking whips and chains? Are you asking to beat me with something? Brand me with a hot poker? Peel away strips of flesh?"

She twists her napkin. "No. It's nothing like that."

"Ella, your eyes are telling a thousand stories, but I can't read your mind. You've gotta talk to me. Tell me what you want from me, and I'll let you know if I can give it to you."

"This is a *necessity*, not a desire. If you want me, you need to let me take the reins."

"There's no question I want you, but honesty's crucial here. Let's be clear about our intentions so there are no misunderstandings."

"I need you to be restrained," she whispers, her lower lip trembling.

Yours was a test. Her words fit themselves into place. She wanted to see how I'd handle being tied up. The alarm bells in my head start to ring.

I cross my arms over my chest. "You'll only feel safe enough to go to bed with me if I'm tied up?"

"Correct."

The hairs on my neck stand on end. My head, my gut, and every muscle and nerve ending join forces, screaming for me to get the fuck out. Common sense begs me to walk away from her.

But I can't.

Because the fucker beating in my chest is telling me to stay.

She needs me.

The affirmation echoes with each throb of my pulse. I'm no stranger to loneliness. I don't want Ella to be alone tonight. And after the month I've had, solitude is the last thing I need.

"I'll do it."

"You really mean that?"

I stare into her eyes. "Yeah."

"If we do this, I'll have sex with you. *Not* the other way around."

I frown. "What do you mean?"

"I decide the position, the pace, and the intensity. I can touch and kiss you however I want, but you may *not* kiss me."

"At all?"

"Correct. I don't kiss on the lips, and I hate being touched."

"Why?"

"The reason doesn't matter."

"It matters to me."

She holds up a hand. "It can't."

"So, basically, you just want me to lie there while you have your way with me?"

"Yes."

"How is that pleasurable for you?"

"Don't worry about me. My pleasure's not your concern."

"Sex is a two-way street. I'm more than happy to reciprocate."

She crosses her arms. "I'm not doubting your abilities, but if you want me, that's the way it needs to be."

"If you need control, I'm willing to give you some. I'll let you tie me up, but here's what can't happen." I lean forward in my seat, pinning her with my gaze. "You will *not* blindfold or gag me in any way. Those are hard limits. Understood?"

Eighteen

A decision, a hotel room, and a reminder

Ella

I admire how easily Garrett sets boundaries. Everything from his tone to his posture conveys an assertiveness I'd give anything to be capable of.

"I hear you loud and clear, Garrett. Now that we understand each other, I'll ask you once more. Are you willing to put aside your desires in favor of my needs?"

Clenched jaw. Forehead lines. The visual cues of his hesitation speak volumes. His gaze darkens as doubt and certainty battle for the upper hand.

The human brain amazes me. I love the twilight before we reach a decision. The space between what we think and our ultimate response. We're wired to crave symmetry, but our desires don't always align with our needs or what's good for us. It's a tug-of-war between chaos and order. Equilibrium is often unattainable. If and when we reach it, that balance is delicate. We can't exist in a vacuum. Outside forces will always threaten the harmony we think we've found. No matter how tightly we grasp those fleeting moments of stability, they slip through our fingers.

Sometimes I wonder why we cling to order if chaos is inevitable. What would happen if we surrendered to the imbalance instead of fighting it? Can we embrace the fluid nature of symmetry? Sure. Is it risky? Of course. The fragile balance between risk and safety is another ideal we dig our claws into. But maybe we have it all wrong. What if the true danger lies in stagnancy?

Garrett teeters on the edge of the unknown. Deliberations are under-way, but his jury is still at odds over me.

"I asked you a question."

His nod is nearly imperceptible. "Let's make it happen."

Equal parts terrified and relieved, I stand and reach for my purse. He grabs the check, and we head to the front counter. He yanks his wallet from a pocket, but I tell the hostess to charge our meal to my room before he can pay.

His brows come together. "I wanted to treat you."

"This isn't a date," I remind him.

"Last I checked, they weren't mutually exclusive," he mutters, following me from the restaurant.

We ride the elevator to the eleventh floor, his gaze never leaving mine. Alone in the cramped space, his stare is more intimate than any sexual en-counter I've experienced.

I peer into his eyes, feeling my defenses weaken. My past tells me to fortify them and push him away, but I can't. The twisted paradox comman-deering my self-control makes me ache to lower my drawbridge for once. Still, that resolve is tumultuous at best.

I'm seconds from snatching my armor and running.

I've never willingly gone to bed with someone other than Paolo. No one understands my dysfunction or the full extent of what I've been through. Not even Paolo, and he's the man I've known longest, the one I've felt safest with.

Until now.

It doesn't make sense that I feel safe with Garrett. The man's a stranger, but I *know* him nearly as well as I know myself. The inexplicable pull sur-passes any force I've ever felt.

Knowing his gaze is locked on to my ass as we walk down the hall to my room, I can't help but sway my hips a little.

He sucks a sharp breath and follows me inside. "You're killing me."

I lock the door behind us.

Garrett removes his jacket and tie, draping them over the desk chair. He kicks off his shoes and waits at the foot of my bed, fists clenched at his sides. "Ready when you are, Cupcake."

"Take off your shirt."

He unbuttons the white dress shirt with sure fingers, then slides the material from his broad shoulders and drops it onto the bed. My gaze travels over his body. Like mine, his nipples are hard, and his chest is heaving. A smattering of dark hair covers the muscular expanse of olive skin. I follow the trail down his chiseled abdomen to where it disappears beneath his waistband.

"Are you Italian by chance?" I ask, noticing the similarities in our complexions and hair color.

"No. I'm first generation Irish Israeli."

"You're stunning."

"Thanks. So are you." He smiles, and I lose the ability to think.

I point. "Take off your belt and give it to me."

"Yes, ma'am." He unfastens the belt and slides it from the loops of his pants. Smirking, he hands over the length of leather. "Promise not to spank me with this?"

"Spanking's not my thing." Hitting him is the furthest thought from my mind. All I can focus on is the enormous bulge in his pants. The anticipation ignites me, heat blooming between my thighs. I grip his waistband. "Take these off."

Fingers now fumbling, he works the button free and lowers the zipper. The pants fall to his ankles, and he steps out of them, shoving them aside with a foot. He stands before me, wearing nothing but boxer briefs and socks.

The man's body is gorgeous. He's hotter than any celebrity I've encountered or the fitness models I've seen. My gaze drops below his waist, and I wonder if his penis is as beautiful as the rest of him. The thought makes me even wetter.

I point to his socks. "You know what to do."

He tugs them off, nearly losing his balance. "Whoa."

His quick recovery hop amuses me, because I'd be lying if I said I was the picture of steadiness. The heels I practically live in feel suddenly foreign.

Kicking off my stilettos, I nod to the king-size mattress. "Get on the bed."

"How do you want me?" he asks, his voice low and husky.

"On your back. Rest your head on the pillows." I retrieve two silk scarves from my bag. "Stretch your arms out to the sides."

Garrett does as I ask, settling against the luxe red comforter. "No blindfolds," he reminds me.

"I want to see your eyes, not hide them."

Nineteen

Orgasms, a betrayal, and a craving

Garrett

"I'm sorry it has to be this way." Ella clasps my wrist with cool finger-tips, hands trembling as she ties her scarf around it.

Her knot is tight. Not circulation-cutting tight, but damn close. She secures the opposite end to a bedpost, and our eyes meet as she makes her way to my other side. Lust, fear, and vulnerability swirl in her gaze, but I'm the vulnerable one now.

I've never allowed someone to tie me up. A small voice in my head chastises me for not mentioning my whereabouts to Lena, like I've been insisting she do since her return from Alaska. Here I am, tied to a hotel room bed, and no one's the wiser. Hopefully, I don't wake up in a bathtub missing a kidney. It's not like me to be this trusting. I don't even know this woman, and I've given her my literal underbelly. What if she kills me?

Or worse.

I shudder as memories of that dingy basement resurface. The hum of fluorescent lights and stench of wet cardboard. The way my vision blurred with pain when I tried to scream for help around the length of fabric that choked and gagged me.

That motherfucker stole my innocence. My dignity.

"Are you cold?" Ella asks, voice soft with concern.

"No."

She ties the scarf around my other wrist. "What's wrong? You're giving me a weird look."

"Are you planning to kill me or harvest my organs?"

Her brows fly upward. "Of course not." She slowly lowers my wrist and settles on the edge of the bed, her turquoise gaze searching my face. "Why the hell would you think that?"

"Oh, you know, reasons and stuff."

She cups my cheek in a move that's far more tender than anything I've experienced. "Tell me what's on your mind."

"Why do you need to tie me up?"

"We went over this, remember?" She points to the restraints. "These have nothing to do with you. It's a *me* thing."

"You sure?"

"I promise." She tilts her head to the side. "Reconsidering?"

"No. Just figured I'd check. You know, cover my bases."

"I want you, Garrett, but this is the only way I know how to let my guard down enough to make it happen. Can you understand that?"

"Yeah, baby. I got it."

"Good." She kisses my forehead, then stands and grasps my wrist, extending it out to the side. She fastens it to the bedpost and lightly trails her nails up my arm. "Now, how about you keep quiet and let *me* cover your bases?"

I open my mouth to respond, but the words escape me when she unzips the back of her dress. With a sultry smile, she allows it to glide to her feet, exposing a red lace bra and panties. The lingerie is set against a backdrop of dewy olive skin, and her body's more beautiful than I could've imagined. My cock, having recovered from my momentary internal struggle, stands at attention.

"Red's your color. It's also my new favorite."

She toys with her bra straps. "You're saying I should keep this on then?"

"No, I want everything off." I lick my lips, dying to taste every inch of skin in front of me. "Immediately. If not sooner."

"You're not running the show, remember?" She smiles and slides the straps over her shoulders in an agonizingly slow tease.

"Yeah." I nod to my wrists. "You've made that clear."

"As long as we're on the same page . . ." She changes tempo and tugs the lace cups down, freeing full breasts I ache to touch and kiss. She unhooks the bra, then drops it onto the floor.

I didn't think it was possible, but my cock is even harder. My gaze follows the curve of her waist, lingering on the soft, womanly hips I'd love to hold on to while I thrust.

"Fuck, you're stunning, Ella."

"Thank you." She slides out of the panties and drops them by the dress. My gaze drifts between her legs, but she crawls up the bed to me before I can savor the view. Her lips meet my throat, and her mouth moves over me like a flame. The heat of her breath mixes with sensuous flicks of her tongue, making me moan.

"You taste good," she murmurs, teeth grazing my collarbone. She slides a hand over my chest, down my abs, stroking me through my boxers.

"Oh, fuck, yes." My hips lift off the bed, pressing into her touch.

She toys with my waistband. "You feel better about this now?"

I groan and thrust my cock against her hand instead of answering.

"Good." She tucks her fingertips beneath the elastic, feathering them on my skin. Her pupils are dilated, cheeks flushed, full lips parted. She flicks her tongue out to wet them. "For a moment I thought you wanted to stop."

"Nah, baby. I'm all in." My body's strung tight, humming with lust.

Ella palms my cock and strums my chords, sliding her hand up and down. Right now, I want her to play me hard. I need her to lick me. Suck me. Ride me. Fuck me. She can do whatever she wants.

She yanks the boxers to my thighs and uses her teeth to remove them the rest of the way, lightly nipping my kneecaps and ankles on her way down. Tossing the underwear aside, she hungrily eyes my cock, then grips me, stroking and massaging the underside with her thumb. "I never knew I could want someone this badly."

"Feeling's mutual, Cupcake," I say on a gasp. "Now fuck me before I lose my mind."

She reaches for the condom on the nightstand, tears open the wrapper, and slowly rolls it onto me, her eyes never leaving mine. Her grip on my cock and the languid fluidity of her movements tell me I'll be lucky if I last thirty seconds. Hell, it'll be a miracle if I even make it that long.

She straddles my hips and leans forward to check the knots at each wrist.

Her nipples brush my chest. I want to palm her breasts, drag my thumbs over those nipples and pinch, kiss, and suck them. I want to taste every goddamn inch of her. The fact that I can't touch her is driving me insane.

Absolutely fucking insane.

"Tight enough for you?" My voice is someplace between a growl and a whisper.

"That's a more appropriate question for *you*." She lines up the head of my cock with her pussy. "Don't you think?"

"Yeah, well I—"

She takes me to the hilt in one smooth motion, stealing my words. My breath. My sanity. This was no slow easing in. No gradual lowering of her body onto mine. Nope. She climbed into the fucking saddle and took off in a gallop. Whip cracking, spurs digging. I'm balls deep in ecstasy. She's so hot and tight, I'm ready to come apart at the seams.

"Holy fuck, you feel good," I rasp, unable to believe I'm lucky enough to have this gorgeous woman on top of me.

Ella squeezes my hips between her thighs and trails her nails down my chest. Tendrils of hair tickle my skin as she leans forward and clamps her hands on my shoulders.

She rolls her hips in circles. "Do you like this better?"

Lost in the blue-green of her eyes, I moan something incoherent.

Her smile widens as she slowly lifts herself. "How about this?" She slams her body down onto my cock.

I can feel my eyes go wild. "Oh, fuck."

"You like it harder. Good to know." She does it again, and my pelvis flexes upward to meet her. She shakes her head. "I control the pace, remember?" Another downward thrust accompanies her whispered reminder.

I grunt a reply of sorts and struggle against the restraints, my arms stretched to their limit.

Yeah, I remember your rules, Cupcake.

But God help me, it's hard. I can't stifle the guttural groans and moans ripping from my throat. This is unlike anything I've ever experienced. My submission heightens every sensation, from her pussy's viselike grip to the way her thighs squeeze my hips. The pleasure radiates from my dick to my toes, and I swear it's enough to kill me.

She tightens her muscles and changes pace, slowly circling her hips as she leisurely grinds my cock. Her eyes are closed, with butterfly lashes resting on her cheeks. Little sound escapes her parted lips.

She's a quiet lover. Damn near silent. I'm used to my women screaming their pleasure. Not Ella. Her breath hitches on soft gasps as she brings herself to the edge. She picks up speed, telling me she's getting close. Nails digging into my shoulders, she arches her back and lifts until she's nearly free of me. She slams her hips down, breath leaving her in a rush.

"You gotta slow down, baby." I moan as she repeats the movement. Harder this time. "Fucking—fuck—"

I clench my jaw, fists, the muscles in my legs. Ass cheeks, you name it. Holding back this orgasm is like deflecting a tidal wave with a surfboard. Ragged moans rip from my throat, and I can't stop them. I love fucking, but I've never been on the receiving end. My surfboard's about to break in half.

"Let yourself go," she gasps the words.

"Not until you do."

She meets my gaze. "Move your hips with me."

I slam them upward. It only takes a few thrusts for her to shatter into an orgasm.

"Oh! Garrett—" Her head falls back. "Don't stop . . ."

The surfboard splinters into pieces and the pulsing spasms of her pussy bring me under.

Over.

Sideways.

Meeting her thrust for thrust, I bellow something incomprehensible and come harder than ever in my life.

She's still moving.

It's too much ecstasy. Ella climaxes a second time, whimpering my name as she collapses forward. She rests her head on my chest and clings to me, both of us gasping for breath. Her body continues to flutter around my cock, rippling with the aftershocks of her orgasm.

Neither of us says a word. Not that I'm able to speak. Seemingly content in the saddle, she makes no move to dismount. Instead, she weaves her arms around my neck and holds on to me like she wants to crawl inside my body. Her warm breasts press into my chest, gasps gusting my skin with each rise and fall of her shoulders. Her hair is fanned out, the silken strands tickling my sides.

Ella annihilated me. Nothing compares to the rawness I feel. *Nothing.*

I don't consider myself a lovey-dovey post-sex kind of dude. My experience with intimacy involves a "she orgasms, then I orgasm, then someone gets the hell out" approach. None of that lingering in the afterglow bullshit. But here I am, aching to run my fingers through her hair and breathe her in as she falls asleep in my arms. I actually *want* to snuggle. What reality is this?

Too bad I'm still restrained.

After a few minutes, she kisses my neck, then slowly presses herself up to her elbows. She stares down at me, her eyes mirroring what I'm feeling—a mixture of satisfaction, yearning, and vulnerability.

"Thank you," she whispers, feathering her fingertips over my shoulders and chest, again with that tenderness I can't explain but crave more of.

I never realized how much I wanted someone to touch and hold me. Caress me like I matter. Until now.

"Ella, I'm at a loss for words."

She plants a tender kiss on my cheek before moving off me to sit on the edge of the bed and stretch. She's fucking radiant. Her beauty knows no match. I want to draw her. Paint and sculpt her.

As if sensing my thoughts, she peers over her shoulder with a smile. "Why are you looking at me like that?"

"Because you're a work of art."

Ella laughs and steps into her dress, making me wish I were the fabric brushing her skin. "Why thank you. You're not too shabby, yourself. And by the way . . . your gravitational pull was stronger than I expected."

"Likewise. You just rearranged my solar system." I cock my head to the side. "Why are you getting dressed?"

"Because I'm chilly." Standing, she zips the back of her dress, before tossing her hair over a shoulder. "They keep this hotel way too cold."

"Come over here and let me warm you up."

I need this woman in my arms more than my next breath.

She shakes her head and resettles on the edge of the bed. "Sorry. Doesn't work like that."

"Oh? And why not?" When she doesn't answer, I jut my chin at her. "Lemme guess, you don't cuddle?"

"Not really." She chews her lip like she's ashamed of her admission. "I've never actually cuddled with anyone. Ever."

"*Seriously?*"

"Yeah."

I'm a bona fide sex fiend, but even *I* have cuddled a time or two. Maybe she really doesn't like being touched. Or maybe the idea of postcoital intimacy threatens her femme fatale veneer. God forbid someone sees through her facade.

"It's okay, Ella. You can snuggle with me. I won't tell anyone. It can be our little secret."

Her body goes ramrod straight. "What did you say?"

"I said, nobody has to know what we do. How about you untie me so I can kiss you senseless?"

She lurches to her feet, her eyes going cold. "Like I said before we started, I don't kiss."

"Then let me hold you."

"No." Head darting from side to side, she snatches her purse and clutches it to her chest. "This was a mistake."

"Hold up. What are you doing?"

"Going home." She rushes for the door.

I strain against the scarves at my wrists. "Uh . . . wait a minute. Aren't you gonna untie me first?"

Hands shaking, she reaches for the doorknob. "I . . . I can't."

"You're joking, right?"

She pulls the door open and glances over her shoulder, panic written on her features. "I'm sorry. I need to go."

"Ella Sammons, get back in here and untie me. This isn't funny."

Her eyes well with tears. "I can't."

"Don't walk away from me!" I sputter, yanking my arms.

"I'm so sorry." Her agonized whisper reaches my ears as she exits into the hallway.

The door clicks, and I stare after her in stunned silence.

She just gave me the best sex of my life, and now she's leaving me strung up like a naked Jesus? I hold my breath, waiting for this sick joke's punch line. This can't be real. She wouldn't leave me tied to a bed, butt naked and bewildered. Her bra, panties, and shoes are still on the floor by the desk, for fuck's sake.

She really didn't fuck and flee.

Right?

After twenty minutes of trying to remain calm, I resign myself to the fact she's not coming back. I tug on the restraints, and the fuckers dig into my wrists.

"You've gotta be kidding me."

How could she just leave?

It looks like I'll need to MacGyver my way out before the hospitality workers come to clean the room. Last thing I need is some stranger in a maid outfit climbing aboard. I glance down at myself. The condom's still on, even though my hard-on packed its bags and followed Ella out the door.

First, I try brute strength. That serves only to tighten the knots. The scarves look and feel like silk, but they must be some weird anti-rip synthetic shit. Tendrils of panic squeeze my lungs.

In hopes of putting some slack in my bindings, I scoot my body closer to the headboard, then drag myself to a kneeling position using my abs and legs. It works. Marginally.

Too bad it's a fucking king-size bed.

Ignoring the pain, I clench my jaw and force my arm to bend. I pull my left wrist to my mouth and loosen the knot with my teeth, just enough to pull my hand out. Once that wrist is free, I untie the other. Gasping, I kneel on the bed and examine the bleeding gouges on my wrists.

After gathering my scattered garments, I yank them on while muttering various obscenities to myself. Finally dressed, but too sweaty and flustered to wear my suit jacket, I drape it over my forearm instead. My gaze lands on Ella's red bra and panties.

A better man would march out the door and leave them alone. Too bad I'm not a better man. I snatch the lace garments and stuff them into my suit jacket pocket. After all, I deserve a fucking souvenir for what she put me through.

The doorknob slams against the sheetrock behind it when I fling the door open and stalk down the hall. A hotel worker eyes me as I pass. I flash them a don't-fuck-with-me scowl before continuing on my merry way.

I press the elevator call button and glance at the mirrored doors while I wait. My hair's disheveled, with pieces haphazardly falling in my face. My shirt's an unbuttoned, wrinkled mess, and my exposed nipples could cut glass. I draped the belt over my neck because I couldn't get it on. Now I realize it's because my pants are inside out. The revelation triggers one of those maniacal laughs steeped in disbelief.

I'm still laughing when the door slides open, barely holding it together as I step inside and sag against the wall. The elevator stops at the next floor. A pair of drunken, tuxedo-clad guys enter—obviously enjoying the aftereffects of an open bar wedding.

"Good for you, man!" One of them claps my shoulder. "Looks like you had a fun night."

"You have no fucking idea," I grit out.

The other guy nudges me. "Hey, bro, you know your pants are inside out?"

"Yeah, I realize that. Thank you."

We reach the ground floor and I cross the lobby. Dodging a guy with a luggage cart, I push through revolving doors and step onto the sidewalk.

I stomp all the way to my Jeep, my brisk strides placing distance between me and the twilight zone mindfuck I experienced. Am I acting like a toddler? Maybe. But I don't care. My mood is all over the place as I reflect on what happened. I'm ready to laugh some more, maybe even cry or punch a wall. What the fuck was I thinking, allowing her to tie me up?

I've had my share of walks of shame, but this takes the cake. Only it's not shame I'm feeling. It's a power struggle between anger and intrigue.

I broke my own damn rules.

Here I let down my guard to mitigate her vulnerability, only to have her exploit mine? She turned her back on me. While I'm furious, there's something oddly amusing about Ella's betrayal. She fucked me in every sense of the word. Yet somehow, a sick, twisted part of me wants her more.

I slide into the Jeep and toss my suit jacket onto the passenger seat. A flash of red captures my attention. Ella's bra and panties peek out from my pocket. I snatch the lingerie and stuff it into my glove box before I do something stupid like call her.

Sighing, I rest my forehead on the steering wheel and squeeze my eyes shut.

She's like a drug. Even though I know damn well she's not good for me, I'm desperate to indulge in her.

Or a bottle of whiskey.

Twenty

Regrets, collateral, and cut ties

Ella

I'm exhausted. I know I should sleep, but I can't. Lying on my side beneath the warmth of my comforter, I follow the sway of my grandfather clock's pendulum. Back and forth. Back and forth.

Funny, it matches the chaotic flux in my head.

I wasn't prepared for a flashback freight train to ruin what I shared with Garrett. A barrage of twisted memories replaced my peaceful afterglow with shame and disgust. I didn't expect the panic to rise like a cresting wave, drowning out rational thought.

But it did. In a big fucking way.

It can be our little secret. Nobody has to know what we do.

Those words hit me like a bucket of ice water. I lost count of the number of times I heard them whispered in my ear. That hot, stale breath at my neck. His heavy weight on top of me, crushing my body and spirit.

Garrett doesn't have any idea what I've been through. I should've warned him about my triggers. He had no way of knowing how those words would affect me. I know he meant nothing by them, but I had to leave. I needed to place as much distance as possible between me and my past.

After I closed the hotel room door behind me, I ran barefoot down the hall. I didn't stop running until I was behind the wheel. The drive home was accompanied by a deluge of tears. Hell, I'm still crying, but now they're tears of regret.

I can't believe I left him there, naked and tied to a bed.

What the fuck is wrong with me?

I walked out on him like a cheap prostitute, when what I wanted was to fall asleep in his arms. He wanted it too. I could tell by the way he pressed his head to mine, hugging me the only way he could. The emotion written on his features touched something inside me that has never been touched.

But I left.

It will be a long time before I forget the panic in his eyes. I fucked things up before we even had a chance.

It's better this way.

I made the right decision.

The affirmations do nothing to stop the tears from rolling down my cheeks. Knowing Garrett would brush them away if he were here, makes them fall faster. It's been years since I cried this hard.

God, I wanted to kiss him. More than that, I wanted to let him kiss me. That has never happened before. I've never wanted to let myself be vulnerable. Not even with Paolo, and I've known him for years. I *connected* with Garrett. He has the power to break down my walls. I crave his closeness, his warmth, but he deserves better than a broken shell.

My phone buzzes with a text. I canceled my lunch date with Alessia because I'm not hungry, and I don't have the energy to leave my bed. I know I'll need to force myself to clean Mario and Luigi's tank later, but that's really all I can handle today. The thought of interacting with another human is too much for me. While I hate disappointing Alessia, I can't handle her bubbly personality right now. I need peace. Quiet. Darkness. I peek at my phone to discover it's not her anyway.

It's Jenna, my friend who manages the Wayfarer nightclub. We've hung out a bunch over the past few months in preparation for Burlesquerade. We're not super close, but she's a nice person. Jenna is someone I'd consider opening up to—*if* I were the type of woman who opened up—but we haven't gone deeper than surface level. Regardless, women need to look out for each other, so I'd given her my spare room key last night—just in case. My stomach flip-flops as I unlock the screen.

Jenna: He was gone when I got here.

Thank God.

Me: Okay, thanks.

I asked her to grab my stuff but didn't give her any particulars. I simply claimed I had an emergency and needed to leave abruptly. I can't even imagine Garrett's embarrassment if she'd walked in on him strung up like that.

Jenna: I'll stop by later with your shoes and overnight bag. I couldn't find your underwear though. Are you sure you left without them?

Me: Yes. They were by the shoes.

My dress did little to block the wind, and the blast of frigid air on my bare ass added insult to injury when I ran to my car like a scared animal.

Jenna: Well, they aren't here. I just double-checked.

Me: Thanks for looking.

Great. Where the fuck is my underwear?
Maybe Garrett flushed them down the toilet in a fit of rage. Or burned them. It doesn't matter. I'll never see him—or my undies—again. I guess I'll have to consider the missing lingerie collateral for my foolishness.

Tiny dust particles drift in the beams of sunlight filtering through my blinds. They float so carelessly, weightless and free. That's how I felt after sex with Garrett. Backlit by his desire and our shared pleasure, peacefully drifting through time and space. Then my trauma eclipsed the freedom, blanketing us both in darkness.

My phone buzzes a second time. Groaning, I reach for it, ready to silence the damn thing so I can wallow in peace.

Except it's not Jenna. Or Alessia.

The sight of the name I assigned to Garrett makes my heart leap into my throat. Holding my breath, I read the texts.

Prodigy:Y ou may want to work on your knot technique. That, or give up on any fishing boat aspirations.

Prodigy: What the fuck happened?

Prodigy: How could you leave me like that? Do you realize the mindfuck you put me through?????

My stomach plummets to the floor. I clutch the phone. He deserves an answer, but what can I possibly say?

Prodigy: I know you're reading these. Don't you DARE ignore me! I deserve a fucking explanation.

I type my reply with shaking fingers.

Me: I'm not good for you.

Prodigy: No shit.

Me: I'm sorry I had to leave.

Prodigy: You didn't have to leave. You CHOSE to. There's a difference. You fucking hurt me, Ella.

My body shakes on a sob. Hurting him was the last thing I wanted, but I needed to protect myself. Of course, now that the smoke has settled, and it's clear there was nothing I needed protection from, the magnitude of my fuckup disgusts me. I'm a train wreck, mangled and twisted. The kind that brings rubberneckers out of the woodwork. Too bad I don't have the luxury of looking away.

Me: I'm sorry.

Prodigy: Do us both a favor and lose my number.

Twenty-One

Gingerbread, a confession, and a promise

Garrett

Parking in our neighborhood can be a real bitch. I leave the Jeep two blocks over and trudge down the sidewalk to the brownstone. As I drag my sorry ass home with burning wrists and heavy limbs, I think about how much easier it would be to take an Uber.

Even though she has a brand-new Subaru, Lena rarely drives it. She's a mass transit kind of girl. She's always telling me I should use the subway more often. Nope. Not happening. For one, I can't deal with the stench. New York City's underworld reeks. She's immune to smells, courtesy of time spent in a hospital, but I'm most definitely not. I can almost hear her voice in my head. *But you'd save money on gas and it's better for the environment.*

While she makes a valid point, I won't get rid of my Jeep. I need an accessible way out. A getaway car. I won't allow myself to be stranded somewhere. Or, you know, tied to a bed naked and whatnot.

I round the corner and spot Wes dragging a load of evergreen brambles out the front door. I have no clue why he's up at this hour, let alone doing arborist shit. Lena mentioned he still hasn't adjusted to the time difference between New York and Australia. Clearly, his sleep schedule is as bizarre as mine.

I meet him at the bottom of the stoop. "What's up, Dundee? It's a little early to be grooming shrubbery, don't you think?"

His eyes widen. "Whoa, mate. You look rough. Fun night?"

"Yep." I point to the branches. "What are you doing?"

"Well, *someone* insisted on getting a specific tree, even after I measured and told her it was too tall. I had to saw off some branches."

"Sounds typical." When Lena gets an idea in her head, there's no stopping her. I tap my watch. "But it's the ass crack of dawn, dude. Why are you doing this now?"

"I figured I'd get rid of them before she wakes up. This way I won't be as tempted to tease her about her 'perfect' tree."

I snort. "You're actually surrendering an opportunity to fuck with her? Are you sure you're feeling okay?"

He flashes a cocky grin. "I feel great. Gotta pace myself with the jokes, or else I'll piss her off. Besides, I'd much rather fuck her than fuck with her." He tosses the branches into a pile by the trash cans. "Oh, and by the way, she's expecting you to make gingerbread cookies later."

"You should make them with her. I'm not in the mood today."

"Nope. I've got six strands of lights to untangle. You two are making them, and I plan to eat them." He holds his hands up in surrender. "Listen, I'm not gonna step on any toes. That's your gig, mate. I've heard all the stories. It means a lot to her."

A heavy sigh deflates my chest. "Looks like I'm not getting off the hook."

"Not a chance." He grins and elbows me. "Don't forget your Grinch apron."

I'm still getting used to the idea of someone knowing these details about my relationship with Lena. She and I have no secrets, and while the full-disclosure approach has saved my life more than once, I can only imagine the anecdotes she's filled him in on.

"Oh, it's ready. I ironed the fucker and everything. But you can wear the antlers this year, Emerson."

Wes wags his brows. "Been wearing them in bed for days."

I snort a laugh. "If I hear her call you Santa up there, I'm calling the cops."

"Actually, it's Comet," he informs me, galloping in place like he's riding a reindeer. "She's not big on beards."

"Jesus Christ," I mutter, shaking my head.

"She's yet to call me *that*."

Hours later, after a scalding shower and pathetic excuse for a nap, I head for Lena's living room with the requested extension cord in tow. Wes is on his stomach beneath the spruce, fiddling with the tree stand clamps. Hermione, obviously smitten with the guy, is there to "assist." The plump feline settles her body on his forearm and laps at the tree water.

"Should your cat be drinking this water, love?"

"No, she should not," Lena replies from the kitchen.

"You heard her. Now, go on." Wes nudges Hermione, who rubs her face on his jaw as she passes.

"Watch out for her, she's a real flirt," I tell him with a chuckle.

"I'll take it. The other one's plotting my death." He points to where Harry sits on the arm of the couch—with narrowed eyes and a menacing scowl.

"That's because you're bedding his mama."

"No, seriously. He tried to trip me on the stairs. I almost stepped on the poor bloke's tail." He returns Harry's petulant scowl—like the cat truly gives a fuck he's making faces at him—before meeting my gaze again. "Would've served him right though. Last night he jumped on my dick while I was sleeping. Thank fuck I had a blanket on me." He flexes his fingers in the air, simulating claws.

I give a sympathy cringe. "That's almost as bad as catching it in your zipper."

I've been through some crazy shit, but I've never had my dick clawed. Although there was a chick with braces who did a number on me in college. That experience wins for worst blow job.

Lena enters the room wearing a red Christmas apron. She's in her glory and I must admit, it's damn cute.

"Hey, Gar. Thanks for bringing the cord." She hugs me tightly.

"Got you covered, Mrs. Claus." I nod to the tree. "Looks nice."

"It's perfect, right?"

I smirk. "Perfect height and everything."

"Shut up." She elbows me in the ribs. "I had a vision for this year's tree."

"Looks like lover boy made it happen."

Wes snorts and scuttles from beneath the tree. He fixes the green velvet tree skirt and brushes pine needles from his jeans. "I'm known to make things happen. Do you have a broom, love?"

"Whoa, you guys need some privacy?"

Wes laughs.

Lena gives us an eye roll. "You two are impossible."

"But you love us," Wes reminds her, shaking pine needles from his shirt. He pulls a few out of his hair and flicks them at me. "The tree's been up an hour and there are already needles everywhere."

"I've been trying to convince her to get an artificial tree for years."

Lena shakes her head. "And what do I tell you every year about that?"

"Yeah, I know. That's why I bought you those pine-scented candles."

"Not the same," she insists, retrieving a broom and dustpan from the hall closet.

Wes reaches for them. "I've got this, love. You two make those cookies. I'm hungry."

"Who says I'm gonna let you have any?" she asks over her shoulder as she sashays toward the kitchen.

"Oh, you will, sunshine."

I laugh and follow Lena to the kitchen, where she has everything spread out for gingerbread cookies. As always, she prepped the fragrant dough the night before. I wash my hands, then roll it out with her grandmother's old wooden pin.

I point to the selection of cookie cutters. "Are we doing just people this year, or animals too?"

"You tell me. Bestiality is your thing, not mine."

"Well played." I reach for a reindeer. "Bestiality, it is."

"Oh! I almost forgot." She hands me the theater-themed cookie cutter she bought me. "We need to make some *Prodigy* ones."

I squeeze her shoulder. "Thank you. This is cute."

"I'm so proud of you."

"Means a lot, Leens. Thanks."

Wes enters the room and heads for the fridge. "Have you got any more of that cider, love?"

"Third shelf on the left."

He withdraws the jug of apple cider. "Anyone want some?"

I nod. "Yeah, man. Thanks."

"No, I'm good," Lena says, her brow furrowing. "Mother of God."

"What's wrong?" Wes and I ask in unison.

Her widened eyes snap to mine. "What the hell happened to your wrists?"

Fuck. I tug my shirtsleeves down. "Nothing."

Lena snatches my hand and shoves the fabric up my forearm. "What caused these gouges?"

"I'm fine. It's nothing."

I can count on one hand the number of times I've lied to Lena. Now's one of them. I'm light years from fine. Ella's departure fucked me up.

Badly.

All day, I've been fighting the urge to head to Ralph's Tavern. A little Jameson or Tullamore would do me well. I can almost fucking taste it.

But I resisted, knowing Lena would smell the whiskey on me. I don't want to disappoint her. More than that, I know myself well enough to know I wouldn't stop at a sip. I could swim in a lake of booze and still not be satisfied. I wouldn't realize I was drowning until the surface froze over, trapping me beneath the ice.

Thankfully, I'm still safely perched on the edge, but if I keep finding myself in shitty situations, it won't be long before I venture onto the ice. The temperature's rising. History has proven I can't see the thin spots when I'm skating.

Lena's jade gaze burns into me. "What's going on, Gar?"

"I already told you, it's *nothing*."

"Bullshit. What the fuck happened?" Shoving the shirt higher, she points to the old scarring on my forearm, her eyes watering. "You promised me you'd never do it again."

"I didn't. It's not what you think."

I haven't cut myself in years. Not since she begged me to stop after my stint in the hospital at seventeen. I'll never forget how she clung to me, sobbing her eyes out until I swore to give up all my knives. To this day, she still counts the ones in my knife block whenever she enters my kitchen.

"You promised," she whispers.

"I didn't do it, Leens." I hold my hand over my heart. "I swear to you."

"Then how'd it happen?"

Wes sets a glass of cider in front of me. "Looks a lot like rope burn."

Thanks for blowing my cover, asshole.

I planned to fill Lena in later. Privately. Now feels awkward as fuck. I look away as heat floods my face. I never blush.

"It, uh, well . . ." I clear my throat. "It kinda happened during sex."

"Oh. My. God." Lena grips my chin and turns my head to face her. "Garrett Liam Casey."

"What?"

"Seriously?" She gapes, her panic fading into the background. "You sustained injuries while *fucking*?" When I don't answer, she succumbs to a fit of laughter—complete with her trademark snort.

"It's not funny," I mutter.

"You mean to tell me that 'he who requires control in all things' allowed someone to tie *him* up?"

"I'm not telling you anything right now."

"It's written all over your face." She cackles and turns to Wes. "You should've seen him at the gala. He got one look at her, and his world stopped turning."

I hold up a finger in protest. "Not true."

"Bullshit. Your eyes were glued to her ass." She laughs and playfully ruffles my hair before addressing Wes once more. "Then, he pulled me onto the dance floor so he could show off his moves." She twirls, performing a mini salsa by the sink.

"Also, not true."

"Sorry, mate, but I saw the footage. I'm gonna have to agree with Lena on that one."

"Her booty awakened his loins, and he nearly gave me a friggin' hernia doing his mating dance out there." Lena dramatically shakes her ass and struts around the kitchen. "Oh, c'mon, Gar. Tell me I'm wrong. You totally used me to show off your moves."

I throw my arms up in surrender. "What can I say? Dancing's the closest thing to sex. And *your* inability to keep up is hardly a reflection on me."

"Oh, I keep up just fine. Right, Wes?"

"You got that right, sunshine."

"TMI, people." I laugh and plug my ears.

She pulls up a stool. "So, I take it she called you?"

"She more than called me. She rearranged my musculature and fried a few synapses."

"Tellllll meeeeeee."

"Not right now. I'm still . . . processing."

"Process faster because I wanna know."

Wes claps my shoulder. "A run-in with the 'ever-elusive Ella' explains your appearance this morning."

I stare out the kitchen window. "I'm in over my head with this one."

"Over your head? How?" Lena asks, leaning forward.

Wes chuckles. "She's relentless, isn't she?"

"Yep."

"Quiet, you." She nudges him and turns back to me. "How are you in over your head?"

"In every way imaginable."

She arches a brow. "Because she's kinky?"

"This wasn't kink."

"Specifics?"

When Lena wants to know something, she finds out. Rather than deal with the aggravation of her following me around all day, I cut my losses.

"She tied me to a bed, fucked me into oblivion, and walked out the door."

Lena's eyes widen. "She got dressed and left?"

"That's what I just said, isn't it?"

"Wow. That's like the flip side of 'wham, bam, thank you, ma'am.' I can't believe she did that."

"Oh, it gets better." I can taste the bitter amusement in my tone. "She left me strung up like a virgin sacrifice."

"Wait, she left you *naked?*" Lena's voice is shrill now. "Fucking *tied up?*"

"Affirmative."

"Holy shit." Wes settles on a stool at the island. "Why the hell would she do that?"

"Your guess is as good as mine."

He rakes a hand through his hair. "How'd you get out of there? Did the maids come or something?"

"That's what I was worried about—some hotel worker getting on top. I pulled the knots with my teeth and Houdini'd my way out."

Lena shakes her head, her lip curling in disgust. "That woman is on my shit list."

"Yeah, mine too."

She grips my shoulders. "Stay away from her. I don't care how great the sex was. She's not good for you. I don't like the look in your eyes."

I sigh and run both hands over my face. "I know. That's why I told her to lose my number."

"But did you delete *her* number?" Wes eyes me, his royal-blue gaze searing my skull.

"Not yet."

His lips twitch at the corners. "Something tells me you'll be going back for more."

"He'd better fucking not." Lena tightens her grip on my shoulders. "I mean it, Gar. If you go there, you're setting yourself up to fall . . ." *Off the wagon.* She doesn't need to utter the words. Her eyes finish the sentence.

"No shit."

"After everything you've been through, why would you even consider putting yourself in that position?"

Because I'm tired of being lonely.

Because I need someone who's as fucked up as I am, and Ella fits the description.

Because I like to punish myself.

Because Ella needs me too.

"I dunno," I mutter.

"You're gonna sit here in my kitchen and lie to me?" She releases my shoulders and crosses her arms. "You *do* know."

"Because I felt different when I was with her, and for the first time since Carissa, I wanted *more.*"

"More what?"

"More than a hard fuck," I snap, knotting my hands in my hair. "I want to feel something other than pain, okay?"

"I don't want you to get hurt—"

"Let me worry about that."

"Gimme your phone. I'll delete her number for you." She holds out her hand.

I shake my head. "Not ready to do that yet."

"Seriously?" Disbelief colors her voice. "I don't understand you sometimes."

"Look, I'm not gonna seek her out, but if she comes to me with a damn good explanation for the stunt she pulled, maybe I'll hear what she has to say. I know it's crazy, but I need to see how this plays out."

"Even if she wrecks you?"

Wes touches her arm. "Calm down, love. He's a big boy. He can handle himself."

"You have no idea what he's been through, Wes," she whispers, her eyes welling with tears. Her body shakes as they spill over. "You don't know how it felt to almost lose him."

I pull her into my arms. "Leens, honey, stop. Please don't cry. I know you worry, but I won't let anyone drag me down that rabbit hole again."

"You promise?" Her whispered plea breaks my heart.

I'll never shake the terror of nearly losing her in Alaska. I can't imagine how I'd feel if the tables were turned, and *she* was the threat to her safety. No, I won't put her through that shit again.

"Yes." I tighten my arms around my best friend and kiss her forehead. "I promise."

Twenty-Two

An assignment, jealousy, and a megaphone

Ella

My boss pops his head into my office on Monday morning, wearing an ear-to-ear grin. "Guess who's going to be on the forefront of our fusion of film and newspaper reporting?"

"I'm sorry, what? You lost me there, Harvey. Too many *f*'s in one sentence."

"May I come in?"

"Of course." I point to the chair in front of my desk. "Make yourself comfy."

He settles, cup of coffee in hand, and continues to smile as he speaks. "Well, I talked to my buddy Jerry Goldfield over at Eastpoint Studios. You remember his cameraman, Lance? You worked together a few years ago?"

Lance Pines had a major crush on me. The only reason I tolerated his attention—and attempted a few casual, *group* dinner dates—was because he's Austin Pines's cousin. Austin vouched for his character, so I let down my guard a smidgen. In truth, Lance was beyond sweet. Everything a normal woman would want.

Except I'm not normal.

"Yes, I remember him."

"Anyway, Jerry got the contract to produce an exclusive documentary about the makings of a Broadway show. Lance will do the filming, but as you know, he's super shy. Jerry wants someone there whose writing and interviewing skills are stronger. Someone whose photography really shines. Jerry and I go way back. He's one of my best friends, so when he reached out, I couldn't refuse him. Besides, he enjoys your work immensely." Harvey's smile widens to the point where *my* face hurts. "Especially after reading your article about *Prodigy*."

Just the mention of Garrett's show has my body tensing. "Uh-huh."

"So, naturally, you were the perfect match."

"Bear with me, Harvey. I haven't had enough coffee to follow your spiel. What exactly did you sign me up for?" I take a long, slow sip of my java, savoring the dark roast's chocolaty notes.

He laughs. "Sorry, I got ahead of myself. You and Lance Pines will work together to film a documentary. You will do the interviews and photography. He'll handle the videography." He excitedly rubs his hands together. "It will be perfect. This is a tremendous opportunity for you, and it will give the *Tribune* the boost we need. Since you already have a rapport with Garrett Casey, everything sort of fell into place."

I choke on my coffee, coughing and sputtering as the liquid dribbles from my mouth.

"Whoa. Take it easy." Harvey hands me a tissue. "You're not supposed to inhale your drinks."

I mop at my chin and the splatter on my desk. "You want *me* to make a documentary about *Prodigy*?"

"Earth to Ella. Do you read me?" He snorts and cups his hands around his mouth, then makes a bunch of alien spaceship beeping noises. "Yes. You're spearheading the *Tribune's* involvement in the project. Jerry's calling it *Prodigy: Inside Scoop.*"

Houston, we have a problem.

"I don't think I'm the right person for the assignment."

"Don't be silly. Not only is *no one* better qualified than you, but you have what it takes to make our newspaper shine. I mean, you've already got the connections and the finesse. Your talent knows no match." He points to me. "I'm not just saying that because I want something from you. I think you know me well enough to know I mean it."

Praise comes easily from Harvey, which is one of the reasons I love this job. It's nice to feel like I'm worth something as a journalist. The last thing I want to do is let my boss down. Especially since he's the one gunning for me to get the promotion I've been working toward. If it were up to Harvey alone, I'd already have the job. Too bad there's a committee of chauvinists who run the paper's parent company, Mercury Communications. The CEO, Hans Mercury, being the worst of them. While I agree this project *is* an incredible opportunity, there's no way I can handle it. I already ruined my rapport with Garrett.

"Trace may be a better candidate," I say, thinking of a male colleague with far more film experience. "He did that Costa Rica documentary a few years ago."

Harvey shakes his head. "Entertainment, theater especially, is *your* wheelhouse. *You* are the one who I want to represent the *Tribune.*"

I am so fucked.

I force a swallow. "I understand."

"I knew you would." He leans in with a conspiratorial grin. "And since I know you're always up for a challenge, I convinced Jerry you can lure Elias Hawke into the open for an exclusive interview."

He's out of his mind if he thinks that's happening.

I blink through my disbelief and clear my throat. "Elias Hawke has *never* given an interview. To anyone. I mean, the guy refused an appearance on *Good Morning America*, for God's sake. And *The Today Show*. Let's not forget *USA Today*, *The Wall Street Journal*, or *The New York Times* and their unsuccessful attempts to feature him."

"I know." He claps, bouncing in his seat like a little kid who just learned it's time for ice cream. "That's why it's going to be epic!"

"I'm sorry, but I can't commit to that. The documentary is one thing, but I'm not about to stalk some author who hates the press."

He straightens, the smile fading from his face. "Sorry, Ella, you know I always give you an out, but this one's nonnegotiable."

"He's a recluse, Harvey. How the hell would I find him? And even if I do, what makes you think he'd agree to speak with me?"

"I suggest you find a way to work your magic."

It's one thing to know you're fucked. But somehow, putting my predicament into words makes it really hit home. Vocalizing the shit show I've gotten myself into wasn't on tonight's agenda. Paolo called when I was leaving the office, and before I knew it, I was seated on a barstool at La Bussola, spilling my guts.

I rest my head in my hands and groan.

He pours me another wine. "Bella, you really know how to fuck yourself over."

I peek at him from between my fingers. "What am I going to do?"

"Keep it professional and do your job."

I chug the contents of my glass. "But he hates me."

I haven't even *begun* to process the part of my assignment that involves luring Elias Hawke from his hidey-hole, so I left those details out of my vent session. Maybe if I keep things to myself, I can pretend Harvey didn't task me with an impossible mission. Then again, smoothing things over with Garrett isn't plausible either.

I am unbelievably fucked.

His eyes darken, and he crosses his arms over his chest. "Maybe you should've thought about the potential consequences *before* you took Gerard to bed."

The sharp edge of jealousy in his tone isn't lost on me. I probably shouldn't have gone into as much detail about what happened.

"It's Garrett."

"Whatever." He leans in close, lowering his voice so only I can hear. "Ella, blind acceptance is unrealistic."

"What are you talking about?"

"You can't expect every man to handle your . . ." He flails his arm around, trying to find a word that won't piss me off.

"Handle my what?"

"Restrictions."

"He handled them fine."

He lifts a dark brow. "Did he?"

"Well, sorta. Until I walked out on him, obviously."

He grips the edge of the bar, fire flashing in his eyes. "I know you, Ella. I was there. I saw the terrified young woman with no place to go. Not every man is like me. You can't expect others to understand without explaining your past."

"My past is no one's business but mine."

"True, but it bleeds into every aspect of your life."

"No, it doesn't."

He sighs, and his expression softens. "I'm not here to argue with you, but I want you to really think about what I'm saying. Not a day goes by when you don't feel the impact of what you went through."

"That girl ceased to exist at seventeen. I'm not her anymore."

"As much as you try to erase what happened and reinvent yourself, she lives on in you. Her pain is your pain. I know you don't want to remember, but you can't run from yourself. And if you ever want a healthy relationsh—"

"I don't want a relationship." I cross my arms over my chest. "I don't need anyone."

Paolo's gaze burns into mine. "You keep saying that, but you know damn well everyone needs someone sometimes."

I reach for his hand and squeeze it. "That's why I have you, caro. You understand why I am the way I am."

He's the only man who understands me. I was a fool to try a sexual encounter with Garrett. I never imagined the experience would trigger me how it did.

It can be our little secret. Nobody has to know what we do.

His words struck a dark chord, the pain reverberating like my abuse happened yesterday—not thirteen years ago. It didn't matter that I *knew* he was talking about cuddling. The urge to flee overpowered logic and reason. For a moment, I was back in that apartment, begging the bastard to stop.

Garrett had no way of knowing my inner torment. I still can't believe I left the poor man tied to the bed. I can't blame him for hating me.

"I do understand, and I'll always be here for you." Paolo sighs heavily. "But sometimes I need a little more than you can give."

Right. I'm a selfish bitch. He caters to me and my ludicrous restrictions, but the man deserves a more fulfilling sex life.

"I'm sorry," I whisper, staring at my hands.

"Don't be sorry." He tips my chin up and smirks. "One day I'll convince you to marry me. Until then, I'm happy to keep business as usual." He points to the calendar hanging behind the bar. "By the way, my mother expects you at Thanksgiving brunch *and* dinner."

"I'll be there." It's not like I have anywhere else to go. "What can I bring?"

"Just yourself. Everyone looks forward to seeing you."

"Thanks." Regret flattens the smile twisting my lips. I should really stop sleeping with my best friend. The man should have a girlfriend to spend his holidays with, not a train wreck like me. It's clear I'm fucking with his head. I don't have the energy to explain my reasons to him, so I change the subject. "What time is your sister coming home?"

"Not sure." He cocks his head to the side. "Oh. I almost forgot. How come you didn't tell me she broke things off with Dr. Fuckface?"

"Huh?" I feign innocence, unsure of how much he knows.

"Don't be coy. Alessia said she told you the day it happened. You didn't think to mention it?"

"First off, it wasn't my news to share." My inner feminist rears her head and dusts off her armor. "*And* she asked me to keep my mouth shut. Also, her love life really isn't your business."

He lifts a brow. "Really?"

"Yes, really."

"I've got news for you, bella. If it involves *my* sister, it's my business."

"Yeah, okay. What else should I report back to you about, Mr. Almighty-Member-of-the-Patriarchy? Do you need to know about her menstrual cycle too?"

"Fuck no." He pretends to shudder. "I don't need any of those visuals."

"Oh, grow up." I give him an exaggerated eye roll. "I honestly don't know how she deals with all seven of you overbearing, brutish men. Not to mention your dad."

Paolo shrugs and sips his wine. "She's used to us."

"And that's *exactly* why she needs a woman like me to share her secrets with," I retort smugly. "Alessia deserves an unbiased confidante who doesn't meddle."

He swirls the wine in his glass. "Are you telling me you approved of her relationship with him?"

"My approval doesn't matter."

"Let me rephrase. Did you *like* that fucking moron?"

"Absolutely not. He's a pompous bastard who doesn't deserve to breathe the same air as her. I knew he was shady from the get-go. She's better off alone."

"At least we can agree on that."

"We agree on lots of things, caro." I rest my hand on his forearm and give him a quick squeeze. "Like how incredibly fucked I am with this documentary. I mean, what if I get to the theater and Garrett tells everyone I'm a psycho?"

"Is he twelve, or a grown-ass man? I didn't think you went for the kiss-and-tell types."

"I don't go for any types," I mutter.

He waggles his eyebrows. "Except tall, dark, and handsome."

His observation forces a smile from me. "I mean, he's gorgeous, so . . ."

He snorts. "Please. Gregory isn't hideous, but he's definitely not a god."

"It's *Garrett*. And you haven't slept with him, so your assessment is inaccurate."

"I'll take your word for it." His tone scrapes down my spine, but it's his expression that makes me regret my statement. "Listen, all you need to do is act professionally. Ask your questions, take your pictures, and write your story."

"That's the problem. I'm not *writing* a story, Paolo. It's a fucking full-length documentary."

"You've already interviewed Gideon, so focus on the rest of the cast. *Especially* the gorgeous blond one."

I chuckle. "Don't you worry. I'm over here fangirling Tess McPherson too."

"Good. Give *her* your attention instead of Griffin." He crosses his arms. "No one wants to look at him anyway."

Oh, Jesus Christ.

"I shouldn't have said anything. I didn't mean to make you jealous."

"No, I'm glad you told me. You know you don't need to censor yourself with me. As far as what I'm feeling? Label it whatever you want." He shrugs and pours himself another wine. "My point is, stop worrying about this assignment. This isn't your first rodeo. You know what you're doing and how to conduct yourself. Besides, you'll have the camera guy with you as moral support. You already know him, and you said he's nice. At least you won't be alone or stuck with some misogynistic fucker."

He makes a valid point. While there are plenty of monsters in the entertainment industry, Lance isn't one of them. No, he's sweet and kind—a true gentleman. I'm well acquainted with theater's dark side.

They say keep your friends close and your enemies closer. Well, that's exactly what I did when I pursued a career in the same arena as my former abuser.

Back then, I was a vulnerable child. I couldn't defend myself, so I endured the abuse for four years. I suffered in silence because I didn't have a voice.

I have a megaphone now. Every story I write, every event I attend, feels like fighting back. The more visibility I gain, the louder I become. Thirteen years later and I'm fucking thriving. Right under his nose. I can only imagine how uneasy it makes him, knowing I could expose him at any point. But that won't happen. I'd much rather make him suffer.

It's called power. And I'm stepping into mine.

Knowing my presence—and success—makes the man who hurt me increasingly uncomfortable, is the sweetest kind of vengeance.

Twenty-Three

A feminist, a sanctuary, and a prayer

Ella

Lance Pines is the southern gentleman I remember. Polite, soft-spoken, and considerate. Everything I *should* want. He's engaged now, so that train already left the station. Too bad I didn't climb aboard when I had the chance.

He holds open the door to the Compass Theater with a smile. "Have you met any of the cast before?"

My stomach does another flip-flop, like it's been doing for the past week—ever since Harvey assigned me to the documentary and the impossible "interview that shall not be named." Thanksgiving came and went, but I could barely eat the dinner I helped Paolo's mother prepare. Here it is, Monday evening, and I can't remember the last full meal I've eaten.

"I interviewed the male lead."

"This is his first Broadway production, right?"

"Yes." I don't elaborate because I'm focusing all my energy on remembering to breathe.

Lance points to a staircase that leads to the theater's lower level. "Tom

Berkley said there's a meeting room downstairs. I guess that's where every-one will gather until rehearsals move further along."

"Uh-huh."

He eyes me, his baby blues narrowing. "You okay?"

"Yeah. Why?"

"I don't remember you being this quiet the last time we worked together."

I release a heavy sigh. "I've never done a documentary like this. I usually interview people and write my story later. I don't want to disappoint Harvey if my on-camera persona leaves a lot to be desired."

It's mostly true. Although, I'm sure I'd be fine if I weren't interviewing a man who I left tied naked to a hotel room bed.

"That's understandable. Think of it this way." He motions to the two of us. "You're the outgoing one here. Trust me, my awkwardness will make you shine."

"You aren't awkward, Lance."

He snorts. "That's mighty kind of you, Ella, but we both know you're tellin' a fib. There's a reason I'm *behind* the camera."

"For what it's worth, I find shyness in a man refreshing."

Again, it's a realization that would've been helpful *before* he got engaged to someone else. But what is my life if not ironic?

We descend to the theater's underbelly in silence. Thanks to previous assignments at this venue, I'm familiar with the long, dimly lit corridor that leads to the meeting room Lance mentioned.

"Good evening, Ms. Sammons and Mr. Pines." Tom Berkley greets us in the hallway with a broad smile. "I'd like to chat for a moment before in-troducing you to the cast."

"Absolutely." Lance extends his hand. "Nice to see you again, Mr. Berkley."

They shake. "We're going to be seeing a lot of each other. Please call me Tom." He turns to me, his grin widening. "Ms. Sammons, I was thrilled with the article you wrote about Garrett Casey."

The winged battalion in my gut takes flight. "Thank you. It was an in-teresting interview."

"He's quite the character, so I can only imagine."

Oh, you have no idea.

"Listen, I'm not sure what guidance Jerry and Harvey gave you, but I have some requests of my own."

Lance shifts the camera bag on his shoulder. "Sure thing. Let us know what you want, and we'll make it happen."

"Obviously, Garrett Casey is a first-time Broadway actor. Since *Prodigy* is also a new production—and based on a bestselling novel—it's a perfect vehicle for the birth of a star. We'd love if the documentary could capture that transformation."

Lance tilts his head to the side. "So, you're sayin' you want us to focus on him?"

"Yes."

My inner feminist bristles and rears her head, making me stiffen my spine. "With all due respect, Tom, Ms. McPherson deserves equal screen time. She's an extremely talented actress and we should recognize her as such. We wouldn't want *Prodigy* to have a reputation for being sexist."

"No, of course not." Tom meets my gaze in earnest. "I apologize if my request seems sexist. That's certainly not my intent. Let me try to explain where I'm coming from. Ideally, we want everyone to have their moment. Tess is *already* Broadway's sweetheart. She has a phenomenal reputation and a huge following. Garrett is essentially an unknown."

"You want us to make him a *known*," Lance drawls, rubbing his chin. "Put him in the spotlight, so to speak?"

"Precisely. I guess you could call Garrett my newbie passion project. I see a lot of potential in him, so I'm taking him under my wing." Tom straightens his bow tie. "*Prodigy*'s plot centers on Xavier Crane's demons. We witness his fall from grace and his redemption. Since Garrett so perfectly captures the essence of the dark professor, it's important we use this opportunity to showcase him."

Fuck me.

"I understand." I tuck a lock of hair behind my ear. "I'll try to paint him in the best light."

"I have faith in you, Ms. Sammons."

"Please call me Ella."

"All right, will do." Tom squeezes my shoulder.

The touch turns my stomach, and I suppress the urge to flinch. Thankfully, he removes his hand before my shoulders acquaint themselves with my earlobes.

He gestures to the meeting room. "C'mon, let's go inside. I can't wait to see the cast's reactions when they learn they're going to star in a documentary *and* a groundbreaking Broadway production."

"Wait a minute." I stop short, making Lance collide with my back. My skin crawls with the brief contact. I reflexively take a huge step forward and pivot to face the men. "Are you saying—"

"I haven't mentioned anything to my people yet." Tom's green eyes sparkle with mischief. "But that's about to change."

My stomach bottoms out. Not only does Garrett hate me, but now I'm taking him by surprise?

I shrink back against the wall as Tom opens the meeting room door. "Excuse me a moment. I need to use the restroom."

He eyes me over his shoulder. "It's down the hall on the left. We'll see you inside." He and Lance enter the room.

My brisk stride carries me across the concrete, stilettos clicking in a staccato of nerves. I rush into my chosen sanctuary and latch the door. Sagging against a metal stall, I take a few moments to catch my breath.

I'm a survivor.

I control the situation.

No one can take that away.

I repeat the mantra until my breathing regulates. After a quick once-over in the mirror, I splash cool water on my wrists, then wet a paper towel. I dab at my temples and the back of my neck.

I can do this.

I'm a professional.

My hair's out of whack, so I snag my brush to tame the flyaway strands. Next, I smooth on a coat of siren red, my preferred lip color. I recite my affirmations once more, then toss in a few Hail Marys for good measure.

It looks like stilettos, red lipstick, and a virgin are my weapons of choice in tonight's faux confidence arsenal. Let's hope they don't backfire.

Twenty-Four

Turkey, testicles, and a bomb

Garrett

Tess stuffs the remainder of her sandwich in her mouth, smiling while she chews. Whatever she's eating smells divine. My stomach growls for the second time since I arrived at the theater.

I nudge her. "You look like you're in heaven."

Nodding, she swallows and chugs some water. "It's the last of my leftovers from Thanksgiving."

"Nice. Did you have family in town?"

"No. My roommate and I cooked a turkey. It wasn't nearly as good as my mama's, but it was better than nothing. How about you? What did you do for the holiday?"

"I had dinner at my friend Lena's. Then she had a big Friendsgiving party on Saturday night." I pat my empty stomach. "I'm all turkey'd out."

"Friendsgiving?"

"Yeah. She's not close with her family either, so she invited a bunch of friends and coworkers. It doubled as a surprise belated birthday gathering for her boyfriend. We all hung out and stuffed our faces."

"That sounds wonderful."

"It was."

The party was relatively drama-free, until my idiot cousin flirted with Wes's sister, and Jake nearly blew a gasket. Lena made me run interference with Connor to keep him away from Isla. Jake seemed fine by the end of the night. *The poor bastard needs to get his shit together and decide what he wants.*

Finished eating now, Tess picks up her script and points to the page. "Oh, my goodness! Did you see the part where I slap you?"

Tom handed out a revised version of our script when we arrived. He mentioned something about making it more impactful. Evidently, he'd shied away from some of the more controversial stuff in Hawke's novel, but made a last-minute decision to add it back in. *I'm curious what changes he's made and how it will affect my character.*

"I must've missed that." I scan the page. Sure enough, Annaca Collins smacks Xavier Crane in the face. Twice. *That definitely wasn't in the original version.* "That'll be interesting. Have you ever hit anyone for a show before?"

She shakes her head. "I've never hit anyone, period. How about you?"

I snort. "No comment."

Her sapphire-colored eyes sparkle with amusement. "You do seem like the rascally type, Mister Garrett."

Oh, you have no idea.

"What can I say? I've been known to push some buttons."

"From what I know of you so far, I'm sure you're a professional button pusher." She secures her flaxen mane in a ponytail. "But I still can't see myself hittin' you."

"I'll be extra obnoxious that day to give you incentive. Maybe put some mice in your locker or something." I wink, grateful for our easy camaraderie. Especially after the brewery snafu.

She giggles. "I'm not afraid of mice. Clowns, on the other hand . . ."

I curl my lip. "Yeah, fuck clowns. Don't even get me started on them."

"I'm sure we'll figure somethin' out. Maybe you can taunt me with my childhood nickname."

"Dare I ask what that might have been?"

She wrinkles her nose. "I was always a bit disheveled, so my brothers called me Messy Tessy."

I bark out a laugh. "You realize it was a mistake to tell me that, right? I'm obviously gonna have to annoy you with that on a regular basis."

"Don't push your luck, Mister Garrett." Tess lifts an eyebrow in challenge. "Unless you wanna make me slappin' you a habit." She looks up as Tom enters the room with a tall, sandy-haired man who's carrying a tripod and camera bag. "I thought we already did our cast photos for the playbill."

"So did I."

Tom clears his throat. "Okay, people. I've got some exciting news. This fine gentleman is Mr. Lance Pines. He works for my friend Jerry Goldfield over at Eastpoint Studios. Be sure to get acquainted because Lance will be your shadow until *Prodigy's* debut."

"What do you mean, our shadow?" Tess asks.

Tom points to the guy's camera bag. "Lance and his colleague are filming a documentary."

One of our castmates, a dark-haired guy whose name I can't remember, leans in. "What kind of documentary?"

"Glad you asked, Emmett. The project's title will be *Prodigy: Inside Scoop.* It's essentially an exposé on the makings of a Broadway show that will air the week *Prodigy* goes live."

Excited murmurs rise from our group.

Tom smiles. "Most people don't know the behind-the-scenes stuff, the hours of hard work that go into a production of this scale." He holds up our new script. "The public doesn't get to witness the transformation from words on a page to blockbuster performance. But we do. Now's our chance to show them what it takes to be Broadway's highly anticipated breakout." He motions to us. "And if I have my way, we'll add some Tony awards to our accolades."

"Shit, I'd give my left nut to win a Tony," I mumble.

Tess snorts. "Keep your nuts, Mister Garrett. You might need them one day."

I chuckle and elbow her. "You're too much."

"Something funny, Garrett?" Tom pins me with his gaze, making me feel like I'm back in high school, being reprimanded by my history teacher for passing notes to Lena.

Straightening, I clear my throat. "No. I was just—"

The door opens, and in walks the *last* woman I expected to see. I struggle to breathe as Ella takes her place beside Lance.

His colleague.

Your shadow until Prodigy's debut.

My director's words reverberate against my skull like wayward tennis balls, before slowly yielding to comprehension. My stomach hits the floor. The hairs on my arms and neck stand on end.

"Ah, here's the woman of the hour." Tom drapes his arm over Ella's shoulders.

Something flashes across her face, but her posture remains statue still. Rigid. Unyielding. Her piercing blue gaze locks with mine, swirling with regret, fear, and other emotions I can't name.

My breathing and heart rate kick up a few notches. From my tingling scalp to the tips of my toes, every inch of my body zings with awareness. Heat and anger arrow down my spine, tightening my balls. Even my traitorous dick joins the party.

I'm beyond fucked.

"People, this is the lovely Ella Sammons. She's a photojournalist with the *Tribune*, and she'll be the voice of our documentary. Ella will interview the entire cast many times throughout this process, with special attention given to our leads. Everyone already knows the ethereal Tess McPherson. Her reputation precedes her."

Tess flushes. "Thank you, Tom."

"No need to thank me. I speak the truth. But I've got another truth bomb for you folks." Tom motions to Lance and Ella. "By the time these two are done working their magic, Garrett Casey and the rest of the cast will be household names."

Twenty-Five

An exit, a cover-up, and a punch to the stomach

Ella

Garrett lurches to his feet and stalks from the room without a word, the door slamming shut behind him. As the thud of his heavy footsteps echoing down the hallway reaches my ears, there's no mistaking his stomp, not even through solid oak. A shaky breath expands my chest.

Tom blinks. "That was unexpected." He gestures to Tess, who bears the same wide-eyed expression as everyone else in the room. "Is he all right?"

She clears her throat. "Um, I think he's not feelin' well."

Her attempt to cover for him is sweet, and I'm sure Garrett would appreciate it if he were still here. She stares at his empty chair like it holds the answers to the questions everyone's asking.

Lance turns to Tom. "Maybe he isn't pleased with the idea of our documentary?"

Gee, you think?

Tom shakes his head. "I'm not sure what's going on. That was out of character for him. Please accept my apology on his behalf. And to address your comment, Lance, I can assure you Garrett doesn't have a choice. The documentary is happening regardless of his—or anyone else's—feelings about it."

Well, okay then.

Tom drones on for another twenty minutes about documentary logistics, general *Prodigy* housekeeping stuff, and the rehearsal schedule. Everyone listens intently. Tess keeps stealing furtive glances at the door.

Garrett still hasn't returned.

When Tom finishes his spiel, he steps out to make a phone call. Lance and I continue to make our rounds, introducing ourselves to *Prodigy's* cast and crew. I keep a mental note of everyone's names. We reach Tess last.

I extend my hand. "Ms. McPherson, it's so wonderful to meet you."

She clasps my palm and gives me a firm shake. "The pleasure's all mine, Ms. Sammons."

"Please call me Ella."

"Sounds good, Miss Ella." She smiles. "And you're welcome to call me Tess."

"I'm curious about your thoughts on the documentary. Have you ever done anything like this?"

"No, this is a first for me. I'm excited, and admittedly, a little nervous. I think people will be expectin' more glamour, so the reality will surprise them. Audiences don't know how much work it is. Mostly, I hope I'm not a bore."

"I don't think you have anything to worry about," Lance says with a reassuring smile.

"You're from the South?"

He nods. "Yes, ma'am. Tennessee, to be specific."

"I'm from Georgia." She eyes me. "And how about you, Ella?"

"California." I opt for my standard answer and quickly change topics. "Have you worked with any of your castmates before?"

"No."

"What's the deal with your costar?"

Lance's question makes my stomach flip-flop. I shift my weight. My pointy security blankets are suddenly pinching my toes.

"I honestly don't know. He was perfectly fine one minute, and the next . . . well, you saw." She points to Garrett's empty seat. "I hope you can forgive his rudeness. Mister Garrett's not usually like that. If anything, he's the opposite. Kind, easygoing, and funny. I don't know what's gotten into him. He's really quite sweet."

Something in her tone nudges my consciousness.

She likes him.

Images of them together flit through my mind. Limbs tangling, chests heaving. His hips thrusting upward to meet her body's movements like he did with me. The way his eyes fluttered when he orgasmed. His groans and gasps of pleasure.

The responding gut punch of jealousy shocks me. Who am I to be possessive of Garrett? The man clearly hates me. Not that I can blame him.

The more I think about that night, the crazier I feel. Why couldn't I have just kissed him? Why didn't I let him hold me? Why did a simple statement send me running for the hills? Truth is, I already know the answer. I can flee all I want, but my history has been nipping at my heels for over a decade. One of these days my demons will outrun me.

As much as I need to shield myself, there's a huge part of me that's sick of hiding. No one has ever looked at me the way Garrett did when we had sex. He saw inside me, through me. There was no hiding from him. God, how I wanted his hands on me, his arms around me. Most of all, I craved his warmth.

But I ruined it. The look in his eyes when I closed that door, broke my heart. I left the man tied to a bed, naked and pleading. Still wearing the fucking condom. I walked out with zero explanation. Now I'm encroaching on his dream job.

The fury etched into his features tonight tells me it's going to be a fun year.

Twenty-Six

A partridge, a scapegoat, and a booty call

Garrett

I toss my keys on the end table and kick off my shoes, finally home after my director dropped the bomb on us at rehearsal. I still can't process it. All I understand right now is the urge to drink.

I noticed all seven liquor stores I passed on the way from Manhattan to Brooklyn. The signs in the windows beckoned me with their come-hither neon glow. That doesn't even include the three bodegas that sell a selection of booze. And Ralph's Tavern down the street. Seven liquor stores, three bodegas, and one bar. It's like a fucked-up version of the "Twelve Days of Christmas," except my partridge is a bottle of whiskey.

I came so close to sipping the nectar. I stopped my Jeep at the curb outside bodega number two, and again at liquor store number six.

But I resisted.

Finally safe at home, I feel like I ran a marathon. My battle with alcohol dependency is an uphill climb, and I'm getting tired of the struggle.

I strip out of my work clothes and snag a pair of gym shorts before heading downstairs. I need to burn off some energy before I do something stupid. My fist collides with the bag like an affirmation. The strikes come fast and hard, each one reverberating to my gut. I'll pummel the fucker until I can't stand anymore if it helps fight the cravings.

The seven liquor stores, three bodegas, and lone tavern drift through my mind again. Ralph's is only a few blocks away. It wouldn't take long to get there—five minutes at most.

Maybe I can convince Teddy to let me have a shot.

Just one.

I'll beg if I need to.

The siren's call of the liquor fills my head. I hit the bag even harder, blinded by the sweat running into my eyes. The red leather scapegoat absorbs my strikes and eggs me on, swinging back for more.

One drink won't kill you.

No one would even know.

You'd feel much calmer with some alcohol in your blood.

By nature, I'm a lover—not a fighter. I'm the one who puts the fires out, often described as cool, calm, and collected. Even-tempered and rational, I think things over before I react. Assertive, but not aggressive. Cunning, but not conniving. My approach is one of restraint, carefully calculated and precise.

I displayed *none* of that tonight, when I marched out of rehearsal like a fucking prima donna. I'm furious with myself for throwing a tantrum. I still haven't returned Tom's calls because I have no clue how to explain myself.

Hey, so, your documentary chick and I have a history. She once tied me to a bed, fucked my brains out, then left me strung up like a virgin sacrifice. It triggered all kinds of crazy shit from my past, and now I can't stop thinking about alcohol.

Yeah, nope.

Some dark, dangerous part of me has awoken from its slumber. Ever since Ella walked out on me, chaos has been surging through my veins, waiting to catch fire. Seeing her tonight was the lit match I never saw coming.

I strike the bag one final time with a guttural bellow, then collapse onto my weight bench. Panting, I reach for a towel to mop at the sweat on my face. I chug my water and wait for my heart rate to return to normal.

But I don't cool down. Not even a little.

Just one sip. Call it a nightcap.

I should be exhausted. I should retreat upstairs to shower and climb into bed. Instead, I grab my phone and dial Anya's number without thinking.

She answers on the second ring. "Casey. It's been a hot minute since we talked."

"Where are you?" I ask, my voice husky with need.

"Home. Why?"

"Come over."

"Not tonight. Work was a shit show, and I'm already in my jammies."

I grip the phone tighter. "Red, please."

"You don't sound like yourself. You okay?"

"Far from it."

"Go upstairs and talk to Lena," she suggests with a yawn. "She's always good at cheering you up."

"Lena can't give me what I need right now."

"And you think I can?"

"I *know* you can."

Her low chuckle reaches my ears. "It's been a while since you called for a fuck. I figured our romps were on hiatus."

I clench my jaw. "Just come over. Please."

"Have you been drinking?"

"Not yet, but that's where I'm heading."

"The cravings are that bad?" Her softened tone tells me I'm getting through to her.

"It's the worst they've been in a long time. You gotta help me, Red. I'm going out of my mind."

"I'll be right over."

One tiny sip, my addiction whispers.

Twenty-Seven

An agreement, a hard fuck, and an offer

Garrett

Anya meets me at the brownstone's front door, wearing jeans and an NYU hoodie. She secured her auburn hair in a messy bun, and she's already removed her makeup.

Stepping inside the shared foyer, she points to my gym shorts. "Boxing?"

"Yeah." I mop at the sweat running down my chest. "Sorry I didn't shower yet." I usher her into my apartment with a hand at the small of her back.

"It's fine. You'd need another one, anyway." She watches me close the door behind us and slide the dead bolt. "Expecting visitors?"

"Just you."

She nods to the ceiling. "Lena's sleeping, I presume?"

"Dunno. I'm not worried about her right now. Like I told you, she can't give me what I need."

"You gonna tell me what you *are* worried about?"

I cross my arms over my chest. "Nope."

"Funny, you claim I'm part of your inner circle, but you're shutting me out." She props her hands on her hips. "Talk to me, Casey."

"I didn't call you over here to talk."

"You know I'll gladly fuck you into the next decade, but that's not getting to the root of your problem. And as your AA sponsor, it would be helpful to know what's going on with you." She advances on me, her body brushing up against my erect cock. Her gaze burns into mine as she strokes me through the material of my shorts. "Don't worry, Casey, I'll give you what you need. But you're gonna talk to me afterward. Got it?"

"Yeah." Right now, I'd agree to just about anything.

Her other hand traces the ridges of my abdomen before gripping my waistband. "How do you want me?"

"You know the answer to that."

Gasping, I flop facedown onto the cushioned floor mats in my gym, finally spent. Anya is where I left her, draped over my weight bench, her fingertips brushing the floor. I lost track of how many times we fucked.

"You okay?"

"Uh-huh." She gives me a thumbs-up. "You?"

"Nope." I peel off the condom and fling it in the trash can's direction. It misses the mark, but I don't have the energy to do anything about it.

She presses herself up and crawls over, plopping beside me. "Tell me what's up."

I search her face. "I'm sorry if I was too rough with you."

"Don't be. I begged for it. You needed an outlet, so you used my body. It's a simple concept."

"I'm an animal. Why am I so fucked up?"

"Do you want me to list all the shit you've been through?" She touches my shoulder. "We're all animals, honey. Some of us are simply better at being caged."

"I need more than a cage. I hope I didn't hurt you."

"You didn't. The sex was amazing, as always."

"Don't lie to me. I can see it on your face."

She pushes herself up onto her elbows, then brushes the hair back from my forehead. "What you see isn't pain. It's frustration. I thought I could fuck the notion of booze right out of your head and make the cravings a distant memory. It's always worked for you in the past, but something's changed. I can tell by your eyes that it didn't work this time."

"My weakness isn't your fault."

"You're not weak, Garrett. I fucking hate when you say that. Do you think *I'm* weak when I'm having a tough time with my cravings?"

"No."

"Then show yourself the same compassion. It's a disease. You've been fighting so hard for years. If I thought it would help, I'd gladly come over here and distract you every night. But I won't let my solution add to your problem. You need to ask yourself what's got you reaching for the bottle in the first place."

"I don't know." What I really mean is I don't have the energy to explain it.

"*I* don't need a reason, but you aren't making it better by lying to yourself. You *do* know." She runs her fingers through my hair. "Also, you need to come to more meetings. I know it's hectic with work and rehearsals, but it's important to carve out time for recovery."

"Yeah."

"And once you figure it out, try to avoid whatever's triggering your cravings."

That's going to be hard since said trigger will be my shadow until *Prodigy's* opening. Guilt nudges my conscience for not coming clean about the Ella encounter to Anya. I'll tell her eventually. I'm too exhausted right now.

She grips my chin. "I'm picking you up Wednesday night at six for the meeting."

"Can't do Wednesday. I've got rehearsal."

"Fine. Saturday morning then. Be ready."

"Okay, but it'll have to be the eight a.m. one." I raise a brow at her. "And *you* don't like to get up early."

"As your sponsor, I'm willing to make an exception for your recovery." She kisses my cheek before sitting up. "I'm heading home. Night, Casey." She climbs to her feet and heads for the stairs.

"Anya."

She looks over her shoulder at me. "Yeah?"

"Thanks for having my back."

"Always. You're stronger than the booze, Garrett. Remember why you stopped in the first place. And you can always call me to talk, you know."

"I know. Thank you."

She points to the ceiling. "Go clean yourself up and get some rest."

"There's no rest for the wicked."

Twenty-Eight

A penis parade, a heart-to-heart, and a padlock

Garrett

Everything aches. My head, my muscles, my dick, all of it. Not even the scalding forty-five-minute shower helped soothe me. I dry off and wrap a towel around my hips before heading to the kitchen.

"Your milk was expired." Lena's voice makes me jump and nearly drop my towel. She's seated on the counter reading a magazine, swinging her legs like a kid on a too-tall stool.

I snatch the terry in time and sag against the doorframe, clutching my chest. "Woman, are you *trying* to kill me?"

"No. The opposite, actually. I brought you some groceries." She points to my phone on the counter. "You would've known I was coming if you checked your texts."

"I haven't looked at my phone yet today."

"No kidding."

I gesture to my towel. "You almost saw my dick."

"I've seen it like a hundred times before."

"It's literally only been a handful of times. And they were all accidental.

You make it sound like I parade my—admittedly perfect—junk for your perusal on the regular."

She snorts a laugh. "Perfect penis perusal parade. Imagine if that was a thing?" She sets down her magazine and straightens. "I vote we make it official. You can design shirts for us. We'll proudly wave pink penis pom-poms at passersby."

Lena's love of alliterations never ceases to amuse me.

"You're insane." I chuckle, shaking my head. "Where do you even come up with this shit?"

"I mean, you've given me plenty of material over the years. Plus, I see a boatload of ass cracks and ball sacks at work, so you could say the territory's familiar." She flashes me a grin. "Anyway, I didn't know your milk was past its prime when I went to the store, so you'll need to pick some up."

"You didn't have to get groceries for me."

She arches a brow. "Really? And what did you plan to eat this week?"

"I have food."

"Cereal, pickles, and pork rinds don't count. And like I said, your milk was bad, so that left the latter two. If you keep eating all that sodium, your blood pressure will skyrocket. Then I'll need to do your shopping *and* medicate you." Her jade eyes search my face. "How are you doing this morning?"

"Other than the near heart attack you gave me, I'm fine. You?" I open the fridge, which is now fully stocked with meats, cheeses, yogurts, and a variety of fresh produce. "Where'd you find these white carrots?"

"They're parsnips, Gar."

"Same difference." Tightly gripping my towel, I pad over and wrap her in a one-armed hug. "Thank you."

"You're welcome." She peers up at me. "You really need to eat better."

This sweet woman cares more about my health than I do. Lena makes sure I go for an annual physical, and my twice-yearly dentist appointments. She's always stocking my pantry, fridge, and medicine cabinet. She brings me home-cooked meals several times a week, and always has a sixth sense for when I'm struggling. Which is why she's here right now.

"What's going on?" she asks, her gaze burning into me. "Something's wrong."

"What makes you think something's wrong?"

She rolls her eyes and hops off the counter. "Seriously?"

"Yeah." I pivot to face her while tucking my towel, so it stays up. "Sounds like you've already made up your mind about how I am, so let's hear it."

In classic Lena fashion, she props her hands on her hips. "Well, for starters, you got home from rehearsal way earlier than I expected you. Then, you didn't answer any of my texts last night or this morning."

"I didn't feel like talk—"

"Wes said you were going apeshit on the punching bag last night."

I cross my arms over my chest. "Wait. How'd he know that?"

She narrows her eyes. "You gave him a key, remember? You said he could use your gym whenever he wanted. Anyway, he went downstairs to use the treadmill and said you were like a cage fighter on 'roids."

My scalp prickles. I was so caught up in my anguish, I didn't even notice him. That means I was unaware of my surroundings, something I never allow to happen.

"Please tell him to announce himself next time."

"He did, Gar. He asked if you were okay, but you didn't answer him. He figured you were upset about something and wanted space, so he came back upstairs." She points to my ceiling. "*Then* we had to listen to Yowling Yolanda swinging from the light fixtures. Don't even get me started on how unethical it is to have a sexual relationship with your AA sponsor. I mean, what the actual fuck? Yolanda should know better than that."

"Her name is Anya, for fuck's sake. And clearly"—I thump my fist on my chest—"*I'm* no study of ethics."

"I just don't think it's a good idea."

"Fucking my sponsor seemed more appropriate than a bottle of whiskey. Also, the volume level serves you right for what I've been dealing with lately."

"What's that supposed to mean?"

I fling my hands upward. "You up there screaming and Dundee's battle cries." My face grows hot, so I cross my arms again. "It's unnerving."

A slow smile curves her lips. "Payback's a bitch, isn't it? How do you think I've felt all these years with your harem?"

"I don't have a harem."

"Whatever. My point is, you got home early, ignored me, pummeled your bag, *and* called your phone-a-fuck. Something's wrong." She taps her watch. "I don't have plans today. I'll gladly follow you around until you talk to me."

As much as she aggravates me at times, Lena's persistence saved my life more than once, so I owe it to her to be honest.

Sighing, I plop onto a stool. "The cravings are bad."

Lena settles on a different stool and gently touches my arm. "How come?"

"Because I'm fucked up."

"No, you're not."

"We'll have to agree to disagree."

I take a deep breath and fill her in on the documentary situation and my subsequent tantrum. I tell her about how I wanted to walk to Ralph's last night and beg Teddy for a shot. I unload everything that's been pent up since my hotel room, naked-Jesus fiasco.

To her credit, Lena maintains a neutral expression while she listens. The only evidence of her shock is what registers in her eyes. "You have a lot on your plate, Gar."

"Yup." I pinch the bridge of my nose. "And to top it off, I savagely—and *very* unethically—fucked my AA sponsor on my weight bench." Rubbing my temples, I rest my forehead against the counter. "I lost control. I was really rough with her, Leens. I'm disgusted with myself."

"Did she ask you to stop?"

"No. If anything, it was the opposite."

Lena places her hand on my shoulder. "Then don't beat yourself up for that aspect of it. The lack of ethics, on the other—"

"You know what the worst part was? I *still* wanted a drink afterward. Pure physical exhaustion was the only reason I didn't find myself on a stool at Ralph's."

"I'm worried about you. When's your next appointment with Dr. Ortiz?"

"Friday."

"And what about your AA meetings? I know you've missed a bunch. If you don't want to go alone, I'll go with you."

"I know. Thank you. Anya is making me go to the one on Saturday morning."

She reaches for my hand and interlaces our fingers before tightly squeezing. "You are stronger than the alcohol."

"Everyone keeps saying that, but I honestly don't know anymore."

"Well, I *do* know. You're a fucking warrior, and I'm not about to let you forget it." She squeezes my hand even tighter. "I'll always be here for you."

"Yeah, but how much longer will I have you around?" The words leave my lips before I can stop them. *Fuck.* I did not want to open this can of worms so early in the morning.

"What the hell are you talking about? You make it sound like I'm terminally ill."

My chest deflates on a sigh, and I bang my forehead on the counter a few times. "Wes is gonna move you to Australia."

"You really believe that?"

"It's only a matter of time. He'll whisk you away, and I'll never see you again. You'll settle down, have a couple of kids, and I'll be a distant memory. That's the way it goes. Things change, people grow up and move on."

And I'm always the one left behind. The broken little boy who isn't worth sticking around for.

"Look at me, Garrett."

I study the insides of my eyelids instead. Lena digs her nails into the back of my hand.

"Ow." My gaze snaps to hers. "Why'd you claw me?"

"Because you're shutting me out." Pain flashes across her face. "For the record, Wes and I have discussed this issue at length. I've made it clear that New York is my home. I plan to keep this brownstone. I'm more than just the woman dating Wes Emerson—I have a life, an identity of my own."

"How does he feel about that?"

"He said *I'm* his home. He doesn't care where we live as long as I let him fly to Australia to surf every now and then." Her eyes fill with tears. "I can't believe you think I'd abandon you."

"It's just that I—"

"You will *always* be in my life. You once told me I was the beacon of light that saved you. Well, guess what? You're my rock. You're the anchor that keeps me grounded. I adore you, and that's never gonna change. I'm not moving away. I told Wes I'll happily spend a few months of the year in Australia, but I'm not uprooting my life here. So, whether you like it or not, you're stuck with me."

"Thanks, Leens," I say softly. "I love you."

"I love you too. Please don't worry about me abandoning you. I'm nothing like all the other assholes who've failed you. It pisses me off and hurts my feelings that you'd categorize me with them."

"I know you're not like them, and I'm sorry I hurt your feelings. I guess I just . . . don't want to die alone."

"Are *you* terminally ill?" she probes.

"No, of course not."

"What's with the fatalism? Why are you letting your mind take you there?"

"I'm really fucking lonely."

"Maybe you should think about dating. I can arrange something with one of my nurse friends. I know for a fact Kristie thinks you're sexy as fuck. She told me so after Friendsgiving."

I shake my head. "Please refer back to the part about how fucked up I am. I couldn't hook up with one of your friends out of principle. What if things ended badly, and I made shit awkward for you at work?"

She cocks her head to the side. "*Or* what if you meet the love of your life and live happily ever after?"

I snort at the absurdity of her statement. "Do you hear yourself right now?"

"Um, everything I'm saying is completely valid. You need to stop closing doors before they have a chance to open." She waves a finger in front of my face. "Except when it comes to Ella. Keep *that* door closed. Throw a few padlocks on the fucker too."

Twenty-Nine

A confrontation, an amendment, and a tsunami

Ella

It's Wednesday evening. I've been dreading this moment since we left the theater on Monday. Now we're back, and it feels like I'm walking into battle.

Lance hands me my notebook as we prepare to enter the theater's meeting room. "So, what's your goal for tonight?"

To survive the encounter without having a panic attack. "Um, I'd like to shadow Tess and get a feel for her character."

I toyed with the idea of telling Lance I have a history with Garrett—as explanation for my jitteriness—but decided against it. One almost date and awkward fuck hardly counts as history, right?

"Huh?" Lance asks, furrowing his brow.

"What?"

"You just said 'right,' but I didn't hear the first part."

Great. I'm already losing my mind. "You should probably ignore me for the rest of the night, Lance. I'm clearly off my game."

"That's okay. You're entitled now and then." He smiles. "Hopefully, the cast won't throw any fits, and we can actually accomplish something." He holds the meeting room door open for me as we slip inside.

Garrett and Tess are rehearsing a scene. The staff has rearranged the room to accommodate props for Xavier Crane's private basement office at the university where he works.

Tom Berkley stands nearby, directing, as directors do. "Tess, I want you to put your hands on your hips and give him a dose of defiance. We can assume Annaca's inner monologue is something like, 'How dare he speak to me like that, just who does he think he is?' Remember, he's called her character into question, and she's not having it."

He motions to the script he's holding. "To recap, Xavier and Annaca had an altercation during class, where he criticized her for not singing to her potential. Garrett, I love how you delivered your lines. 'Either give it your all or get out. There's no place for mediocrity in my classroom.' Your rude snarl was perfection. Tess, keep in mind that although Annaca fights to suppress her tears, she's furious Xavier publicly embarrassed her. She goes to his office after hours to confront him about his behavior. Let's pick up where she walks in. Garrett, go ahead." He points to the desk nearby. "Why don't you sit so we can get the full effect?"

Garrett nods and settles in the chair, then looks up at Tess with disdain. "Ms. Collins, as stated in the syllabus, my office hours are by appointment only."

"Then let's set up an appointment," she drawls.

"I'm booked."

"Well, I suggest you pencil me in, or I predict a meeting with the dean in our future."

"Are you threatening me, Ms. Collins?" Garrett grinds out dangerously.

"I dunno, did you humiliate me, Professor Crane?"

"You'd better learn to deal with criticism if you think you're going to make it in my class. Or in life, for that matter."

"The same could be said for you."

"Excuse me? Only an idiot would dare to criticize me. I'm not thrilled with your attitude."

"I'm not thrilled with yours either, and as a paying customer, I suggest you change your tune," Tess replies coolly.

Tom speaks up. "Garrett, I want you to come out from behind the desk and advance on her. Tess, you'll slowly back away from him. Annaca is toeing the line here. Is she wrong in her feelings? No. Is her response to the situation appropriate? Not exactly. She's a dichotomy of emotion. Half of her wants to challenge Xavier, push his limits. On the flip side, she wants to submit. Xavier is also torn. He's infuriated, but it meshes with a healthy serving of intrigue. Like Annaca, he wants to see how far he can push her. Little does he realize, but Annaca can push back. Go ahead."

As instructed, Garrett darkens his expression and rises. He slowly approaches Tess, who backs away from him until the desk blocks her retreat. He looms in front of her, with less than a foot of space between them. It's a move that would send me running for the hills. Tess plays up her countenance with a nervous flip of her hair over her shoulder.

"I'm not sure I heard you correctly, Ms. Collins." Garrett's voice rumbles down my spine. "What was that you were saying about changing my tune?"

"I'd prefer our encounters to be respectful."

"I'm not concerned with your preferences."

Whoa. Talk about an imbalance of power. Xavier is a domineering bastard. His behavior would never fly with me, but there's a subset of the population who will eat this shit up. As a survivor, I'm a bit more sensitive to this kind of dynamic. I lived it for four years.

"You've made your lack of concern for me quite clear. For the record, you don't intimidate me," Tess drawls sweetly.

Tom's decision to have Tess keep her accent was gold. It adds a layer of spice to Annaca's character.

"Okay, Garrett, now you're going to kiss her," Tom instructs, rubbing his hands together in excitement.

Puzzled, Garrett eyes his director. "Tom, if I may pause here for a moment. I need some clarification on the script. I've read through the newest version. We're only in the beginning of the first act. I thought Annaca was the one who kisses Xavier after the concert scene. Isn't that a few scenes from now?"

"Yeah, I'm wondering the same," Tess chimes in.

"Originally, yes. But you guys possess such intense stage chemistry, I'm considering even more adaptation to the script. It was hard to visualize on paper, but I'm dying to explore the sensuality aspect after seeing the two of you in the flesh. Let's try it, and then we'll iron out the details as a team."

When Tom Berkley has a vision, there's no stopping him. It's clear he has something brewing in his genius mind, so it would be wise for Garrett not to obstruct the path of his artistic direction.

"All right, you're in charge. Tell me what you want from me," Garrett says, looking over his shoulder. His expression darkens when he spots me, and I suddenly have difficulty filling my lungs.

"Okay, let's start with Tess. At this point, Annaca has retreated as far as possible. Her tush rests on the edge of Xavier's desk. She's challenged the dark professor, and he took the bait. He looms in front of her, seething. She insists that he doesn't intimidate her, but we know that's only partially true. She's most definitely intimidated. Entwined with her trepidation is an intense attraction. Xavier is wickedly handsome, domineering, and volatile. But Annaca can sense a sadness within him. A pain so deep, it draws her closer. His web snagged her the moment she walked into his classroom. Her sense of self-preservation begs her to escape, but deep down, she craves capture. Are you with me, so far?"

Tess nods. "Absolutely."

While I can't read his mind, Garrett's turbulent expression resonates with my thoughts. The script's uncanny parallel to our relationship is more than a little unnerving.

"Garrett, I know you can amp this scene up. Xavier is a man who's accustomed to controlling the people and situations around him. He runs the show, quite literally. Now, this petite, fiery blonde enters his domain with her youth and beauty, her immeasurable talent, and he's transfixed. With little more than a glance, she's moved him in ways he didn't expect. Factor in Annaca's defiant refusal to back down, and she's more than ruffled his feathers. She's plucked him bare, and he's terrified. But his fear goes hand in hand with an all-consuming desire. You got me?"

"Yes."

"So, at this point in the scene, Xavier is staring down at Annaca in challenge. She's pushed him to the edge. His body is on fire with lust. She doesn't falter, and those crystal-clear sapphire eyes unravel him. The last tethers of control are slipping through his fingers. She's just informed him he doesn't intimidate her. Garrett, I want you to make her understand the error of her ways. Tess, repeat the previous line and we'll go from there."

"You've made your lack of concern for me quite clear. For the record, you don't intimidate me."

"That's unfortunate. You lack the self-preservation necessary for survival in this class."

"And *you* lack the ability to handle me."

"Don't test me." Garrett's tone is volcanic as he advances on Tess. "You might get more than you bargained for."

"There's no bargaining here. You've already demonstrated your inability to cope with a challenge."

"Excuse me?" His chest heaves with his breaths, and he clenches both fists at his sides.

"What's the matter, Professor? Did I strike a nerve?" she croons innocently.

"And now . . . the beast pounces," Tom interjects with a wicked grin. "Garrett, show me what you've got. Repeat that line, Tess. I want you to taunt him a bit."

She smirks and eyes her costar. "What's the matter, Professor? Did I strike a nerve?"

Garrett absorbs her soft moan of surprise as he seizes her lips in a kiss. He presses his body up against her and weaves his fingers into her hair. Everything inside me catches fire watching the scene unfold. I've never let anyone touch me, but I can almost feel his hands on my body, his tongue in my mouth. I suck in a sharp breath as heat blooms between my thighs and clawing need surges through my veins.

The dark professor kisses his pupil fiercely, but it's not enough for Tom.

"Cut!" He approaches the pair. "Let's try that again. I want more from you this time, Xavier."

Garrett rubs at the back of his neck and gestures toward where Lance and I are standing. "Sorry, Tom, but it's a little challenging to act out the scene with an audience."

Tom barks a laugh. "Who do you think we'll be filling the chairs with? Mannequins? You've been on stage before. Isn't the point to have an audience?"

Garrett clears his throat. "I'm not accustomed to having one so early in the game, that's all."

"I think it's great practice. We need to knock our audience's socks off, blow their fucking minds. Xavier is consumed by a tsunami of lust. I need you to embody that desire. Crest and crash over us, pull us under. I want *impact*."

"If you want a tidal wave, I can definitely make that happen. My concern is Tess's comfort level."

"She can handle it. Right, Tess?"

"Yes," she replies breathlessly.

"Good. Now, make me proud. Tess, once more with the line, please."

"What's the matter, Professor? Did I strike a nerve?"

Garrett lunges, hauling Tess up against him. He kisses her with fervor, one hand tangling in her flaxen locks, and the other gripping her hip. After a moment, he clears the desk with a swipe of his arm and presses her torso back. He climbs on top of her without skipping a beat, even as books and a metronome crash to the floor. Tess threads her fingers into his hair and wraps her legs around him.

"Hot damn," Lance murmurs from beside me. "Now, *that's* a kiss."

Thirty

A fantasy, a dismount, and the Lincoln Tunnel

Garrett

All I can focus on is the soft body beneath me, the tongue sliding against mine. Nails digging into my scalp. The way Ella's legs pull me closer and how I ache to bury myself deep inside her again and again, until she screams my name. I flex my hips, grinding my hard cock between her thighs.

"Holy. Fucking. Shit." Tom's voice echoes in the distance. "Okay, Garrett and Tess, you guys nailed it."

Garrett and Tess.

Tess.

Oh. My. Fucking. God.

Tess!

"Fuck! Sorry." I roll off Tess so quickly, I clear the edge of the desk and plummet to the floor, landing flat on my back. My skull slams the concrete with a thud, making my teeth rattle. The instant pain sends a wave of nausea crashing through me. My vision gets hazy as a chorus of voices echoes in my brain. I taste blood.

Tom stands over me, his face blurring in and out of focus. "Are you all right?" His lips move, but it sounds like he's in the Lincoln Tunnel. "Answer me."

I blink a few times. Then everything goes black.

Thirty-One

A hard-on, a head injury, and some puke

Ella

This is like driving past the scene of an accident. I don't want to see what's in front of me, but I can't look away. The chilling reality of an unconscious Garrett makes it hard to breathe. I rush over to the desk.

"Someone call 9-1-1," Tom barks, kneeling beside Garrett. "Son of a bitch. He's out cold."

A cast member yanks a phone from their pocket. People gather around us, everyone talking at once. I'm too focused on Garrett to worry about the proximity of other males.

"Did you hear his head hit the floor?"

"Do you think he has brain damage?"

"What if he can't play the part anymore? Will they recast?"

Tess sits up, wide eyed and disheveled, her chest heaving. Her lips are swollen, cheeks pink from the scrape of Garrett's stubble. She swings her legs over the edge of the desk and hops to the floor. "What on earth just happened?" She grips my shoulder to steady herself, off balance from getting up too fast.

"I dunno, Tess," Tom mutters. "Did you bite him or something?"

She kneels beside Garrett and touches his forehead. "Of course not. One minute we were doing the scene, and the next . . . well, this."

Tom motions to the people crowding us. "Okay, folks. Let's call it a night. You can head out. We'll take Friday off and start fresh on Monday." Cast and crew members scatter like roaches. He points to Lance. "Can you please go upstairs and wait for the paramedics?"

"Sure thing." Lance jogs from the room.

"Tess, do you know where the fridge in my office is?"

"Yes." She rises and heads for the hallway.

"Go grab something cold from the freezer. I don't think I have any ice packs, but we'll make do with whatever you find," Tom calls after her retreating form.

He scrubs a hand over his face and looks up at me. "This isn't what I meant when I told him to crash over us."

I have no clue what I'm supposed to be doing, so I shift my weight and stare at Garrett's face. His hair's sticking out every which way. Dark lashes fan his flushed cheeks. His lips are parted, and slow, deep breaths expand his chest.

"Can you hear me, Garrett?" Tom speaks to him in a soothing voice, while prying one of his eyelids open. Given my eyeball aversion, the act makes me cringe and pivot toward the door.

Tess reenters after a few moments, carrying a frozen burrito. She hands it to Tom. "Cold beans should do the trick."

I risk a glance as Tom gently lifts Garrett's head and gives him a burrito pillow.

"I knew there was a reason I asked Helen to buy these things," he says with a chuckle. "I never imagined my lead would need a bean compress though. That fall was something. I wonder what the hell came over him."

"I think I know what happened," Tess whispers.

He lifts an eyebrow. "What do you mean?"

"He got carried away. He . . . uh, he was a bit . . ." Redness creeps over her cheeks and down her neck. "He was . . ." Her gaze snaps to mine in a silent plea for rescue.

"Aroused?" The jealousy simmering in my stomach makes the word cling to my tongue.

She nods. "He knows I felt it, and I think that embarrassed him. I'll bet that's why he jumped off me so fast."

I have intimate knowledge of how it feels to have his hard length pressed between my thighs. God, how I ache to feel it again. The chances of that happening are next to impossible. Besides, it looks like he's interested in her now.

My chest tightens. "Maybe he was caught up in the scene. How can you be sure he was aware of"—I flail my arm, searching for words other than *his huge erection*—"his arousal?"

"He apologized before he fell, so I can only assume that's what he meant."

Tom chuckles. "The poor guy's having a shitty night. First, I gave him a hard time for a lackluster kiss. Then he gave me the luster and wound up with a hard-on and a head injury. I hope this isn't an omen for the show."

"Do you think he has a concussion?" I ask.

"I don't know, but I heard his skull hit the floor pretty damn hard."

I peer at Garrett's face. "So did I, and I was across the room."

Garrett groans, and his eyes flutter open. He quickly squeezes them shut. "The fuck?"

Tom pats his arm. "You fell, bud."

"You scared the sugar-honey iced tea out of me, Mister Garrett."

"My fucking head," he mumbles, attempting to sit up.

Tom holds him in place. "Sorry, but you aren't going anywhere until the paramedics check you out."

"Please tell me you didn't call an ambulance."

Tess grimaces. "We had to. You may have a concussion."

"I'm fine." He sits up suddenly, then clutches his head. His body lurches, and his eyes go wild. "Oh, fuck." He frantically scans the room, but it's too late—his night gets worse.

I can't even react as he empties the contents of his stomach onto my designer stilettos.

"Oh my goodness!" Tess launches to her feet. "I'll grab paper towels."

Garrett rolls to his side. Nausea seizes his frame, and he gags, the sound snapping me out of my stupor. Nothing motivates quite like warm vomit seeping between your toes.

I sidestep him as he retches again, my feet squishing in puke.

"This was all I could find." Tess bounds into the room with a wad of napkins and hands them to me.

"Thank you." I kick my shoes off and wipe my feet, stifling the gag that wants to break free. Barf-covered toes notwithstanding, I'm concerned. I've been around enough injured Benicasa boys to know vomiting is a textbook concussion symptom.

Garrett groans. "My fucking head."

Lance returns with a pair of uniformed men equipped with a wheeled stretcher. Tom and Tess bring them up to speed.

"I can walk," Garrett mutters as the paramedics examine him.

"Bullshit. You can't even sit up," Tom says. "*And* you just puked on Ella's feet."

"Wait." Garrett stiffens and jerks his head to the side. He narrows his eyes like he's spotting me for the first time. "Why's *she* here?"

His confusion's concerning in and of itself, but his disdain annoys me. "You know why I'm here. Also, I think 'sorry I puked on you' is a bit more appropriate," I snipe, returning his glare. "But I'll let your lack of courtesy slide since you're hurt."

Tom addresses the paramedics. "He's disoriented. We're concerned he has a concussion."

"He'll get checked out at New York General. They'll do a CT scan to assess the extent of his injury. He'll likely be admitted overnight for observation."

"I'm fine. No one needs to observe anything." He crosses his arms over his chest, his frown deepening.

"Au contraire, mon frère." Tom squeezes his shoulder. "This isn't up for debate."

The paramedics load a glowering Garrett onto a gurney and push him from the room. Tom follows close behind, as Lance and Tess linger, making small talk about Southern cooking.

The evening's events replay themselves in my mind, with flashes of the kiss scene tormenting parts of me that ache to be claimed. A blinking light on the floor catches my attention. Stooping, I snatch the busted cell phone that skittered a few feet away from the desk and pocket it.

My better instincts tell me to chase after Garrett and hand it over.

But I don't.

Thirty-Two

A lecture, a visitor, and a bulldog

Garrett

I don't have time for a concussion. Nor do I have the energy to listen to Lena's traumatic brain injury dissertation right now, but since I'm stuck in a hospital bed, connected to tubes and wires, I don't have a choice.

She leans over and grips my chin. "Your ass will do everything these doctors tell you, or you'll have to deal with *me*."

"I have to deal with you, regardless."

She squints. "This is serious, Gar. I'm not trying to be a bitch—I only want you to be safe. The last thing you need is a blood clot. You have swelling and a slight brain bleed. It isn't something to fuck around with."

I gesture to the beeping monitor. "Does it look like I'm fucking around?"

"Why are you so angry?"

"I'm not."

"Bullshit." She settles on the edge of my bed. "Talk to me."

"Let's see, I dry humped my costar on a desk—boner in full force—then gave myself a motherfucking concussion. After tonight, and how I flipped out about the documentary on Monday, it wouldn't surprise me if Tom kicked me out of the show. To top it off, the doctor said I can't be on a computer for like a week, so how the fuck am I supposed to do my *actual* job?"

Lena squeezes my ankle. "I get it. Did you reach out to Nate yet?"

"Yeah. I'm sure he'll pick up the slack at Hudson Graphics, but I hate letting my team down."

"You aren't letting anyone down."

I roll my eyes. "Uh-huh."

"Please stop being so hard on yourself. You can't be everyone's prodigy."

"Uh, are you new here?"

"Nope. I have a quarter century's worth of Garrett Casey experience, so I know my shit." She leans in. "Which is why I'll remind you that your health—and recovery—takes precedence. Fuck everything else."

"It's not that simple, Leens."

"How are your cravings?"

"Horrendous."

"How can I help?"

I open my mouth to answer, but movement in the doorway snags my attention. My breath catches as I lock gazes with a pair of Caribbean blues.

"Knock, knock."

Lena's head swivels toward the door, and her body stiffens. "Hello, Ella. How can I help you?"

"I came to speak with Garrett."

My best friend stands and crosses her arms over her chest. "Now's not a good time. Brain injuries don't respond well to stress."

"I have no intentions of stressing him, Lena. I simply want to talk."

"Like I said, now isn't a good time." The ice in Lena's tone makes *me* shiver. I can only imagine its effect on Ella.

"All right then." Ella holds up my missing phone and meets my gaze. "I found this under the desk in the meeting room. The screen is busted, but I assume it's still working because it's been making a lot of noise. I planned to drop it off at your office tomorrow, but since I didn't want you to miss any important client calls, I stopped here on my way home instead."

I clear my throat. "Thank you. I appreciate that."

Lena holds out her hand for my phone. "I'll hang on to it for him. Screen time is currently prohibited. You know, traumatic brain injury and whatnot."

Oh, for fuck's sake. "I'm fine, Leens."

She arches a perfect eyebrow. "Who's the trauma nurse here?"

"No one's debating your credentials, but I have a business to run."

"Not tonight, you don't." She turns back toward Ella. "Thank you for dropping off his phone, but he really needs to rest."

"I couldn't agree more." Ella places the device in Lena's palm. "Feel better, Garrett. I'll see you next week." She turns toward the door.

While my head aches like a bitch, I'm curious to hear what she has to say.

"Ella, wait." The sudden acceleration of beeps gives away my racing heart. Lena eyes the monitor, then shoots me a glare, but I keep my focus on Ella. "What did you want to discuss?"

Her gaze darts between Lena and me. "It's nothing. We can talk another time."

"What if I wanna talk now?"

I touch Lena's arm. "Can you please give us a few minutes?"

"You two can have all the time you need . . . *after* I speak to Ella outside."

"Leens," I warn, clenching my jaw. "Behave."

Lena points to the hallway. "Ella, come with me."

Thirty-Three

A gatekeeper, a priest, and a divine intervention

Ella

I step into the hallway outside Garrett's hospital room. Lena follows, closing the door behind us with a loud click that does nothing for my nerves.

She stops in front of me and crosses her arms over her chest. Her rigid stance tells me this won't be a light-hearted chitchat. "Why are you here?"

Even with me in stilettos, she's taller. Maybe it's because she's playing the role of gatekeeper, but I've never felt this intimidated by a woman.

I peer up into her eyes and inject false calm into my voice. "As I mentioned before, I came to return Garrett's phone."

"What did you want to talk to him about?"

Are you his spokeswoman? Beating back the snark that wants to break free, I give her a tight smile. "That's between him and me."

"Are you planning to fuck with his head some more?"

"Excuse me?"

Her eyes narrow into slits. "I know what you did after Burlesquerade." She steps closer to me. "And you have no idea how it affected him. Now, I'll ask you again. Are you gonna fuck with his head?"

I'm rendered mute by the shock of him sharing such intimate details with her. The icy fury in her gaze makes my stomach bottom out.

"Got nothing to say? Well, I've got *plenty*." Her nostrils flare as she jerks a thumb toward Garrett's door. "That man has been through hell and back. His recovery is precarious at best. I won't let you—or anyone else—derail him."

My voice finds me again. "I admire Garrett's commitment to sobriety. I would never jeopardize his recovery."

"But you *did*." She waves a finger in front of my face. "So, you'd better think long and hard about how your actions affect people."

Intimidation yields to indignance as I stiffen my spine and look her square in the eyes. "I'm not sure who you think you're speaking to, but I don't appreciate you making it sound like I waved a glass of whiskey under his nose. I left after a consensual adult encounter. End of story."

"No, it's not the end of the story, Ella. He gave you his trust, and you left him tied up. Alone and vulnerable. Fucking naked." Lena's face turns red, and she blinks back tears. "You have *no idea* what he's been through."

"With all due respect, neither of you can fathom what *I've* endured. I feel terrible about hurting him, but I had to leave."

"Why?"

"My reasons are none of your business. While I don't need to justify myself to anyone, I came here because Garrett deserves an explanation. We have no choice but to work together on *Prodigy*, and I don't want things to continue being awkward."

"Wait." She cocks her head to the side. "Are you saying you didn't take on the documentary project to taunt him?"

I blink a few times, attempting to process her words. "I'm sorry, *what?*"

"I dunno, but it seems a bit coincidental you're suddenly involved with his Broadway dream. How'd that come about?"

"Are you insinuating I'm trying to somehow infiltrate his life?"

"You tell me."

Is she serious?

"I was *assigned* to the documentary, Lena. I tried to get out of it, but my boss didn't give me a choice. Why the hell would I torment Garrett? What kind of woman do you think I am?"

She stares at my face for a long moment before speaking. "Truth is, I don't know you at all. I have no right to make any assumptions about your character or motives." She sighs heavily, her posture softening. "I'm sorry I haven't been fair to you, but I need you to understand something. I know Garrett better than anyone else. His wounds run far deeper than you can imagine. I've seen him at rock bottom more than once."

"Guess what? I've been there too."

"I'm sorry to hear that, Ella. And I apologize for being bitchy. Bottom line, Garrett's my family. I will do everything within my power to protect both the man, and the broken little boy inside."

While Lena's ferocity for Garrett moves me, I'm unnerved she thinks of me as a femme fatale on a mission to destroy her best friend. I came here to explain myself to him, but she's taken the wind out of my sails. The fact remains he has a concussion, so maybe tonight isn't the best time to burden him with my shit.

"He needs to rest. I'll talk to him another time." I adjust my purse on my shoulder and step around Lena. "Good night."

She says something, but I don't hear it over the clicking stilettos of retreat. I need some air. A glass of wine. It was a bad idea to attempt a visit tonight.

I ride the elevator to the ground floor, staring blankly at the lit number panel. The hollow ache in my chest radiates to my abdomen. I press a hand to my lower belly, lingering on the scar from thirteen years ago.

My past is full of shitty decisions.

A glass of wine somehow morphed into church. While I missed the evening Mass by a few hours, the chapel is still accessible. I quietly make my way to the candles near the statue of Madonna and child. It's easily the most beautiful sculpture in Saint Jude's Cathedral. I frequent the church when lighting my weekly candle for my grandmother and the son I lost. Yes, I was just here last night, but this feels like the right place for my current mood. Besides, Saint Jude is the patron saint of the lost cause. It's fitting I'd choose this church as my sanctuary. My sliver of peace in the chaos. After today's insanity, I need a little solace.

I recite the Hail Mary in my head, select a candle, and watch the flame flicker to life. "*Ti amerò per sempre*," I whisper, making the sign of the cross. *I will love you forever.* It's something my grandmother said to me as a child— back before Mamma and I left Italy.

I suppress a wave of emotion and head for my usual pew. The Roman

Catholic cathedral is one of the more beautiful churches in the city. It's a lofty, ornate structure, filled to the brim with intricate carvings and vivid stained glass. Saint Jude's is only a few blocks from my apartment, which is also a bonus. I've spent many evenings seated in a pew at the back, quietly reflecting on my life.

I left the hospital in a daze. My mind keeps spinning its wheels, desperate for traction. *You have no idea what he's been through.* Lena's words echo in my head. I know his parents died from suicide, but she made it seem like there's more to Garrett's story. My heart aches for him. We make quite the pair—a couple of broken souls trying to cope with childhood trauma.

While I plan to explain why I left the hotel, I doubt I'll tell him my whole truth. I've never uttered the words to anyone other than Paolo and Father Angelo, who approaches on my left, carrying my empty Tupperware container.

The priest smiles as he settles in the pew beside me, dressed in the lavish purple robes typical of Advent. He hands me the container. "Thank you again for the soup. It was delicious. Just what the doctor ordered."

He missed Sunday's Mass because he wasn't feeling well. I made a batch of turkey soup and dropped it off that afternoon, along with a bottle of vitamin C and some cough medicine.

"You're very welcome. Are you feeling better?"

"Much better. It was just a chest cold." He taps his watch. "This is late for you, Ella. Is everything all right?"

"I'm okay, Father. Just caught in my head again, that's all."

His warm brown gaze searches my face. "Anything in particular?"

"Christmas is coming."

Although I've tried to erase all memories of my past, there are some too cherished to discard. Christmastime in Italy is what I miss most about my native land. The carefree times before my childhood was tainted. Closing my eyes, I envision the sparkling lights and decorated trees. I can almost smell the aromas of freshly baked biscotti, pizzelle, anise cookies, and struffoli. My mouth waters at the memory. I can still hear my neighbors cheerfully greeting one another with wishes of *Buon Natale.* But, like the double-edged sword typical of my reality, the holiday's annual reappearance drowns out the good memories with a glaring reminder of the loss I *chose.*

Alone in the concrete jungle of New York City, I never feel more isolated than at Christmas. I crave warmth, affection, and family, but I'm an orphan in every sense of the word.

Garrett's an orphan too. He battles the kindred demons of loneliness and vulnerability. Like me, he keeps his torment locked beneath the surface. The shadows in his eyes pull me closer, making me want to heal him.

Who am I kidding? I can't even heal myself.

I gesture to the lush poinsettias on the altar. "It always hurts more when those flowers show up."

He nods. "It's hard to believe how fast the years go by."

Father Angelo is aware of my past, but I've never delved into the nitty-gritty reasons behind my decision. I still don't fully understand them.

Regrets are a bitch.

The hollow feeling wraps around my lungs. "Yeah, it's crazy to know if things were different, I'd be raising a teenager."

"You made the best choice for you at the time. I'm sure it still hurts, but don't forget God has a plan for all of us."

"I'm starting to think God has a sick sense of humor," I mutter, flipping through the psalm book in my lap.

"What makes you say that?"

"Everything. Nothing. I don't know, Father." I meet his gaze. "I feel so lost."

I've tried to get Garrett out of my head, but I can't. I thought I could fuck him out of my system. It didn't work.

"That's because you won't allow anyone to find you, Ella. You keep everyone at arm's length when what you really need is some closeness." He tilts his head to the side. "What about Maria Benicasa's son? I know you two are friendly. Isn't he a suitable partner?"

A heavy sigh deflates my chest. "Paolo is a wonderful man, but he's just a friend. He deserves better than me. I'm the one who isn't suitable."

He rubs his chin. "What about your singer friend Josh?"

"You mean Jake?"

He nods. "He seems like a nice young man."

"Jake is one of my dearest friends." A rueful smile curves my lips. "I'm afraid he's also the butt of one of God's jokes."

"How so?"

"He's helplessly in love with his best friend's little sister."

"That's a shame. You two would have attractive children."

I snort a laugh. "You crack me up, Father."

"Well, it's true." He eyes me. "If Jake isn't an option, why not get to know someone from work?" He straightens like a light bulb went off in his head. "What about that man you interviewed recently? The one in the new Broadway show? I read your article. It seemed like he intrigued you."

He's mentioned reading my work in the past, but I never imagined it was a regular occurrence. Either he can read my mind, or my story wasn't as discreet as I thought.

I'm not about to lie to my priest, so I say, "He more than intrigues me, Father, but I've already ruined things with him."

"Ruined them, how?"

"Trust me, you don't want to know."

He chuckles. "That's fine. You can tell me all about it in confession on Sunday."

Nope. Not happening.

"Let's put it this way. I hurt him and unknowingly jeopardized his sobriety."

"Did you ask for forgiveness?"

"Not yet."

"What are you waiting for?" His eyes sparkle with mirth. "If he gives you any trouble, send him my way. Sister Mary Catherine and I will straighten him right out."

I laugh at the thought of the grumpy old nun he loves to bicker with. She's an endearing type of miserable—the kind of woman who'd grab a man by the ear, drag him into her office, and lecture him until his eyes crossed. I'm sure she'd have a field day with Garrett.

Between us on the wooden pew, my phone loudly buzzes with a text. *Prodigy* flashes across the screen.

"Oh my God." I clap a hand over my mouth. "Sorry for taking the Lord's name in vain, but the guy we were talking about just texted me."

Father Angelo's smile widens. "I find it interesting he contacted you while we were discussing him. I smell a divine intervention."

"Maybe." My cheeks get hot, and I peek at the message.

Prodigy: Why did you leave AGAIN?????

As much as I want to reply, I don't want to be rude to Father Angelo. I hate when people bury their noses in their phones instead of having a conversation.

I set it back down and meet his gaze. "Tell me more about this divine intervention. Should I dig out my rosary beads for good measure?"

"I'd never tell you *not* to do the Rosary, Ella."

"Good point. I'm sure it's in your job description."

"Most definitely." He chuckles and smooths his robes. "Personally, I enjoy praying the Rosary."

"Oh?"

"I'm a sucker for repetition. I find it comforting." He rubs his stubbled jawline. "Bad day? There's nothing like a few Our Fathers to cheer you up. Toss in a Glory Be and everything is right with the world."

If only it were that simple. While I frequent this church, my feelings about religion itself are more nebulous. Catholicism was so deeply ingrained in me as a child in Italy, that it has always been part of my life. Yes, I find comfort at this cathedral, but it has more to do with the setting and priest than my beliefs. The "Catholic guilt" and constant judgment I experienced in the past, isn't present in this parish. Father Angelo is a progressive man, inclusive and unassuming. He makes me feel welcome here. Safe and cherished. I can't say I'd come as often if it were anyone else behind the altar. While I identify as Catholic, the truth is, I don't know what I believe anymore. I recite old prayers out of habit because they help keep my grandmother's memory alive.

I give him a weak smile, wishing I could attain the level of comfort true believers receive from religion. "I'm more of a Hail Mary kind of girl."

"Makes sense. Many ladies are." He motions to the pew's leather-bound prayer book. "Listen, maybe reciting prayers doesn't comfort you much, and that's fine. Do whatever brings you peace, be it cooking, exercise, a good book. I just think it would be helpful if you got out of your head a little. Trust in your ability to read people. There are good men out there, I promise."

"I'll take your word for it." My phone buzzes, drawing my attention once more. "It's him again."

"Well, I'd better go water my flowers." Father Angelo rises and points to the altar. "I'm sure they're thirsty." He flashes me a wink. "And I wouldn't want to impede any divine pairings."

"It's just a coincidence."

"Keep telling yourself that, Ella. Good night, dear. Be kind to yourself."

"Good night, Father. I'll see you Sunday with more soup. I'm making pasta fagioli this weekend, and I think you'll love it."

"I always look forward to your cooking." He pats his tummy and heads down the center aisle.

Smiling, I pick up my phone to read Garrett's message.

Prodigy: Seriously, please tell me why you left.

Me: You need to rest.

Prodigy: Was Lena rude to you?

Me: Don't worry about me.

Prodigy: Just so we're clear, I wanted you to stay.

My heart somersaults in my chest. Maybe there is hope for his forgiveness.

Thirty-Four

Relief, an explanation, and a mea culpa

Garrett

I slept like shit. Between the beeping and having my vitals checked every hour, I'd be shocked if I got more than forty-five minutes of rest. My head throbs like a bitch, and my vision keeps getting hazy, so there's that too.

A petite, redheaded nurse enters the room, wearing a scrub top with cartoon cats all over it. "Good morning, Mr. Casey. You have visitors, but I need to check your blood pressure first."

It must be Lena if she's worried about me blowing a gasket. I peek at her name badge. "Thanks, Cheryl, but you can tell Lena I'm still pissed at her."

I desperately wanted to hear what Ella had to say.

Lena relayed their conversation, and how Ella disclosed that her boss assigned her to the documentary. I genuinely thought she took the job to toy with me. She told Lena she's hit rock bottom in the past. Maybe that's why she's so cagey.

I can't believe Lena chased her off. Then again, she nearly ripped Carissa's throat out when I told her about the affair. Even now, years later, she practically foams at the mouth when my ex's name comes up in conversation. But

Ella isn't Carissa. She's not an icy, entitled snob who likes to fuck her boyfriend's college roommate behind his back.

Cheryl smiles, adjusting her rhinestone-encrusted, cat-eye-shaped glasses. "It's not Lena, dear." She wraps the cuff around my upper arm and inflates it. "I already updated her by phone when she called to check in."

Since Lena is my health care proxy, and she works at this hospital, it's easy for her to keep tabs on me.

"One fifteen over seventy," she murmurs, deflating the cuff. "That's excellent."

"Oh good. Make sure she knows that, so she stops giving me shit for eating salt."

"Lena said she'll be here this afternoon. You can tell her yourself." She chuckles and nudges me. "I'll send your visitors in." She heads for the hallway.

A few moments later, a familiar face appears in the doorway, making me smile. "Excuse me, we're looking for Professor Crane." Tom steps into the room. "There he is."

Tess follows close behind. "Howdy, Mister Garrett."

Oh, great. My smile fades, and my face grows hot.

She stops at my bedside. "How're you feelin'?"

"I'm okay," I croak, unable to meet her gaze. "I'm sorry I fucked up rehearsal."

Tom pats my arm. "Stop it. We've got plenty of time before *Prodigy* debuts. You need to focus on getting better."

I quickly fill them in on my concussion status, the tests I've had, and the time frame for recovery.

Tom's cell rings. "Excuse me, but I need to take this. It's my wife. Oh, Helen with her impeccable timing," he mutters, leaving the room.

Now or never.

"Tess, listen . . ." I force a swallow. "I want to apologize for last night."

She waves me off. "Don't worry about it."

"I'm sorry I got carried away. I didn't mean for that to happen." I pick at the tape securing a tube to my hand. "I hope I didn't make you uncomfortable."

"It's fine."

"It's just that I was thinking about—"

"I've seen how you react when Miss Ella enters a room. You don't have to explain."

I blink a few times. *How the fuck does she know?*

Tess smiles and flashes me a wink. "Your secret's safe with me."

"I'm, uh, well . . ." I clear my throat and try again, "Is it that obvious?"

"I knew something was up after you stormed out on Monday. I watched both of your reactions to one another last night. And good *Lord.*" She grins and fans herself. "Y'all have enough sexual tension to burn down the theater. Heck, if it helps make our scenes more authentic, I'm all for it. You can pretend I'm whomever you like."

A laugh bursts from my lips. "You're awesome, Tess."

"I'm serious." She rubs her cheeks. "But shave next time because your whiskers are sharp. Also, if you have any single friends who kiss like that, send them my way."

I laugh harder. "I'll see who I can round up." I meet her sapphire-colored gaze with a smile. "Thanks for being so cool. I was worried I ruined everything."

"You didn't ruin a darn thing."

"I can't believe you knew I was thinking about her."

She chuckles. "Apparently, you didn't hear yourself moan her name during our kiss scene."

"Oh, Jesus." I clap a hand to my face.

"Nope. It was definitely, 'Oh, Ella.'" She giggles and squeezes my shoulder. "Like I said, don't worry about it. Just buy me some face cream."

"In my defense, I didn't know Tom planned to change up the script. I thought we had several weeks before the kiss scene. I promise to shave before the next rehearsal."

Tom returns, and the three of us chat for a bit before they head out. Meanwhile, I'm dizzy with relief over Tess's reaction to my rogue boner. It's bad enough to have a skull-busting headache. Factor in my panic over a sexual harassment situation, and I was stressed the fuck out. At least I don't have to worry now.

I'm lucky to have such an easygoing costar. The earlier awkwardness dissipated as soon as she cracked a joke. I rub at my stubbled jaw and ponder a face cream care package of sorts. Just to fuck with her a little. I'll get her some aloe and wound dressings too.

A knock turns my attention to the doorway.

Ella stands at my room's threshold, carrying a brown paper bag. "Good morning."

"Hey." I sit up straighter, and the heart monitor beeps a little faster. "Come in."

She approaches my bedside. "I won't keep you long, but I wanted to bring you some breakfast. I can't imagine the hospital serves anything worth eating." She hands over a bag from Nikolai's Bakery, and the aroma of warm carbs greets my nostrils. "It's an everything bagel."

"Thank you so much."

"You're welcome. Since I wasn't sure if you like butter or cream cheese, I brought both. They make a chive cream cheese that's simply delicious."

Nikolai's Bakery is one of my choice eateries. Their assortment of carbs, warm and room temperature alike, is my definition of comfort food. Lena and I adore their bagels. We've been known to eat the chive cream cheese with a spoon.

I pop the lid on the cream cheese and give it a sniff. "Mmm. The chive one is my favorite."

"Oh, good. That means I've done something right for once." She gives me a rueful smile. "Listen, Garrett—"

"Sit." I point to the chair at my bedside. "Stay a while."

She bites her lower lip. "I need to get to work."

"Tell your boss you got stuck in traffic."

"You're persistent."

I motion to the chair. "It's one of my best qualities."

"I suppose Harvey won't can me if I'm a few minutes late." Ella lowers herself into the seat. Her eyes lock with mine. "Garrett, I'm sorry. For everything."

"Thank you." I lean over to peek at her cherry-red heels. These are different from the ones she wore last night. "I'm sorry I barfed on your shoes. I'm happy to replace them if they're ruined."

"It's all right. Please don't worry about it. I have more shoes than I know what to do with."

"Are they all pointy death-trap stilettos?"

She laughs. "Most of them, yes. I have a few pairs of flats, and some sneakers, but I only wear them at home."

"How come?" My stomach growls, and I glance at the bag. "Would you think I was rude if I devoured my bagel right now?"

"Of course not. Nourishment is part of healing." She watches me slather a ridiculous amount of cream cheese on my bagel. "To answer your question, flats make me feel vulnerable, which is something I despise. It's hard to explain, but those few extra inches of height are my security blanket. Even though it's counterintuitive."

"How so?"

"Well, I can't exactly *run* in heels."

Who is she running from? And why?

Confessing to one's weaknesses is a big no-no in the Garrett Casey hypervigilance playbook.

Rule number one: never expose your soft underbelly to the enemy. It's the principle I'm least likely to abandon—except when it comes to Ella. There's no denying her ability to disarm me, and despite Lena's urgings, I'm not sure I'd classify her as an adversary in the first place.

"It sounds like you and I have similar relationships with vulnerability."

"I hate it," she whispers.

"Same. So, your kamikaze footwear is an empowerment tool?"

"Exactly."

"You can also use the spike heels as a weapon, if need be," I inform her around a mouthful of warm dough.

"There's that too. I imagine a stiletto to the eyeball would hurt."

I jerk my thumb toward her feet. "Taking one of those to any ball would suck." I hold up a finger. "Just so we're clear, I am *not* volunteering for a junk shot in the name of research."

She laughs, and the sound warms me. "You're too much."

"Been told that before."

She studies my face for a moment, making me wonder what stories my eyes are telling. "I'm sorry I left the hotel room that night. It had nothing to do with you. To be honest, I'm so fucked up it didn't occur to me that my actions might hurt you."

"Were you afraid of me?"

"Not you, specifically. Just the situation and your words."

"My words?" I frown, trying to remember our postcoital conversation. "What do you mean?"

"I'm referring to when you said, 'It can be our little secret. Nobody has to know what we do.' It made me—" She takes a few slow, deep breaths. "I had a flashback."

About six hundred questions collide in my brain, but all I can manage is, "A flashback?"

"Yes. An extremely vivid one. I felt raw. Exposed. My every instinct screamed for me to run, and the panic took over. I wasn't thinking clearly." She twirls a piece of hair between her fingers and stares at the strands instead of making eye contact. "I guess I have trouble with intimacy."

You don't say.

"Makes two of us." I search her face. "What happened to you?"

Her breath catches. "I can't talk about it right now. Just know that my leaving had nothing to do with you." Our gazes meet and her eyes are damp. "I'm sorry I jeopardized your sobriety."

I want to tell her it has always been hanging by a thread. My past is the canyon waiting to swallow me whole when I finally unravel and fall. Her abandonment was simply another pair of scissors. Since she's clearly dealing with some shit of her own, I muster up a weak reassurance instead.

"It's fine."

She grips the hospital bed's guard rail. "I realize I have a certain reputation. I've heard the whisperings. My actions haven't helped matters, but the woman I portray in public isn't who I truly am."

"What reputation?" I'm curious to hear how she perceives herself.

"I don't let people know me, and it frustrates them. Am I mysterious? Yes. I carry myself that way for a reason. Call it a defense mechanism if you'd like, but I don't keep people at arm's length to toy with them."

"I'm not worried about your reputation because I don't care what other people think. I make my own decisions based on experience. While I get that you have your reasons for keeping people out, I won't lie and say you didn't fuck with me."

Her lip quivers. "I'm sorry."

"What do you need protection from?"

"The world."

I lean in. "Why? Is someone hurting you? Are you in danger?"

"Not anymore." Ella shakes her head. "I appreciate your concern, but please don't allow me to mean something to you."

"Let me decide what holds meaning in my life. If you're so determined to not have an impact, why bring me food?"

"Because I can't stay away from you." Her whispered confession makes my heart race.

"Then, don't." I lean in closer, the bagel long forgotten. "But we need to clear something up. I have a long history of being left behind. You can't imagine some of the shit I've endured. If you need control of the bedroom situation, I'll let you have it. To be honest, I'd let you do just about anything you wanted to me. But"—I hold up a finger—"*don't* walk away from me. Never turn your back and leave me in a position of vulnerability again. That dismissal cuts me deeper than you realize."

"It won't happen again."

"Also, don't censor yourself with me, okay? I want to know what's on your mind. If you don't like something, speak up. Use your voice, Ella. I swear I'll listen."

"I'll do my best." She fiddles with her necklace. "Please try not to use those specific words around me."

It can be our little secret. Nobody has to know what we do.

One thing's for damn sure, those words will never again cross my lips in her presence. My brain aches with the questions I need answered. *Who hurt her? When? For how long? Is she safe? How can I help her?*

"I'm sorry I freaked you out. I just wanted to hold you."

"I know."

"Why'd you leave me that way? You could've at least untied me."

"Like I said, I was scared," she whispers, blinking back tears. "I'm *always* scared."

"What are you afraid of? Did you think I'd hurt you?" When she doesn't answer, I soften my voice. "I'm not a mind reader. You've got to tell me, so I don't unknowingly trigger you again."

"I think the better question is what I'm not afraid of. It's a smaller list." She looks away.

I study her for a moment. She's right—the air of mystery and her sultry confidence are a front. Inside, she's a terrified little girl who's slowly showing me parts of herself that others don't see.

"I hope you realize I'd never hurt you," I whisper, bending to catch her gaze. "You don't need to be afraid with me."

"I think that's why I'm drawn to you."

"Thought it was the Garrett Casey gravitational pull?"

"There's that factor as well." She gives me a sheepish smile. "And you adapted to my needs with ease."

"Trust me, there was nothing easy about it, and I wouldn't have done it for just anyone. Understand that, Ella. I let down my guard for you. In the spirit of reciprocity, I hope you can lower some of those walls and let me in."

"I can't make any guarantees. My fears and insecurities are so deeply rooted, I don't remember a time before them. Mine was not an ideal childhood."

"I can relate. The shit show continued through my teens and early twenties."

She straightens, the journalist inside her taking over. "When did you start drinking?"

If she's more comfortable wearing her reporter hat, I'll let her interview me all day long. Maybe I can slip in a question of my own now and then.

"At twelve. It was a coping mechanism."

"My God . . . that's so young."

"Like I said, my world was upended long before my tenth birthday."

"When did you stop drinking?"

"Not until I was twenty-three."

"I imagine college was a struggle." Her compassion-filled eyes search mine.

"Yes and no. The studies came easily but my relationships suffered. I was a functional alcoholic. I don't remember earning my bachelor's, but I was sober for the better part of my MBA courses."

"Look at you now—you own a business and scored the lead in a Broadway show. I'd say you've done well for yourself."

"I'm a work in progress. It's been a long road to recovery. Thanks to my addictive personality and trio of demons, it's a road I'll keep traveling."

"Trio of demons?"

"Alcoholism, depression, and anxiety. Not a day goes by without having to deal with at least one of those fuckers."

"I admire how easily you talk about it."

"For the most part, I'm an open book and full-disclosure kind of guy. Why waste time with mystery?"

"Have you always been like that?"

"No. I used to keep *everything* locked up. My inpatient stay at Bellevue changed that for me."

Her eyes widen. "You were hospitalized?"

The morbid fucker inside me loves seeing people's reactions when I divulge my psychiatric history. It's amazing how quickly compassion yields to judgment. Ella's questions come from a place of concern, so I keep talking.

"Yeah. Nine years ago. And once during my teens."

"I'm sorry you dealt with that."

"Don't be. It was the best possible thing for me. My fucked-up waters run deep. Sometimes, spilling my guts is the only thing that keeps me from drowning. Don't get me wrong—I'm selective with the people I trust, and I still leave some shit buried in the name of self-preservation. We all do. But extensive therapy and AA meetings have helped tremendously. I'm sure you can pick up on this vibe, but I'm a huge advocate for mental health services."

"Yes, I can tell. I think that's wonderful. I wish Jake were more open about his struggles."

"Tell me about it."

Hands down, Jake Bennett is one of the most anxious people I've ever met. He's what I call a closet sufferer. He doesn't have much choice as a celebrity in the spotlight. Society is hesitant to embrace men with mental health issues.

She sighs. "But who am I to talk? I'm one of those time-wasting, lock-away types."

"Would've never guessed."

"I'd love to hear the rest of your story."

I lift an eyebrow. "What do you want? Plot synopsis? Chapter outline?"

"I want the unabridged version"—she glances at her watch—"but I'm afraid it will have to wait for another time. I should really get to work before Harvey gets worried."

"When can I see you again?" I sweep my gaze over her body. "And I'm not referring to rehearsal."

Her eyes widen. "You'd actually consider it?"

"I find it comical you seem surprised by that."

She flushes and wraps her arms around herself. "It's just that, well, after seeing your kiss last night, I assumed you were interested in Tess. I mean, it was . . . um . . . quite something."

"I wasn't thinking about Tess."

Her breath catches, and her widened gaze snaps to mine. "Oh?" Her shoulders rise and fall faster. She licks her lips. "Who was on your mind?"

"Take a wild guess." After a brief visual journey of her curves, I find her eyes once more. The sea of lust swirling in them mirrors my ache to lose myself inside her.

She opens and closes her mouth a few times, but no sound comes out.

I lean in close. "You should see what I'm capable of *without* an audience."

Thirty-Five

A piano, a foodgasm, and a revelation

Ella

Bryant Park has always been one of my favorite places in the city. Even at Christmastime when everything aches. I love the hustle and bustle of shoppers perusing the glass-enclosed vendors. The holiday music spilling from the speakers. The aroma of roasted chestnuts and hot cocoa. It's ironic how the season's cheer and excitement help to fill my life's emptiness. I watch smiling couples gliding hand in hand on the ice and can almost feel their warmth. A bittersweet pang of jealousy tightens my chest. I want someone to spend the holidays with.

Garrett's office building looms in the distance. I've got a clear view from my position near the skating rink. There was a text from him when I woke. He's still in the hospital but hopes the doctor will discharge him later this evening or tomorrow. I think I'll stop by to see him after I finish my shopping. I took today off from work, as one does when they need a mental health day.

I pause at a vendor selling hand-painted Christmas villages and tree garb. Every year I put up a tiny tree in my apartment to help lighten my mood. The artificial spruce curates my favorite ornaments, including my annual new addition. I browse the dangling beauties in search of one worthy of hanging with the previous twelve. My gaze settles on a miniature grand piano. The delicate brush strokes and perfect tiny keys are a thing of beauty.

"That was easy," I say, making my way to the cashier. Smiling, I hand over the ornament.

"Ah, I love this one," the woman murmurs. "I painted it for my grandson. He inspired a whole collection of pianos."

"Does he play?"

She nods. "He just started last year. I may be biased, but he's quite good."

"That's wonderful. My dear friend, Jake Bennett, is a piano wizard. You may have heard of him." I don't typically name-drop, but I'm proud of Jake's talent.

Her eyes widen. "Oh, I've more than heard of him. I've seen him in concert twice. My grandson *idolizes* him. Jake Bennett is the reason he started playing piano in the first place. In fact, Jake was Gabriel's very first concert." She beams, her smile lighting up the little shop. "I took him to see the Christmas special at Radio City Music Hall last year."

"Ah, yes. That was an incredible show."

"Gabe memorized the sheet music for 'Desert Rose' in under a week. You should hear him play."

I withdraw a business card from my purse and hand it to her. "I want you to hang on to this. I'm sure you've heard about Jake's community center?"

She nods. "The Phoenix is a wonderful project."

I lower my voice like what I'm telling her is scandalous. "I heard from a little birdie that Jake himself will be giving private piano lessons."

"Oh, my goodness! Really?"

"Yes. Children must qualify for the Phoenix's music mentorship. There will be an application procedure in place to ensure only serious pupils are accepted. I think you should have your grandson apply when the time comes." I point to the card she's holding. "And tell the powers that be, Ella gave her personal recommendation." I flash her a smile. "I'll put in a good word on my end too."

Her eyes tear up. "Thank you so much, honey. That would be Gabe's dream." She wraps the ornament in tissue paper. I reach for my wallet, but she waves it away. "I want you to have this one. On me."

"Oh, I couldn't. Please let me pay for your beautiful artistry."

"I insist. Merry Christmas." She places the piano in a paper bag and hands it to me.

"Thank you," I whisper. "Merry Christmas to you and your family. Tell Gabriel to keep playing."

I ride the elevator with my purchases carefully tucked beneath my arm and glance at the to-go container I'm holding. I don't know what prompted me to buy Garrett lunch, but here I am. I hope he likes Mediterranean food.

The elevator dings, and the door slides open. I meander down the hall to Garrett's room, pausing outside.

Fuck.

Lena is here again. Recalling our previous encounter, my confidence deflates like a popped balloon. I may as well be barefoot because my stilettos do nothing to bolster it. She doesn't like me, and I'd be willing to bet her distaste runs even deeper now that I'm trying to regain Garrett's trust.

I take a fortifying breath, steel my shoulders, and knock on the open door.

Garrett looks up. "Ella, hey. Come in."

Lena eyes me from where she's seated on the foot of his bed. "Hello."

"Hi." I turn my focus to Garrett. "I brought you lunch. There's an amazing gyro place in Bryant Park—"

"Opa's gyros are my favorite! I go there *at least* twice a week. That spinning meat slab is heaven on a stick."

Lena snorts. "You kill me with your descriptions sometimes."

"Do you have a better one?"

"Not really," she says with a giggle.

Garrett smiles up at me, warmth infusing his features. "Thank you."

"You're welcome." I hand him the bag. "I wasn't sure if you like tzatziki sauce, so I asked Nick to put it on the side."

He grins. "I love their sauce."

"I'll keep that in mind for future reference. How are you feeling?"

"My head still hurts, but the swelling's mostly gone. I should be able to go home tonight."

I glance at the beeping machines he's connected to. "Wouldn't it be safer if they monitored you for longer?" I hate the idea of him suffering a complication down the road. "What if you pass out or something?"

"Nah. I'm in tip-top shape."

"He still needs to be monitored, but his scans have improved, so it doesn't have to be in an inpatient setting. He can finish out his recovery at home. There are symptom checklists and whatnot to help. Plus, he has me," Lena explains.

I must look confused, because Garrett clarifies with, "Lena's a trauma nurse. This shit's in her wheelhouse."

"Oh, that's right." An anxious part of me settles, knowing he'll have someone to keep an eye on him. "Do you anticipate any issues?"

"No. He should be fine." She gives him a pointed glare. "As long as he follows directions and actually rests."

He salutes her. "Yes, Queen Leens."

Their dynamic reminds me a little of mine and Paolo's, making me wonder just how close their relationship is. My chest tightens. Who am I to be jealous? I have no claim to him. Yet somehow, the thought of Lena in Garrett's arms makes my palms sweat.

"Okay, well, I won't keep you. I'm sure we'll talk once you're cleared to return to rehearsals."

Garrett frowns. "You literally just got here."

I motion to Lena. "And I dropped by unannounced, so I don't want to interrupt your visit."

"Puh-lease. I hardly count as a visitor," Lena says with a chuckle. "I'm meeting Wes for lunch. You aren't interrupting anything." She rises and presses a kiss to Garrett's forehead. "Keep me posted on your discharge and let me know when to pick you up."

"Will do. Thanks, Leens."

"Bye, Ella."

"Enjoy your lunch date," I say. She smiles and gives us a wave before leaving. I turn to face Garrett, who's watching me closely. "What?"

"You all right?"

My breath eases out of me. "I am, now."

"Ah, gotcha. I figured it had something to do with Lena being here."

"I don't think she likes me much," I mutter, twisting a piece of my hair.

"She's prickly toward you because she loves me. Lena has always been fierce where I'm concerned." He points to the open door she left through. "You must be growing on her because she would've lingered if her hackles were up."

"She has a lunch date," I remind him.

He points to his gyro. "And thanks to you, so do I." He juts his chin toward the chair at his bedside. "You know what to do."

"Thought you didn't date?" I settle in the seat, folding my hands in my lap.

"I don't. But I'm always open to change." He eyes my wool coat. "How about you take that off and stay a while?"

"I really shouldn't. You need to rest."

He gestures to his bed. "I've done nothing but rest for days, Cupcake. Make yourself comfy. I don't bite."

His devilish grin tells me otherwise, but I slide my coat off and drape it over the back of my chair. "You're persistent."

"It's part of my charm." Chuckling, he opens the food container and slathers the gyro with tzatziki sauce. He breaks it in half, wraps one piece in a napkin, and hands me the warm pita and meat conglomerate. "Eat this."

"You're a bit bossy too, Mr. Casey," I murmur, accepting my portion.

"Funny, that's *also* part of my charm." He takes a bite of gyro, and his throaty moan reverberates to my clit.

I squeeze my thighs together to combat the sensation. A look of sheer bliss transforms his features as he chews. Even dressed in a hospital gown, connected to tubes and wires, with messy hair and a scruffy jawline, Garrett is *still* breathtaking. A groan rumbles from his chest. Then another low moan. No joke, the man is giving the diner scene from *When Harry Met Sally* a run for its money. Those amber eyes flutter in an apparent foodgasm, and I've never seen—or heard—anything sexier.

Well, except that time we had sex. That was way hotter. My heart races with the memory, and I need to remind myself to breathe.

"Mmm-mmm-mmm. Oh, God, *yes*." His gaze locks with mine. "So. Fucking. Good."

I get it. Nick's gyros are to die for, but Garrett's sounds are doing something to my insides. Hands shaking, I take the tiniest of bites, careful not to drip sauce onto myself. He moans *again*, making me flush and nearly drop my gyro.

"I'm glad you're enjoying your food, but can you maybe be less vocal about it?"

He watches me while he chews. Swallowing the bite, he chugs some water. "Why?"

Because it's turning me on. "Because it's unnerving."

"Why's that?" He licks his lips. Then licks some sauce off his fingers. "You've heard me moan before."

"Garrett." His name leaves my lips unbidden, and I'm not sure if it's a warning or a plea.

His lionlike gaze burns into me. "I'm listening."

"Huh?" He's got me so flustered I don't know my own name, let alone what I planned to say.

"Talk to me, Ella. Tell me why I've got you squirming." He motions to the space between us. "Because I don't have the time or energy to keep tip-toeing around this."

"For one, I'm not squirming. Also, no one's tiptoeing around anything. You're lying in a hospital bed after a traumatic brain injury. This is hardly the setting for moans and innuendo."

"Oh, yeah?" His wicked smirk makes him even sexier. "And why not?"

I stiffen my spine. "Because it isn't."

"That's not an answer."

"Jesus, Garrett. What do you want from me?"

"I already told you. I wanna know what's on your mind."

"Forgive me if it's a little hard to think when you look at me like that," I huff the words, well and truly off my game now.

His smile widens. "Like what?"

"The way you stare sometimes."

He sets down his gyro. "You mean when I'm envisioning your legs thrown over my shoulders, those sexy death-trap shoes by my ears?"

My breath rushes out of me. The visual does nothing to cool my heated body.

And he's not done.

"Or when I imagine you straddling my face, grinding your wet pussy on my tongue." His gaze sweeps the length of me. "Or on your hands and knees in front of me so I can watch my cock filling you?" He leans in close, and my inner muscles clench. "You need to be specific because I give you a lot of looks, and they all share a common denominator."

"And that is?" My breathless voice is equal parts wanton and uncertain.

"I want you, Ella. I haven't stopped thinking about you since the gala. There's something between us, and I know you feel it too. You've gotta tell me what's on your mind so I don't fuck up."

"I'm a disaster," I whisper, forcing a deep breath. "My mind's a dark place."

"Mine too, baby."

"I have heavy baggage."

"Suitcases turn me on."

I laugh in spite of myself. "You're insane."

"The psychosis is real." His expression sobers. "In all seriousness, feel free to unload. I'm a good listener."

We sit in silence for a few beats while I consider his offer. Over the years I've confided in Paolo, burdened him with pieces of my past. I haven't known Garrett for long, but his willingness to bear some of the weight puts me at ease. He's not forcing me to talk. He's giving me an option to use my voice. I get to choose who I share myself with this time.

Sometimes there's power in being vulnerable.

I take a fortifying breath and meet his gaze. "I've been through some . . . trauma. Wounds that won't heal."

He nods and shifts his position to face me. His neutral expression is at war with the pain in his eyes. Or perhaps it's recognition. Understanding. Compassion. Whatever it is, it resonates inside me, dismantling pieces of my fortress.

"As I'm sure you've noticed, I have a turbulent relationship with sex. I loathe it as much as I crave it because I don't like to be touched. Kissing isn't my thing." He lifts an eyebrow, so I clarify, "Let me rephrase. I enjoy kissing—it's *being* kissed that's the problem. I won't let you kiss me, so please don't try."

"Got it." His eyes focus on my lips. "What else?"

"I need to be in control of the sex."

"So you've mentioned." Releasing a heavy sigh, he rubs a hand over his face, then purses his lips like he's struggling to choose his words. After a moment, he clears his throat. "Listen, if you want something to happen between us again, I'm all in, but it can't be like it was last time."

My stomach bottoms out. "What do you mean?"

"I'll let you take the reins, do whatever makes you feel comfortable, *but* you can't tie me up again. That part is nonnegotiable. It dredged up way too much shit from my past. Stuff that needs to stay buried for the sake of my sobriety. I hope you can understand."

I nod slowly as hundreds of questions circle my brain.

His eyes burn into mine. "I'm sorry if that means we can't have sex, but it's a boundary I need in place."

Boundaries are sacred. They deserve awareness and respect—not pressure. I won't do anything to jeopardize his sobriety.

"I understand," I whisper.

"I'd much rather us get to a place where restraints don't even cross your mind. Fear has no place in the bedroom, Ella. I want you to trust me, and I'm willing to put in the work, but I need you to be open and honest. You don't like something? Tell me. If I'm saying or doing something wrong? Communicate. No more fuck and flees, okay?"

"It won't happen again." I press a hand to my heart. "I promise."

"Thank you." His posture visibly relaxes.

"Most man-on-top sexual positions are out of the question," I blurt. "And you can't put your hands on me unless I tell you to."

"That's fine. I'm a bit of a voyeur anyway." His wicked grin unravels me as he makes a show of folding his hands behind his head. "You can ride me all day long, Cupcake."

"Noted." The visual heats me, making me cross my legs.

"I'm serious. Whatever you need. I won't break your rules."

My dam crumbles with his willingness to respect my boundaries, unleashing a cascade of truths.

"I'm afraid of my own shadow. I'll flinch if you shout or loom over me. Outside of Paolo, Jake, my boss, and my priest, most men terrify me. Especially, big, tall ones capable of overpowering me. It's even worse if they're loud."

He stiffens. "I wouldn't call myself loud, but I'm six-three and well built. You're saying I terrify you?"

"No, no. *You* don't terrify me. It's the things I feel when I'm around you that scare me. You make me hope for normalcy. Ache for a connection, instead of the self-contained life I lead. I don't understand it, but you make me *want* to be vulnerable. That's never happened before." I stare into his eyes for a few moments. "You scare me because I'm out of my element. The control I'm so desperate for seems less critical when it comes to you, and I've never willingly relinquished control."

Garrett listens with his whole body as the river of confessions flows from my lips. He soaks them up, absorbs me, and for once, it's fucking liberating to dump my shit at someone's feet.

The freedom's a high I need to chase, so I keep going.

"I've never had a conventional relationship. No one has ever made love to me. I've never been *in* love. Hell, forget boyfriends—I've never even been on an actual one-on-one date."

His eyes widen, but he doesn't say anything.

"So, yeah. I'm a little unsteady where you're concerned." I point to his sobriety bracelet. "And given your circumstances, I'm probably not the healthiest influence." I squeeze my eyes shut and whisper, "We're a bad idea, Garrett. I should stay the hell away from you. Yet somehow, when I look into your eyes, I want to pull you closer. There is so much of me inside you."

"Look at me." When I meet his gaze, he continues. "Ella, I'm no stranger to trauma. That's the thing about pain—sooner or later you've gotta confront it. I'm not there yet. From what I can tell, neither are you. But I do know this. I won't knowingly do anything to hurt you. If you let me, maybe I can take some of your pain away."

"How?"

"When I'm feeling better, I want to take you on a date. A real date. No expectations of sex or anything else. Let me hang out with you. We can go anywhere you want. We'll do whatever you feel like doing. Be it dinner, a museum, the zoo, or yoga."

I lift an eyebrow. "You'd do yoga?"

"Sure, I would. I'm flexible as fuck. I've done it many times." His eyes glitter with mischief. "My sun salutations are on point, and you should see me in downward dog."

I laugh. "You're too much."

"Thanks . . . I guess?" He chuckles and rubs his jaw. "I know I'm pretty intense sometimes."

"I like your intensity."

"I like *you*, Ella. And I want to know you better. I'm happy to do things on your terms. Like I said, you tell me what you want, and I'll make it happen."

I bite the inside of my lower lip. "I'm kinda shitty at making decisions."

"Do you want me to plan something?"

"Yes. I'd really like that."

His smile transforms his face. "Consider it done. But you need to help me out by telling me some of your interests. Give me a few more, besides the obvious like photography and writing."

"Food. I *love* cooking, eating, studying its history. I enjoy wine, but I wouldn't want to put you in any uncomfortable situations. I love art and music, even though I'm shitty at both."

"Not true. I've seen your photography."

"Thanks. I categorize that with work. By art, I mean, paintings, drawings, and sculptures. I'm a sucker for anything related to women's rights and female empowerment."

"Ever burn any bras?"

"Oh, hell no. I need them."

He laughs. "I was kidding about the bra burning, but you sound like Lena. She has a love-hate relationship with her breasts."

"A lot of us do."

"I'm a feminist, myself. Maybe it's a product of having a female best friend for a quarter century, a female AA sponsor, and a woman psychiatrist, but I relate well to women. Oddly enough, most of my trust issues are also related to women."

Mine too. "How so?"

"Well, for starters, my mother abandoned me. She knew she was all I had left, but she took her life anyway. Then, my aunt dismissed me. Wendy acted like I didn't exist and turned a blind eye when I needed her. Last, but certainly not least, my ex's betrayal fucked me up for years."

"What happened?"

"I came home early from a business trip to surprise Carissa with an engagement ring. I found her in our bed with my college roommate. Oh yeah, and she was already three months pregnant with his kid. I guess they'd been fucking under my nose for over a year."

"Oh my God," I whisper, my heart aching for him.

"Yep." He stares out the window. "I moved out of our apartment that night. Two days later, the company I was working for laid me off. I lost my woman, my home, and my job in under a week. I spiraled *hard* after that."

"When did this happen?"

"Nine years ago. After the fallout, I moved in with Lena and started my own business. But I haven't had a relationship since."

"Aren't you . . . lonely?"

His pain-filled eyes snap to mine. "Absolutely. I've found staying busy helps. It's easy to forget about the loneliness when my free time is practically nonexistent."

"You're an intensely sensual man. Surely, you must have a release for all that pent-up energy?"

"Yeah. That's why I self-medicate."

"With what?"

"When boxing and running don't work, I turn to sex. I have a couple of friends who I call when the need arises. I've known them for years and trust them implicitly. Even so, we never cut corners with safety. There's one who always has my back when the alcohol cravings get to be too much. She's also my AA sponsor, which may or may not be a conflict of interest. But whatever. Over the years, I've successfully turned to Anya instead of the bottle."

"When was the last time you had to call her for sex?"

"Honestly?" Shame, and perhaps a hint of regret, twists his expression. "This past Monday after I stormed out of rehearsal."

"Oh." My mouth goes dry with the thought of him sleeping with someone else. We weren't together then, so it shouldn't bother me, but it does.

"Ralph's Tavern is down the block from my place." He holds up his thumb and forefinger. "I was this fucking close, Ella. I could almost taste the whiskey. Boxing didn't cut it. I turned to the next logical option."

"Which meant calling your AA sponsor to fuck." The statement sits heavy on my tongue.

"Yeah."

"Did it help?"

He looks away. "It did."

"Why not reach out to Lena?"

"What? Nooo." Horror flashes across his face. "I don't sleep with Lena."

"I didn't mean for sex, but now that we're discussing it, have you two? I mean, she's beautiful."

Forget beautiful—she's stunning. Lena has the kind of natural beauty that takes your breath away. It's no wonder Wes Emerson is enamored with her.

"No way. We've never even kissed. While I admit she's gorgeous, our relationship isn't like that. She's sacred to me. I'm extremely protective of her. No joke, I'd die or kill for her in an instant."

"Yeah, I picked up on that at the gala."

"It may seem strange to outsiders, but she's as much a part of me as I am of her. She's not blood, but she's my family. And unlike my mother, aunt, and ex, Lena has *never* turned her back on me." His expression is as fierce as his tone. "I'm sure she'll soften toward you once you get to know her."

"Let's hope."

"No, really. She's cool as fuck. Lena's the type of woman you want in your circle. I'm sure you have friendships like that?"

Oh, how I ache for more meaningful female friendships. Alessia is one of the few females in my circle, and she's practically family. Sure, Jenna is sweet, but our bond is surface level. I missed out on the sleepovers and girl talk so many women grew up with. I don't know how to behave around other women, so it's difficult to connect with them. I'm well aware it has something to do with how I carry myself, but I've yet to find an acceptable alternative. I can't let down my guard, be warm and inviting, while still shielding my wounds. It would be like a knight riding into battle wearing half of his armor. It's so much easier to linger in my comfort zone: Ella the enigma, armed with lipstick and stilettos.

A laugh of irony leaves my lips. "This may surprise you, but aside from Paolo's mom and sister, other women tend to avoid me. Most of my friends are male. I realize that seems counterintuitive with my fear of men, but I kinda have a sixth sense about who the good ones are. I'm closest with Paolo and Jake."

"Jake's a great guy. I'm not sold on Paolo."

"Oh? And why not?"

He narrows his eyes. "He wants you."

I shake my head, secretly pleased by his jealousy. "I've already been down that road with him."

"What road is that?" He searches my face. "More importantly, are you still going down it?"

I chew my lip. "You sure you want my answer?"

"Probably not but tell me anyway."

"Paolo was there for me during a challenging time in my life. His friendship has always been my haven. One day it morphed into a little more. We've been sleeping together for about five years. I keep telling myself I'll stop, but there are times when the loneliness gets to be too much. Times when it's like an aching, bone-deep emptiness, and I feel like I can't breathe." I stare out the window for a moment. "Humans aren't meant to be solitary. In many ways, Paolo's been a mentor to me. We all need someone sometimes, and he's the only one I trust. He's my safe place."

"But?"

"He deserves more than I can give. He's very family oriented. He needs someone to settle down with, and we both know I'm not that person."

"I get it. When was the last time you got together?"

"It's been a little over a month." I fiddle with my necklace, pondering how to phrase my next statement. "So, listen, this may seem a bit presumptuous—" I squeeze my eyes shut. "Never mind. Forget it."

"Yeah, no. That doesn't fly with me, Cupcake. Tell me what's on your mind."

Speak up.

Use your voice.

Demand respect.

A few deep breaths expand my chest. "If we pursue something together, I need us to be exclusive. I don't want to compete with your fuck buddy."

"There's no competition. Going forward, it will be you and *only* you." He motions between us, gaze darkening. "Exclusivity goes both ways. I don't share well either."

"I won't sleep with Paolo again. You need to understand our closeness though. He's important to me, and he's a big part of my life. You can't get jealous if we spend time together." I wave a finger at him. "I saw you glowering when we were at La Bussola."

He smirks. "Who, me? I don't glower."

I roll my eyes. "Uh-huh, sure."

He laughs. "Okay, maybe a little. But in all seriousness, Anya is my AA sponsor, and a close friend. I see her on a regular basis. We share a love of running, and since Lena despises it, Anya's my go-to for that."

"I understand. I'm glad we got that conversation out of the way. I hope one day you can appreciate Paolo for what he did for me in the bedroom."

He lifts a brow. "And that was?"

"Let's call it a transformation. Like I said, I struggle with intimacy. He's the only man I've ever *allowed* close to me in that capacity."

His eyes widen. "So, when you said he was a mentor, you meant that literally?"

"Yes. He taught me everything I know. He introduced me to pleasure. Paolo redefined my views of sex and showed me it could be on my terms. It didn't have to hurt. I could *want* it to happen, ask for it even. And I could just as easily refuse it. His patience and understanding carried me out of the darkness, but I still have a long way to go."

"You were—" Swallowing, he tries again. "Someone hurt you sexually?"

"Yes." I nod slowly, my head a heavy weight on my neck. "I'm a rape survivor."

The words crackle in the air between us, but as my flashbacks after our first time together proved, I can't hide this part of my history anymore. While I'm not ready to give him any details, he should know my truth. He deserves a piece of my puzzle. If nothing more, it'll serve as explanation for why I ran out on him that night.

Garrett's eyes burn with emotions I can't read. Resting his arm on the bedrail, he holds out his hand, palm open and inviting. He doesn't speak or reach for me, just patiently waits, his gaze locked with mine.

His gesture is a request—not a demand—and one I'm happy to fulfill.

"It was a long time ago." I place my hand in his, tentatively interlacing our fingers. His warm, firm touch is a haven. "And *very* few people know that about me, so please don't repeat what I've told you."

"My lips are sealed." He tightly squeezes my hand like his strength will erase my reality. "I can't even begin to express what I'm feeling." Outrage colors his voice. "I truly have no words . . ."

"Yeah, same." A nervous laugh breaks free. "Vulnerability for the win."

His throat moves on a swallow. "I have so many questions."

"I really can't answer them right now. I may never be able to."

"I understand. I won't push you, but I want you to know something." His fiery gaze caresses the part of my soul I'd left for dead. "Ella, if you let me, I can be your safe place too."

Thirty-Six

Lions, a spiral, and a word of advice

Garrett

While it's old and tattered, and the information is out of date, the issue of *National Geographic* I found beneath a stack of magazines in my psychiatrist's office doesn't disappoint. Who knew learning about a pair of man-eating big cats from the late-1800s could be so fascinating? I, for one, had never heard of the maneless Tsavo lions. Then again, my experience with cats is limited to Harry and Hermione, Lena's pets. And the sleek black stray that showed up on my stoop again this morning.

I like lions. They prowl around and fuck shit up, then spend their days lounging in the sun after taking down a wildebeest or two. I'm enjoying this article tremendously. Of course, I'm not supposed to be reading *at all*, which is probably why my brain hurts.

I was treated to a rare ride in her Subaru when Lena picked me up from the hospital last night. I'm not allowed to drive for a week, so I endured a spirited lecture on the ride home, and on the way here this morning, about the importance of following my post-concussion protocol. I'll take Lena's lectures over my family's dismissal any day—at least she gives a fuck—yet here I am, out of her sight for ten minutes and my dumb ass is already breaking the rules.

Dr. Lola Ortiz opens the door to her office. "Okay, Josh. You take care of yourself. I'll send the prescriptions to your pharmacy this afternoon."

Her patient, a gruff-looking guy with a full beard, mumbles his thanks as he leaves.

Lola pops her head into the waiting room. "Garrett, hello. Do you mind if I run to the café next door to grab a bagel before our session? I skipped breakfast, and now I'm famished."

"Go for it." I return my magazine to its rightful stack, leaving it on top of the pile so other folks can be enlightened about Tsavo lions.

She smiles and holds the door open for me. "You can go ahead and get settled. I'll be right back."

"Take your time." I step past her into the office and close the door.

Lola's space isn't your typical psychiatrist's lair. For one, there's no couch. A bamboo hammock is strung between two beams on the far side of the office. I've never lain in it, but she's told me some of her patients prefer it over the sage-colored velvet armchairs positioned in the center of the room. Her desk, which she only uses for paperwork, is situated in the corner. The muted lighting and aromatherapy remind me of a day spa. Tranquility fills the lungs with every breath, a salve for the unhealed wounds within. With bonsai trees, trickling water sculptures, and plants galore, the Ortiz Center for Mind Wellness is a fucking oasis. Soothing music floats from hidden speakers, the wooden flutes and wind chimes coaxing the truth from your lips while sending your troubles away.

This is my safe place.

I settle in my usual spot, the supple leather chair facing the other ones. It's Lola's chair. I'm the only patient who's allowed to sit here. She learned early in the game I'm more forthcoming without my back to a door. I shut down when I sense a threat, whether imminent or imagined.

The framed forest prints, potted ferns, and twiggy wall art whiz past me as I use the chair to its full potential. My office chair is harder to spin, so I love this one. It reminds me of the times when my mom would take me to the merry-go-round in the park by our home. She'd push me on the swings and make sure I didn't fall off the monkey bars. We'd grab ice cream on our way home. We'd laugh and sing all the way to our driveway, chocolate ice cream dripping onto my shirt. She'd dig out the sidewalk chalk and let me make murals by her car. My love of bridges, landscapes, and portraits decorated our pavement from the moment the snow melted in spring, until the first flakes of winter fell. *You were born to be an artist, my love. Never lose sight of your talent.* I squeeze my eyes shut against the faint echo of her voice in my head.

Those were the good old days, back before she abandoned me.

Lola returns, to-go coffee mug and paper bag in hand. "Should you be spinning with a concussion?"

I snort and use my foot to stop me. "Probably not."

She plops into one of the armchairs, withdrawing an everything bagel from her bag. "I feel rude for eating during our session, but my previous patient had to listen to my stomach growling the whole time. I didn't want to subject you to that."

"It's all good. Don't worry about me—I'm well fed. Lena forced an egg sandwich on me this morning."

"She's still taking care of you, I see."

"Yeah. She kinda loves me."

"We should all have friends like Lena."

The hint of sadness in her tone makes me wonder about her life. She's a cool chick. I'd be shocked if she didn't have a boatload of friends. She's also incredibly attractive, so it wouldn't surprise me if dudes were lining up to date her. Then again, she works six days a week. This practice is her life. She probably doesn't have time for relationships.

"So, what's new?" she asks, tucking a strand of hair behind her ear. She's wearing it down for once.

I point. "I like the red."

Ever the chameleon, she once again changed the prominent streaks of color gracing her mahogany-colored waves. Her highlights were electric blue when I saw her three weeks ago.

"Thanks." Her star-shaped diamond nose stud flashes with her smile. "I was bored."

"I'm surprised you didn't get a new tattoo."

A bunch of silver bangles jingle when she holds up her wrist and points to the elaborate compass inked into her skin. "You've seen this one, right?"

"Yeah. It suits you."

"Thanks." She focuses her espresso-colored eyes on my face. "Talk to me."

Those three words are the first ones she ever said to me, and it's how we begin every session. With Lola it's not a case of "let me psychoanalyze your problems away," it's a conversation. A give-and-take that somehow has the power to disarm even me.

I'd briefed her on the phone when I changed my appointment from Friday to Saturday, so she knows the gist of everything that's happened during the past few weeks.

Sighing, I twist my bracelet in circles, massaging the leather with my thumb. "I'm in over my head."

"So, pull back."

"I can't."

She arches a perfect eyebrow. "You can't, or you won't?"

"A mix of both."

Lola bites into her bagel and watches me while she chews. "Why do you think you're so drawn to her?" she says after a swallow.

"Because she's just as fucked up as me."

"Seems counterintuitive, given your distaste for drama. With everything on your plate, I'd think you'd want to simplify your life."

"Yes and no."

She chuckles. "You've gotta give me more than that, Garrett."

"I guess, in some ways, it feels like maybe she can understand me better than someone without baggage. She's obviously seen darkness, so my shit won't be as much of a shock. Not having to navigate someone's reaction to my history simplifies things. Sorta."

Even though we rarely touch on my childhood abuse—I shut down whenever she brings it up—Lola knows every detail, courtesy of my hospital records. Outside of Child Protective Services, the first responders, law enforcement, and medical professionals who handled my case, I've only confided in two people about what happened to me.

Lena knows the whole story. So does my cousin, Connor. I figured he deserved a reason for why his older brother was sentenced to twenty-five years in prison. I've shared bits and pieces with Anya over the years, but I never disclosed the abuse to my ex. Deep down, I knew I couldn't trust Carissa with my secrets. An ironic concept, given that I'd considered marrying her.

Lola dabs her mouth with a napkin. "I can see your point. The issue is going to be about navigating *both* of your trauma."

"Yeah." I rub my jaw. "That's where it gets complicated. Like, okay, her parents are dead, so she understands loss. But they didn't kill themselves, so she might not grasp the betrayal and all the other shit that comes with suicide. You know, like the fucking abandonment."

She nods, sadness washing over her features. "Right."

Lola lost her twin brother to suicide by train when they were only twenty. She's in her midthirties now, and the loss still hits her hard. Like me, Julio also battled alcohol addiction, depression, and anxiety. That's part of why Lola and I jive so well. She gets me.

We met during my stay at Bellevue Hospital, after my second suicide attempt. Raw from Carissa's affair and pregnancy, out of a job and place to live, I was detoxing. *Hard.* To top it off, I was in the clutches of severe PTSD. Incessant flashbacks and nightmares from childhood haunted me to the point where jumping off a bridge felt like the best option.

That's the thing about rock bottom. It's a dark, lonely place. I was one of the lucky ones, able to see the sliver of light in my darkness, hear the voice telling me not to let go. That voice was Lena's, and I'll forever be grateful to her for saving me. Through the chaos, I clung to the whispers of peace that told me my fucked-up existence was worth hanging on to.

Inpatient psych was rough for a man who requires control. While I understood the protocols necessary for suicide-risk patients, I hated them. My every move was under a microscope, like they feared I'd bust through my window's iron bars and plummet to my death. I get it. I *was* high risk, but that didn't make their scrutiny any easier.

The other doctors I encountered lacked Lola's compassion. They pegged me as a drunk jumper incapable of turning my life around. Maybe they were jaded. Or perhaps they didn't want to deal with my detoxing. I'll never know.

Lola wasn't like them. Fresh out of her psychiatry residency, she came to see me every day for six weeks. I later found out I reminded her so much of her brother, that I felt like a second chance. She couldn't save *him*, but she made it her mission to save *me*. She kept tabs on me after I was discharged. I was the first patient she called when she opened her own practice. While I'm still fucked up, I've made a shitload of progress under her care.

"Ella doesn't have addiction issues, so that might be another source of tension," I mutter.

"What do you mean?"

"I'm talking about the shit I do to cope with my cravings."

Lola nods and sips her coffee. "You're referring to your appetite for sex, I presume?"

"Yep." I cross my arms over my chest. "It's gonna be a problem."

"How do you figure?"

"Let's be real, we're a disaster waiting to happen. Rape survivor, plus sex addict, equals a bad fucking idea." I meet her gaze. "Pun intended."

"You're not a sex addict." She leans forward in her seat. "We've been over this. You're a recovering alcoholic who uses sex to temper his cravings. There's a significant difference. Your brain's reward center is still held captive by the neural pathways of addiction. It's been conditioned to respond to those habits, making them automatic. By turning to sex, you've replaced one habit with another. The good news is, while your alcoholism was self-destructive, your sex life isn't as problematic as you think." She purses her lips. "Except—"

"Yeah, yeah, I know. I shouldn't be sleeping with my AA sponsor."

"Listen, I'm not knocking Anya as a person. She's been an important part of your recovery. While I understand she's dealing with some issues of her own, you've added a layer of complexity to your relationship that doesn't need to be there. It's time to make new pathways, Garrett. You can't keep running the same trail wearing different shoes."

"Jesus, do you really have to hit me with the truth bombs so early in the session?"

She laughs. "That's how I roll."

"Let me ask you something. It's a little weird because that's how *I* roll."

"Hit me. I like weird."

"Is there any reason you'd feel afraid to have sex with me?"

Lola blinks a few times before raising her eyebrow. "Care to clarify?"

"I mean, in a different life, at a different time, would you be afraid to go to bed with me?"

She straightens in her seat. "Are you propositioning me?"

"No, definitely not." I rub my temples. "That came out wrong. Bear with me a moment while I figure out what I'm trying to say." I take a deep breath. "Basically, I need a woman's opinion on something, and I can't ask Lena."

"I'm listening."

"Okay, so, if you were a woman—" Shaking my head, I try again. "I mean, you *are* a woman, obviously. If you were a *different* woman, and you just met me, would you find me intimidating? Let's say I was me, but you didn't know me the way you do. I'm talking first impressions here."

Lola taps her chin in thought. "Define intimidating."

"I mean it in the sexual sense. Suppose we'd gone on a few dates, and it was clear things were progressing in that direction. Would there be some trepidation? Again, this is hypothetical. It's not you and me I'm talking about—we're strangers who just met. Would you, as a woman, be afraid to sleep with me? If so, what is it about me that would hold you back? Be specific."

"Okay, I think I understand what you're asking now. Before I answer, I want to take a step back."

"Alrighty. I'm stepping back." I shuffle my legs like I'm doing just that.

"Are you asking me this stuff because you're trying to make sense of Ella's reaction to you?"

Ding-ding-ding.

"Yes."

"You can't do that, Garrett. The correlation isn't cut and dry. Remember, Ella has a history of trauma. Survivors—especially rape victims—don't always behave how we expect them to. Sometimes they avoid any encounters where sex could be a possibility. Other survivors cope by becoming hypersexual. There's no standard reaction because everyone processes trauma differently. Intimacy can be complicated for those who *haven't* been victimized, but for the people who have? It can be damn near impossible. Sexual dysfunction, asexual behavior, and hypersexuality are all common among rape survivors."

"I just need to know how I'm coming across. Am I doing something to make it worse for her?"

She shakes her head. "It isn't about you."

"I don't want her to be afraid of me."

"You can't control how she responds to you." Lola motions to me. "I understand why you'd think you're the cause of her struggles, but you can't put that responsibility on your shoulders. Everything circles back to her trauma. Her rapist desecrated her mind and body. She lost her agency, her voice. Control was stolen from her in the most brutal way possible. *That* is what made her the way she is."

"But it feels like I'm making it worse."

"Listen, you know me well enough to know I'm not a bullshitter, so I won't lie to you." She steeples her fingers in front of her lips and stares out the window for a moment before speaking. "Are you intense? Absolutely." Her eyes lock with mine once more. "But your intensity is *not* a bad thing. It's fundamental to who you are, and after everything you've been through, it's no wonder. I wouldn't classify you as threatening, but that's not to say some people won't feel threatened by you."

"But—"

She holds up her hand. "Again, you cannot control someone else's feelings and reactions. I know this is a hard concept for you because you crave control."

"Yeah."

"You don't just crave it; you equate it with survival."

"Nail on the head," I mutter, spinning my bracelet in circles on my wrist.

"What happens when you lose control? What happens when you can't achieve perfection?"

"I spiral."

Spin. Spin. Spin. Everything's a motherfucking circle.

Her dark gaze burns into mine. "And when you spiral, where does that take you?"

"Back to the booze."

"What happens if you let your alcoholism take over?"

"In the long run?" I rub the back of my neck. "I die."

"Can you understand why this pattern of thinking is detrimental to your recovery?"

"Yes. No. Maybe." My chest deflates on a sigh. "I don't know."

"Because you can't control everything, Garrett. Life is a tug-of-war. It's about balance. You need to learn how to loosen your grip and allow someone else to pick up some of the slack. Not everyone out there will hurt you. There are people willing to help you pull. Give them some of your rope."

"Yeah, right." I cross my arms over my chest. "So they can hang me with it?"

"No, dear. You do that to yourself. I want you to make new pathways." She points to my head. "Find new trails in the forest because the ones you've been using lead to quicksand."

"I'm getting some hard-core *Princess Bride* vibes right now."

She squints. "You always do that."

"Do what?"

"Crack jokes when you're uncomfortable hearing the truth."

"Gee, you think?" I run both hands over my face. "There's nothing like being slapped upside the head with the reality of my shortcomings."

"Yeah, well, that's what you pay me for."

I snort. "True story. Since I'm paying you and all, how about you help a guy out with this pathway business. How do I stay away from quicksand?"

"Stay out of the fire swamp." She rolls her eyes. "Duh."

A chuckle bursts from my lips. "You're great. You know that, right?"

She pats herself on the back. "I've been told that a time or two. Listen, in all seriousness, I want you to relinquish some control to love. Release a few of your doubts and learn to trust. Rely on someone else. Stop striving for perfection because it's *not* attainable."

I hold up a finger. "Never say never."

But the thing is, in my heart of hearts, I know she's right. Too bad I can't get my brain on the same page.

No matter what I do, it's never enough. I'll never be good enough, smart enough, funny enough, strong enough. No accomplishment will make me worthy of love. My parents' unconditional love turned out pretty fucking conditional when they left me behind. I wasn't enough for Wendy and Jim, or they would've protected me from their son. I wasn't fast enough to escape Sean's torment, or cunning enough to outsmart him. Carissa's cheating proved I wasn't enough for her either.

I've spent almost two decades overcompensating for those failures. My quest for perfection and the drive to become indispensable consumes me at times, but I'm seeing the payoff.

I'm keener, stronger, and faster than most men my age. My company is thriving, but I keep honing my craft, learning new software as the money pours in. My well of jokes never runs dry, and I chase people's laughter like the sound itself will heal me. I'm a better friend—always there when someone needs me. Whiskey dick is a thing of the past, and if Anya's screams are any indication, I'm a damn good fuck.

Every design I create, dollar I earn, smile I induce, and orgasm I wring out is a stepping-stone to perfection. I won't settle for less. I learned the hard way incompetence leads to failure. My biggest failure? Addiction.

Booze is a slippery fucking slope, and I'm not willing to slide again. I cling to everything I've achieved, chased, and fought for, because it all boils down to my survival. One sip—one stumble—and I'll wind up at the bottom of the abyss, dead like my father.

Lola's voice breaks into my thoughts. "Bottom line, you've got to stop reaching for something you can't grasp. You can't be everyone's prodigy, Garrett. The sooner you accept who you are, understand your limits, and stop trying to be perfect so the people in your life don't abandon you, the faster you'll find peace."

"You say it like it's easy."

"No. It's hard as fuck." She holds her hand over her heart. "And I understand it'll be the biggest personal challenge you ever face, but I believe you have what it takes to make these changes. Think about it. You've already given up some control professionally. I'm really proud of you for finally offering the partnership to Nate."

"Thanks."

"I mean it, Garrett. That's major progress for you. Now all you have to do is keep up the momentum in your personal life. Keep taking those baby steps. You'll get there."

"I'll try."

"Don't try . . . do."

"Okay, Yoda." I flash her a smirk. "But you never answered my question."

She smiles. "I hoped you'd forgotten."

"Not a chance."

"Let's see . . . To an outsider, you carry yourself in a way that projects a certain confidence. A self-assuredness that permeates your entire being. Some people are drawn to confidence—others fear it. You have no say in who does which. From a female standpoint, I think it's safe to say you're brutally handsome, and you move with a swagger that promises sex."

"Why does everyone keep saying I have swagger? What the fuck does that even mean?"

"You give the impression you'd be a lot to handle in the bedroom."

My face gets hot. "That isn't exactly false . . ."

"So, can you understand why that fact alone could be terrifying for a rape survivor?"

I nod slowly. "Yeah. I get it. What can I do—what trail can I blaze—to help her understand I'm not a threat?"

"Respect her boundaries. Don't passively listen when she speaks, make the effort to really *hear* her. Not just what she's saying, but the shit that's left unsaid. Give Ella back her power by surrendering some of yours." She gives me a pointed stare, those eyes piercing my psyche like always. "And I highly recommend you take sex out of the equation."

Thirty-Seven

A grill, a delivery, and tiramisu

Garrett

The man is a literal genius.

I've lived here for nine years. As in, almost a *decade*. But it was the Aussie transplant, who's been in town for a month, who had the brilliant idea to buy a grill. I can't believe I never thought of it.

I point to the rack of ribs sizzling on the metal grate. "Do you think they need more barbeque sauce?"

Wes flips our steak, then nudges at the ribs. "Lena told me not to drown them." Grinning, he reaches for the bowl of mesquite deliciousness he concocted. "But I kinda like my meat *saucy*."

"Don't we all?" I hump the nearby umbrella table, knocking over my can of seltzer in the process. "Fuck."

His laugh echoes through the tiny courtyard behind the brownstone. "You're hilarious."

"Makes sense." I snatch the can and set it upright. "I always wanted to be a comedian."

"Really?"

"Nah. Just fucking with you."

He snorts and turns his focus to the ribs, shaking his head as he flips them. "Sometimes it's hard to tell when you're being serious."

"I know. I always use that to my advantage."

Companionable silence stretches between us. I flick at the miniature icicles clinging to the chain-link fence that separates our yard from the neighbor's. I pull one off and turn it over in my hand. The ice glistens in the fading light of the low winter sun as my skin's warmth melts it. Icicles and snowflakes are nature's artwork. It's too bad they have such a short lifespan. Winter is a tragically beautiful season.

A soft mew turns our attention to the little cedar shed I built a few years ago. "Oh, look. It's you again," I say, as the reappearing black cat saunters over to us. "What's going on, buddy?"

Wes points to the grill. "He smells our food. He was here yesterday when I grilled some shrimp." He tosses him a piece of chicken. The cat gobbles it up and peers at Wes expectantly. "You like barbeque, too, huh? Smart bloke." He peels off another piece and drops it. "Next thing we know, you'll be sniffing around for lobster tails."

I motion to Wes. "So, *you're* the reason he lingers on our block? Here I thought it was because Joan across the street always puts out tuna."

The cat weaves between my legs, purring loudly. He peers up at me and squints before rubbing his face on my jeans.

Wes holds his hands up in surrender. "Don't blame me. I only fed him the one time." He jerks his chin toward the furry motorboat that's now lying on my feet. "I dunno, mate. He seems to have an affinity for you."

"What can I say? I'm a pussy magnet."

Wes throws his head back, his booming laugh startling our feline friend, who bolts across the yard and disappears behind the shed.

"What's so funny?" Lena steps through my sliding glass door onto the patio.

"Garrett's being pervy." He zips his cardinal red parka to his throat and fixes his scarf.

She hands him a platter. "That's nothing new."

I give a dramatic curtsy and swig the few sips of seltzer that survived my assault on the table.

Ever the blue-ribbon championship rooster, he puffs his chest up and motions to the grill. "How do they look?"

That's the thing about men. We take tremendous pride in *all* our meat and love hearing about it. *"Damn, that steak looks good!"* registers pretty fucking close to *"You have a huge dick!"* on the male ego meter. At least, that's the case for me—and Wes, apparently.

"Um, great. But I thought you were doing a dry rub?"

"Nah." He juts his chin at me. "We like our meat *wet.*"

My laugh sends seltzer out my nose. The bubbles burn like a bitch, making me scrunch up my face like a rabid pug.

"Seriously?" Lena rolls her eyes. "Is everything about sex with you two?"

Wes watches her hungrily. "Haven't heard ya complain yet, sunshine."

With my nasal membranes on the road to recovery, I laugh and clap his shoulder. "I love this guy."

Lena's posture relaxes, and the smile that curves her lips is one of pure elation, showing just how much my approval means to her. She wraps her arms around me. "I knew you would."

I've spent a lot of time with Wes since my return from the hospital. Despite all our digs and banter, he's a genuinely caring guy. He brought my phone in to have the screen repaired, checked in on me when Lena ran errands, and since I'm not cleared yet for a run or lifting weights, we've walked through Brooklyn every day the weather allows. He even asked my opinion before buying the grill I wish I'd thought of. We've discussed nearly everything there is to discuss, touching on the shit we went through with our exes. I don't usually connect this easily with another dude, so it speaks volumes about his character.

Returning Lena's hug, I kiss the top of her head. "I could still kick Dundee's ass though."

Wes flexes his enormous biceps, their size visible even beneath layers of goose down. "In your dreams, Casey."

My phone buzzes with a text.

Nate-Dawg: I'm here. Let me in.

Me: ?

Nate-Dawg: Your Jeep's outside, but no one answered the door.

Me: Be right there.

"Who's that?" Lena asks.

"Nate is here for some reason. I'm gonna let him in."

Wes skewers the steak. "Tell him to stay for dinner. We've got plenty."

I head inside and make my way to the front door. It's not like Nate to drop by unannounced. I'm curious to see what his impromptu visit is about.

I unlatch and open the door. "Yo."

"Hey, man. How are you feeling?" He juts his chin toward the huge, insulated bags he's carrying. "Lemme in. This shit's heavy."

I step out of his way. "What's all that?"

"Food for you."

"Since when do you cook?" I ask, following him into my kitchen.

He chuckles and sets the bags on the island. "It's not from me."

Lena and Wes enter the room from the back staircase that leads to the courtyard. They greet Nate, and Wes places our platter of meat on the counter.

"You hungry, mate?"

"Thanks, but I have plans tonight." A grin overtakes his face as he meets my gaze. "I'm taking Daria out."

"Good for you, Nate-Dawg." I unzip the totes and withdraw several glass-lidded casserole dishes. Each one has its contents labeled with a piece of masking tape. I frown at the unfamiliar handwriting. "I'm confused. Who made these?"

Nate empties the second tote and lines more containers up. "The incredibly gorgeous delivery person was also the chef. She wanted me to pass along this message." Pursing his lips, he flutters his eyelashes at me. "Nourishment is part of healing."

"Ella?"

"Bingo." He motions to the plastic containers with blue lids. "These can go in the freezer. They're the same as what's in the casserole dishes but parceled out into lunch portions."

"Holy—"

"I'm not done," Nate singsongs, holding up a hand to silence me. "I memorized her instructions. Keep your trap shut so I don't fuck them up. Okay, the dish with the olives on it contains tortellini with pesto sauce. You'll notice the color is slightly different from your typical pesto. That's because she wasn't sure if you had any allergies, so she skipped the pine nuts in favor of sunflower seeds." He rubs his stomach. "She let me try some, and it's fucking delicious."

"Pesto is one of my favorites."

"It gets better." Nate holds up a red bowl. "These are pumpkin ravioli in an apple sage butter sauce. She *made* the pasta herself. Like, from scratch."

"Wow," Lena murmurs. "That's dedication."

"Yep." He points to a green crock. "This is an escarole and white bean soup with homemade ditalini noodles. There's aged parmesan and pancetta in it. If you haven't had pancetta, she said it's like bacon." He takes a deep breath and gives a flourish with his hand. "And last but not least, the rectangular pan contains a special *nonalcoholic* tiramisu she created. She had to make several batches in order to get the flavor just right."

I sink onto one of the stools, my eyes stinging for some strange reason. No one other than Lena has ever shown me this much care and consideration. "I'm blown away right now. I can't believe she did this for me."

He straightens like a light bulb went off in his head. "Oh! I almost forgot." He pulls a long beanbag thing from the bottom of the smaller tote. "This is supposed to help with headaches. You store it in the freezer, and then plop it on your head if you're in pain. I'm pretty sure she said it's filled with rice." He chews his lip. "I don't remember though. Anyway, you can also stick it in the microwave and use it for sore muscles. It smells like lavender and chamomile. She got it from the little aromatherapy shop in Bryant Park."

Wes meets my gaze. "She must really want to make amends."

"We've already talked, and I told her things between us were cool." I open and close my mouth a few times, trying to find words for what I'm feeling. "She didn't need to do all this for me."

Nate starts loading containers into my freezer. "Well, she said you two got off to a rough start, and she still feels terrible. She wanted to make sure you know how sorry she is."

My throat works on a swallow, eyes stinging with emotion I didn't know I was capable of.

Once all the lunch portions are put away, Nate grabs the tote bags and tucks them under his arm. "I'll return these to her on my way past the *Tribune's* office tomorrow. Try not to break any of her dishes, dude. Women are funny about things like that."

"Damn right, we are. Don't lose the lids to her containers either. Mismatched Tupperware is annoying as fuck," Lena chimes in.

"I can't believe she did this. For *me*," I whisper.

Nate stops in front of me, placing both hands on my shoulders. "I was also impressed that she went to these lengths. I mean, she could've just had pizza delivered to you. Instead, she painstakingly prepared homemade meals, all while keeping your sobriety in mind. I asked her *why* she did it. Because, well, we all know I'm nosy. You know what she said?"

"What?" My gravelly voice betrays everything I'm trying so hard to hide.

"Garrett is worth it."

Lena gives an appreciative nod, her smile reaching the corners of her eyes. "All right, I've officially taken Ella *off* my shit list. She's now in a probationary period. I'll continue to reassess."

Thirty-Eight

A painful discussion, a threat, and gratitude

Ella

I knew it would be a difficult conversation, but I never imagined it being *this* hard to explain to Paolo why our relationship dynamics must change. When he called me earlier to suggest we get together at his place, his tone told me exactly what he had in mind—another night tangled in his sheets.

Those days are over now. Things are evolving with Garrett, and I need to see where they lead. While it would be so much easier to dodge the issue, I refuse to disrespect the friend who helped me through the darkest time of my life. Paolo deserves my honesty. I agreed to meet him after work but rerouted us to La Bussola. To talk.

Judging by his reaction, this wasn't the conversation he was expecting.

Paolo finishes his wine and stares into his empty glass for a moment, a mixture of pain and frustration twisting his features.

Silence stretches between us.

"Please say something," I whisper.

He sets down his glass with a heavy sigh. "What do you want me to say?" His brown eyes lift to mine. "That it doesn't bother me?"

"I want you to be truthful, caro."

"All along, I've wanted this for you. With all the shit you endured, and how it *still* haunts you, you deserve a step toward normalcy. I want you to open your heart to someone and find happiness. I *want* you to find love. And maybe I'm selfish" —he blinks a few times and looks away—"for hoping you'd find it with me." His whisper sends tears sliding down my cheeks.

"No. I'm the selfish one. You were nothing but patient and kind. You've always been my haven, and I hate that I've hurt you."

"I'll be fine." He meets my gaze once more and forces a weak smile. "I always knew you wouldn't marry me."

"I'm sorry I fucked with your head. I didn't mean—"

"Does he know?" His expression sobers along with his tone. "Have you told him what happened?"

"He knows I'm a survivor," I whisper. "But I haven't told him . . . *everything.*"

He tilts his head to the side. "Why not?"

"Because I'm not ready to share that part of me yet."

"Do you think half-truths and omissions will be enough for him? Or will he push for more?"

Deep down, I know Garrett will respect my boundaries. He's given me no reason to believe he won't. But Paolo makes a valid point. I haven't been transparent with Garrett, and he deserves better. The trouble is, I've spent so many years trying to forget my past, that I don't know when—or *if*—I'll ever be ready to rip those wounds open again.

When I don't answer, he leans in close. "Is he someone *worthy* of lowering your guard for?"

"Yes." That, I can say with certainty. "Garrett's a good man, Paolo. He's been through some shit of his own, though. It's complicated."

He reaches for my hand, and I place my palm in his. "I won't lie to you and say I'm not hurt. But that's my problem. Bottom line, I only want you to be safe and happy. If he can give you that, then I guess it's something I'll need to come to terms with. But listen to me closely, bella." Paolo's eyes lock with mine, burning with an intensity I've never seen from him. He squeezes my hand in a vise grip. "If he *ever* hurts you the way you've been hurt, or even comes close, he's dead. And believe me when I tell you, they will *never* find his body."

"I know. I'm making messes today," I tell my fish while feeding them. Not only did I spill their food, but it will take a while to scrub my mascara off the couch cushions. I'm sure I look like a puffy-eyed raccoon from all the crying I've done since leaving La Bussola. It breaks my heart knowing I've hurt Paolo.

I should've known his feelings ran deeper than mine. Though, honestly, part of me did. But I selfishly chose to ignore that fact when I continued to have sex with him. What kind of woman does that make me?

More importantly, where does that leave my friendship with Paolo? Will we lose our closeness?

After cleaning up the fish food, I resettle on the couch and hug my knees, terrified my best friend will write me off like I deserve. A fresh sob escapes me at the thought of not having him in my life.

My phone rings on the coffee table, so I blindly reach for it to silence the ringer. A quick glance at the screen tells me it's Garrett. I draw a deep breath to compose myself before answering.

"Hello?"

"Ella."

"How are you feeling? Is your head okay?" I wipe my nose on my sleeve, then continue my barrage of questions, "Are you still dizzy? Have you been resting?"

"Hey, slow down, Cupcake. Are you all right? You sound upset."

I sniff and force my ragged voice to soften. "I'm good. My allergies are bugging me." I mop away the remaining tears with a tissue, hoping my little fib will deflect his attention. "How are *you?*"

"I'm feeling fine. Better than fine, actually. Nate just stopped by."

The food!

After my Paolo fiasco, I'd forgotten about this afternoon's delivery to Garrett's office. I spent my day off yesterday shopping and cooking, and I loved every minute of it. But I won't lie. My nerves were a mess, riding the elevator to his eleventh-floor suite. I almost chickened out when those doors slid open to reveal the Hudson Graphics sign. If it weren't for Nate's warm greeting, I would've tucked my tail and ran.

"Did he explain everything like I asked him to? I probably should've written it down for him."

"He did." He clears his throat. "Ella, I can't tell you how much your gesture means to me. No one's ever done something like that. I mean, yeah, Lena makes sure I don't starve, but she's family. I've never had a woman go to such lengths for me."

That's no surprise, given his rotten ex and what he's told me of his dismissive family. It's a relief knowing he at least has Lena to look after him. And me . . . if he'll let me.

"I'm sorry that's the case, Garrett. You deserve all that and more. Believe me, it was my absolute pleasure. I think I told you how much I enjoy cooking."

"You did. But you left out the part about what a *phenomenal* chef you are."

"Wait, you've already tried some?"

"Damn right, I did." He chuckles. "And as much as it pained me, I managed to share a little with Lena and Wes."

"Sharing is caring and all that jazz. I hope they liked it."

"Are you kidding? I practically had to chase them out of here. In all seriousness, the food is amazing."

His praise warms me. "Thank you. I'm glad you like it. Did you try the tiramisu?"

"It's to die for. And knowing you went out of your way to find a nonalcoholic recipe . . . I don't think you understand how deeply you've touched me." If his gravelly tone is any indication, my efforts weren't in vain. "I mean this from the bottom of my heart, thank you for thinking of me."

"You're welcome. Lately, it seems that's all I do." The whispered confession passes my lips before I can stop it.

"I'm right there with you, Cupcake."

Thirty-Nine

Decisions, a souvenir, and a savior

Ella

Garrett pulled out all the stops in the secrecy department. He's on his way to pick me up for our date, but I have no clue where we're going or what we're doing. He meets each request for clues with a "you'll see."

Today is Saturday. It's been ten days since his fall. He's concussion symptom-free, or so he claims, which is the reason I agreed to move up next weekend's plans. He missed Monday and Wednesday's rehearsals, so I haven't seen him since the hospital released him last Friday.

While I'm not typically a phone person, we've talked each day, the conversation coming easily for the first time in my life. I'm sure it has something to do with his sense of humor or the deep rumble of his voice in my ear. The prospect of spending the night with him exhilarates me.

As if on cue, my phone buzzes with a text, sending my heart rate into a gallop.

Prodigy: I'm here.

Me: I'll be right down.

Prodigy: Please wear something other than stiletto death traps.

Frowning, I glance at the pair of red heels I'd chosen.

Me: Psst . . . this clue would've been helpful earlier.

Prodigy: You can pack them, but boots would be more appropriate for today. Don't forget your camera.

I toe my stilettos off, wondering what he's planning that requires boots. Now I'm reconsidering my outfit too. It never occurred to me I'd need something more casual than the black dress I slipped on. It hugs my curves, yet shows less than my usual amount of cleavage, so I figured it would be perfect for most date settings. The zipper's a bit of a bitch to undo. I really don't want to change.

Me: What about clothes?

Prodigy: You're welcome to come naked. However, I think you'll be more comfortable in something casual.

Me: I'm already wearing a dress. Should I change?

Prodigy: You do you, Cupcake. We'll make it work.

Feeling somewhat flustered, I step into my heels once more, then snatch my overnight bag, quickly stuffing sneakers, boots, and more casual clothes inside. I already packed three outfits, sexy lingerie, and a multitude of toiletries.

Better to be prepared.

Camera bag in tow, I blow my fish a goodbye kiss, then hurry downstairs, my breathing becoming more challenging with each step. I imagine first-date jitters are common, but this isn't just my first date with Garrett, it's my first official date *ever*. Pretty sad for a woman who's twenty-nine.

Crisp air greets me as I step outside onto the sidewalk in front of my building. Garrett's Jeep is idling at the curb.

He hops out when he sees me. "Good morning, gorgeous."

"Hey. Good morning to you too."

He chuckles when his gaze lands on my shoes. "You couldn't help yourself, could you?"

"What can I say? I'm a creature of habit."

"I get it. I'm just teasing you." He opens the passenger door for me, then reaches for my bags. "Let me take those."

"Thanks." Handing them over, I slide into the luxe leather seat, pleased to discover its warmth. "Oh, wow."

"Wow, what?"

"The seat's already warm."

"Got you covered, Cupcake." He winks. "A warm hiney is a happy hiney. Now buckle up." I can't help but laugh as he closes the door and makes his way around the front of the Jeep. He hops inside and points to a button on his console. "*Butt,* if you don't want a toasty tush, the switch is right here."

"You *crack* me up," I deadpan.

"Well played." He laughs. "I'm impressed."

"Don't get too used to it. My joke arsenal is barren. So, are you ever gonna give me a hint about what we're doing?"

He pulls a pair of aviators from his visor and wipes the lenses with his shirt. "It all depends on your answer to my next question." He puts on his sunglasses and shifts to face me. "Sweet or savory?"

"Huh?"

"Answer the question."

"What does it pertain to?"

A wicked grin curves his lips. "You'll see."

"I suppose if I had to choose, I'd pick sweet."

"Good answer." He checks his mirrors, puts the Jeep into gear, and pulls away from the curb.

I allow a few minutes to pass before giving him an expectant nudge. "Well? You still haven't told me anything."

"You gotta be patient, Cupcake." He heads down Park Avenue toward Grand Central Terminal and cruises past a few taxis. I admire how easily he navigates the Manhattan traffic, like the congestion doesn't faze him.

Garrett turns onto W. 42nd Street, taking us past the side of the New York Public Library heading toward Broadway. We pull up outside Compass Roasters, a coffee shop near Bryant Park.

He turns off the ignition. "You hungry?"

"I had oatmeal, but I'm sure I can make room."

"Good. Since you chose sweet, we're starting our date at my favorite java joint. They have the *best* gourmet cupcakes." He points to his office building looming down the block. "I come here every day for my afternoon pick-me-up." He unbuckles and opens his door. "Come inside with me."

The aroma of coffee and confections greets me as I follow him into the café. He stands beside me when we take our place in line, his warmth radiating into me. "Have you ever been here before?"

I shake my head. "I've probably walked past it a hundred times, but I've never been inside. I'm surprised you trek all the way over here when Starbucks is much closer to your office. You know, being a self-proclaimed man of efficiency and such."

He laughs. "I make a lotta proclamations, don't I? You can probably ignore the bulk of them because I usually don't know what I'm talking about."

"I beg to differ."

"Thanks for the vote of confidence. Yeah, Starbucks is closer, but I prefer it here. I admit, I'm totally biased because my friend Geneva owns the place, but I always try to support local businesses, especially when they put out a kick-ass product." He points to the glass cases loaded with decadent cupcakes, cookies, and brownies. "Not only are their coffee and baked goods amazing, but Compass Roasters *feels* like a small-town coffee shop. They remember their customers' names and usual orders. I like that personal touch. I strive for it with my own business. There's too much disconnect out there. It's nice to have a warm, inviting oasis to escape to. I'm slowly learning I'm not a city boy at heart."

"You crave connection and inclusion, the sense of community that's often absent here."

"Right." His gold eyes lock with mine. "Because despite millions of people, the city's fucking lonely sometimes."

I tentatively slip my hand into his and interlace our fingers. He squeezes tightly, like my touch is the only kindness he's ever received. I lift our hands to my lips and press a kiss to his knuckles. His breath catches, and the longing in his eyes mirrors the ache inside me. I'd say something, but nothing feels worthy of the invisible current flowing between us.

This man is going to be my undoing. And God help me, I look forward to coming undone.

With our hands still intertwined, we move closer to the counter as a unit. I've only lived in Rome and New York City. Small-town life is a foreign concept for me. If it's anything like the welcoming vibe that permeates Compass Roasters, I'll pack my bags in an instant.

The café boasts an eclectic charm, from the gleaming wood tables, decoupaged with pieces of antique maps and covered in shiny lacquer, to the tile compass mosaic adorning the wall behind the counter. The ceiling is painted navy blue, with constellations stenciled in shimmering gold. Billy Joel's "Why

Should I Worry?" blasts from the speakers. A strawberry-blond barista is all smiles, chatting with an elderly customer as she prepares his latte.

She spots Garrett and waves. "Hey! Haven't seen you in a while."

"Took some time off."

He'd mentioned during one of our phone calls that he feels like an idiot for getting a concussion, so it makes sense he wouldn't elaborate. I give his hand a reassuring squeeze, and he brushes his thumb over my knuckles in response, his appreciation as clear as if he'd put it on a billboard.

"Good for you." She gives him an approving nod, and her earrings sparkle in the vintage pendant lights. "I'll be with you in a moment. You want your usual?"

He grins. "Sure do."

"What's your usual?" I ask, scanning the chalkboard drink menu.

"My friend Lincoln turned me on to the dirty chai. It's a chai latte with espresso. Geneva always puts whipped cream and cinnamon on mine."

"That sounds delicious. I'll have the same."

"Hot or cold?"

"Well, since it's chilly out, I'd better get a hot one in case the hiney warmer stops working."

"Good call." He laughs and points to the cupcakes. "Do you have any allergies or flavors you don't like?"

"No allergies. I'm not huge on lemon, but everything else is fair game."

The gentleman in front of us leaves, so we approach the counter. Garrett releases my hand to retrieve his wallet, and I pocket one of the café's business cards. Suddenly hungry, I peruse the treat menu, intrigued by the creative dessert names like Bombshell Blondies and Orgy Bars.

Geneva pours milk into a steel pitcher and sticks it beneath the frother. "How's it going, Garrett?"

"So far, so good." He motions to me. "I'd like to introduce my beautiful date, Ella, to the deliciousness of your baking skills. This is her first time here."

"Listen to you, with the flattery again. Nice try, but I'm still not gonna tell you our secret recipes." The warmth in her smile is at odds with her ice-blue eyes. "Hi, Ella, I'm Geneva. Welcome to Compass Roasters. What can I get started for you?"

I can't put my finger on it, but there's something familiar about her. I've interviewed hundreds of people and attended countless events, so it's possible we've met before.

"Nice to meet you, Geneva. I'd love to try a large cup of Garrett's usual."

"The dirty chai is always an excellent choice. Do you want a happy ending?"

"Excuse me?"

Geneva giggles. "Sorry. I forgot you're a first-timer. Happy ending means whipped cream."

"In that case, absolutely."

She turns to Garrett. "What size do you want? Also, is this for here or to go?"

"I'd like a large as well. We'll have them to go, please." He points to the cupcakes. "We'll also take one of each kind, except for the Mellow Yellow Limoncello."

"You got it."

My eyes widen when she retrieves a box from beneath the counter and starts loading it up. I touch Garrett's arm. "There are only two of us. We're getting *thirteen* cupcakes?"

"Good point. Fourteen is way better. Even numbers are superior, am I right?" He rubs his jaw and studies the display case. "Geneva, can you please add a second Moaning Mango?"

"Sure thing."

These aren't your standard-sized cupcakes. No, they're massive—like saucers—and the man is buying *fourteen*. It's a damn good thing I threw some yoga pants into my bag.

I peer up at him. "Are you hungry?"

He licks his lips and sweeps his gaze over me, sending a shock wave of heat through my body. "I'm always hungry, baby."

The box of desserts sits heavy on my lap as we resume our travels. I pat the lid. "How will we know which one's which?"

"The pamphlet thing in there explains all the flavors. Plus, the wrappers are color coded." He looks over at me when we stop at a red light. "North or south?"

"For what?"

"Pick one."

"Um, north."

"Excellent." He hands me his phone. "Tap on the Spotify icon and choose our journey's soundtrack."

"How can I select appropriate mood music when I don't know where we're going?"

"You *do* know." His teeth flash with his coy smile. "We're heading north."

I peer at the four playlists on the screen: Due North, Going South, East Bound, and Wild West. "I'm detecting a theme here. Let's see, since we're going north . . ." I touch the corresponding playlist, and the acoustic version of James Bay's "Wild Love" fills the Jeep. "Ooh, I adore this song." I adjust the volume, then search his face. "Did you make these playlists in preparation for our date?"

"Especially curated just for you." He clears his throat. "But that particular song makes an appearance on all four of them."

It's one I've listened to on repeat. Hearing the first few chords and Bay's romantic lyrics stirs a deep longing inside. Hope springs to life, knowing Garrett added it for me.

"How come?" I whisper, desperate for validation. I can't be the only one who aches like this.

His eyes briefly lock with mine, then dart back to the road ahead. He lays his open palm on the console between us.

An invitation.

Once again, he's giving me a choice.

I slip my hand into his. "Are you gonna sing it for me?"

"Do you want me to?"

"Yes." My insides flutter with the thought.

"I'll think about it." He winks and points to a road sign. "East or west of the Hudson River?"

"West."

"That was quick. I expected some questions."

"Maybe I'm starting to trust the process."

His answering smile melts my insides. "Sounds like I'm doing something right."

"You're doing a lot of things right, Garrett. Our outing reminds me a little of those Choose Your Own Adventure books I read when I was younger."

"That's exactly what I was going for." He presses a button on his steering wheel to lower the music a few notches. "You wanted me to plan something, and while I'm more than happy to whisk you away and romance the hell out of you, I wanted to give you control of every aspect."

"So, let me get this straight." My smile infuses my voice. "You plan to romance the hell out of me?"

"That's the goal, gorgeous." He points to the steering wheel. "I've got this, but make no mistake, *you* are the one in the driver's seat. I'm talking brakes, gas pedal, drive, park, neutral, and reverse." He squeezes my hand. "It's all you, Ella."

"Does that mean you had something in mind for each option? Like, say, if I'd picked south first?"

"I've got something for every combination of directions and gear shifts." He looks over at me with a wicked grin. "Time for your next question. Mountains or valleys?"

"Hmm . . ." I twirl a piece of hair and consider my options. While I'd love to see the mountains, I certainly don't want to climb one. I'd rather not get winded and sweaty on our first date—unless it happens in a bed. Since I don't know exactly what he has in mind, I figure I'll err on the side of caution. "Let's do valleys."

"Sounds good. Hudson Valley, it is. One of my favorite places on earth."

The conversation flows easily, and I'm totally relaxed, nestled in his warm leather seat. We talk about our education, careers, and future aspirations. I tell him more about my freelance work. I even disclose my dream of authoring a book about my experiences with misogyny in the entertainment industry.

He looks over at me. "I say, go for it. You can be the voice for women who can't—or won't—use theirs."

"Maybe someday." I release a wistful sigh. "I'm not sure most people are ready and willing to listen to what I have to say."

He brushes his thumb over my knuckles. "I will always listen."

Just like that, the gauntlets and chain mail fall to my feet. The growing pile of armor I've shed should scare me. Instead, I'm seconds from ripping my helmet off. I never imagined meeting someone who could loosen the barbed wire encasing my heart, but here he is.

Our journey north on the New York State Thruway continues for about two hours before Garrett takes the Saugerties exit. The trees and wildlife grow in number as he travels the winding roads. Mountains loom before us, the distant, cloud-kissed peaks appearing almost blue. Scattered rays of sunlight bathe the frost-bitten range.

I point. "Those are the Catskills, right?"

"Yeah, but don't worry. Since you picked valley, I'm not taking you to the ski slopes this time."

"That's good because I don't know how to ski in the first place," I say, thanking my lucky stars I made the choice I did. Although, the thought of hot cocoa and a crackling fireplace in a ski lodge sounds appealing. Especially if it involves a warm bed too.

"Maybe I'll teach you someday. I did a lot of skiing with Lena's family when I was younger. We grew up a bit northwest of here in Windham. Have you ever ventured upstate?"

"No, not at all."

He nods. "We're currently in Ulster County, the home of New Paltz, Kingston, Woodstock, Saugerties, and more. This whole area is part of what's known as the Mid-Hudson Valley."

"I've definitely heard of Woodstock." The eclectic small town is a mecca for the arts and music.

"Excellent. I'm thinking we'll have dinner there."

I point to the box of cupcakes in my lap. "Dinner's a long way off. When do we get to try these?"

"Soon."

After a few miles, we arrive at a place called Opus 40. Garrett explains that it's an environmental sculpture park featuring forests, meadows, a quarry museum, and most importantly, a sprawling, walkable bluestone sculpture.

"When you mentioned you enjoy sculptures, I knew you needed to see this place. That's also why I told you to bring your camera. I think it's their off-season, but I arranged for a private viewing. It's just you and me, baby."

I blink at him. "How on earth did you manage that, when you had no idea which direction I'd choose?"

"I have my ways." He cuts the engine.

Equal parts dumbfounded and impressed, I gape through the windshield at the bluestone ramps, walkways, and pedestals before me. The dusting of snow is already melting as temperatures climb toward the forties.

Garrett points to my shoes. "Please tell me you packed boots or sneakers."

"I have both." I toy with the hem of my dress. "But I should've listened to you and worn jeans."

"Yeah, you're gonna be cold." He motions toward the building across the way. "There are restrooms in there. You should probably change."

"Hold these." I hand him the box of cupcakes, then unbuckle and reach for my bag, pulling it into the front seat. The strap catches on my to-go cup's lid, spilling my chai. There wasn't much left, but it's enough to flood his cup holder. "Shit! I'm so sorry." I grab the cup and turn it upright, setting it in a different cup holder.

"No worries." He yanks open the glove box and pulls out a wad of napkins. He stuffs them into the cup holder to soak up the chai but doesn't seem to notice when my missing lingerie flutters to the floor.

"Aha!" Retrieving the red lace garments, I hold them up and meet his gaze. "I was looking for these. I had a feeling you took them."

He snatches them back before I can blink and stuffs them under his shirt. "Sorry, baby. Finders, keepers."

I raise an eyebrow. "But they're mine."

"Not anymore. You left them behind. They're mine now."

The feminist in me should be indignant, but she's nowhere to be found. Instead, there's a wanton goddess exhilarated by the prospect of him keeping something so intimate. I smile as she sashays into focus. "And what, exactly, do you need them for?"

"I dunno, maybe I'll jack off with them?" The wicked gleam in his eyes tells me he's probably serious. "I haven't decided yet."

I pretend to pout. "At least let me keep the bra. I like how that one fits."

"I'll think about it." He winks and nods to my bag. "You gonna change?"

"Yes." I withdraw socks and a pair of black leggings. "I'll pull these on and wear them under my dress." I hike the material up to my waist and slip into the pants.

Garrett's pupils dilate, his eyes roaming my exposed thighs and black silk panties like he's ready for us to move to his back seat.

I take my time covering up because I enjoy the way he looks at me. "You know, a true gentleman would avert his eyes."

Those gilded orbs snap to mine. "I'm not a gentleman."

"Oh?" I prop my heel on the dashboard and tug on a sock. "I'd say you had me fooled, but that was before I knew you were an underwear thief. Now I'm convinced you're a scoundrel."

His eyes darken. "You have no fucking idea."

"How about you tell me what's on your mind?"

"Visions of you straddling me."

I switch legs, pulling the other sock over my toes. "Too bad it's broad daylight." My gaze lands on the growing bulge in his jeans. "Because I'd be more than happy to oblige."

"We could always relocate to somewhere more private and come back here later." The heat in his tone makes my insides clench.

After two hours in a car together, listening to the rumble of his voice and breathing his scent, my desire has reached its flash point.

All we need is a match.

I glance at the empty parking area. Garrett's Jeep is angled away from any buildings, and he has tinted windows. No one can see or hear us, so why not seize the opportunity to be close to him?

I give him a sultry smile, then grip the waistband of my leggings. Lust flares in his gaze when I slide them off. Feeling more empowered than ever in my life, I slip out of the panties too.

He waits, chest heaving while I take the cupcakes he's holding and place them in the back. I pull my lingerie from beneath his shirt and toss it by his bag.

"We *could* relocate." I unbuckle his seat belt and reach across him to adjust his seat, staring up into his eyes as he slides backward. "But I want you *now*."

He doesn't move or say a word. He simply watches me from beneath his sinfully long lashes. I snag a condom from my purse, then pop the button on his jeans and unzip them. I motion for him to lift his hips so I can shove the denim down. His boxers follow, freeing his hard cock. A bead of moisture eases from the tip, but I resist the urge to take him into my mouth. I stroke him instead, pressing a series of kisses to his neck and jawline.

I love how he feels like silk-covered steel in my hand. I could luxuriate in the sensation for hours, but we're cramped in a vehicle. In a relatively *public* location. Efficiency must take center stage now.

But later, I'm going to take my time with him.

"We have to hurry." I nip his earlobe, then make my way toward his throat. He groans and tilts his head back, exposing more of himself to me. I pause for a moment to roll on the condom, then swiftly straddle his lap. My breath hisses out of me as I ease down onto him. He's thick and long, the fullness almost too much.

"Oh, fuck, Ella." His reverent whisper reaches my ears when I take him to the hilt. He grabs the Jeep's *oh shit* handle with one hand, while the other clutches the console.

I roll my hips, still kissing and licking his neck like I'm starved for his taste. He groans again, the sound a primal reminder of the restraint he's showing. The muscles of his shoulders flex with his grip on the car. I wrap my arms around him, bracing myself with the headrest as I move. My downward thrusts force gasps from me.

Clinging to him, I bury my face in his neck and let my body take over.

"You feel so fucking good," he rasps. "Ride me harder."

I pick up the pace, all too willing to ramp up the intensity. One would think my experience on top would strengthen my thighs, but it doesn't take long for them to tire.

I lift my head to meet his gaze. "Help me."

"Tell me what you need."

"You take over." I clamp my hands on his shoulders and arch my back, spreading my thighs as wide as the space allows.

Using the handle and console as leverage, Garrett jacks his hips upward, delivering a powerful thrust.

"Yes, just like that. Don't stop." My whimpered pleas match my body's growing desperation. "Garrett, please . . ."

"I've got you, baby." Sweat glistens on his forehead as he powers into me.

Our mixed gasps and groans, and the frenzied slap of our bodies fill the Jeep. His eyes never leave mine, peering into my soul like he's taking a blade to what remains of my barbed wire. Piece by piece, the rusty sections encasing me fall away.

My savior wields weapons of molten gold, forged in kindred pain. He breaches my stronghold's final defenses with frightening ease. Yet, as the walls crumble around me, I welcome their destruction.

It's one thing to spend years hiding behind your own armor. There's a certainty there. Knowledge and steadiness. It's me against the world, and the only person who can fail me is myself. I've never considered allowing someone else to stand guard. No one was capable.

Until Garrett.

For the first time in my life, I've found the shield I crave.

Each thrust takes me higher, stroking and rubbing the places deep inside, making me swear my body was made for him. But it's the intensity in his eyes that sends me over the edge.

I whisper his name as my release takes my breath away, throwing the gates wide open. The drawbridge is down, the moat's dried up, and I'm completely at his mercy.

Shock waves of pleasure radiate to my toes. I cling to Garrett's shoulders as his thrusts pick up speed. Muscles tensed, he white-knuckles the cup holder between our seats, knocking his phone to the floor. He nearly pulls the grab handle off his roof as his body coils even tighter. Another upward thrust, and he explodes, my name leaving his lips on a ragged moan. Clamping my thighs around him, I pull him deeper into my body.

Garrett's orgasm is the most beautiful thing I've ever witnessed. Eyes fluttering closed in ecstasy, head thrown back, he's lost to the pleasure. And when he meets my gaze after pouring himself into me, I hand over the silver platter holding my heart.

I thought the way he looked at me before was intense, but it pales in comparison to the reverence in his eyes now.

"God, Ella, what are you doing to me?"

I collapse against his chest, my body still gripping his pulsing length. We're both gasping. My head is turned toward the window, and his heart races beneath my ear.

It takes a few minutes for me to notice he's still holding the handle.

I lift my head. "You didn't touch me."

"I recall being given rules."

And he followed every single one. He respected my boundaries without being asked. Right now, I'm not so sure what barriers still apply. We're closing in on a new frontier. My maps aren't accurate anymore.

People often claim a smile is disarming. My experience has proven smiles bring manipulation masquerading as warmth. Garrett isn't smiling. His expression is raw, vulnerable. Naked, yet still fully clothed. A lot like how I'm feeling. Something changed between us in this car. We gave each other something much deeper than mind-blowing sex. We exchanged pieces of our souls.

And, so help me God, I want to give him more of mine.

"Some rules have changed." I gently unwrap his fingers from the handle and guide his hand to my hip. I repeat that with his other hand, reveling in his warmth on my skin. "Almost all of the rules have changed," I whisper.

He searches my face, his tentative grip on my body telling me he's afraid of making a misstep. "When do I find out the new ones?"

I cup his jaw and brush my thumb over his lower lip. "I'll let you know as soon as I figure them out."

He nods, and his body relaxes, fingertips splaying apart. "Permission to hold you?"

I melt deeper into his chest. "Permission granted."

He tightens his arms around me, holding on to me like I'm treasured. But he's got it all wrong. *He* is the treasure.

"*Tu sei il mio tesoro.*"

"I don't know what you're saying, but it sounds beautiful," he whispers.

"I said, 'you are my treasure.'"

His breath catches, and he pulls me closer. We sit in comfortable silence for a few moments. I think he's about to say something when his chest expands on a deep inhale, but he starts to sing instead.

The lyrics to "Wild Love" pour from his lips as his decadent voice fills the vehicle. Every word soaks into me, filling the emptiness until it overflows in rivers down my cheeks.

I cling to Garrett like he'll vanish if I let go. The dashboard clock reads 11:11. One day in the future I'll look back on this moment for what it is. And I'll be able to say with one-hundred-percent certainty that I knew the very minute I fell in love.

Forty

A song, a sculpture, and a look

Garrett

Ella's body trembles in my arms. Tears roll down her cheeks, and she clings to me for dear life as I finish the song's last verse.

I tilt her chin up to look into her eyes. "I didn't mean to make you cry."

"These aren't sad tears." She sniffs and quickly brushes them away.

"Promise?"

Instead of answering, she grips both sides of my face and kisses me full on the lips.

I've wanted to kiss Ella since the moment I first saw her, so I can't stop myself from moaning. I allow her to lead, only parting my lips when her tongue nudges them open.

Her hands weave into my hair as she deepens our kiss. Tongues stroking and sliding, we sip from each other's mouths like they hold the healing tonic we crave. I've never been big on kissing. It was always an emotionless prelude to what I really wanted. Right now, with Ella's lips on mine, time stands still. I'm feeling things I've never felt. I'm not so sure I'm worthy of the woman in my arms. But I do know this. Ella's kiss is everything I didn't know I needed.

I'm still inside her and hard as hell. She rocks her hips in a fluid grind, her kiss becoming more desperate by the second. I follow her lead, absorbing the sensation of her pussy squeezing me. As much as I want to explore her body, I won't take more than I'm given. I keep my hands still, satisfied with the embrace she's allowed.

She feels so right in my arms. Warm and soft, yet stronger than anyone I know. She's a fragile fortress.

I groan into her mouth as her movements gain speed, the fluid rhythm now frenzied. Her kisses get more erratic, her breath coming in short bursts.

She breaks our kiss and arches her body, nails digging into my shoulders as she comes. She doesn't moan or scream, just sighs like she's releasing a breath her lungs held trapped for an eternity.

My cock is so sensitive, the first flutters of her pussy send me flying. "El, baby, *fuck.*"

Her body's spasms carry me through until we're both spent, panting and pulsing in each other's arms. My head sags against the headrest, a kaleidoscope of stars swirling behind my closed eyelids.

"*Il mio tesoro per sempre,*" she whispers at my throat.

She translated the first part before my song, and I've listened to enough Pavarotti in my lifetime to know *per sempre* means forever.

My treasure forever.

Other than my friendship with Lena, I've never been anyone's treasure. I've never considered the possibility of forever because people always leave me behind. I'm the afterthought who's easily dismissed.

I'm not sure if Ella's words come from the heart or if they're orgasm induced, but I do know how deeply they resonate inside me, echoing to the dark corners of my soul. People haven't shown me too many tokens of affection, so I'm going to cling to this one—this woman—for as long as she'll let me.

We've been exploring Opus 40 for nearly an hour, awed by the stonework sculpture's enormity. I love Ella's appreciation for art in all its forms, and how she lights up when she talks about it. I can't wait to see all the pictures she's taken.

She gestures to the Catskills. "Have you ever climbed any of these?"

I point. "I've been to the top of that one. It's called Overlook Mountain. There's a fire tower and the ruins of an old hotel at the summit. I have some pictures I can show you when we get back to the city. On a cloudless day, the views of the Hudson River are spectacular. Here's a fun Garrett fact for you. I was in the tower, looking out over this beautiful valley, the day I decided to name my company Hudson Graphics."

"It's a perfect name." She smiles, sunlight glittering in her eyes. "I love fun Garrett facts. Keep them coming."

"You gonna reciprocate? I'd love to decode some mystical Ella mysteries." I want to know everything about this woman.

"Maybe." Her lashes flutter with her coy smile, but she doesn't offer any clues.

"I'll take you up there when the weather gets warmer," I say, deciding not to push my luck in the mystery department.

"I'd love that. I've never been hiking."

I rub my jaw. "We may have to ease you into that one and do a few milder hikes first. It's like two and a half miles uphill—not exactly a breeze for a beginner. Plus, there are rattlesnakes."

She wrinkles her nose. "I'm not a fan of snakes."

"Yeah, you gotta stay away from downed trees and rock walls. They like to hide out there."

Eyes widening, she points to the bluestone beneath us. "You mean rock walls like these?"

"Don't worry, Cupcake. I'll protect you from those snakes." I flash a wolfish grin. "Although you had no trouble wrangling mine."

She laughs and playfully shoves my shoulder. "So, you're saying I should add snake charmer to my résumé?"

"Fuck yeah, you should. Put it between musculature rearranger and synapse fryer." *Right beside heart stealer and soul soother.* I clear my throat and change topics before I start spilling my guts. "Are you getting hungry yet?"

"Actually, yes. That oatmeal's a distant memory."

"You know what that means, right?" I raise a brow at her.

"Oatmeal's a shitty breakfast?"

I laugh. "Not where I was going, but yeah. It's certainly not eggs and bacon."

"I prefer sausage." She keeps a straight face, but the amusement in her tone is clear. "Of course, that's irrelevant right now. Back to your question."

I blink a few times, too distracted by her pun to speak. She's funnier than I gave her credit for. I'd be willing to bet she doesn't let too many people see her silly side. It warms me to know I'm seeing parts of her she keeps hidden away.

She tilts her head to the side. "You said, 'you know what that means, right?' and I'm still waiting for the answer."

"Oh, yeah. Sorry, you distracted me." I give her a stupid grin, feeling lighter than ever in my life. "It's question time again. Do you want actual lunch, or should we gorge ourselves on cupcakes?"

A slow smile curves her lips. "Can we do *both*? I'm dying to sample those cupcakes. However, we need something substantial before all that sugar. You know, maybe something healthy?"

"You want a salad, I can make that happen. Burgers, lobster, sushi, you name it. Say the word and it's yours."

"Are you always this accommodating?"

"No."

"That was a quick answer." She stares up at me, her eyes filled with longing.

I could swerve around her statement and keep things light and fluffy, but I'm a blunt guy. Pretending doesn't serve anyone, and I don't have the energy to put on a show. Something tells me she needs to hear my explanation. She deserves to know she's the exception to my rules.

"Ella, I haven't dated anyone in nine years. Like I told you, my history involves lots of casual sex. No strings. No connection. Just fucking for the sake of fucking." I fling my arm toward the parking area. "*Nothing* that happened in that Jeep was casual for me. No part of this adventure is typical. I don't do feelings. Romance. Hope. It's not who I am. But somehow, since I've met you, I'm learning that maybe I don't know myself as well as I thought." I stuff my hands in my pockets to keep from stroking her cheek. "You make me want all those things. You are an anomaly."

"You're my mirror, Garrett." She steps closer and wraps her arms around my waist, resting her head on my chest. "I could've said those exact words."

"One day you'll understand we have more in common than you realize." After years of the torment nipping at my heels, she could be the person I finally bare my soul to. The thought both terrifies and soothes me. "So much more."

She tightens her arms around me, and while I'm desperate to return her embrace, I'm still unsure of the types of touch she'll allow.

"Permission to hug you?"

She looks up at me. "New rule. You can hug me whenever you want."

Relieved, I pull her close. "I like this rule."

"Me too, tesoro."

I rest my chin on top of her head, and she melts against me. We stand in the cold December wind for several minutes, until a particularly frigid blast of air makes her shiver.

"C'mon, Cupcake. Let's get food."

"Only if you promise to turn on my hiney warmer when we get in the car."

Tinker Street is the central vein of Woodstock, lined with cafés, bistros, shops, and galleries. Shoppers hustle along the sidewalks, armed with their purchases. The holidays are coming, and the artsy small town is the perfect place to snag unique gifts. I need to pick up something for Lena's birthday while we're here.

For lunch, Ella selected a Middle Eastern restaurant situated on the corner. We picked a private table by a window overlooking the sidewalk so we could people-watch.

Ella peruses the menu. "You mentioned coming here in the past. Did you try the falafels?"

"They're awesome. I'm torn between those and the Israeli breakfast."

"Why don't we order one of each? Then we can share."

I close my menu. "Works for me."

We place our orders when the waiter reappears, then chat about things to see in the area.

"How come you know this town so well when you grew up in Windham? Isn't it kinda far from here?" She removes the lemon wedge from her water glass and offers it to me.

I squeeze some juice into my water. "It's not too far. But to answer your question, I lived near Woodstock during the summer before college. I stayed with a buddy of mine whose family owns a cabin. They moved to Denver, but kept the property, converting it into an Airbnb."

"I thought you lived with Lena's family?"

"I did, but that was from age thirteen to seventeen. I stayed here afterward." I rub my jaw, pondering how deep I should delve into my explanation. "I went through some shit at my aunt and uncle's when I was thirteen, so Lena's family took me in. Things got complicated once her brother moved to Tokyo."

"Why?"

"Trevor was a good buffer. He kept their drunk father in line. Once Trev moved, Roger treated Adele, Lena's mom, like shit. I got involved after a particular incident when he went after Lena. Everything sort of imploded."

"He was abusive?"

"Yeah. It was mainly verbal abuse. The day I got my driver's license, Lena and I went joyriding in the junker I'd saved up for. When we got home, we walked in on her parents fighting. We saw Roger hit Adele. Lena got between them, so he slapped her and threw her against a wall."

"Oh my God. What did you do?"

"I jumped on his back and put him in a headlock. Mind you, I was a scrawny seventeen-year-old kid. He probably would've killed me once he got free. Adele called the police, which took the wind out of his sails. I dragged Lena out of there, and we drove for hours, both crying."

"That's terrible."

"It got even worse once we returned."

Her eyes widen. "It doesn't sound like it could get much worse."

"One would think that, but I can assure you, it did." I release a dark chuckle. "While Lena and I were gone, her father told the police *I* attacked and kidnapped her. They were waiting for us when we pulled into the driveway."

"*What?* Where was her mother for all this?"

"Spineless and mute. The bastard had her so terrified, she didn't utter a word in my defense. Lena lost her mind when the cops put me in cuffs. That's when Adele finally opened her mouth. So, yeah, that sorta put an end to my days of living there. I stayed around here for the summer, then moved to the city for college."

I'll never forget the feeling of betrayal. As much as I tell myself I've forgiven Lena's mother, there's a part of me that hasn't. Adele abandoned me that day. If it weren't for Lena, they would've tossed me in a cell for a crime I didn't commit. The ordeal fucked with my head for a long time. And I was already fucked up to begin with. To this day, Lena is the only woman who has ever had my back unconditionally.

"It sucks because Lena's mom was like a mother to me up until that point. I lost my mom when I was seven, and my aunt didn't give two fucks about me. Adele filled that void for a few short years. I get that she was a victim too, but it still felt like a slap in the face."

"That's understandable. Tell me about your mom." She reaches for my hand and gives it a squeeze. "If it isn't too painful for you."

"It's painful, but I'm able to talk about it now. It's been like a quarter century. I should really be over it. But I guess I'm not." I take a long sip of water, gathering my thoughts. "There's no closure with suicide. The what-ifs and whys still take over my mind. For years, I was convinced it was my fault. I wasn't enough to keep her here, you know?"

"I don't think it had anything to do with you, tesoro."

"She *knew* she was all I had left, but she still abandoned me. It's hard to believe I *wasn't* part of the issue. I've gotten most of those thoughts out of my system, thanks to regular therapy. I know I wasn't a shitty kid. I did what I was told, helped around the house, used my manners. Dad spent a lot of time at the bars, so Mom was my sun and moon. It always hits me hardest on her birthday, the anniversary of her death, and Mother's Day, obviously."

"There's no time line for grief."

"Yeah. You probably didn't wanna know all that when you asked, so I'll switch gears and give you the basics. Mom grew up in Tel Aviv, Israel. She met my father during a trip to Ireland and fell madly in love. They married in Dublin, then moved to Pennsylvania a few years later. Her name was Arielle Zahavi."

"What did she look like?"

"She had long, shiny black hair, olive skin, and gold eyes like mine. My mom was exceptionally beautiful."

"What about your dad?"

"His name was Liam Casey. He was tall with dark hair, blue eyes, and a really deep voice. I remember him being jovial and fun when he was around. But like I said, he spent more time at the bars than at home, so I was closer with Mom."

"Do you have pictures of her?"

"Yeah, one. It's in a lockbox at home. I stole it from my aunt's photo album after my cousin burned all of my pictures."

Her mouth drops open in horror. "That's rotten! Why the hell would he do something like that?"

"Sean is a sadistic psychopath. The darkest kind of evil. He tormented me for seven years. First verbally, then it grew physical. I was his favorite punching bag." *And ashtray.* My back burns at the thought, making me stiffen in my seat. I force a few deep breaths as my throat starts to close.

Ella squeezes my hand, then interlaces our fingers. "Where is he now?"

"In Attica prison. He got twenty to life after he nearly killed me."

"Mother of God! That doesn't seem long enough."

"Yeah." *Ticktock, motherfucker. It's already been twenty years.* The sickening thought ricochets through my mind, making the hairs on my neck stand on end. My stomach hits the floor with the realization I could come face-to-face with Sean again.

Her eyes lock with mine. "Are you okay?"

No. "There's a possibility he'll be eligible for parole in the next few years." The words scrape past my lips on a tortured whisper. "I don't know what the fuck I'll do if that happens."

You're not a kid anymore.

You can defend yourself.

"Try not to think about that now, tesoro." She grips my hand even tighter, pulling me from my inner tailspin. "It's not a definite."

"Let's hope."

She shifts in her seat and gnaws her lower lip, brows deeply furrowed. "What happened next?"

"The state removed Connor, my youngest cousin, and me from the home because clearly Wendy and Jim were incapable of providing a safe place for us to live. Connor was only four when I went to live with them, making him eleven when everything happened. He stayed with his dad's parents, and I went to Lena's. His brothers, Brian and Brendan, were already eighteen, so they did their own thing. Sean was twenty-one at the time."

"Did Sean ever target his brothers?"

"He had some scuffles with the twins, but they could hold their own. I was more worried about Connor."

"Did he hurt him?"

"No. I made damn sure of that. I went out of my way to keep Sean's wrath focused on me."

"You protected Connor."

"I did my best to shield him when the violence escalated."

"Where the fuck were your aunt and uncle?" she snaps, fury burning in her eyes.

"Jim was a trucker, so he was barely ever home. He was nice enough when he was around. Wendy is my mother's half sister. I think she despised me because I looked so much like my mom. Who knows her reasoning? She wasn't overly mean, just dismissive and kinda cold. She worked in the local hospital's billing department during the day, then waitressed at night to make ends meet."

"So, who watched . . ." Her voice trails off when realization dawns. "Sean was your babysitter?"

"Yup. Lucky me, right?"

"Why didn't you tell someone he was hurting you?" she whispers, her eyes growing damp.

I stare at my hands for a few beats, remembering how I'd practice making a fist beneath my desk at school. How I'd punch my pillow each night and pretend it was Sean's face. How I prayed one day I'd have the courage to hit him back. How I begged my dead mother's memory for the strength to stand up for myself.

Yeah. That never happened.

Noticing my silence, Ella brushes her thumb over my knuckles. "Why didn't you ask for help?"

"Because he threatened Connor's life if I opened my mouth." The admission comes out on a strangled whisper, and I hate how weak I sound. Clearing my throat, I stiffen my spine and meet her gaze again. "I couldn't let myself be responsible for something happening to him. Connor was, and still is, a man I consider my brother. He's the only Geraghty I keep in touch with. No one could protect *me*, but I could keep him safe. So, I did. I dealt with the abuse for years. Until Sean went off the deep end."

"Did Lena know what was going on?"

"Not for a long time."

Ella slides my sleeve up before I can stop her and brushes her hand over the scarring on my forearm. "Did he do this to you?"

The marks shouldn't be noticeable with how dark my arm hair is. They're either more obvious than I thought, or she's super observant. Then again, I'm not used to people paying attention to details about me.

"Well? Did he?"

I hesitate, afraid of what she'll think if I tell her the truth. "Do you really want to know?"

"Yes." Her fingertips feather over my scars, tracing each one, like her touch alone can erase them.

I clear my throat and stare at the flickering candle between us. "Those are all me. It was how I coped with the fear, anger, and pain. Something I *could* control. I kept it secret for over six months by always wearing long sleeves. Of course, that went out the window when I spilled cocoa all over myself one day while hanging out with Lena."

"How so?"

"She grabbed one of her brother's shirts for me to change into, but I refused to take mine off, even though it was saturated." I meet Ella's pain-filled gaze. "You've met Lena, so you know how feisty and persistent she is. She knew something was up and practically forced me to undress. I remember standing there in her bedroom, wearing nothing but my boxers. She cried when I showed her the wounds I'd inflicted and the ones from him. I begged her not to tell anyone. She wanted me to sleep over, but I couldn't leave Connor alone with Sean, so I went back home." I swig my water, the coolness soothing my throat. "It took a couple days, but Lena convinced me to tell Wendy what was going on."

"How did she respond?"

I stare at the ice cube melting in my glass. "She blew me off. Told me I was an ungrateful brat for trying to stir up trouble in her family. She wouldn't listen when I tried to show her the cuts and bruises. Wendy called me melodramatic and said I needed to grow a set of balls. I was, and I quote, 'lucky to have a roof over my head and food on my plate.'"

"You were a *child*," she whispers, as a tear rolls down her cheek. "Food, clothing, and shelter are basic requirements for survival."

"Oh, I had clothes. Hand-me-downs from Brian and Brendan."

The waiter arrives with our food and looks between us awkwardly while setting our plates on the table.

Ella brushes her cheeks and smiles up at him. "Thank you. This looks delicious." He leaves, and she returns her attention to me after unwrapping her silverware. "My heart breaks for you, tesoro. I wish I had the power to change your past."

And now I feel like a total dick for ruining today's uplifting mood.

"I appreciate that, Ella." A sigh heaves from my chest. "Listen, I'm sorry. I didn't mean to unload all my shit onto you. Our date wasn't the time or place for that. I'm supposed to be romancing the hell out of you. Instead, I've made you cry twice."

She scoots her chair closer, so we're side by side. "Please don't apologize. You *are* romancing me. I feel more connected to you than anyone in my life." She reaches for the hand that's closest to her and presses a kiss to my knuckles. "Feel free to unload on me anytime."

"The same goes for you."

She gives me a small smile. "Thank you, but I probably won't do much of that. I have an extremely hard time talking about my past. I'd rather not dredge up old pain, you know?"

"Fair enough. Just know I'm always here to listen."

"Thank you." She smiles and plops a falafel onto a smaller plate for me. "I can't wait to try these. I wonder if they're anything like the food truck near my office."

I slide some eggs, baba ghanoush, and tabbouleh onto her plate, then tear off a piece of pita for her. "I'm gonna eat the hell out of this feta cheese."

"I love feta."

"I never met a cheese I didn't like."

Ella laughs. "Come to think of it, neither have I." She bites into the falafel, and her eyes flutter closed as she chews.

Jesus Christ, the woman even chews sexily. I bet she looks stunning when she flosses her teeth.

"Good?" I ask, as images of Ella readying herself for a shower dance through my head. She probably runs a brush through that silky hair I'm dying to tangle my fingers in. My cock twitches to life, making me shift position.

"Amazing. Way better than the ones I've had in the city."

"Have you thought about what you'd like to do for the rest of the day?"

She lifts an eyebrow. "You aren't going to give me another this or that?"

Her tone holds an edge of hopefulness, telling me how much she enjoys being given options. The freedom to choose empowers her, and there is nothing sexier than an empowered woman. Except that woman naked on top of me.

"Oh, absolutely. I was just gunning my engine before resuming my quest to sweep you off your feet."

Her smile could melt even the hardest of men. I never considered myself a softy, but here I am. As long as she keeps smiling, I'll be the softest, fluffiest, most cloudlike motherfucker that ever walked this planet.

"You're doing it again," she murmurs, a blush coloring her cheeks.

"Doing what?"

"Giving me one of those looks."

"Do you want me to stop? I could probably dial it back a few notches if necessary."

She clamps her hand around my wrist. "Here's another new rule. Never stop looking at me that way."

Forty-One

Candles, carbonara, and a command

Ella

Garrett holds the door open for me as we leave a candle shop, carrying beautiful wax creations intended as Christmas gifts. We've walked all along Tinker Street, drifting in and out of boutiques and galleries. We spent quite a while in one particular store because Garrett wanted to find a suitable birthday gift for Lena. I marveled at the handmade jewelry displayed in glass cases like artwork. He bought a gorgeous pair of chandelier earrings with a matching amber ring, and a chunky silver bangle. The man has seriously good taste.

My dress looked ridiculous with pants beneath it, so I opted to leave them in the Jeep before lunch. A gust of wind chills my legs, making me regret that decision. And why the hell did I wear stilettos?

We make our way toward the municipal lot where we parked. I'm eager to kick off these shoes and warm my ass again.

"Okay, Cupcake, it's question time." His breath crystallizes in the frosty air. "We're heading for four o'clock, which means we should probably start pondering our dinner options. Before we do that, you're gonna need to decide where we stay." He unlocks the Jeep and opens the door for me. "Remember my friend's cabin I mentioned during lunch?"

"Yes."

"Well, I tentatively reserved it for the weekend. However, if you'd feel more comfortable in a hotel, we can certainly do that instead. You won't find the super ritzy ones up here like they have in the city, but there are a couple of nice places to choose from."

"I've stayed in many hotels, but I've never been to a cabin. Let's do that."

He grins. "Great choice. There's a massive stone fireplace in the living room. Jonah said he had a firewood delivery last week."

The idea of cozying up with Garrett in front of a crackling fire makes me swoon. There's something innately romantic about cabins. Of course, I've never been to one, but I've always dreamed of owning a rustic log home.

I flutter my lashes at him. "If you build us a fire, maybe I'll kiss you in front of it."

He clenches his hand on the edge of the door. "Ella, I'll rebuild the Colosseum if it means I get to kiss you again."

The fire in his eyes sends a flare of heat to my core. This man is so passionate and full of life, I can't imagine not having him in mine.

"Let's start with a fire, tesoro."

Pure longing infuses his features. "I love when you call me that."

The man aches for love and acceptance. To be cared for and treasured. He craves connection as much as I do. I'm still reeling from our conversation at lunch. I can't fathom the depravity he endured. The broken little boy inside is screaming for attention, and so help me God, I hear him.

I stroke his cheek. "It's freezing. Get in the car."

He closes my door and makes his way to the driver's side, easing into the crisp leather seat. He starts the engine and looks over at me. "Since we're staying around here, that means we can try one of the other restaurants I told you about. You mentioned something about pasta earlier."

"What if . . ." I chew my lip as a plan comes together in my head.

"I'm listening."

I meet his gaze. "Let me make you dinner. I never get to cook for anyone, and I guarantee my pasta will be way better than anything we can find in a restaurant. I'm not bragging, by the way, just stating a fact."

"I've tasted your food. Trust me, you've earned bragging rights."

His praise warms me and bolsters my confidence, making me want to show off a little. I learned how to cook from Italy's finest chef, so I know my way around a kitchen. Give me some basic ingredients, and I'll tantalize one's tastebuds with ease. Tonight's the perfect occasion to prepare a meal that would make my grandmother proud.

The overwhelming urge to nurture Garrett, serves only to fuel my fire.

"We can stop at a grocery store for ingredients before we head to the cabin. Now that you've seduced me with visions of a warm hearth, I kinda want to stay in tonight."

He starts the ignition. "Let's make it happen."

Garrett reenters the kitchen with a smile. "It smells incredible in here." He stops beside me, where I'm standing in front of the stove. "Are you sure you don't need me to do anything?"

"I need you to relax and let me feed you." I point to the meat sizzling in a pan. "I'm glad they had pancetta. Bacon works, but I like to make my carbonara authentic."

"Then I'm surprised you let me get angel hair instead of regular spaghetti."

"Who am I to deny such a simple request?"

We visited a local grocery store before riding the short distance to his friend's cabin. It was a normal, domestic outing, yet I enjoyed it immensely. Garrett pushed the cart while I gathered everything I needed for Gigi's carbonara recipe. The store's impressive selection of cheeses made my mouth water.

He leans against the counter. "I started a fire."

"Perfect." I give the boiling pasta a quick stir, then tend to the bowl with the egg and cheese mixture that will become our sauce. "You're watching me."

"Am I freaking you out? I can go in the other room. I know you said you hate when men loom over you."

"No, I want you to stay. You aren't looming. I'm just not used to an audience while I cook." I blow a wisp of hair out of my face, then tug the elastic from around my wrist. "Long hair sucks sometimes."

He holds out his hand. "May I?" I must look confused because he clarifies with, "My braid skills are superior to most women's."

"You're asking to braid my hair?"

He chuckles. "You catch on quickly."

I place the hair tie in his hand, still perplexed. Then I remember he's had a female best friend since childhood. Of course, he can do hair. "Let me guess. Lena taught you?"

"Yeah. She had hair down to her butt when we were kids. She could do a regular braid on herself but none of the fancier ones. She showed me how to do them on one of her Barbies."

"You played Barbies?"

"Damn right, I did. It was better than getting my ass kicked at home. Plus, Lena's very imaginative, so our Barbies had grand adventures. Not going to lie, I miss it sometimes."

My heart clenches at the image of them playing together. "That might be the cutest thing I've ever heard."

He laughs. "Well, fuck. You should see me at a tea party."

"Did you guys play dress-up?"

"Sure did." He snorts. "It got interesting when she discovered makeup. Nearly lost an eyeball once to a mascara wand." He briefly scrunches his eyes closed at the memory. "She felt *so* bad about it. She came after me with washcloths to try to clean everything off. Meanwhile, I resembled a drugged-up raccoon. The look on her older brother's face was priceless." He stretches the elastic between his fingers. "French, fishtail, or Dutch?"

I turn off the burner for the pancetta and give the egg and cheese sauce a stir. The pasta is almost done. "What is a Dutch braid?"

"It's an inverted French braid. You pass the hair strands from underneath, so the braid sits on top instead of woven beneath the hair."

"Let's do that one." I spin so my back is to him, tossing my locks behind me.

"You got it." He starts near my forehead, and the first brush of his fingers through my hair sends goose bumps over every inch of my body. My breath catches when he gently gathers the strands by my temples and begins weaving them together. "Let me know if it's too tight."

"Uh-huh." I melt against him, like a flower leaning toward the sun.

What is this ecstasy? His touch is not at all sexual, yet my body hums with awareness that reverberates to my core. I'm not making it easy by leaning on him, but I'm afraid my legs will give out if I don't.

"You like this," he murmurs, incorporating another piece of hair.

"What clued you in?" My breathless voice betrays my desire as well as the hardened peaks of my nipples.

He feathers his fingertips over the nape of my neck as he works his way down. "You have beautiful hair, Ella. It feels like silk and smells amazing." He finishes the braid and steps back. "Voilà."

I reach up, my fingers exploring his handiwork while my body weeps for the loss of his touch. Since when do I want a man to touch me?

"Thank you." I spin around to meet the satisfaction in his eyes. "New rule. You're welcome to play with my hair whenever you'd like."

A wicked grin curves his lips. "I'll keep that in mind."

The stove timer beeps, drawing my focus to the meal I'm supposed to be cooking. I quickly turn off the heat, then drain the pasta, reserving some water. I add the drained pasta to the skillet with the pancetta. Next, I add a little of the reserved water, and the egg and cheese mixture. "It's very important to pour this on the pasta while it's still hot," I explain, mixing until everything's creamy. "This way, the pasta's heat, and the residual heat of the skillet, take care of any egg that's still uncooked. Raw eggs are dangerous, you know." I continue stirring as I add a little parsley, then point to a stool at the kitchen island. "Have a seat."

Garrett settles, his gaze following as I move around the kitchen gathering dishes and silverware. I fix plates for us, setting his in front of him, before pouring our waters.

Once everything's ready, I slide onto the stool beside him. "*Buon appetito, tesoro.*"

We clink our glasses together, and then I wait, a mix of excitement and fear churning in my belly. It will crush me if he doesn't like it.

Garrett takes a generous bite, and his eyes flutter closed while he chews. He moans low in his chest, making me silently rejoice. "This. Is. Divine."

I couldn't stop my smile if I tried. "I'm so happy you like it."

"No, seriously. It's the best carbonara I've ever eaten."

Heat rises up my neck and cheeks. "Now you're using flattery as a weapon."

His eyes snap to mine. "I would never use any weapon on or against you."

"I didn't mean it like—"

"This isn't smoke and mirrors, Ella. I mean everything I say." The ferocity in his gaze matches his tone. "Today has been one of the best days of my life."

"Mine too," I whisper, reaching for his hand. I interlace my fingers with his. "Thank you for spending time with me."

"I don't like the term 'spending time' because it implies losing something. Like the seconds, minutes, and hours that pass are somehow being used frivolously. Think about it. You spend money, and you wind up with less in your wallet, which sucks. Being with you feels like the opposite. Like I'm earning or winning a prize."

I stare at him in stunned silence. I doubt he realizes how deeply his words affect me. Hearing him so perfectly vocalize what I feel when we're together makes my eyes water.

He rubs his chin in thought. "What if we call it *sharing* time together? Because it's really an exchange. We fortify each other with pieces of ourselves as the time passes, so everything balances out. Like I said, it's winning, but we're both the victors."

I love you.

Garrett's fork clatters to the floor when I grab his cheeks and pull his lips to mine. As my pent-up desires, hopes, and needs spill over, I kiss him with everything I've got.

Groaning, he pulls me into his lap, mirroring my kiss with equal passion.

We're a balance—a *bilancia*—teetering between the darkness of our pasts and the bright potential our future holds.

I wrap my legs around him and grind into his lap, pressing against his hard cock. My body clenches with a level of need I've never known before. He threads his questing hands into my hair, loosening my braid. I want his hands all over me, his fingers and cock inside me.

I break the kiss and stare into his eyes. "Take me to bed."

He stands, lifting me with him. Like a koala, I tighten my arms and legs around him as he carries me down the hall to the cabin's bedroom. He sets me down and closes the door, then turns to face me again. "What do you need?"

"You." The confession leaves my lips with ease. "I need *you*."

Garrett is everything I've ever needed. He's the kind of man I prayed for, but never dreamed of finding. He not only understands my limitations and boundaries, but he also respects them. He understands and respects *me*. As a human being. And as a woman. The more time we spend together, the less I remember my pain. With Garrett, I'm formidable—not broken.

He crosses the room and sits on the edge of the bed. "Come here."

I move into the place he's made for me between his legs. Since he's seated, I'm taller, which I'm sure he did on purpose. His attention to detail, and genuine concern for my comfort, makes me fall deeper in love with him.

He peers up into my eyes, his molten amber depths filled with heat. "Tell me what you want from me, El."

"Undress me."

He reaches behind me and locates my dress's zipper, slowly tugging it down. The crisp air on my exposed back makes me shiver. Garrett pauses, searching my face for a moment before unzipping me all the way. "Say the word and I'll stop."

"I know. Keep going."

He grips the front of my dress near my shoulders and peels it from my body, allowing the garment to fall at my feet. His breath catches at the sight of my lingerie. He unhooks my bra, then slowly slides the straps down. It's not a move born of hesitance. No, this is a carnal man savoring the moment before he uncovers the treasure he seeks. Heat flares in his eyes when he finally drags the black lace to my hips.

My nipples tighten in the cool air.

"Fuck, you're beautiful," he whispers, his shoulders rising and falling faster with each breath.

He tosses the bra aside, and his gaze caresses my skin. He's waiting for my permission to go further, which makes me want to grant him every liberty.

"Touch me."

Garrett lifts his eyes to mine, watching my reaction as he places both hands on my shoulders. He skates them down my sides, then back up again, edging closer to my breasts.

My body aches for him. I've never been this turned on, or felt this powerful, in my entire life.

His movements are agonizingly slow as he tests the waters. He's still wading in the surf when I'm ready for his deep dive. He brushes his thumbs over my nipples, making me gasp. I bite back my moan when his warm palms finally cup my breasts.

I point to my panties. "Keep going."

He grips the waistband, dragging them down over my hips. His gaze lingers between my thighs, and when he licks his lips, I *feel* it.

I kick the thong aside and step even closer to him. "Put your hands on me. I want them all over my body."

Garrett feathers his touch over my hips and thighs before finding my chest again. He rubs circles on my nipples with his thumbs. "May I kiss you?"

I lean forward to meet his lips, but his mouth surrounds my nipple instead. Gasping, I stare down at him in shock. His eyes flash to mine, and he waits, but there's no way I'll stop him. Not even a freight train barreling in our direction could make me ruin this moment. A satisfied groan rumbles from his chest when I clutch the back of his head and pull him closer.

With one hand clamped on my hip, and the other splayed across my lower back, he licks and sucks my nipples, rubbing his tongue over the hardened peaks. The scrape of his stubble, alongside plush lips and a devilish mouth, ratchets up the sensations on my skin.

"Oh, Garrett, that feels so good."

He switches sides, and the hand that was on my hip travels lower, barely grazing the top of my pussy. He traces my C-section scar, and we lock gazes again. The question in his eyes is clear.

"Uterus stuff." It's a half-truth, but that's all I can give him right now. One day I'll bare my soul to him. Until then, I'll focus on handing over my body. "Touch me."

"I've got you." He strokes my clit, the gentle exploration making me gasp. "Does it feel good?"

"Yes."

But I need more. I flex my hips into his touch, silently begging him to take it further. As if hearing my pleas, he presses the pad of his thumb to my clit and rubs circles, careful to match his tongue's rhythm on my nipple. A soft whimper escapes me when his fingertips approach my body's entrance.

I clutch his shoulders, and he increases the pressure on my clit, stroking and rubbing until my knees buckle. I'm seconds from climax when he releases my nipple with a loud pop.

"You still with me, baby?"

"Please don't stop."

"Open your legs for me."

I step my feet hip-width apart, desperate for more of his touch.

"No, no, Cupcake." He presses my thighs open, wedging his knees between them so I'm straddling his lap. "When I tell you to open for me," he spreads his legs wide, bringing mine as far apart as they'll go, "I mean like *this*."

I'm naked, completely exposed to him as he eases a long finger inside me. A second one joins, and he pumps them in and out, his thumb massaging my clit.

"Oh, Garrett, *please*."

I never imagined I'd beg a man to touch me or give him free rein of my body, but I've completely surrendered myself to Garrett.

He's rewriting my every rule. The more control I give him, the deeper he embeds himself in my heart.

"You're so wet for me." He grazes his teeth on my shoulder. "Ride my hand how you ride my cock. I want to feel your pussy squeezing my fingers." He massages me inside without easing up on my clit.

I flex my hips into his hand, grinding against his fingers until I explode, gasping his name. He keeps moving, coaxing my body to ecstasy.

"Look at me." His voice is thick with lust, and when our gazes meet, I swear he can see my soul. He cups my jaw. "I want to be so deep inside you, we forget to come up for air."

"Can I hold the reins?"

He places his free hand over his heart. "Always."

I grip his shirt. "First, get naked."

Garrett withdraws his fingers at my command, and I climb to my feet. He swiftly sheds his clothes into a pile on the floor. His powerful body is a thing of beauty, all muscles and ridges. His cock is huge and hard, and I need him inside me.

I point to the middle of the bed. "Kneel."

He scoots to the center and rests on his knees as instructed. I snatch a condom from my bag and tear it open, then crawl up the bed to him. Dipping down, I grip his cock and lick the head. He's leaking for me, the warm saltiness something I never thought I'd like.

"Oh, fuck." His groan reverberates to my clit.

His thigh muscles tighten, and a needy sound escapes him as I bob my head a few times. I take him to the back of my throat, cupping his balls as I move. I only give him a few strokes before pulling back to stare up at him from beneath my lashes.

Wild with lust, he knots his hands in his hair and tugs. "Why'd you stop?"

I brush my lips on the head. "As much as I'd love to suck you off right now, I need you inside me more." I press myself up and roll on the condom. "But don't worry. I promise to blow your mind—and cock—some other time."

"Give me your mouth, Ella."

I clasp the back of his neck and kiss him. Our tongues tangle for a moment before I break off the action again.

Eyes wide, and nostrils flaring, he forces a few breaths. "You're killing me."

"I like you too much to kill you, tesoro." I pivot so my back is to him, then lower myself to all fours. I meet his gaze over my shoulder. "Besides, I'd much rather fuck you."

"Holy shit," he croaks, realizing I'm about to let him take me from behind. "How'd you know this is my favorite position?"

"Because you're intensely primal, and it seems fitting you'd want it this way." Some hedonistic part of me wants to see him unhinged. I give a casual shrug as I grip his cock and line us up. "Let *me* do it until I tell you otherwise. Got it?"

He nods. "Hands off?"

"No. I want you to hold on to me."

His warm palms settle on my hips, and I flex them back, taking the head of his cock inside. I repeat the motion a second time, drawing him even deeper. His breath hisses out of him, and he tightens his hold. The third time, I slam my hips back and take him to the hilt.

"Oh, *fuck*." His fingertips dig into my flesh.

I set a languid pace, fluidly rolling my hips. I'm already sensitive from his fingers, so his thick cock stretching and filling me feels amazing. I arch my back and drop to my elbows, deepening the angle. My movements become jerkier as the pleasure gains traction. My orgasm hovers on the horizon.

"I love watching you take my cock."

The explicit words, uttered with such gritty desire, transform me. Gone is the woman who was content to run the show. I'm ready to hand over the reins. Garrett's in the saddle now, and I want him raw.

Feral.

Unrestrained.

Stilling my hips, I claw at the bedsheets, desperate for the release I need. "You take over," I say on a gasp. "Fuck me."

"How do you want it?"

"Hard." I want to feel him in my chest.

He grabs a fistful of my ass. "Then open your legs, and let that pretty pussy take me deeper."

This time, I spread my legs wide apart at his growled command.

"Yeah, baby, just like that. I wanna see all of you." He trails his fingertips down my crack, circling dangerously close to my ass.

I gasp when he strokes places no one has ever touched. He rubs and teases, the sensations unlike anything I've felt before. Arching my back, I press into his touch.

"You like that?"

"Yes."

"Good to know." He caresses each ass cheek before tightly squeezing the globes. "I'm gonna fuck you now." He rolls his hips in a fluid grind, faster and harder with each rotation. "Tell me to stop if it's too much. You promise to do that for me?" He pulls back slowly and waits.

"Yes."

He surges forward with a groan. "Fuck, you feel good."

"Oh, God, Garrett," I whimper.

"Keep moaning my name. Say it again and again." He pulls back until I'm nearly free of him and circles his hips in a deliberate tease. "I need to hear you."

"Garrett."

He squeezes my ass. "Say it louder."

My legs give out when he slams into me. "*Garrett*."

He lifts my hips back up and falls into a pounding rhythm. His name tumbles from my lips on gasps and whimpers as his thrusts force the air from my lungs.

"Say it." He groans and moves faster, hips slapping where we meet. "Tell me you *know* who's fucking you."

Each thrust takes me higher, my body coiling tighter. Burning hotter.

A little more friction. More pressure.

Until I explode.

"Garrett!" I bite the comforter as I come, my pussy spasming around him. My knees give out as bursts of light and color flash behind my eyes.

His pace doesn't falter. "Who's fucking you, Ella?"

Forty-Two

A climax, a fire, and a motive for murder

Garrett

Ella whimpers my name as her body quakes and shudders. Her pussy's rippling hold on my cock makes me want to roar.

I slam inside her. "Who's fucking you?"

"*Garrett.*" The blanket she's biting muffles her breathless reply.

I tighten my hold on her hips, watching her luscious ass bounce with each thrust. I can't help but give the cheeks another squeeze. This position is my kryptonite.

"Oh, God." She squirms, clawing at the bed until the fitted sheet comes loose. "You're gonna make me come again."

I reach around her to rub her clit. All it takes is a second for her to explode. She writhes beneath me, her throaty moans tightening my balls.

Two more strokes, and I'm gone.

"Ella, honey, fuck." My cock jerks as I lose myself inside her on a guttural groan. I collapse facedown onto the mattress at her side, panting and covered in sweat.

Her head is turned toward me, lips parted as she tries to catch her breath.

Her hair is a wild mess, but it only makes her sexier. Her flushed cheeks give her a luminous glow.

I've never seen a more beautiful woman.

I brush the hair off her face. "Are you okay?"

"Uh-huh." She nods and traces my jawline with her fingertip. "You?"

"Yeah." Unfamiliar feelings swell inside me, making me pull her close. There are a million things I want to say, but I can't find the words, so I tighten my arms around her.

She shifts so she's draped over me, her head resting on my chest. "Your heart's racing."

"Because you're holding it."

"*Ti amo, tesoro.*" The whispered confession flows over me, coating my soul, and soaking into my heart. Her eyes capture mine, and my future dances in those Caribbean-blue depths. "*Tu sei la mia anima gemelli.*"

The first part of her statement echoes in my mind, making me beg every deity that it rings true. She lost me on the second half.

"I don't understand what you're saying, baby."

She kisses my collarbone. "I'll write it down for you later. Then you can look it up if you so choose."

"Let's try this again." Ella sets my plate of carbonara in front of me with a smile. "Do you think you can control yourself this time around?"

"I'm pretty sure you're the one who pounced earlier."

She pops her plate into the microwave. "Did you try to stop me?"

"Fuck no. That's crazy talk. I'll let you climb up my body all day long."

She sweeps her gaze over me. "I can't help it. You drive me wild."

"Ditto, Cupcake." I point to the white T-shirt she's got on. She's not wearing anything beneath it, and the outlines of her hardened nipples tease me through the fabric. "You look sexy as fuck in my shirt."

"Thanks." She juts her chin at me. "We match."

While I'd love to walk around shirtless, I don't want her to see the scarring on my back. It's a heavy conversation I don't want to have right now. Feeling safer covered up, I pulled on a shirt and boxers after my shower.

The microwave beeps, and she withdraws her plate, smiling as she makes her approach. "I'm so hungry." She settles beside me, scooting her stool closer to the island. The motion sends droplets from her damp hair onto her chest, making it even easier to see her body.

"You're so fucking beautiful."

She flushes. "Eat your food, tesoro."

The pasta tastes even more amazing after exertion. We eat in silence, both too famished to talk.

I rest my palm on her bare knee after I finish. "That was absolutely delicious. You are a culinary goddess, my sweet."

"Thank you. I'm glad you enjoyed it. I'm always happy to cook for you." She traces the veins of my hand. "Did you add more wood to the fire?"

"Sure did." I squeeze her knee. "We can eat our cupcakes in front of it."

"I can't believe we haven't touched them yet." She glances at the microwave clock. "I was sure we'd have at least two gone by now."

"The night is young." I stand and grab our plates, then motion toward the living room. "Go warm up. I'll take care of the dishes."

Ella joins me at the sink, pulling the dish towel from its hook. "It'll go faster if we do it together."

With me washing and her drying, we complete our task in no time. We head for the living room, ready to relax by the fire.

She plops onto the love seat and tucks her legs beneath her. "This is lovely."

Settling beside her, I study her face. "What are the rules for right now?"

"There aren't any."

"That means I'm free to hold you?"

"Of course."

I drape my arm over her shoulders, and pull her close, kissing the top of her head. We stare at the dancing flames in comfortable silence. She feels so right, snuggled up against me. I don't want this weekend to end. I want her to always be in my arms.

Visions of her on her knees in front of me hijack my brain. How she arched her back and spread her legs wide for me. How her lush ass bounced with my thrusts, and the way she reacted when I let my fingers wander. She hasn't learned all her body's secrets yet. I can't wait to help her uncover them.

It felt so fucking good to hold on to her hips and really let loose. I worried I'd be too intense, but she took my cock like it was made for her. I loved watching it stretch and fill her pussy.

I shift position, adjusting myself as I move. "Ella."

She looks up at me. "Hmm?"

"I, uh, just want to clarify something. Earlier, in the bedroom, I didn't make you say my name because I'm one of those dudes who get off on hearing it. That's not me. I mean, don't get me wrong, I definitely enjoyed hearing it, but that wasn't why I kept asking you." I clear my throat to stop myself from rambling. "I needed to hear my name because I couldn't see your eyes."

"My eyes?"

"Yeah. I had no way to gauge whether you were in the present. I needed to make sure you knew it was *me* and not the man who hurt you."

She takes both of my hands in hers. "Oh, I knew it was you, Garrett." She bites her lower lip and releases a shaky breath. "With every thrust."

I tip her chin up and search her eyes. "Did I push you too far? You're a quiet lover, so, like I said, it's hard to gauge."

"You pushed me, but it never reached a level I was uncomfortable with. I would've told you to stop. Besides, that was never the offending position. It was always missionary." She looks away. "That's the one I can't handle."

A sinking feeling creeps into my gut. "When you say it was *always* missionary, are you telling me it happened more than once?"

Her eyes meet mine, and the pain I see inside them takes my breath away. "Truthfully, I lost track of how many times it happened. I stopped counting at a hundred." She shakes her head. "But it was always the same—his heavy weight on top of me, crushing me into the mattress."

I open and close my mouth a few times, but no words come out. Her revelation eviscerates me.

"And as for being a quiet lover, well, I guess that's a learned behavior."

I blink through my shock and tilt my head to the side, still speechless.

"I lost my virginity with a knife to my throat. Making noise was never an option for me."

A wave of nausea slams through me as I process her statement. My pulse throbs in my ears. I clench and unclench my fists, ready to hunt the motherfucker down and bludgeon him.

"Who is he?"

Give me five minutes alone with the man and I'll peel the flesh from his body. Chop off his dick and feed it to him. And then, while he chokes on his own cock, I'll set him on fire and watch him burn.

"That's not something I'll ever tell you, so please don't ask." She squeezes her eyes shut. "I'll take his identity to my grave." She stares into the flames once more. "Besides, it was a really long time ago."

I need to know more. Who is he, and more importantly, why is she protecting him? Bottom line, I need to find the motherfucker and make him pay for what he did.

"How old were you?" My voice is rough and foreign.

"It started a few weeks after I turned thirteen, but I endured it for almost four years." Her hollow tone slices through me. "That's why I'm so fucked up. Childhood trauma has a way of doing that to a person."

Thirteen.

Just like me.

Her face gets blurry. My rapid blinks do nothing to stop my eyes from burning. I pull her close, like my hug has the power to erase what she told me, but I know better than that. Just like my demons still haunt me, she'll never be free from those memories.

I rest my chin on top of her head to hide my watery eyes. "I'm so fucking sorry."

"Don't be sorry. You're the first person who makes me want to *live* instead of just exist."

"You do the same for me." A tear drips onto her hair, soaking into the soft mocha strands. I hold her tighter as another one rolls down my cheek. I'm not a crier, but I'm so torn up by what she told me, I could fucking weep.

Four years. The bastard raped her for four *years*.

Forty-Three

Tears, a fire, and old scars

Ella

Garrett tightens his hold on me and draws a ragged breath. His body shudders, making me look up at him. A tear slides from beneath his closed lids, his expression twisted in pain.

"Tesoro," I whisper, touching his cheek.

He opens his eyes but doesn't say anything.

"Are you all right?" I didn't anticipate his strong reaction to my truth. Especially when others didn't believe me.

"I'm good." He drags a hand over his face to wipe the tears. Red-rimmed golden orbs meet mine. "The smoke is burning my eyes."

"There's hardly any smoke. It's all going up the chimney."

"I guess I'm, uh, overly sensitive to some things." He clenches his jaw and stares into the fire.

"Look at me." I wait for our gazes to lock before speaking. "I didn't tell you to make you upset."

"I know." He reaches for my hand and interlaces our fingers. "I wish I could go back in time and prevent it from happening to you."

"I appreciate you saying that."

"I want justice for you."

I shake my head. "I don't need justice. I need peace."

"How does someone have peace without justice?"

"I created my own by cutting ties with my past. I reinvented what I knew of myself and redirected my focus. The only way I've been able to survive is by burying my pain and moving forward. That's how I find peace, Garrett. By *surviving*."

"But that's like sticking a Band-Aid on gangrene. The wounds still fester."

"Maybe." Shrugging, I stare into the fire again. "But when a Band-Aid is your only option, you use it."

He squeezes my hand tighter. "I will *always* give you options."

"You've already more than demonstrated that."

"What else can I do? What would bring you more peace?"

"Keep being the man you are." I cup his cheeks, peering deep into his eyes. "The healing started when I met you."

"Ella, I—"

I silence him with my lips. The kiss sends fire through my veins and my body takes over. I press on his shoulders, making him lie back. I follow without breaking our kiss, and move to straddle his hips, plastering my body to the front of him.

Like always, he allows me to lead, his lips and tongue moving to the rhythm I've set. He hardens beneath me. Rearing up, I pull at his shirt, tugging it off him. He does the same with mine, and our lips meet once more. The warmth from his bare chest radiates into me.

We kiss like we've never been hurt. His hands roam up and down my back. I grind against him, desperate to feel him inside me again.

It seems ironic that sex is my love language. The very thing that once hurt me is what I now crave most.

Garrett grips my ass and flexes his hips against me. "I want you so fucking bad."

I shove his boxers down, freeing his cock. "I'm on the pill, and I trust you."

"I trust you too." He rolls his hips, dragging his shaft through the wetness gathered between my thighs.

Our lips connect, and I swallow his groan as he slides into me. He feels so warm, so perfect, inside me. He digs his fingertips into my ass cheeks while moving his hips with mine.

I need him deeper, so I widen my legs and grind into his upward thrusts. He moans and holds me tighter, his kiss growing more urgent by the second. My clit rubs against his pubic bone and my body grips his cock, but I want more. No, I *need* more.

This is what desperation feels like.

Two souls, meant to intertwine, tightly coiling together. The closer we get, the more heat we make.

The flames burn brighter and hotter until I shatter, gasping his name. He bucks his hips wildly beneath me, carrying me through my climax until he's ready to blow.

"Look at me." His low growl commands my attention.

The thrusting stops, and his body goes rigid. He squeezes my ass, pulling me deeper as he pours himself inside me.

I will never tire of watching this man come. I love how his golden orbs seem to deepen in color when he detonates, and how he holds my gaze like our eyes share the secrets we aren't ready for our lips to reveal. Our souls lay themselves bare every time our bodies come together. The current flowing between us is charged with unspoken promises. Confessions and affirmations. Everything we're afraid of latching on to. We crave acceptance, healing, and love. We yearn for understanding. That ache, in its purest of forms, manifests as hope.

Bold, beautiful hope. It's something I've only recently become acquainted with. Lying here, watching it flicker to life in the gilded mirror beneath me, is the greatest gift I've ever been given.

It means he feels it too. He's starting to trust the promises his heart is making. He believes we can be something together.

I tighten my muscles around him, as if answering his silent pleas. He's etched himself into my heart, and I want to hold on to him forever.

With Garrett, I dare to hope.

"Tesoro," I whisper, stroking my thumb over his lower lip. "*Tu sei la mia anima gemelli.*"

You are my soul mate.

I lurch upward in bed, escaping the clutches of a horrible nightmare. Someone was being tortured, and I couldn't save them. Rubbing my eyes, I blink in the darkness and try to catch my breath.

Agonized moans reach my ears, and it takes me a moment to realize I wasn't dreaming. The torture is real, and it's coming from the man in bed beside me.

I flick on the nightstand lamp.

Garrett's curled on his side, gasping, and covered in sweat. His eyes are scrunched closed, tears seeping from beneath his lids. "Please stop." The terror in his voice makes my blood run cold. "*Please.*"

"Garrett." I stroke my hand up and down his arm. "You're having a bad dream. Wake up, tesoro."

He groans and rolls to his stomach, then pulls his legs beneath him, balling himself up like a terrified armadillo. "Mama, help me."

Unable to witness another moment of his suffering, I shift to my knees and scoot closer. "Garrett, wake up. It's just a night—"

My mouth drops open when I see them.

Dozens of small, round scars cover his back. Some white and flat. Others pink and raised. Spaced out, and in clusters, they mar his beautiful olive skin.

We've been naked together. How is it possible I haven't seen them before now? It dawns on me that I never had the opportunity to explore his body because I was always on top. The only time we changed positions, he was behind me. Now I understand why he insisted on wearing a shirt after his shower. He went to bed with it on but must've stripped it off in his sleep.

"No!" He tucks himself even tighter, like he'd crawl into the mattress if he could.

Tears fill my eyes, blurring the marks, as a sickening realization settles in my stomach. This isn't a nightmare—it's a flashback. Sean did this. That monster repeatedly held a lit cigarette to his back. These scars serve as evidence of his torture. A constant reminder.

I've noticed how Garrett looks over his shoulder and sits with his back to a wall. I've seen the way he scans a room as if searching for the nearest exit. How his phone and keys are never far from reach. I haven't missed his flinches and the shadows that darken his features whenever someone mentions childhood. Like me, his torment continues to haunt him, even after two decades. It's no wonder he turned to alcohol.

"Oh, tesoro." My hand flies up to stifle my sob.

I crawl around him to get a better view, pausing near his butt. My heart clenches, and another sob escapes me, knowing the agony he endured. I stroke my hands up and down his back like my touch can erase the marks. Soothe his pain and heal him.

I'd give up my soul if it meant I could've saved him from this atrocity. How could someone do this to a child? What kind of sick fuck inflicts this harm on an innocent? There's a special circle of hell for people like Sean. I'd love the opportunity to send him there.

My tears drip onto Garrett's skin as I count the scars, pressing a kiss to each one.

He unfurls his body, extending his legs so he's lying flat on his stomach. "Thirty-seven."

I cling to him tighter as my heart cracks down the middle. I keep pressing kisses to his back until my lips have touched all thirty-seven scars. I repeat the cycle a second time, then drape myself over his body, unable to stop my tears from flowing.

Forty-Four

Shame, healing, and coupledom

Garrett

Scars tell a story. For most people, they represent minor injuries and mishaps from the past. Like that one on your knee from when you fell off your bike the first time after you *insisted* you didn't need training wheels anymore. The one on your finger from when you thought you'd help your mother chop vegetables but stupidly grabbed the knife by the blade. Or the one on your arm from that time you tried to befriend a feral cat. I have plenty of those scars. The normal, benign reminders of childhood stupidity. Little boo-boos that healed quickly but still left their mark as lessons learned. I wish all of mine were that innocuous. My body is a trauma roadmap, full of dead ends and detours. Bent signs and rusty mile markers. From the wounds I inflicted on myself, cutting to chase away my pain, to the ones from Sean's wrath, my skin is marred with postcards from the road trip to hell.

Before tonight, Lena was the only woman who ever shed a tear over my scars. Carissa never gave a fuck. She simply handed me a list of plastic surgeons and urged me to "do something about it," like there was a magic eraser that could give me a flawless body. Her reaction was the polar opposite of my best friend's compassion. Lena helped her mother clean my wounds and change my dressings after I got out of the hospital. I remember how hard she cried when she rubbed burn salve on the raw, charred blisters. The experience awakened a protective ferocity inside her, and she credits those few months of my recovery as the reason she became a nurse.

Feeling Ella draped over me like a warm blanket, her tears soaking into my skin as she kissed each mark twice, was the comfort I didn't know I needed. My breathing and heart rate return to normal. The tension eases out of my body, and my demons retreat to the dark corners of my mind.

So, this is what it's like to be cherished instead of abandoned and dismissed. Her nickname for me means treasure. That's how she treats me—like I matter. My pain, fears, and desires all *matter* to Ella. Her concern for me is genuine. Her affection is real. With her, I hold value.

I am enough.

I didn't know it was possible to fall for someone in the span of a day. It seemed so unrealistic before I met her, like the shit in fairy tales. I'm not used to happy endings. My reality breeds wolves and warlocks. Monsters who eat your heart and steal your soul. The kind of evil that breaks you. How is it possible a woman who's as broken as I am holds the power to put me back together? And how the fuck have I survived this long without her?

"Thank you for caring." For a big man, my voice is awfully small right now. "It means a lot to me."

"I wish I could make them go away." The pain in her voice tells me it isn't because she finds me hideous. No, this is true empathy.

"Me too." I turn my head to the side, finding her watery gaze. "I'm sorry you had to see me like that. It's been a long time since my last nightmare. I think our talk earlier stirred things up in my head."

"Never apologize for something you can't control." Her fingertips travel my skin, feathering over the marks. "I hate that you have to see these permanent reminders of what he did to you."

"Yeah." I fiddle with the edge of my pillowcase. "And those are just the visible scars."

She rolls off my back and lounges beside me so she can look at my face. "When you say that, do you mean there are more hidden from view, or are you referring to psychological trauma?"

"Both."

"Did he burn you other places?"

"No. Those are the only burns, thankfully." The compassion in her eyes coaxes the truth from my lips. "The rest of my scar tissue is internal. Like I told you, we have much more in common than you realize."

"Oh, God," she whispers, as the pieces fit themselves together in her mind. Squeezing her eyes shut, she pulls me closer. "Please tell me he didn't."

I burrow my head beneath the pillow, suddenly unable to look her in the eyes. Or speak.

I'll talk about most of the crazy shit I've experienced, like my mental health struggles and my battle with alcoholism. My parents' suicides and the repercussions I suffered. The Carissa fiasco and my subsequent tailspin. My own suicide attempts.

But *that* incident? The shame still silences me, even after twenty years. The memories live in the darkest recesses of my soul, and I will do everything in my power to keep them buried there. I don't discuss the details with Lena, my psychiatrist, or anyone else, because I'm determined to carry the burden myself. That's how I've survived—by suppressing my torment and shouldering the weight of my truth. Over the years I've learned pain, fear, and self-loathing are heavy as fuck.

Ella knows the physical and emotional aftermath of sexual assault. She understands the irreparable harm another person can inflict. We've seen the same darkness. Though it goes against two decades' worth of self-preservation, I want her to know all the parallels we share. I need her to *know*, beyond the shadow of a doubt, that she's safe with me.

She removes the pillow from my head and gently runs her fingers through my hair. "I've found peace without justice. You got justice but haven't found peace."

"I don't think I ever will."

"Believe me, I get it. Like I said earlier, that's why you have to create your own peace."

"Is it wrong to want vengeance too? Am I a shitty person for hoping he gets his in prison?" I roll to face her, the confessions pouring from my lips. "For years I've fantasized about him getting his ass kicked by other inmates. Being shanked in the yard. Jumped in a bathroom. Having someone do to him what he did to me. I want him to suffer a horrible death, so I can be the first person to piss on his grave. Does that make me as much of a monster as him?"

"No, I think those feelings are natural." She brushes the hair back from my face, then strokes my cheek, her touch so tender it makes my eyes burn.

"I've had them too. My emotions have run the gamut from anger to acceptance. I've gone through denial and grief. Sadness. Fear. Shame." She shakes her head. "People don't understand what it's like unless they've gone through it themselves or had it happen to someone close to them. They can't fathom why it's so difficult to talk about. I wish more people would realize not everyone has the freedom—or desire—to speak up."

"Yeah." I rub my jaw, annoyed by the whiskers that showed up in a matter of hours. My eyes find hers and hold her gaze. "Please don't share what I've told you with anyone. Lena, Connor, and my doctor are the only other people in my life who know, and I'd like to keep it that way. I told you because you make me want to bare my soul."

"You make me want to bare mine too," she whispers, pressing her hand to her chest. "And I promise I won't breathe a word to anyone."

"Thanks." I hold out my open palm to her, and she clasps my hand, interlacing our fingers. "I want you to feel safe with me, Ella. I need you to trust that I will always follow your rules and give you options. I may fuck up now and then, but I'll never hurt you. Please tell me you believe that of me."

"I do."

"Good." A relieved sigh deflates my chest. "Listen, I know this is technically our first date, so it's probably a bit early for this conversation, but I need to know where we stand."

It's also the middle of the night. But, since she already witnessed me in the throes of a nightmare, and now knows my darkest secrets, it feels appropriate to make things even more weird. Go big or go home, right?

"Are you asking if we're a couple?"

"Yeah, I guess I am." I clear my throat. "I realize it's kinda awkward—"

She holds a finger to my lips. "I have no experience with relationships. If anyone's awkward, it's me. And if I recall, we already discussed being exclusive."

"Exclusivity is different from coupledom. We agreed to only have sex with each other, but I want more than that." I squeeze the hand I'm holding and brush my thumb over her knuckles. "I want to *share* time with you. Heal and comfort each other. Do mundane shit like laundry and grocery shopping together. I want us to learn new things and reexperience old things. Replace our shitty memories with positive ones. Make our own rules. *And* have lots of wild sex."

"That is exactly what I want, Garrett."

I can't stop the grin from overtaking my face. "So, that means you're officially my woman now?"

She cups my jaw. "As long as we get to eat those cupcakes tomorrow, I'll be anything you want me to be."

Sitting up, I throw the covers off us. "Why wait 'til tomorrow?" I point to the nightstand clock. "It technically *is* tomorrow."

Her eyes widen. "Garrett, it's three o'clock in the morning. You want cupcakes *now?*"

"Yes, the fuck, I *do.* Is there a rule stating desserts of the frosted variety may only be consumed between the hours of noon and eight p.m.? Hurry now, Edgar, fetch me the tea and crumpets before it's too late. Oh, bollocks. We've missed our opportunity."

My mock British accent makes her laugh. She pokes me in the side. "No, I don't have any rules about desserts."

"Then you're gonna fucking love mine." I stand and gesture to the door. "C'mon."

She scoots off the bed, her eyes darting between us. "But we're naked."

"Naked cupcakes are the best kind."

Forty-Five

Naked cupcakes, a nickname, and a premonition

Ella

If I ever open a bakery, I think I'll call it Naked Cupcakes.

I admire Garrett's perfect ass while following him to the cabin's kitchen, barely resisting the urge to squeeze it.

He retrieves the box of cupcakes from the fridge and sets it on the counter. "Okay, you've got fourteen options. Make that thirteen. I forgot there are two Moaning Mango ones."

"Which do you suggest?"

"That might be the toughest question you've ever asked me." He rubs his jaw. "Let's see. The only ones I haven't tried are Amaretto Afterglow and Tie-Me-Up Tiramisu, for obvious reasons. All the other ones are phenomenal, so it's incredibly hard to choose. I guess it depends on what you're in the mood for."

"Which one's calling to you most? Maybe your decision will help me make mine."

"Currently, it's a toss-up between Gimme S'More Lovin' and Red-Hot Red Velvet." He purses his lips, considering them both. "I think I'll start with the red velvet one. The cream cheese frosting is to die for, and Geneva adds a creamy center that's so good it makes my eyes cross." He grins, lifting his selection from the box. "Don't worry. I'll share."

I peruse the list. "Strawberry Sex Swing? Caramel Kama Sutra? Cannoli Be You? These names crack me up."

"I know, right? So, this is some cool trivia for you. Geneva is actually a twin. Her sister, Lorelei, owns a sex-themed dessert café upstate called Oral Fixation. They created some of the recipes together. While Geneva limits her sexy stuff at Compass Roasters to cupcakes, Lorelei does it all. In fact, customers must be over eighteen to dine there because shit gets wildly inappropriate. I stopped in one time to check it out. The servers literally talk dirty to you when describing the menu, which is full of scandalously named treats. I mean things like, 'Come For Me Carrot Cake' and 'Multiple Orgasm Cream Pie,' which is amazing, by the way. She's even got dick-shaped cookies—aptly named 'dickies'—and pussy replica cinnamon buns."

"We should go there," I suggest, more than a little intrigued by the concept.

"Oh, we definitely will. They're closed on Sundays, so we'll have to plan another trip up here."

"I'd love that." The idea of future adventures with Garrett makes me giddy. I point to another cupcake name in the Compass Roasters pamphlet. "What on earth is The River?"

"That's a specialty one named after an elite New York City sex club, which you may or may not have heard of because it's not open to the public."

I know of the club, its provocative owner, and her partners through my dealings with the organizers of Burlesquerade. From the whisperings I've heard, Esme DaVinci runs a secret society of sex-positive female business owners with a common goal of empowering women. My friend Jenna is a club member. She's invited me many times, but I've never ventured to The River. I'm curious how much Garrett knows about the discreet establishment.

I peer up at his face. "Tell me more."

"Well, to an outsider, The River is simply a water-themed nightclub. Vetted members, however, have access to the *pleasure* spa, which is essentially a kink club that caters primarily to women."

"Sounds intriguing," I murmur, although I'm not sure I could handle what goes on there. I point to the cupcake. "How does that represent the club?"

"It's a flourless chocolate lava cake, covered in fudgy ganache. When you bite into it, a river of liquid chocolate flows over your tongue."

"Wow."

"Yeah, the club's owner approached Geneva about creating a signature cupcake for their Valentine's Day event last year. They were such a hit, she kept them on her regular menu, and the club added them to their dessert bar."

Garrett's knowledge of the place makes me wonder if he's ever waded into those waters. Since we're officially a couple now, I figure it's my place to ask.

I search his face. "Have you ever gone to The River?"

"Me? No." He shakes his head. "My office manager, Juliana, is a member. She's told me all about it, and by that, I mean the stuff that's *not* protected by The River's nondisclosure agreement."

"Wait. You talk about sex at work?"

"Jules has no filter. And you know how blunt I am. So, yeah, the topic comes up from time to time. Jules and I were friends before she started working for me though. That's why we talk about shit that's not appropriate for work. I keep things professional with everyone else. Except for Nate-Dawg, naturally."

"Would you ever go there?" I ask, eyeing him.

He shrugs. "Maybe, but I doubt they'd let me in. Jules said there's a huge waiting list and a fuckload of prerequisites for membership. Like I said, it's exclusive. And expensive."

I nod, returning my attention to the cupcake list. "What is Chocolate Chip Foreplay?"

"Chocolate chip cookie dough." He flashes a mischievous grin. "Because it's cookie foreplay. *Duh.*"

I laugh and pinch his ass. "Some of us know nothing about foreplay, thank you very much. My experience is limited to what we've done together."

He blinks. "Really?"

"Yes, really."

"Hold on. You're saying I'm the *first* dude to finger fuck you?"

Heat crawls up my cheeks, and my body clenches with remembered pleasure. "Garrett, you're the first man I've ever *allowed* to touch my breasts or between my legs. So, to answer your question, yes, you're the first one to finger fuck me."

"I'm confused. You've slept with Pasquale. Are you saying he didn't touch you?" Shock colors his tone.

I roll my eyes. "Pasquale? What is wrong with you men? He does the same thing with your name."

"Oh, does he? I'm curious what your Italian buddy says about me."

"Jealous much?"

"Maybe."

"First of all, his name is Paolo. And if you must know, I only allowed limited touching. Basically, I let him put his hands on my waist while I rode him."

"Interesting." He circles me, his gaze roaming my naked body, lingering on my pussy. "So, Pietro didn't go down on you then?"

"Absolutely not. I've never let *Paolo*, or anyone else, do that. My abuser wasn't concerned with my pleasure. Oral sex is the one thing he never forced on me. I think that's why it feels so sacred. It's the only first I still have left to share with someone." I straighten my spine. "But it's far more intimate than anything I'd ever be comfortable with."

Garrett stops in front of me, and the smile that curves his lips is pure sin. "I've got news for you, Cupcake. One day, you'll ask me to."

I roll my eyes, pulling the cannoli-flavored dessert from the box. "Keep telling yourself that."

"Do you wanna know *why* I call you Cupcake?" He licks his lips. "Out of all the world's possible nicknames, do you know why I selected that one in particular?"

Now that he mentions it, I am curious. It does seem off the beaten path as far as pet names are concerned.

I raise an eyebrow. "Because you think I'm sweet?"

He shakes his head and holds up his cupcake. "From the moment I saw you at Jake's gala, I wanted to unwrap you." He slowly peels the wrapper down, like he's undressing the cake, and traces his finger over the ridges left by the paper. "I wanted to know your secrets."

"My secrets?"

"I imagined tasting every inch of you." Eyes locked with mine, he lifts the cupcake to his lips, then slowly, deliberately, drags his tongue through the frosting.

His moan hardens my nipples, and my lungs stop functioning. My pussy becomes wetter by the second, watching him swirl and flick his tongue. He twists the cupcake in his hand until he's licked it clean of frosting, then takes a bite, his molten gaze burning into me while he chews.

He swallows and steps closer to me. "I want to make your body come apart in my mouth."

"Is that so?" My breathy voice makes me sound like a phone sex operator.

"I'll make it so fucking good for you, Ella." Breaking the cupcake in half, he plunges his tongue into its creamy center and goes to town, lapping at its core.

I can't stop my gasp. Heat blooms in my lower belly and my inner muscles quiver. The visual alone makes me swear I can *feel* his tongue on my clit. My breasts rise and fall with each breath, and I can barely remain upright. I can't imagine what it would be like having his face between my thighs.

Garrett looks up at me and licks the frosting from his lips. "I'll make you come so many times, my name will be your new favorite prayer." He dives back in, and his eyes flutter closed. This time, his moan is deeper and more primal, matching his tongue's enthusiasm.

"Holy fuck," I whisper.

He lifts his head, wiping his mouth with the back of his hand. "And when your pussy can't handle any more of my tongue, you'll come on my cock."

He pops a chunk of red velvet into his mouth, watching me while he chews.

I prop my hands on my hips and pivot my body toward him, drawing his attention to my breasts. "I thought you were going to share. You did all that teasing, and now you plan to leave me hanging?"

He breaks off some cake and brings it to my lips. "That wasn't teasing, baby."

"Oh? Then what was it?" I go out of my way to lick his fingers as I accept his offering.

Heat flares in his eyes. They dart to his cock, then meet mine once more as he hardens between us. "Call it a premonition."

"What, exactly, do you think you're prophesying?" I know damn well what he's talking about, but his dirty talk turns me on.

Garrett doesn't just use innuendo; he drops explicit truth bombs, his words splintering my expectations. He shatters the ceiling of my lust with every wicked statement, pushing me higher and hotter than I thought possible. I've never felt a desire this potent.

Right now, I want more shrapnel.

I trail my fingertips down his chest. "Besides, you haven't shown me your crystal ball."

"I'll show you any ball you wanna see, Cupcake."

"Tell me more about these visions you speak of."

"Which one do you wanna hear about? They all involve my tongue in your pussy." His words send a flood of heat between my legs.

"Whichever comes to mind first."

"I want you to sit on my face," he presses his palms to his cheeks, "so I can feel your soft thighs hugging me."

"That won't be happen—"

"Or I can spread you out on the table and eat you like a feast." He points to his ears. "Trust me, I'll lick your pussy so good, you'll hold on to these and pull me even closer." His eyes sweep over me. "Imagine it, baby. Me sucking on your clit, thrusting my tongue deep inside you, making you scream my name. What do you think would happen if I added a finger or two?"

I can't breathe or think, let alone answer.

"I bet you'd pull my head closer." He feeds me more red velvet. "Like I said, one day you'll ask me to do all those things to you."

"Will I?"

"You will." He brushes his fingertips along my jawline, tipping my head up so he can stare into my eyes. "And that's a fucking promise."

"I like promises," I murmur, eyeing the rest of his cupcake. "Especially when they come from you."

"Likewise."

I suck his finger into my mouth when he feeds me another bite. "Mmm-mmm-*mmm*."

The man is a picture of lust, from his pupils and parted lips to his heaving chest and taut abdomen. He doesn't reach for me or move closer. He waits, arms at his sides and eyes focused on my face.

Pleased I've got him under my spell now, I hold up my cupcake. "Want some?"

"Yes." He swallows. "To every possible meaning behind your question."

Smiling, I peel the wrapper and bite into my treat with a moan. "I *love* cannoli."

"I've got one you're more than welcome to."

"Good to know." I point to the stool behind him. "Have a seat."

He settles with his back to the counter and rests his elbows on the granite. We're eye to eye now, and the heat in his could burn down the cabin.

I swipe my finger through the frosting and bring it to his lips. "Open up, tesoro."

He complies immediately, licking and sucking the cannoli cream off me. I remove my finger with a loud pop, then gather more frosting. His mouth drops open to accept it, but I smear it on his nipples instead. Leaning forward, I press a trail of kisses from his collarbone to a nipple, then lick the frosting off. I give him a hard suck just because I can.

"Oh, *fuck.*" His head lolls back as I lick my way to his other nipple.

"Keep your hands off and let me love you." Pressing his knees apart, I drop to mine in front of him.

Our gazes meet, and his widens when I plop some frosting on the tip of his cock. I grip him, licking and sucking until the frosting is gone.

Then I do it again.

Garrett's legs shake on either side of me. "You're killing me, El."

I abandon my cupcake on the counter, then take him to the back of my throat. His breath rushes out on a groan, making me feel like a goddess. It's a heady power I wield, sucking the most sensitive part of his body. I enjoy having him in my mouth almost as much as I love feeling him fill me.

Almost.

My pussy clenches in agreement, and I bob my head a few more times before rising. "I'm really selfish, so I need to stop now."

"Huh?" His bewildered gaze begs me to keep sucking him. "Why?"

"Because I want you inside me."

"Then what the fuck are you waiting for? Get on my dick."

"I suppose since you worded it so eloquently . . ." I climb into his lap, facing him. Our shared moans fill the kitchen when I slide down onto him.

I roll my hips in a slow grind, the delicious friction igniting me.

But I want more.

"Put your hands on me, Garrett."

"Thought you'd never ask." He wraps me in his arms and tugs my body close.

I love how his hugs envelop me in warmth. There's safety in Garrett's arms, understanding and trust. And judging by how he strokes my back so tenderly, I'd dare say his embrace holds affection too.

That possibility makes my heart soar.

"New rule. My man is allowed to touch me, unless I tell him otherwise."

"Another great decree." He slides his hands to my ass and squeezes, pulling me deeper into his lap.

I reach for the cupcake and bite into it once more. Instead of feeding Garrett a morsel, I leave the rest of the cake behind and kiss him. Deeply. Like I want to crawl inside him. I wrap my arms around his neck, weaving my fingers into his silky hair. Using the stool's rungs to brace my heels, I move my body up and down while we kiss.

I crave this connection we share. He fills me so fully, so perfectly. Not to mention what he's doing to my heart.

"New rule. Never stop kissing me."

"I'm more than happy to make that a reality." He threads his fingers into my hair and cups the back of my head, deepening our kiss. He takes the lead, licking into my mouth like he's starved for me.

Our lips taste like mascarpone and lovemaking. Surrender and freedom. Indulgence and healing. Rich, creamy decadence that curls my toes. This kiss is different from all the ones before. Maybe it's because we've learned more about each other, divulging some of our darkest secrets. Or perhaps it's because he's my man now. Whatever the reason, as his tongue urgently slides against mine, a peculiar and wonderful thought settles in my head.

We'll serve cupcakes at our wedding.

Forty-Six

A tangled web, an escort, and a request

Ella

I stare at the lit buttons on the elevator's control panel, the butterflies in my belly going haywire. How will I tolerate watching Garrett and Tess together without letting on that it bothers me? How will I be able to keep my hands—and lips—off him while being in the same room?

I haven't seen him since he dropped me off at my apartment yesterday evening, after an amazing Sunday together upstate. We slept in, had breakfast in bed, then had more mind-blowing sex before touring the countryside.

When I mentioned my love of architectural photography, he took me to dozens of sites in Ulster County. I photographed churches galore and several bridges. We stopped in the historic city of Kingston, so I could see the Senate House, and a Dutch church that has been around since the mid-1600s. We even visited an old-fashioned covered bridge on our way to New Paltz. Then, we crossed the Hudson and had dinner at a world-famous culinary school.

This past weekend was the best experience of my life, and I look forward to sharing many more adventures with Garrett.

We both agreed it would be best to keep things professional at the theater. Our involvement may be viewed as a conflict of interest when it comes to producing the documentary. I've lived my whole life with discretion. Why does it seem so impossible now?

Lance waves his hand in front of my face. "Hello? Did you hear me?"

"I'm sorry, I completely missed what you said."

"I asked if you think Garrett is fully healed from his concussion."

"I'm sure he's fine. Otherwise, they wouldn't have cleared him to return to work and rehearsals."

He also had no trouble fucking my brains out, but I keep that little morsel to myself.

The doors slide open, and we head for the meeting room. I force a deep breath and follow Lance inside. Everyone's gathered around Professor Crane's desk, chatting excitedly.

My eyes lock with Garrett's, and he gives me a secret smile, melting my insides.

"Ah, it's the woman of the hour." Tom's boisterous greeting surprises me. "We were just talking about you."

"Oh? And why might that be?"

"We were discussing the most beautiful theaters in the country. Garrett said you mentioned being from Santa Barbara, so we were curious if you've been to the Granada Theatre?"

My stomach bottoms out when my lie comes back to bite me in the ass. I've never even been to Santa Barbara, let alone visited the venue. But I *did* tell Garrett that's where I'm from.

I lied to the man I love.

Of course, we didn't know each other when I gave the fabricated birthplace, but it sickens me now, knowing I've been dishonest with him. Bile rises in my throat when I remember Santa Barbara isn't the only detail I haven't been truthful about. I told him my mother is dead. She may be dead to me, but she's still very much alive, somewhere in Philadelphia. I also conveniently left out the part about me *being* a mother. Given his issues with abandonment, I'm sure learning I gave up my child won't be well-received news.

Look at me, all tangled up in the web I've woven. One thing's for damn sure, I need to right these wrongs as soon as fucking possible. Garrett deserves my honesty.

I have no clue how I'll do it, but sooner rather than later I need to tell him my *entire* story—not just the parts I want him to know.

Everyone stares expectantly. Meeting my gaze, Garrett tilts his head to the side and lifts an eyebrow.

Right. I'm supposed to speak.

I clear my throat. "Sorry. I had to think for a moment. No, I haven't been there."

Tom nods. "That's too bad. The next time you make a trip home, you'll have to check it out."

"I'll be sure to."

Another lie. How easily they tumble from my lips.

He claps twice, making me jump. "All right, people. How about we get down to business?"

Lance and I observe from the room's perimeter as a dark-haired guy with piercing blue eyes takes his place at Garrett's side. They're joined by Tess and another blond woman. I've met both actors, but I'm so unsettled by the Santa Barbara discussion, I can't remember their names for the life of me.

"If I'm not wrong, Emmett and Taryn are the understudies for Xavier and Annaca's characters," Lance murmurs, as if reading my mind.

"Yes, that's right. I'm sure Tom wants to whip them into shape after what happened with Garrett."

Tom addresses the pair, "I trust you two have been practicing your lines?"

"Oh, absolutely." Emmett motions to Taryn. "We upped our game after Garrett got hurt."

"Sorry for fucking up our time line." The embarrassment in Garrett's tone makes me want to hug him.

Tom waves him off. "You relax. We've got plenty of time."

The musical director approaches, and the cast practices *Prodigy's* opening number, filling the room with song.

Goose bumps bloom on my skin, listening to everyone harmonize. Despite the number of people singing, I can easily pick my man's voice out of the crowd. It's so deep and rich, like everything about him.

Before Garrett, I didn't think love was in the cards for me. It seemed like a mathematical impossibility to meet someone who truly understands what I've been through. He comprehends my pain, not because he's an empathetic human being, but because he *lived* it. I'm still reeling from the revelation he made in the wee hours of Sunday morning. He didn't share any details, but the shame that radiated from him broke my heart.

Seeing his scars, and knowing the invisible trauma his cousin inflicted, awakened the protective warrior inside me. I can't change Garrett's past, but I'll do everything in my power to make sure no one ever hurts him again.

While he hasn't come right out and said it, it's obvious he blames his mother for what happened to him. Her abandonment was the catalyst for his torment, a pain I can relate to on the deepest of levels. Your mother is supposed to have your back unconditionally. Ours threw us to the lions.

I see myself every time I look at him. He reflects the younger, powerless version of me, and the strong woman who survived. Lately, my survival feels like thriving.

I wonder if he sees pieces of himself in me. Am I a reminder of his vulnerability, or do I reinforce his strength?

Rehearsal drags on, but Lance and I glean several juicy tidbits for the documentary. We interview Taryn and Emmett, both talented and interesting actors. Taryn is an aspiring veterinarian. I'm eager to learn more about her work with animals.

My insides flutter when it's finally time to leave. Everyone files out of the theater, going their separate ways. Garrett edges closer to me on the sidewalk. We already agreed to meet at my place.

He looks up and down the street. "Where'd you park?"

"In the garage on the next block."

"I'll walk you over there."

Lance speaks up. "I parked right next to her, so you don't need to go out of your way."

Garrett hesitates, his irritation briefly flashing across his face. "Okay, cool. As long as she's not walking alone at this hour."

"Are you kiddin'? I'd never let a lady walk alone." Lance points down the sidewalk to Taryn's retreating form. "That kinda thing makes me nervous."

Taryn mentioned her apartment being a few blocks over, but it's late. And dark. Prime habitat for rapists and murderers.

"I'll walk her home," Garrett says, as if reading my mind. "See you guys later." He gives us a wave and jogs after his castmate. "Hey, Taryn, wait up."

Pride swells in my chest, watching my man behave like a gentleman. Mixed with that respect, however, is a twinge of jealousy. Taryn is a beautiful woman. Knowing she's walking off into the darkness with *my* man, makes me uneasy.

I know it's something I'll need to get over—especially once *Prodigy* opens. There's no doubt in my mind Garrett will garner plenty of female attention. The man is magnetic and intoxicating. Not to mention, brutally gorgeous. And kind. Intuitive. Respectful. He's everything a man should be.

He's mine.

"C'mon, Ella. Let's get out of here before it starts to sleet." Lance ushers me toward the parking garage. "Didja notice Tom's cough?"

"Yes, I did. I wonder if he's a smoker."

We had to stop one of our interview segments until he got over his coughing fit.

"He doesn't smell like one. My daddy's a smoker. His hair and clothes hold the scent. Tom always smells nice."

I chuckle and nudge my colleague. "I haven't sniffed him, but I'll take your word for it."

We reach our cars after a few minutes and part ways. I'll see Lance again on Wednesday evening.

I drive the short distance to my apartment and rush inside to freshen up before Garrett arrives. Once satisfied with my appearance, I flit around my living room, tidying it up.

I plug in the strand of lights that illuminate my miniature Christmas tree, laden with the ornaments I've purchased for my son.

His birthday is the day after Christmas. I wonder what he looks like. How much has he grown since I handed him over to the nurses?

Is he a kind boy? Does he enjoy sports? The arts? Music?

Do his parents love him with all of their hearts?

Does he love his adoptive mother as much as he would've loved me?

The thought sends a wave of pain crashing through me, but I quickly tamp it down when Garrett's knock reaches my ears. I head for the door, forcing a few deep breaths to dispel my sadness as I pull it open. His towering frame in the doorway disperses what remains of the clouds.

"Hi," I murmur, peering up at him.

His smile goes straight to my ovaries. "Hey, Cupcake. Did you miss me?"

I practically leap into his arms. "God, yes. Rehearsal was so fucking long."

He laughs. "Tell me about it. They're only gonna get worse when we start having them every night." His hug tightens, melting me into a pool of mush. "I can't stop thinking about you."

"Same here." *I love you.* "*Tu sei la mia anima gemelli.*"

"That sounds so fucking hot, but you still haven't told me what it means."

"Maybe later," I say, between the kisses I'm raining on his neck and jawline. I loosen his tie and pull it off, then frantically work the buttons on his shirt.

He cups my hands to still them. "Slow down, baby. We've got all night."

"Need you *now*."

"In that case . . ." His Cheshire cat grin liquefies what's left of my self-control as he unfastens his belt and removes his shoes.

I unzip my dress and let it fall to my feet before kicking it aside. I spin in a slow circle, giving him a panoramic view of the teal lingerie that I've chosen.

"Fuck." He releases a rough exhale when he spots my thong. "Your ass is so fucking sexy." He follows as I saunter into the living room.

"I wore this just for you. You'll notice the color matches my eyes."

"Oh, I noticed." He grips my hips and tugs my body against him, so my back is flush to his front. He's already hard. "Since you're wearing sexy things, especially for me, how about slipping those death traps back onto your pretty little feet?"

"You want me to wear my stilettos?"

"Damn right, baby. I want them next to my ears while we fuck."

"We'll see about that, tesoro."

Forty-Seven

A warning, a castle, and the twilight zone

Garrett

Ella peels off her lingerie, then crawls toward her pillows, the sway of her hips and lush ass making my dick throb. She looks over her shoulder at me. "You plan to stand at the foot of my bed all night?"

I motion between us. "What are the rules?"

She spins so she's lying on her back with her head resting on the pillows. "You can run the show."

"I love that idea."

She holds up her index finger and pins me with a stern look. "I know you want my legs over your shoulders, or whatever acrobatics you have in mind, but remember, no missionary."

I love that she's setting boundaries for herself and being vocal about her needs. She knows I won't cross any lines, but transparency is key. I need her to know my intentions.

"I planned to kneel in front of you and have you lie back. Is that okay?"

"That's fine. I just can't have your weight on top of me."

"Got it." I strip off the rest of my clothes and prowl around the bed to her. "Can I eat your pussy?"

"*Jesus*, Garrett." Her cheeks turn pink. "Talk about getting right to the point."

"Would you rather I candy-coat it?" I kneel on the bed and flash her a wolfish grin. "My queen, may I please licketh thy clit and feasteth upon thy divine womanhood? I promise to bringeth bountiful orgasms."

"No, you may not licketh—or feasteth—upon any of my womanly parts," she sputters, cupping between her legs like she's truly offended. The heat in her eyes tells me otherwise. "They're off-limits to your mouth."

I've got her flustered now, and it's cute as fuck.

"How about thy bosom? May I sucketh upon thy nipples?"

"*That*, you're welcome to do. The other stuff is off the table. For the record, I'll never *ask* you for oral sex." She sticks out her perfect chin in the world's most beautiful look of defiance.

"I beg to differ, Cupcake."

"You can beg all you want, Garrett. It's not happening."

I know I'm toeing the line between teasing and pressuring her. The last thing I want to do is push her too far, so it's time to back off. My powers of persuasion don't belong in the bedroom with Ella. At least, not yet.

I give an exaggerated shrug. "Okey dokey."

"Really?" She laughs, making her gorgeous tits bounce.

"What?"

"You go from asking to"—she waves her hand dramatically—"*you know*, to okey dokey?"

"You betcha I do, li'l lady." I move to kneel between her parted legs and take a moment to admire her body.

Everything about her is lush and soft. Meaty in the best of ways. I love a woman with curves to hold on to. One day she'll let me go down on her. I'll take my time kissing my way up those pretty thighs. I ache to feel them pressed to my cheeks while I lick her. She'll claw my shoulders and pull my hair to bring me closer.

Her pussy glistens, making my dick even harder. I love seeing her body so wet and ready. She's the only woman I've ever gone bare with. It's an act I've always considered reckless. I know I can trust Ella with my body. Maybe I *am* a daredevil, but I trust her with my heart and soul too.

I just might have the audacity to let myself love her.

"You're giving me one of those looks," she murmurs, drawing my attention to her eyes. "What's on your mind?"

I hesitate, struggling to find the words to describe something so foreign to me. It doesn't serve me—or Ella—to censor myself. Lions don't pussyfoot around. They move with intention.

"I've spent *years* suppressing my emotions. I never imagined saying this, but the safety of numbness no longer appeals to me. You've made vulnerability my ally in under a month. How'd you do it?"

"Is that a rhetorical question, or do you want my answer?"

I feather my fingertips over her calves. "I wanna see if our answers match."

"Well, since we're being candid, it's a lot easier to shed your armor when the other side drops their weapons. I let down my guard in good faith. It only made sense for you to do the same."

"Ditto. Except your answer was more articulate than mine." I lift one of her ankles to my lips and press a gentle kiss to her skin. "Even though it still scares me, I *want* to relinquish control. I wanna *feel* everything with you."

Her eyes reflect my sentiments even before she speaks. "When you say things like that, it's like I'm looking into a mirror and hearing the echo of my own thoughts."

"Yeah." I trace my fingertips up and down her calves, studying the castle tattoo on her ankle. "Do you still feel like a fortress?"

"Yes, but in a different way. Instead of using my walls to keep you out, you've become part of them, strengthening me in ways no one else has."

My chest tightens as I process her words. I press a kiss to her tattoo, exploring the artwork's details because I might tell her I love her if she keeps looking into my eyes like that.

Tattoos are forever, which is why I don't have any. Nothing symbolic in my life has ever lasted long enough to warrant having it inked into my skin. But I'm an artist at heart, so I can appreciate talent when I see it. Ella's tattoo is a gorgeous piece, intricate, yet bold. I squint to read the tiny banner on the castle's gate.

GC.

My eyes widen and snap to hers. "My initials are on your castle."

She blinks a few times. "My grandmother's name was Giada Castiglione. I got the tattoo after she passed away. Castiglione means castle, and she was the strongest woman I knew."

"It's quite the prophetic coincidence she and I share the same initials."

I brush my thumb over the banner, overwhelmed by the urge to prove fate put those letters there for a reason.

"There's nothing coincidental about it," she whispers, pointing to the alarm clock on her nightstand. "It's 11:11."

"You lost me there, Cupcake. Does the number eleven signify something?"

"It depends where you look. Biblically, it's related to chaos, judgment, and sin."

I snort. "Sounds about right. The holy water goes up in flames when I walk into a church."

She snags my hand and gives it a tight squeeze. "On a lighter note, the number eleven represents spiritual awakening and balance."

"That seems more fitting for us."

Her turquoise eyes lock with mine, their intensity taking my breath away. "November eleventh was my grandmother's birthday. It was also the date you and I met. Jake's gala was November eleventh."

"Whoa." A strange feeling washes over me, settling in my bones.

"Whoa is right."

"What are the odds?" My eyes dart to 11:11 on the clock once more. The center colon blinks a steady rhythm like sly winks from the universe. I stare at the glowing blue beacon as the battering ram of awareness hits me. "Ella, *Prodigy* opens on November eleventh of next year."

"Oh my God."

Random trivia floods my brain, all steeped in elevenness. "My birthday is January eleventh."

"Mine is New Year's Eve. There are eleven days between our birthdays."

My scalp tingles when another fact collides with my brain. "Holy motherfucker," I whisper, running both hands over my face. "You're not gonna believe this, but my childhood address in Pennsylvania was two eleven Castle Drive."

She sits up suddenly and presses a hand to her chest, like she's trying to stop her heart from beating through it. The color drains from her face. "I lived on Garrett Street in Queens."

I'm not superstitious. I don't buy into religion. I lost God when my mother died, so higher beings aren't part of my life. I'm not spiritual, and I've never been one for any of the New Agey stuff my friend Juliana is into.

But something is happening right now. Some crazy, twilight zone shit I can't explain or fight.

"Remember when you sang to me in your Jeep?" She doesn't wait for my answer, her words racing past her lips like a delay will silence her. "It was 11:11 then too. I know because that was the moment I fell in l—" Her shoulders rise and fall with a few breaths. "She sent you."

Not even a second later, the time changes to 11:12.

Forty-Eight

Serendipity, an addiction, and three little words

Ella

We stare at one another in silence as the serendipitous whisperings of destiny infuse the air. My grandmother sent him my way. Of that, there is no doubt in my heart. Now it's only a matter of getting him to believe it. More than that, I need him to trust the idea and embrace our possibilities.

How does one approach such a topic?

Hey, so, we've only been official for a few days, but do you want to be mine forever?

"Tesoro, please say something."

Garrett's eyes roam my body, coming to rest on my face. His unblinking stare steals my breath as those twin gold lasers etch themselves into my soul. "You've been saying it all along," he finally murmurs.

"Saying what?"

"*Tu sei la mia anima gemelli.*"

"You don't know what it means," I remind him, secretly proud of his perfect pronunciation. And more than a little flustered by how sexy he sounds speaking Italian.

"I do now. Context clues and whatnot."

"Why don't you tell me what you think it means, and I'll let you know if you're right."

"It means we're soul mates."

"Close. The exact translation is, 'you are my soul mate,' but I'll give your answer full credit."

He motions between us. "What are we gonna do about it?"

I need to know if he feels the same way, or if my cosmic revelations freaked him out. I imagine most new couples aren't discussing soul mates just days after officially entering coupledom. Of course, it really doesn't matter how we feel about it. A fact is a fact.

And if Gigi had anything to do with it, the idea is set in stone. She never liked to be challenged.

I force a deep breath, then release the words with my tension. "How would you like to handle the situation?"

"I wanna test the theory by getting as close to your soul as possible." Desire swirls in his gilded depths as he sweeps them over me. He's still kneeling between my legs, his cock hard and ready. Even though I'm sitting up, his body towers over mine. "Let me see how it feels to fuck my soul mate."

I blink up into his eyes, shocked he's embracing the concept instead of running the other direction. "You still want sex after that mindfuck?"

"I *always* want sex, Ella." He rubs his hand up my thigh. "Your mindfuck, so to speak, only amplified those cravings."

"You're addicted to sex?"

"No." He cups the back of my head and brings our foreheads together. Tightening his fingers in the strands of my hair, he stares into my eyes for a moment before speaking. "I'm addicted to you."

"Tesoro, *tu sei la mia anima gemelli.*"

Garrett slants his mouth over mine, kissing me like his survival depends on it. Like he genuinely believes I can erase every hurt and fill the emptiness he's lived with.

Right now, I'm his food, air, water, and shelter.

Warmth and safety.

He takes it deeper, and I allow him to lead, tongues sliding, teeth clicking. Neither of us closes our eyes, desperate to keep the connection.

I lose myself in a sea of molten gold as another peculiar and wonderful idea floats to mind.

Gold and teal will be our wedding colors.

After a few minutes, he tugs me up to my knees and into his lap, settling back on his heels so my thighs capture his in a straddle. We don't need a map or compass for our bodies to find their way home. He's the key to my lock, and I'm the missing piece of his puzzle. He is strength and certainty, the hope and healing I've ached for. I'm the comfort and nurture he lacked, the haven in his heartache.

A moan interrupts his kiss when he fills me. "Fuck, you feel so good."

We wrap our arms around each other and kiss some more. He turns the key, and I never imagined unlocking a surrender this sweet.

I rock my hips, riding him like a Sunday drive through the countryside. We're in a convertible with the top down, the wind is whipping through our hair, and we don't give a fuck that the other cars are passing us. The sun warms our faces as we sing along to the folk music we're playing. Hands intertwined, we enjoy the sights and each other's company. It's pure, simple comfort, born of emotional connection.

This must be what it feels like to make love.

He kisses his way to my ear, teasing the shell with his tongue. "Lie back for me."

Garrett stays put as I slide off him and rest my head on the pillows. He's kneeling between my legs, a glorious wall of sculpted muscle. It's the position we started in, but somehow it feels more primal, like he's the sinner and my body's the altar. I'm no saint, yet he worships me. His reverence coats my heart and soul.

He respects *and* understands me—the two things I've ached for my whole life. I never thought I'd find someone to give me both.

Gripping behind my knees, he guides my legs around his waist and fills me again.

He clamps his hands on my thighs and works his hips slowly. Each rolling thrust rubs me deep inside. I widen my legs and move with him, beckoning him to let loose.

"You don't know what you're doing to me, Ella."

I grab his wrists, tightening my fingers around them. "Show me. Give me everything."

He digs his fingertips into my thighs and delivers a hard thrust, making me cry out. Then another.

"More."

My moaned plea unleashes him. He slams into me, again and again, making my back arch off the bed. We're racing past the other cars now. Full throttle. I claw his skin, wailing my pleasure as he drives us faster, accelerating past fear and doubt.

The scenery around me blurs, his eyes the only thing in focus. He pushes well beyond the speed limit, weaving in and out of traffic like we don't give a fuck if the cops catch us. Citations and handcuffs don't matter. Not even a jail cell can slow us down. The demons in pursuit gave up miles ago, our heels slowly on the mend from their gnashing teeth.

Nothing stands in our way.

"Come for me," he growls, as we round the final corner before the cliff.

My body meets his command head-on, and we crash in a brilliant display of color and sound. Our car is airborne now, careening through space and time. His eyes remain locked on mine as I shatter, screaming his name over the horns and sirens. My climax paves the way for him.

"Oh, *fuck*, El."

With his head thrown back, muscles tensed, and the sheen of sweat glistening on his skin, he's never been sexier.

This is Garrett unhinged. Raw. Naked beyond the lack of clothes on his body.

My pussy grips him tightly as he releases inside me, still thrusting his hips as he comes. His moans are feral, and the way my name rips from his throat is all the confirmation I need.

He's mine. I am his.

And together, we're unstoppable.

Garrett pounds inside me a few more times, then collapses onto the mattress next to me, chest heaving.

"You all right?" he asks, after a few minutes.

"Yes." I roll toward him and cup his face. "Garrett, I love you."

Forty-Nine

Bacon, Narnia, and husband material

Garrett

Emotions are funny. Too fragile to grasp, yet strong enough to knock you flat on your ass. Hearing those three words leave Ella's lips transforms me.

Her confession is earnest and guileless. The affirmation is real—not an orgasm-induced ploy or sleight of hand.

I'm not the little boy left behind, or an inconvenience to handle. I'm not the man aching to be enough for the woman I thought I'd spend my life with, only to find out she had other plans. I'm not a drunk. Unstable. Damaged. I'm not hiding behind a facade of having my shit together, in hopes my failures won't be exposed, God forbid I let someone down. I'm not a burden to carry, I'm a treasure.

I don't need smoke and mirrors with Ella. She knows the ugliest parts of me.

My masquerade is finally over.

I reach for her hand and press her palm to my chest, my heart racing beneath her touch. "Ella, look at me." I wait for our gazes to meet before continuing. "I need you to know it's here." She nods but doesn't say anything, so

I interlace our fingers and grip her hand tighter. "When I say those words, I mean them."

"I do mean—"

"Let me finish."

"I'm sorry. Go ahead."

"I used to say those words often. So much, they lost their meaning. And for what? Someone who didn't know me. A woman who tossed me aside for another man. Yeah, I still tell my friends I love them, but after Carissa, I vowed never to use that phrase in a romantic sense again." I rest my forehead against hers. "You make me want to scream it from the peaks of the Catskills. Know that and believe it, because *when* I say them to you, they won't come out as a postorgasmic declaration. I won't dilute them. You'll know beyond the shadow of a doubt how I feel."

She cups the side of my face. "My words aren't diluted, tesoro."

"I know." I swallow past the lump in my throat. "That's why you mean so much to me."

I smell bacon. And coffee.

I roll to my side and lift my head, squinting at the clock on Ella's night-stand. It's 7:11. The sight of the number eleven makes me inexplicably giddy. Sitting up, I wipe the sleep from my eyes and stretch. I toss the covers off and pad over to her bathroom, my morning wood in full force like always. After brushing my teeth and splashing water on my face, I admire Ella's fish tank as I make my way through the living room to the kitchen.

Ella is at the stove, humming to herself while flipping bacon. She's bra-less, wearing a white tank top and booty shorts, her sex-mussed hair cascading to the middle of her back. She sways her hips, and my dick twitches back to life.

When I realize she's humming "Wild Love," I lean against the doorframe in silence for a few moments, just watching.

She pulls mugs and plates from the cabinets and sets them on the counter, then cracks two eggs into the frying pan.

"Wakey wakey, eggs and bakey," I announce from the doorway.

Ella whirls around, clutching her chest. "Jesus! You startled me. How long have you been standing there?"

"Long enough to enjoy your song."

"Isn't it *our* song?" she teases, approaching me with a smile.

"Damn right, it is."

She weaves her arms around me and clasps my neck, pulling my lips down to hers. Her kiss is sweet and tender, but hot enough to start my engine. I haul her up against me and deepen the kiss, rolling my hips to make sure she knows how hard I am.

She breaks the kiss. "Breakfast first. I fried a couple of eggs for myself, but I wasn't sure how you like yours."

"What if I want sex for breakfast?"

Laughing, she pokes a finger in my chest. "Too bad. I'm hungry."

I drop my gaze to her pussy and lick my lips. "Me too."

Her cheeks turn a beautiful pink. "Not gonna happen."

There's something incredibly primal about going down on a woman. It's a heady experience to be that intimate with someone, and I can't wait until she allows it. I don't understand those dudes who refuse to give oral because I'd give my left nut to spread Ella out on this counter and lick her until she screams.

"One day, Cupcake."

"Don't hold your breath," she chirps, returning to the stove.

She removes the skillet of bacon from its burner and turns it off before focusing on her eggs. I prowl over and plaster myself to her body, my hard cock pressing into her lower back.

I brush my lips over her ear. "One day, my name will be your new favorite prayer."

"It already is," she whispers, gasping when my lips meet her neck.

I kiss her skin how I'd lick a mixer to get all the cake batter off. Exactly the kind of attention I'm dying to show her pussy.

She cracks three more eggs into the pan and tosses the shells into the trash. I move with her, keeping my body pressed against hers even as she washes her hands and dries them.

"Fried or scrambled?"

Her breathless question makes me slide my hand beneath her shirt to cup one of her lush tits. "That's a hard one. You scramble my brain, so that seems most fitting. However, I won't lie and say a fried egg's not appealing," I lick her neck, swirling my tongue in circles, "Because I *love* when the juices run down my chin."

"Then you eat like a heathen."

I pinch her nipple between my thumb and forefinger. "You have no fucking idea."

"Stop distracting me while I cook."

Her words are in jest, but I immediately back off, moving to settle on a stool at the island. I won't risk pushing her too far. Stop means stop, no matter the circumstances. Our lives would be a lot different if more people abided by those terms.

"Fried eggs please. Do you need help with anything?"

Irony tinges her laugh. "I need help with a lot of things, Garrett. I wouldn't know where to start."

"I meant right now, but now that we're talking about it, have you ever gone to therapy?"

"No."

"You should give it a try. I find it helpful. I mean, I'm still fucked up, but my coping mechanisms have improved. It's nice to have an unbiased outlet."

"I sometimes talk to my priest. He's not biased." She flips an egg and looks over her shoulder at me. "I was raised Roman Catholic, and I've always found church comforting because it reminds me of my grandmother. Saint Jude's Cathedral is kinda my happy place."

"I don't do church."

She lifts an eyebrow. "How come? When's the last time you went?"

"Not since childhood. Wendy and Jim made us go every Sunday to give the illusion their family had their shit together. And, well, you know how that turned out for me."

"Were your parents religious?"

"Yes and no. My dad was Catholic, and my mom was Jewish, so religion was a hybrid experience in our home. I know I was circumcised and baptized, and we celebrated holidays from both faiths, but it was super casual. We didn't go to church or synagogue often. My parents had their beliefs, but they weren't strict followers. However, I remember Easter being a big deal with my father's family. We had relatives visit from Ireland the year my parents died. They were a rowdy crew. I reconnected with some of Dad's family in my twenties. I still have a few cousins in Galway and Dublin."

"What about your mom's family?"

"Wendy is the only one I've ever met. She was raised Jewish but converted to Catholicism when she married Jim."

"You said she's your mom's half sister?"

"Yeah, they shared the same mother. I only know bits and pieces of my family's history, but I guess something happened with my grandparents. I assume it was a divorce because my grandmother left Israel with my mom when she was little. She married Wendy's dad a few years later."

"What about your grandfather?"

"From what I understand, they left my grandfather *and* another kid behind. I once heard Wendy saying Mom has an older sister in Tel Aviv, but she wouldn't give me any information."

Ella's eyes widen. "Your grandmother left her child behind?"

"Yeah. That trait runs in the family. They were probably like, 'hey, I brought you into this world, but I've got other plans now, so you're on your own. Good luck, motherfucker.'"

"Oh, tesoro," she murmurs, turning off the stove.

"It's fine. Everything's good. I'm over it."

"Are you?" Her eyes burn into mine, telling me she's not buying my line of bullshit.

"Not even close," I admit, after a few moments of silence.

She turns her attention to our eggs, glancing at me as she plates the food. "Have you ever tried looking for your aunt?"

"Nope. Having one aunt who didn't want anything to do with me was more than enough. As much as I was curious, I wasn't about to disrupt anyone else's life. It wouldn't be fair to rip some lady's abandonment wounds open, just so I could have blood family. 'Hey, I'm Garrett, your long-lost nephew. Sorry your mom left you behind. Guess what? Mine did too. Isn't it fun to be unwanted? Are you as fucked up as me?'"

"Do you want orange juice? I bought it yesterday," she blurts, turning her back to me. "It's the good kind without pulp."

"Uh, sure." Her abrupt transition catches me off guard, and I momentarily forget my manners. "Thank you."

Ella yanks the fridge open and sticks her head inside. She lingers in there for well over a minute, making me wonder if it's a secret portal to Narnia. Maybe the talking animals are hiding behind the pickles, waiting to lure her in. Aslan would protect her, of that I'm certain. He was a cool lion. Right up there with Mufasa.

Her sniff snaps me out of my movie nostalgia.

"El?"

"Yeah?" Her eyes are damp when she finally emerges.

I rub a hand over my face, feeling like a dick for making her cry. "Listen, I'm sorry for unloading on you again."

Blinking rapidly, she joins me at the counter with our breakfast and juice glasses. "Like I said, I'm willing to carry some of the burden."

"I appreciate it."

"I'm sorry you felt unwanted." She takes a long, slow sip and stares out the window for a few beats, her eyes misting over again. "Your mom loved you with all her heart. Her goal was never to hurt you. She thought she was protecting you."

"From what?"

"Herself? The evil this world holds?" She squeezes her eyes shut, not bothering to wipe the tears sliding down her cheeks. "Only she can answer that."

"She's six feet under, so it doesn't look like I'll ever get my answer," I mutter, my words soaked in the bitterness my soul's been drowning in for twenty-five years. "And instead of protecting me, she delivered me to the belly of the beast. Pretty ironic, don't you think?"

"There's always more to the story. As mothers, we think we know best. Only to find out we were wrong." Her hollow tone sends a shiver down my spine, but it's the pain in her eyes that makes it hard to breathe. "By then it's too late, and we get to spend the rest of our lives regretting those shitty decisions."

I clench my jaw. "An afterlife filled with regret doesn't erase the pain I've lived. Here. On earth. In *this* fucking life. It doesn't make it hurt any less to imagine her up in heaven feeling bad for her choices."

"If she was tormented enough to take her own life, she was well beyond rational thought. She didn't understand the repercussions, Garrett. She had no way of knowing what would happen. I promise she wouldn't have done it if she knew."

I shrug. "Maybe."

We eat in silence for a few minutes. The food is divine, but her mood has gone to shit, and it's entirely my fault. The voices in my head are quick to point out how easily my moodiness could push her away.

No one wants to deal with my Danny Downer shit.

Ella's empathy is one of the things I love most about her. She feels my pain, a connection I thought only Lena was capable of. Once again, she's proven me wrong.

I'm touched by her attempt to soothe me. Maybe she's right, and my mother *does* regret what happened. Too bad that won't change my reality. An ocean of tears can't wash away the scars on my back.

None of it is Ella's fault—or problem—so I need to fix it before she has a shitty day at work.

Apologizing again will only rehash things. I opt for a subject change, pivoting to face her. "What are you doing for Christmas?"

She wipes her face on a napkin. "Christmas Eve is the Feast of the Seven Fishes with Paolo's family. It's an Italian tradition. I told his mother I'd help cook again this year. Afterward, we'll head to Saint Jude's for Midnight Mass."

Jealousy simmers inside me at the thought of her cozying up to Paolo by a Christmas tree. It's hypocritical, since I'm spending Christmas Eve with Lena. Of course, I haven't slept with her, so there's that.

"I see your face," she murmurs, peering up at me. "Before you get all caveman jealous about me and Paolo, you should know I've been spending Christmas Eve with the Benicasas since I was eighteen. I look forward to it. Paolo's siblings are wonderful. His younger sister, Alessia, is one of my few female friends."

"I don't begrudge you your tradition. I'm just—"

"Besides, I already told Paolo the sexual aspect of our relationship was over. He knows how I feel about you."

Something inside me settles. "How'd that conversation go?"

Her shoulders slump. "It hurt him. A lot. I didn't hear from him for a few days afterward. He's always been there, so that loss hit me hard. I cried quite a bit, knowing I'd jeopardized our friendship."

"It takes two to tango."

"Yes, it does, but I didn't listen to my instincts. We shouldn't have crossed that line to begin with. I always had a feeling the sex meant more to him than it did to me, but I guess I didn't realize just how much. I selfishly took the closeness I needed without regard for how it affected him. I feel terrible for fucking with his head, you know?"

I nod, even though I can't relate. Anya was cool when she and I discussed things. Then again, she's just as fucked up as me. Relationships and emotions aren't on her radar. It was never more than sex for us.

"Are you two cool now?"

"I think so. He called me yesterday and sounded like himself." She chuckles softly, then meets my gaze. "By that, I mean, he reiterated his threats toward you."

I straighten, mildly amused by the concept. "Threats?"

"He threatened your life if you hurt me."

"Well, you can tell him he doesn't need to worry about that. I won't hurt you, Cupcake. Ever."

"I know," she whispers. "I hope one day you two can be friends."

Her tone is equal parts anxious and hopeful, telling me I underestimated the importance of her relationship with Paolo.

This must be how Lena felt when Wes and I locked horns. Now *I'm* the one encroaching on a decade-old friendship, going head-to-head with a protective male. My respect for Wes has deepened after finally seeing his perspective. He handled me well, but I can't fathom how much more complicated things would be if Lena and I had a sexual history.

Ella loves Paolo, so regardless of their past, I need to accept he's here to stay. I'm capable of being cordial. As long as he doesn't get in my face, I won't hurt Ella by creating unnecessary conflict. Maybe I'll chat with Wes about it to see if he has any pointers.

She rests her hand on my knee. "What are you doing on Christmas Eve?"

"Lena's having a birthday shindig that night. I was gonna ask you to come with me. Jake will be there with Isla."

"Oh? Are they together now?"

"It's complicated."

"Does Wes know?"

"Nope. Shit's gonna hit the fan when he finds out."

Talk about playing with fire. Wes's protective streak when it comes to his sister rivals mine for Lena.

She shakes her head and stares at her hands while she twists them together. "I hope Jake knows what he's doing."

"Yeah, me too. Time will tell."

Silence settles between us once more as we ponder Jake's circumstances. It's hard enough to keep our attraction a secret at rehearsal. I can't imagine sneaking around full time like Lena told me he and Isla are doing.

"Look at me." I run my fingers through her hair, indulging in its satiny softness. Her gaze flicks to mine, and those bottomless turquoise pools make my heart race. "Are you okay?"

She nods. "If you couldn't tell, I'm a bit emotional."

"Your compassion means a lot to me."

"*Tu sei la mia anima gemelli.* Compassion comes with the territory."

I pull her close and kiss the top of her head. This imperfect angel is reaching places inside me no one's ever touched.

She feeds me the last strip of bacon on her plate. "Are you free on Christmas Day? I'd love to see you."

"I'm all yours, baby. We can hang out in our jammies and watch Hallmark movies."

Her eyes light up. "Really?"

"If that's what you wanna do, we'll make it happen."

Her smile melts my insides. "I'll make you a nice dinner. We can have steak, lobster, anything you want. We'll have cocoa and tiramisu for dessert."

"I don't want you waiting on me hand and foot, El."

"But I enjoy taking care of you."

"I want your Christmas to be special too. Let's cook something together. You can show me your magic, maybe create some of your favorite Castiglione recipes. I just wanna share time with you."

Mischief flashes in her eyes. "We can share time, tesoro, but Gigi's recipes are top secret."

"Fair enough."

She rubs her hands together. "What do you want for Christmas? I have a gift in mind, but is there something you'd like?"

"You."

"You already have me. Pick something else."

"You sitting on my face?"

Ella rolls her eyes. "Seriously? We're back to this again?"

I lick my lips and drag my gaze over her curves. "C'mon, baby, let Santa give you a beard ride."

Nate sits on the edge of my desk, eyeing the feast I've got spread out. "You gonna share?"

"Highly unlikely." I stuff a prosciutto and cheese roll into my mouth. It's a combination worthy of a foodgasm, and I haven't even gotten to the main course yet.

After our breakfast, Ella packed me a lunch fit for royalty, then sent me out the door with a mug of coffee and a kiss.

I would've been thrilled if she slapped some meat between two slices of bread and called it a day. But that's not her style. When Ella makes a meal, she creates more than food. It's an experience. She pours her heart onto every plate and into every container she touches.

Today is no exception. She covered all the bases, from an assortment of meats and cheeses intended as my appetizer, to broccoli with olive oil and garlic so I have a vegetable. There's pasta fagioli in a thermos and a container of chicken parmesan. She even packed some homemade biscotti for dessert.

The best part was the folded-up, handwritten note I found in the bag.

Buon appetito, tesoro!

Tu sei la mia anima gemelli.

Ti amo.

~E

I read her note at least six times before tucking it inside my wallet. It's refreshing to be cherished instead of dismissed. I want to keep her forever.

Nate pouts as I lift another bite to my lips.

Sighing, I hand him a miniature chunk of cheese. "Fine. I'll share."

"Oh, how generous of you. Can you spare a bread crumb or two, my lordship?"

"Maybe if I had bread."

Popping the cheese into his mouth, he points to the biscotti. "What do you call that?"

"That's biscotti, dude. It looks different from those little prepackaged store-bought ones because she made it especially for my dessert. I plan to dunk it in my coffee later."

Amusement glints in his eyes, and the corners of his lips lift into a smirk like they always do when he's about to bust my balls.

"What?" I wave my hand at him. "You're making the face."

"You're happy."

I twist the thermos lid open and breathe in the soup's aroma. "Wouldn't you be?"

"Yeah."

"Then what's your deal?" I sip the broth and moan. "Fuck, that's amazing."

"It's nice to see you happy, that's all."

"Jesus, am I that much of a moody fuck?"

He laughs. "No, asshole. I'm simply making an observation. You're cheerful and smiling on a fucking Tuesday. Love suits you."

"Who said anything about love?"

"Uh-huh." His raised eyebrow calls my bluff, making my face hot. "I'll pretend I don't notice the pep in your step." He motions to my food. "*That* is love."

"She's . . . special."

"Look at you, man. You can't even make a sentence. Of all the words you could use to describe her, you pick special?"

"She's . . . full of compassion and empathy. Nurturing. Soft, yet strong. Flawed, but perfect. Not to mention, indescribably beautiful and a lioness in bed. I'm a *very* lucky man."

Nate's smile is genuine. "I'm happy for you. Do you think you guys would want to do something for New Year's Eve? Daria mentioned having a little get-together."

"Actually, that's Ella's birthday, so I may wanna keep her to myself. I'll ask what she wants to do and get back to you."

I secretly hope she'll want to stay at one of our places instead of hanging out with Daria and Nate. I've got plans to ring in the New Year with a bang. My dick twitches at the thought of all the ways I can make the birthday girl come.

"Sounds good. Did you figure out a plan for her Christmas gift?"

I rub my jaw. "I'm honestly a little stumped. Christmas kinda snuck up on me."

Lena has always claimed I'm an excellent gift giver because I pour a tremendous amount of thought into my gifts. While she's not wrong, as my best friend, she's super easy to buy for and likely biased. I want Ella's gift to do my feelings justice. I need it to be perfect, but nothing I've come up with seems good enough. I'd serve her the world on a platter if I could.

"You've still got five days." Nate slides into the chair in front of my desk. "C'mon, let's figure out this gift situation. I'll help you brainstorm."

I laugh. "You were afraid to talk to women last month. Now you're the gift whisperer?"

"They don't call me husband material for nothing."

Fifty

Ravioli, a surprise, and an envelope

Ella

The tree is lit, my hair and makeup are done, and ingredients for homemade ravioli cover the counter in anticipation of Garrett's arrival. I flit around the kitchen, faster than the nervous butterflies in my stomach. It's not the food I'm worried about, though.

Today is the day I'll grant him his wish. I'm finally going to let him go down on me. He needs to know he has my full trust. It's one of the most important gifts I can give him. I have no idea what to expect, but I've made everything smooth and soft. My body clenches, just thinking about it. I hope I don't let him down.

It's heading on six in the evening. He was supposed to come for breakfast so we could spend Christmas Day together, but he had to deal with some drama at his house. He didn't elaborate, and it wasn't my place to ask, so I really have no idea why he's so late.

The buzzer rings, and I make a beeline for the front door, yanking it open.

Garrett stands in the hallway, wearing a black wool coat and dress pants. Melting snowflakes dust his eyelashes and soak into his inky hair.

His shadowed jawline, and the way his eyes glow in the dim lighting, lend him an air of mystery. Gorgeous doesn't begin to describe him.

"Hey, baby." He ghosts his knuckles down my cheek, then brushes his thumb over my lower lip. "Sorry I'm late."

"It's okay. You're here now, and that's what matters." I brush snowflakes off his shoulders. "Wow. I'm impressed you're actually wearing a coat."

He chuckles. "Well, it *is* a blizzard out there." Smiling, he hands me a package wrapped in metallic gold with a teal bow. "Merry Christmas."

"Buon Natale." I usher him inside and close the door behind us.

He toes his shoes off and leaves them on the mat, then hangs his coat. "I had to park a few blocks over because of the snowbanks."

"I haven't ventured outside today, but it looks beautiful from the window. I love white Christmases." Leading him into the living room, I place the gift beneath the tree, next to the one I wrapped for him. "I hope you brought your appetite."

His smile could liquefy a glacier. "I always do."

I press a kiss to his cheek and breathe in his woodsy, clean scent. "I've missed you."

"I've missed you more, Cupcake." He draws me in for a hug, and I melt against him, elated to finally be in his arms.

I haven't seen him since Wednesday night's rehearsal, thanks to his AA meetings and some work obligations on my end. Today is Sunday. That's far too long for a woman to endure without her soul mate. God only knows how I survived almost thirty years without him.

"It smells good in here," he murmurs, kissing the top of my head. "Like warm cinnamon."

"That's the pies. I made apple and pumpkin."

"I thought we were having tiramisu?"

"I made that too. And sugar cookies." Turns out I'm a nervous baker. I finally had to stop myself so I could shower and look presentable.

He pulls back to study my face. "You're amazing. You know that, right?"

"You flatter me, tesoro."

"It's not flattery if it's true."

I laugh and motion to the kitchen. "C'mon, we've got dinner to make."

He follows, then suddenly stops me in the archway between the kitchen and living room. "Not gonna miss this opportunity."

Before I realize what's happening, he cups my face in his hands and kisses me soft and slow. It takes me a moment to remember the mistletoe I hung this morning. I hang it every year because it's beautiful and Christmassy. This is the first time anyone's ever kissed me beneath it.

Heat arrows down my spine, pooling in my belly. I fist the material of his shirt and pull him closer to deepen the kiss, but he keeps his movements achingly slow. Sensual.

He breaks the kiss long before I'm ready for it to end. "We've got all night, baby."

His silken voice only makes me wetter, the desperation burning through me like a wildfire. What is this clawing need that has taken over me?

"I want you."

"You'll have me as many times as you want." He pats his stomach. "But a man's gotta eat to have that kind of stamina."

"I know you wanted to help, but I already prepped the dough because I was worried about the time."

He grimaces. "I'm sorry I couldn't get here earlier."

"It's totally fine. I'm just telling you because I feel guilty for doing it without you." I motion to the bowls and ingredients. "You get to decide what we put in the middle."

"Would it be too much work to recreate those pumpkin ones you made for me?"

"With the apple sage butter?" I glance at the apples in my fruit bowl and purse my lips, considering the recipe. "That sauce usually needs to simmer for a few hours, but I'm sure we can improvise with something similar. I've got apples and plenty of pumpkin left over from the pies."

His eyes light up. "This is the best Christmas ever."

"Wait until I give you your gifts." My insides quiver, my pussy growing wetter at the thought of his tongue on me.

"You're my gift, Ella. Being here with you is all I want or need."

His words resonate in my heart, calming the butterflies. I wasn't nervous about seeing him, per se, just inexplicably anxious.

We wash our hands, and Garrett rolls up the sleeves of his black dress shirt, rendering me momentarily speechless. I've never seen a sexier set of forearms.

He catches me ogling. "What?"

"You're going to use the rolling pin so I can stare at your arms."

He laughs heartily. "You got it, Cupcake. I'll try to flex as much as possible."

"You can flex your forearms?"

"I can flex anything you want me to flex." He tightens his arm muscles, making a ball of need unfurl inside me. "But I think you'll enjoy my ass cheeks most." He gives the counter a few pelvic thrusts. "They're my favorite muscle to flex."

I clutch the granite, so my knees don't give out. "Can we skip dinner?"

He makes a show of picking up the rolling pin. "Not a chance."

He watches me peel and chop a few apples at warp speed, smirking the whole time. Then I whip up the pumpkin filling.

I've always enjoyed making ravioli. They're much simpler than most people realize, and it's fun to try new flavor combinations for the filling.

I add some nutmeg and cinnamon to the pumpkin mixture, then point to the bowl of dough. "Okay. We're going to roll out two sheets of dough, one for the top, and one for the bottom. By we, I mean you, so go ahead and get started."

"Yes, ma'am." He plops two clumps of dough on the surface I've prepped and begins rolling it out.

His forearms do not disappoint.

"If I ever open my own restaurant, you're going to be my pasta boy. Put your back into it."

He laughs and ups the ante by sticking his ass out. Winking, he arches his back in a vampy parody of a chef, rolling out the dough as if he were making love to it. "Like this?"

"Why are you so fucking hot?" I wave a hand at him. "It's ridiculous, honestly."

He gives me a sheepish grin. "Sorry?"

I circle him, unabashedly staring at his ass as I make my way around the island. "Don't be sorry, tesoro, I'm enjoying the view immensely. Roll the dough a tiny bit thinner please."

Once the two slabs are the right thickness, I show him how to use the pasta roller to cut the dough into strips of uniform width. Using a teaspoon, we plop pumpkin filling in evenly spaced globs.

"You don't want too much because they'll burst. You also don't want the dumplings to crowd one another." Next, we layer strips of dough over top and use our fingers to smooth the ravioli into individual dumplings. "It's important to get all the air out. Again, we don't want them bursting."

I hold up the pasta cutter once all the ravioli are prepped. "Wanna do the honors?"

"Absolutely." Garrett cuts them apart like he's been doing it for years. "This is way easier than I imagined it being."

"I love ravioli. The dough's simple, and you can find any number of filling recipes online. It's fun to experiment with different cheeses and vegetable purées. And I love creating new sauces."

"Would you ever open your own restaurant? I feel like you'd make a killing."

"Here's the thing. On one hand, it's a dream of mine. I *love* to cook. If there was a way to spend my days making gourmet pastas and serving them to people, without all the other bullshit that comes with running a business, I'd do it in a heartbeat." I hand him a fork and show him how to crimp the edges. "I've seen the restaurant industry's inner workings, both as a child with my grandmother's place, and at La Bussola. It's not easy. Especially in New York. I'd hate for the stress of running a business to ruin my love of cooking. I've seen it almost happen with Paolo."

He nods. "It's probably even harder for a family-run business."

"Exactly. How do you keep the quality and authenticity where you want it, all while cutting costs and trying to eke out a profit?"

"Is La Bussola struggling?"

"No, not at all. Paolo would never let that happen. He'll work himself to the bone so that restaurant survives. And that's why I worry. One day his parents will retire, and it will be all on him. He's a brilliant chef, but so much of that is on the back burner now. It's sad to see his talent go to waste."

"What about his siblings? Don't they help?"

"They lend a hand where they can, but they're all busy. Luca's an attorney, Massimo's a DEA agent. Giovanni is a firefighter, and his twin, Marco, is a detective. Matteo's an engineer, and Giancarlo, well, he's the Benicasa wild card."

"How so?"

"He's all over the place. He has two business degrees but chooses to travel the world instead."

Garrett cocks his head to the side. "Doing what?"

"He's an artist—paints murals and portraits for rich people—but I'd say professional flirt is a more accurate job description."

"He sounds cool."

"He is, just a bit flighty. I haven't seen him in ages. I think he's in Los Angeles. I know it bothers Maria that he's not around. She wants her whole family together as much as possible."

A wistful look passes over his face. "Makes sense."

Realizing the concept of family togetherness pains him, I quickly change the subject. "Last, but not least, there's Alessia. We don't see her much because she's in her final year of med school. She's the youngest, and the only girl. Maria and Giorgio desperately wanted a daughter, so they kept going until they had one."

"Damn. *Eight* kids? That's a lot of mouths to feed."

"Having a family restaurant helped."

"Yeah, but still. I can't imagine the grocery bills." He scratches his chin. "I feel bad for Alessia. That's a shitload of older brothers to deal with."

"You have no idea. Paolo's the oldest, and while he's protective, Massimo, Matteo, and the twins have enough testosterone to choke an elephant. Luca and Giancarlo don't pay any attention to her, which is a blessing in disguise. Her love life sucks because most men won't even think of going near her. She's the closest thing I have to a sister."

He smiles and touches my cheek. "I'd say she's pretty damn lucky to have you in her life."

His compliment warms me. "Thank you."

"So, are any of the brothers married?"

"Yes. Giovanni married Tori, his high school sweetheart, last year. Now Maria is constantly begging for grandbabies."

"That's cute."

"Maria is a spitfire. I love her so much. The whole family has been a godsend. I've never met a more welcoming group of people."

"Their names sound so familiar. I feel like I may have met Giovanni at Connor's gym."

"Your cousin has a gym?"

"Yeah, it's called Next Level. He's part owner. I go there sometimes when I don't feel like working out at home."

"Then you've definitely met them. Massimo, Matteo, and the twins are all members."

"Makes sense. The gym has a big cop presence. Connor contracts with the FBI and the other owner is a SWAT team dude. It's probably the safest place in the city. In fact, Wes is making Lena and his sister take Connor's self-defense classes." He rubs his jaw, tilting his head to the side. "You know, now that I think about it, you'd probably benefit from them."

I shake my head. "Not going to happen. A gym full of muscle dudes is trigger central for me."

He presses his lips in a flat line instead of replying. I can tell he wants to push the issue, but he's smart enough not to.

Paolo's brothers are like family. I love them dearly and know any one of them would kill for me. But sometimes, when they're all together, the masculinity makes my skin crawl. They're huge, loud, and more than a little hot-headed. Paolo is different. While he's also tall and well-built, his stature never freaked me out. Same goes for Luca, the quiet, broody one of the bunch.

We plop the ravioli into a pot of boiling water once they're ready, and I turn my focus to the modified butter sage sauce.

"I can't guarantee this will taste as good as it did last time, because I'm totally winging the recipe. It's probably going to be clarified butter with a hint of apple and sage. I may add some cinnamon."

"Butter makes everything better." The wicked smile curving his lips tightens my nipples. His gaze drops to the juncture of my thighs. "I love when it drips down my chin."

My stomach does a backflip. "Pervert."

"You know it, baby." He flashes me a wink. "So, if a full-fledged restaurant is out of the question, you should consider having a pasta food truck. We can travel the countryside and feed people." He holds his hands up like he's displaying a sign. "Ella's Pasta Parlor. Think of the pasta-bilities."

"Maybe one day, tesoro." I stir the butter mixture and release a wistful sigh.

"I think we can make it happen."

"I appreciate your confidence in me, Garrett." The door buzzer rings, startling me. "Can you please get that? It may be the FedEx guy. I ordered something for Paolo's mother, but it hasn't arrived yet."

"I don't think they deliver on Christmas, but I'll check it out." He kisses my forehead and points to the stove. "I'll be your pasta boy and package retriever as long as you keep giving me the sauce."

"Oh, I've got sauce." I shimmy my hips. "But I like it better when you *deliver* the package."

He laughs as he leaves the room. "Well played, Cupcake."

There's something beautiful about melted butter. I love how it seeps into a bagel or slice of toast like the desert soaks up rain. How it melts into a baked potato, and the gratification of dunking a chunk of lobster meat into a ramekin of liquid gold. My love affair with butter is one of the reasons I get my cholesterol checked twice a year. So far, so good. I'll mourn the day when I need to abstain.

Garrett's muffled voice reaches my ears as I add minced apples and brown sugar to the pot. My feelings for caramelized sugar rival my butter love affair, especially when it's intended for pasta. I adore a good medley of sweet and savory. Maybe I'll make dessert ravioli this week.

Wouldn't it be something to start my own business? Images of my pasta food truck dance through my head. People lining up outside to taste my creations. Food is required for survival, but true magic is possible when you take that extra step to transform it into art.

I hum "Winter Wonderland" to myself while I stir, basking in the glow of Christmas. My kitchen is warm and fragrant. Garrett is in my home. And my heart is full.

I spot a piece of apple skin in the sauce and use my spoon to retrieve it, sensing the moment Garrett reenters the kitchen. It's like this every time he walks into a room—a welcome disruption in the force field.

"You're going to love this sauce." I peek over my shoulder at him, puzzled by his stony expression. "What's wrong?"

He stops a few feet away from me and crosses his arms over his chest. Tension rolls off him in waves, his unblinking stare lacking its usual warmth. A muscle pulses in his clenched jaw, but he doesn't speak.

I flick the sauce burner off and set down my spoon, then turn to face him. "Are you okay?"

"I dunno." He narrows his gold lasers on my face. "Forget to tell me something?"

Oh, God . . .

My insides shrivel, but I force a calm exterior. "What's going on?"

He hands me an unmarked, sealed envelope. "I'll ask you again." His icy tone crystallizes the air in my lungs, and the furious disgust in his eyes stops my heart. "Did you forget to tell me something?"

My stomach bottoms out. I open and close my mouth a few times but can't push words past the fear clogging my linen throat.

Garrett advances until there's less than a foot of space between us and points to the envelope. "Your dead mother dropped that off for you. She said it's important health-related information that you should pass along to your *son*." His words slice through me as he cocks his head to the side, his nostrils flaring. "Funny, you never mentioned *him* before. Anyhoo, the late Mrs. Battista seemed *terribly upset* her dear Rosella won't return her calls."

Panic grips me. I stagger backward until my butt hits the counter. I can't breathe through my shock. I changed my phone number years ago. My mother doesn't have my new one. I haven't seen or spoken to her in close to a decade. The last I knew, she lived in Philadelphia.

Why is she in Manhattan?

Why did she have to choose today to show up on my doorstep unannounced?

Better yet, what could be so important she thinks I need to reach out to my son's adoptive parents?

"Tell me something." Garrett's chest heaves with each breath as he closes the distance between us, looming over me like he's eight feet tall. "You're not really from California, are you?" When I don't answer, his expression gets even colder, despite the fury blazing in his eyes. "I asked you a question, *Rosella Battista.*"

"Don't call me that." The words scrape past the lump in my throat.

My abuser liked to whisper my name while he raped me. Over and over again like some sick, twisted prayer. *My little rosebud Rosella, so soft and delicate.* It turns out thirteen-year-old virgins *are* delicate when you repeatedly violate them. To this day, I hate anything to do with roses, and I haven't gone by Rosella since I summoned the courage to leave. My name was used as a weapon for four years. Shards of terror slice my heart, and a part of me dies inside, hearing it leave Garrett's lips.

"What should I call you then? A liar?"

A strangled sob rips from my throat, making me clutch my chest. It would have hurt less if he slapped me.

The worst part is that he's right. I did lie to him. While I wasn't unfaithful, I deceived him, just like his ex. Now I'm caught in the web I've woven for myself.

He leans down so our noses touch. "I bared my fucking soul to you!"

I flinch, cowering from his bellowed thunderclap. The demons of my past tighten their grip on my throat, making me gasp and hide my face.

My fear doesn't go unnoticed.

Garrett takes two giant steps backward and lowers his voice. "I don't even know you."

"You *do* know me," I whimper, peering at him from between my fingers.

"Oh, really? How about we review all the details you left out?" He motions between us. "Go ahead. I'm all ears."

"What do you want me to say?"

"Let's start with the part about your son. Why'd you keep him secret? Where is he? What's he like? Is he healthy? Is he safe and happy?"

"I-I . . . d-don't know."

"Wow." He presses a palm to his chest and slowly shakes his head. "That really hits home for me."

"I'm not in his life for a reason."

"Well, your mother—who magically resurrected herself—thinks you need to find him, so you should probably get on that. Don't worry. He's probably out there somewhere with the rest of us pathetic fucks whose mothers couldn't be bothered with us."

He cracks the emotional dam inside me. I wrap my arms around myself as thirteen years' worth of agony spills over and streams down my cheeks.

"You told me you loved me." His voice breaks, and his shoulders slump in defeat. He takes a few breaths to compose himself, blinking rapidly. "Was any of it even true?"

"I do love—"

"Don't." Squeezing his eyes shut, he holds up his hand to silence me. "Just don't. Your words mean nothing to me anymore."

No one will believe you.

You're lying.

Stop being dramatic.

You're a slut.

Your voice doesn't matter.

You're worthless.

You deserved it.

His eyes are damp when he finally meets my gaze, and hollow resignation replaces his fury. "I bared my soul, and you couldn't tell me your real name. I thought I knew you." His haunted whisper shatters what's left of my heart.

He snatches his keys and heads for the door.

I rush after him. "Please don't leave. I can expl—"

"Too little too late." He holds his hand up to stop me again and deals his final blow. "Save your stories for the next asshole who's stupid enough to believe them."

A moment later, the front door slams as confirmation he walked out of my life.

I sag against the fridge and slide to the floor. When my ass hits the tile, I roll onto my side and curl into a little ball.

The fetal position never saved me from rape. It won't soothe the pain I've brought onto myself now, and it can't heal my childhood trauma. It won't ease the sting of regret or bring my son back into my life. It won't help me start over with Garrett or repair our bond. No, the fetal position can't make truth from lies. It simply isn't possible to unbreak our hearts.

That doesn't stop me from curling tighter. As my tears come fast and heavy, I pull myself a little closer.

Maybe this time I can make myself small enough to disappear.

Fifty-One

A kingpin, a near miss, and a hug

Garrett

I can't believe the bodega near Brooklyn's Prospect Park still stocks my favorite booze. I remember the day I asked them to order the obscure Irish whiskey from a distillery in Galway. I bought the entire case. Here it is, nine years after I stopped drinking, and I'm back to where I started.

I always loved how the owner concealed my purchase in a brown paper bag like he was sending me out the door with absinthe. I wasn't Garrett Casey from rural Pennsylvania, a broken, fucked-up kid. No, in my mind I was a Mafia kingpin during Prohibition, powerful and fierce. I was a man people respected, even if I didn't respect myself. The hint of scandal excited me as much as scoring my next bottle. Even now, my pulse is pounding with the anticipation of what's inside.

Gripping the glass neck, I peel off the paper and withdraw my chosen vice. My eyes caress the familiar label like an old lover. I twist the top off and clutch the bottle tighter, lowering my nose to the rim.

Whiskey is a drunkard's aphrodisiac. The scent alone has the power to bring me to my knees. My forbidden nectar still smells the same. Earthy and rich. It still heats my blood when I pull the smoky aroma into my lungs. I inhale until I'm dizzy, not caring if I lose consciousness. I've got the numbness I crave in the palm of my hand.

This is what coming home feels like.

My addiction is the warm blanket I'm dying to crawl beneath, a refuge amid the chaos I can't seem to escape. My demons dance circles around me, arms spread wide in welcome. I should push them away. Run as fast as my legs will carry me. Instead, I pull them closer, my mouth watering for the reunion I've both dreaded and ached for.

Right now, I'd sell them my soul to make the pain go away.

Who am I kidding? It's hard to believe my soul retained any value after I laid it bare for Ella. She showed me how little it's worth when she couldn't even give me her name. Like a lovestruck fool, I stripped away all my defenses and handed over my heart.

Once again, I bargained with the devil and got burned.

And for what? False affection and empty words? Mistruths and omissions? Lust masquerading as connection? Turns out I never knew the woman behind the mask. Her betrayal eviscerated me, her lies cutting deeper than any knife I've wielded. I still can't wrap my mind around the level of treachery.

Why would she lie about being an orphan to a man who lost both parents to suicide?

Why would she keep her child's existence a secret, and why isn't she part of his life?

How can I love a woman just like my mother?

Was anything we shared real?

Better yet, do any of her claims hold true? She wouldn't lie about being raped . . . would she?

A wave of agony slams into me with the thought. No, she wouldn't lie about that. Doubt and certainty wage war in my head as I lean against the counter and try to breathe.

I left Ella's sometime after eight, then roamed the streets in search of my Jeep, too distraught to remember where I parked. At the time, I thought it wise to walk home from Manhattan during a snowstorm.

That was a stupid fucking idea. Especially since my coat is still hanging on the hook inside her door.

My cravings were quick to rear their heads on my two-hour journey through the elements. The siren call of whiskey lured me past the park to my old supplier—the only asshole open this late on Christmas. I bought some booze and carried it home like a fugitive.

My fingers and toes are so numb they're burning. I can't feel my legs. Pieces of my hair are frozen in clumps, and the rest of it's a stringy mess. My saturated clothes cling to me, chilling my body to the bone. I've never been this cold. My fucking teeth are chattering, but all I can focus on is the bottle in my hands.

I take another slow, deep breath like the vapors alone will scratch this itch.

The fluorescent light above my kitchen sink hums its interrogation. Minutes tick by on the clock overhead, each one echoing in my brain. The fridge rumbles and starts to run, and the furnace kicks on. It feels like the room itself has come alive to watch me fall.

My eyes flick to the cabinets where my old shot glasses live. Will they rejoice at our reunion? What about the glass tumblers? Are they chanting my name?

Does hypothermia make you crazy?

My hands are shaking so badly I nearly drop the bottle. I set it on the counter, tangling my fingers in my frosted hair.

Just one sip.

I should dump it down the drain.

A little nightcap to ease your heartache.

I should smash the bottle.

Just a tiny sip.

I need to walk away.

Instead, I pick up the bottle again, the voices in my head cheering me on. They know how good it will taste. How the numbness will soothe my broken heart and help me forget the pain.

I'm a weak, pathetic bastard incapable of resisting temptation.

I'm a failure. A waste of air and space.

I'm a disappointment to Lena and myself.

My vision blurs. I blink away the tears threatening to fall and lift the bottle to my lips. I've been sober for nine years, four months, and six days. It's a battle I'm tired of fighting. My gaze darts to the clock so I can remember the exact moment the booze finally won.

It's eleven minutes after eleven.

11:11.

I freeze, transfixed by the universe's sick sorcery. Ella would insist it's a message from her dead grandmother. That is, if she's even dead in the first place. The women in that family tend to resurrect themselves. If things turned out differently, I'd be reveling in soul mate serendipity. I don't know what to make of the bizarre coincidence now.

Holding my breath, I watch the second hand travel around the clock's face. The ache in my chest deepens, knowing I lost something I never truly had. I can't blink away images of Ella and me together, our connection in and out of bed, and how we understood each other's pain. My throat burns with the scream that wants to wrench free. I tighten my grip on the whiskey.

How could it end this way?

It's not over. Remember why you stopped.

The thought collides with my brain a second before the minute hand jumps to 11:12. I set the booze down and take a few steps back, eyeing the bottle like it's a wild animal.

The fridge stops running, and another sound reaches my ears.

The treadmill.

Either we have a ghost in this brownstone, or Wes is jogging again. He's been at it all day, which is why I was late to Ella's. I suck at fixing my own life, but my de-escalation powers kick ass. Whatever the reason, I take his heavy, rhythmic footfalls as a sign.

I'm not supposed to fall today.

The enormity of my near miss swells inside me, unleashing the pain I've been trying to suppress since I walked out of Ella's. I choke back a sob and run downstairs, desperate to put some distance between the whiskey and me.

Wes looks up as I burst into the room. "What the—"

I can't feel my hands, so I don't bother with gloves. A guttural bellow rips from my chest, and I pummel the heavy bag like a madman.

I thought I knew Ella. I believed it with all my heart.

My instincts didn't save my mom when I found her in a bathtub full of blood. They didn't protect me from Sean, warn me about Carissa, or make me keep my distance from Ella. How can I trust my instincts to keep me safe? How can I trust anything—or anyone—I believe in?

What about Lena? Why does she stick around?

Am I a burden to her?

What if I've fooled myself into thinking I know her?

Do I really know anyone?

Fists flying, I funnel my pain into the worn leather bag like my strikes alone will save me from myself.

Agony and apathy battle for the upper hand. It doesn't matter which one wins. I lose either way. Droplets from my soaked dress clothes slicken the mats beneath my feet. They groan and squeak as I pivot, adjusting the angle and speed of my punches.

This is how I will protect myself. I don't need a ring to be a fighter. I don't need anyone else to keep me safe. I'm like the lion banished from his own pride. I keep crawling back, hoping for a different outcome, but starvation awaits. Isolation and pain. Only my teeth and claws can save me.

I slip on the wet mat and nearly fall but pull it together and keep punching.

The treadmill beeps and slows. "Garrett, take it easy, mate."

I can't see the bag through my tears. I miss landing a punch, and it knocks me backward. Shoving the wet hair out of my eyes, I quickly recover and go after it again with more fury than before. The bolt overhead creaks with each pendulous swing, but I don't stop.

The pain drives my strikes harder and faster.

Sloppier.

More erratic.

A flash of blue in my periphery warns me of Wes's approach. "You need to calm down. You're gonna hurt yourself."

I ignore his booming voice because I've already hurt myself. What's a little more pain at this point?

My next punch rips the bolt from the ceiling with a metallic screech. The bag goes flying, its chain barely missing my face. The bolt hits the top of my foot, so I kick it. It lands by my free weights, alongside the fallen bag.

Fueled by adrenaline, I release a battle cry and launch myself across the room. I dive for the bag, straddling it as I resume my attack. If I miss it, I'll punch the floor, but I don't give a fuck about my bleeding knuckles.

"Enough!" Wes bellows, hauling me up and backward into his chest. "You're gonna break your fucking hands!"

"Get off me, Emerson," I snarl, still trying to swing at who knows what.

He pins my arms to my sides and drags me to the room's center. "You're off your bloody rocker. I'm not letting go 'til ya chill the fuck out."

Right now, I'm too cold, tired, and weak to fight him, so I slump into his hold.

"Take it easy. Breathe."

"I can't."

"Who's yelling? What was that crash?" Lena clambers down the steps and appears in the doorway, sleep mussed and disheveled. Her eyes widen when she spots us. "Why are you fighting?"

"We're not," I mumble.

She points to Wes. "I was on my way downstairs to get you. Then I heard shit crashing. What the fuck's going on?"

"Not now, Lena," he snaps, pointing to the staircase. "I've got this under control."

Her eyes dart to the fallen bag and chain, then back to me and my bleeding hands. "Gar, are you okay? I can bandage—"

"I'm fine."

I avoid eye contact because I'm ashamed of what she'd think if she knew how close I came to ruining my sobriety. Or if she witnessed me ripping the bag out of the ceiling like a fucking animal. She's never seen me lose control like that.

Probably because it's never happened before.

"Go upstairs, sunshine."

Lena, a woman who doesn't take orders from anyone, gives Wes a nod and slowly backs away. Her eyes linger on me for a moment, but she heads upstairs without a word.

"Garrett, talk to me." Wes lowers us to the floor, but keeps his massive arms banded around me like he's afraid I'll go savage again.

"Everything's fucked."

"What happened? Why are you wet?"

"It's snowing."

"Christ, you're soaked through. How far away didja park?"

"Manhattan."

"Wait a minute." He releases his hold and scoots around me so he can see my face, clamping his hands on my shoulders. "You're telling me you walked here from Manhattan in a bloody snowstorm?"

"Yeah. I couldn't find my Jeep."

His cobalt eyes burn into mine. "What's going on? This isn't you, mate. You're fucking scaring me right now."

"She lied. None of it was true."

"Who lied? Ella?"

"That's not even her real name. It's Rosella." I force a few deep breaths, desperate to keep my composure, but a fat tear rolls down my cheek out of spite. I wipe my face on my damp sleeve. "Her dead mother showed up on her doorstep with a message for the son Ella never told me she had."

"Holy fuck." Wes breathes, gaping at me. "I've known her for eight years and never saw her pregnant. Where is her son?"

"Dunno. I left before the conversation went there."

"Did you let her explain anything?"

I squeeze my eyes shut. "No."

"So, all you've got is unanswered questions. No wonder you're upset."

Upset doesn't scratch the surface. The open bottle upstairs floats through my mind, making me shudder. This is the closest I've ever come to falling off the wagon. I don't know how I resisted drinking that whiskey.

Now everything burns, and I feel like I fought off an army. The open blisters on my hands are bleeding, and I'm sitting on my basement floor, crying to another man.

Merry fucking Christmas to me.

"I don't even know her. Do I know anyone? Is anything real?"

"All right, let's go." Wes climbs to his feet, pulling me with him. "We're going upstairs. You're gonna take a hot shower and go to bed. You can worry about this in the morning."

"I'm fine."

"You're not fine." He leads me out of my gym and follows me up the steps. We reach the main floor of my apartment, and he points down the hall. "Go shower."

"I'll shower in the morning."

"Your clothes are plastered to your body. You're freezing cold, covered in sweat, blood, and God knows what else. Get in the fucking shower."

I stare at my bathroom door, the idea of bathing myself too monumental a task to handle right now.

"Listen, I really don't wanna see your dick, and I don't wanna embarrass you with how much bigger mine is, but if you don't march your arse down that hall and clean yourself up, I'm gonna get in there with you."

A laugh pushes past my chapped lips as I head for the bathroom. "For the record, my dick's bigger."

"In your dreams, mate."

Pausing midway down the hall, I look over my shoulder at him. "Can you do me a favor?"

"Whaddya need?"

"There's a bottle on my kitchen counter. Drink it, dump it, I don't care. Please just keep it the fuck away from me."

He nods slowly. "Consider it done."

After my scalding hot shower, I staggered to my bedroom and put on clean clothes. Now I'm burrowed facedown in my bed, still freezing. Fleece pajama pants and a thermal shirt haven't helped. Hopefully, the extra blanket I layered over top will warm me up soon.

My room is pitch black how I like it. Silent, save for my breaths and heartbeat. Alone with my thoughts, the day's events take their toll. The tears come fast and heavy. Instead of fighting them, I curl into a ball and weep. I haven't cried like this since I walked in on Tony and Carissa.

I cry for the twelve-year-old boy who first snuck a bottle of Irish whiskey from his uncle's liquor cabinet. I remember how he sucked down the amber fluid like a man, ignoring the burn in his throat. That boy drank to forget. He drank to become numb. He drank for control. But it was never enough.

I cry for the kid whose back was marred with cigarette burns, his body violated in the most brutal of ways. An ocean of whiskey couldn't drown out his pain. I remember the searing agony of the torture, and the dulled-down reminder when the force of his vomiting broke the scabs open.

And finally, I cry for the heartbroken thirty-three-year-old man who was foolish enough to think he found love. I weep for his shattered hopes and fragile sobriety. I remember when he felt like he was on top of the world. His happiness only lasted a fleeting moment, and when it fell apart, it splintered.

I can't believe how close I came to erasing nine years' worth of effort. The self-disgust consumes me, burning deeper than any cigarette.

Lena's vanilla perfume reaches my nose before I hear her approach over my blubbering. The mattress dips, and she slides into bed beside me, pulling the covers up to our chins.

"Come here," she whispers, and I roll toward her.

She wraps her arms around me and tugs me close. I bury my face in her chest, my tears dampening the T-shirt she's got on. Body-shaking sobs seize my frame, and I lack the power to stop them.

My fight is gone, abandoned on the basement floor. Suffocating pain is all that remains. Lena runs her fingers through my hair as I cling to her and try to breathe.

She doesn't say a word, just holds me, gently stroking my back. As the only certainty in my life, she doesn't need to speak for me to hear her.

Lena's love is a comfort I'm not worthy of, but I accept her warmth just the same.

Fifty - Two

Morning wood, a voice of reason, and an epiphany

Garrett

Someone's pulling my leg.

Literally.

I squint through the haze of sleep that clings to me, my darkened room coming into focus. I can barely make out Wes's silhouette where he stands at the foot of the bed. Under normal circumstances, a figure looming over me while I sleep is the stuff of nightmares. I'm clearly off my game.

He tugs my ankle again. "C'mon."

"Whassup?" I ask him around a yawn.

"Comfy?"

It suddenly occurs to me I'm wrapped around his girlfriend like a baby opossum. My face is in the woman's bosom for fuck's sake. No wonder I'm so warm.

"Fuck. Sorry." Extricating myself from Lena's hold, I sit up and rub my eyes before crawling out of bed. "Not what it looked like," I mumble, rising to my full height.

Tell that to the morning wood tenting my pajama pants like an overeager soldier's salute. Could I make this any more awkward?

"I made coffee and picked up bagels from Nicolai's," he whispers, seemingly unfazed by the position he found me in. "You should come eat."

I glance at Lena. She's sound asleep, her hair fanned out across my pillow. "What about her?"

"Let her sleep."

Nodding, I follow him into the hallway and close the bedroom door behind us.

I rub my hand over my face and sheepishly meet his gaze. "I'm sorry about that. I swear it was one-hundred-percent innocent, and I meant no disrespect. We both kinda passed out."

"No worries."

"And I, uh, only have a boner because I need to piss."

He chuckles at my blurted statement. "I'm not worried about your dick, Garrett. I know how much she likes mine. Now go piss before ya wet yourself."

Hotheaded Wes Emerson is being uncharacteristically calm about the situation. So much so, I feel the urge to reassure him anyway.

I pause outside the bathroom door and gesture between us. "Just so we're clear, I am *not* a threat."

"I know. I would've come down and got her if I thought you were." He claps my shoulder. "I'll meet you in the kitchen."

I head for the kitchen after relieving myself, and sure enough, there's a full pot of coffee waiting. The whiskey bottle is gone. I don't know what he did with it, and I don't care. The cravings have receded to a dull roar. I'm safe as long as I can't get my hands on anything.

Wes hands me a mug. "I was gonna make coffee upstairs, but it seemed stupid to carry it down here when I knew you had a pot."

"Thanks. I need caffeine more than air right now. I'm so tired and dehydrated, it feels like I have a killer hangover." I pour coffee for us both. "You want sugar?"

"Nah, I'm good." He adds creamer to his mug and leans against the counter, watching me stir. "You look like shit."

"I feel like shit."

"Break any knuckles?"

"Yep. Good thing I'm a righty." I make a fist and show him my left hand. The knuckle of my middle finger is red and swollen, the bony prominence sunken beneath the others. Bruising extends to my wrist. "I didn't even feel it break. But *now* it hurts like a motherfucker."

"You should get that checked."

"There's not a whole lot they can do for it outside of ice and immobilization. I'll ask Lena to splint it when she wakes up."

He nods and sips his coffee. "I've never seen someone lose his shit like that."

"Yeah," I say lamely, staring at my mangled hand. "I'm one of a kind."

"I noticed the bottle was open." There's no judgment in his tone, only concern, but I can feel his blue lasers searing the side of my skull. "I didn't mention that part to Lena."

"Thanks. I appreciate it. I'll probably tell her eventually." I meet his gaze. "I didn't drink any, but you don't know how fucking close I came."

He points to my injured hand. "I think I've got a pretty good idea."

"Thanks for, uh, being there."

"Anytime, mate. Although I hope you don't make a habit of ripping shit out of the ceiling."

"Your woman's gonna be on my ass about that."

"I think we can fix it easily enough."

We fall into a companionable silence for a few minutes before Wes turns to face me. "Any idea what stopped you?"

"Your arms clamped around me seemed pretty effective, no?"

He snorts. "I'm talking about the whiskey. What stopped you at the eleventh hour?"

The hairs on my arms and neck rise, and my scalp prickles with an eerie awareness.

He could have said last minute or final second. He could have used phrases like falling off the wagon or taking the plunge. Plummeting into the abyss. Sliding down the slippery slope. Falling into the rabbit hole. He could have used any other combination of words.

But he didn't.

I stare at his face, chilled and unnerved. I don't know what to make of this twilight zone shit.

"Are you all right?"

"Yeah." I clear my throat. "The clock said 11:11."

He frowns and tilts his head to the side. "Is that your birthday?"

"No. It's a weird numerology thing Ella and I shared. A shitload of strange coincidences involving the number eleven. Can't explain it."

He smirks. "Like the spirits are trying to communicate or something?"

"Or the universe is fucking with my head. You'd shit your pants if you knew the extent of it. Anyway, you said eleventh hour and it wigged me out a little."

"Gotcha." Nodding, he sips his coffee. "So, I've been thinking about something you said last night. How you left without all the answers. If there's anything I've learned from Lena, it's how powerful the benefit of the doubt is. We wouldn't be together if she hadn't put her trust in me." He rubs his jaw. "It's not my place to make assumptions about your relationship with Ella, but my gut tells me there's more to her story. If you love her, you've gotta trust her."

"That's the thing, Wes. I did give her my trust. I told her things only Lena knows. I gave her my fucking emotional underbelly and she stabbed it."

"Did she share anything with you?"

"Well, yeah." I don't elaborate because her history is none of his business. "But she left out some pretty important shit."

"What could be her motives for keeping that information from you?"

"I don't know."

"Did you ask her?"

"Sorta." I did ask, while looming menacingly over her and yelling in her face. Despite my anger, it killed me to see fear in her eyes.

"And?" Wes pops a bagel into the toaster.

"She panicked and froze."

"In her defense, I've seen you angry and it's pretty scary." He gestures to my face. "Especially with those freaky lion eyes you've got in your noggin."

I snort. "My eyes aren't freaky."

"Keep tellin' yourself that, Garrett," he says with a chuckle. "My point is you probably scared her shitless. Did she make any attempt to explain herself?"

"Yeah." I rub the back of my neck. "But I cut her off. I left without letting her explain."

"Yet you're angry you don't have the whole story?"

"Damn it, Dundee."

He laughs and retrieves his toasted bagel, smearing a generous amount of butter on each half. "You see where I'm going with this?"

"Where you're going with what?" Lena's voice makes me jump. She appears in the doorway, twisting her hair up into a bun as she approaches.

"You know, Leens, it would be great if you'd stop sneaking up on us."

"No one's sneaking up on anyone. If you two weren't aware of your surroundings, that's your problem." She eyes the food and grins when she spots her favorite chive cream cheese. "Did I ever tell you how much I love you, Ace?"

Wes wraps her in a hug and kisses her. "Yes, but I wouldn't mind hearing it again."

"Coffee first. Then I'll whisper sweet nothings." She fills her mug and makes her way over to me. "Let me see your hands."

I reluctantly hold them out.

She snatches my left wrist. "Jesus, fuck. There's a knuckle fracture if I ever saw one. Where the hell were your gloves?"

"I dunno. I wasn't worried about them."

"Eat something, and then I'll splint your hand." She slathers chive cream cheese onto an everything bagel and hands it to me. "What's on your agenda for today? Are you going to the office?"

"No. I'll probably wallow in self-misery for a few hours. Maybe sleep some more."

"Skip the misery part, but a nap would do you good. We need to get your Jeep home at some point. Wes and I can do it, or you can come."

"If you guys don't mind going, that would be great. I don't wanna chance a run-in with Ella. I parked a few blocks over from her place. North, I think."

Lena shakes her head. "Directions mean nothing to me. Give me landmarks."

"There was a pizza place on the corner."

"That narrows it down. There's one on just about every corner."

"I'm sorry. That's all I've got."

"No worries, mate. We'll find it." Wes finishes his bagel and swigs what's left of his coffee. "Well, you two chat. I'm gonna go shower." He makes eye contact with me. "Think about what I said."

"Will do."

Lena waits until he's out of earshot before settling on a stool. She pats the one beside her. "Sit."

I plop onto the stool and rest my elbows on the granite. "He's a good dude."

"I know." She ruffles my hair. "You're a good dude too."

"I think you mispronounced fuckup."

She releases a heavy sigh. "I know you're beating yourself up over a near miss, but please don't. Despite all the shit that went down yesterday, you're still sober. That is a huge win. You're a strong man, Gar. I'm really fucking proud of you."

"Thanks," I mumble, resting my head in my hands.

"Obviously, Wes filled me in on the gist of things, so I'm not gonna probe you for information."

"That's a first."

"Um, excuse me, I think I've done an excellent job not being nosy."

"Gold star for sure."

She lightly punches my arm. "I mean well, and you know it." Her expression softens. "In all seriousness, I'm here for you if you need to talk."

"I know. Thank you."

"I'm sorry you're hurting. I wish I could make it go away."

"Yeah, me too. Thanks for coming to see me last night. I hope Wes isn't pissed we slept together."

"He's fine. He knows how close we are."

"He saw us in the bed."

"And?" She arches an eyebrow. "Did he kick your ass yet?"

"No."

"Then like I said, don't worry about it. He cares about you, Gar. You freaked him out last night. You scared me too, and I didn't even see you in action." She wraps her arm around my shoulders. "Wes came upstairs while you showered and set the bottle on my nightstand. I cried when he filled me in on what happened. He knew I was staying with you because I told him not to wait up for me."

"I'm sorry."

"Don't apologize. We're family. I'll always be here for you."

We eat our bagels in silence for a few minutes. The dough soaks up the acid that has been churning in my stomach since last night. I wonder if Ella ate our ravioli without me. The pain of that thought takes my breath away.

"It hurts so fucking much."

Lena's compassion-filled eyes meet mine. "Do you love her?"

"Yeah. Fucking deeply. We connected on a level I didn't think possible. It was so much more than sex for me."

"That's the first time I've ever heard you say that."

"I've never felt it before."

"Not even with Carissa? You wanted to marry her."

I shake my head. "I was young and stupid. Now I'm old, and still stupid."

Lena rolls her eyes. "I'm not even going to address that comment. The self-loathing needs to stop, Gar. It pisses me off."

"Old habits die hard, I guess." I squeeze her knee. "To answer your question, no. I didn't feel anything like this for Carissa."

"Let me ask you something. Do you think it was Ella's goal to hurt you? I mean, was she upset when you confronted her? Or was it more of an 'Oh shit, I got caught' type of response like Carissa had when you walked in on them?"

"Ella panicked initially." I squeeze my eyes shut, thinking of how I behaved. "Then I acted like a total dick and got in her face. She actually cowered from me like I was gonna hurt her."

"Did she try to explain?"

"Yeah. She was crying." I rest my forehead on the counter. "But I called her a liar and walked out."

"Oof."

"Leens, you have no idea what went through my head when I opened the door for a woman calling herself Ella's mother. Then, when the lady said something about a *son* . . ."

"You lost your shit," she finishes for me. "What would Ella have to gain from claiming her mom was dead and keeping her son a secret?"

"I have no fucking clue. All I know is she blindsided me. None of it makes sense."

"Does she know your history?"

"I told her *everything*."

Her eyes widen. "Oh, wow. That surprises me."

"Well." I sigh heavily, debating how much I should share. I desperately need insight, and I know I can trust Lena not to repeat what I tell her. "Ella can relate to my situation. The part I don't talk about."

She nods slowly when my words sink in. "She's a survivor."

"It's how she lost her virginity at thirteen. It continued for four years."

"Mother of God," she whispers, staring at her feet. "That's so fucking young. I'm sick to my stomach right now." Her jade eyes lift to mine. "She's just like you. That's what bothers you most. You feel like you've lost someone who truly understands your pain."

"Bingo."

"Who hurt her?"

"I dunno. She wouldn't tell me."

"Where was her mother when all this went down?"

"Not dead, apparently."

"Shouldn't the mother have protected her? I mean, Jesus Christ, Ella was *thirteen*. Most kids still live at home. When was this happening? How did it go on for four years unnoticed? It was obviously someone she knew well. Do you think it could've been a family member? Or a family friend or babysitter?"

The possibility turns my stomach. I know all too well the pain family can inflict. I shudder as memories assault me.

She notices and wraps me in a quick hug. "How old is her son?"

"No clue. I didn't know he existed until last night. Of course, the scar on her lower belly makes a lot more sense now. She told me it was uterus stuff when I asked about it."

"I mean, it's technically true. A C-section is about as uterus-centered as you can get. Okay, so, we know she's a mom. Where is this kid?"

"She said she's not part of his life."

"Do you think that's by choice?"

I blink a few times. "I didn't give it much thought. I reacted."

She squeezes my good hand. "Just because she's not in his life, that doesn't necessarily mean she abandoned him. You're equating everything to how *you* felt being left behind, but this isn't about you. Not every woman has the same motivations as Arielle Zahavi. You need to consider it from all angles." She tilts her head to the side. "Do you truly think a woman who visited your hospital room with food, *and* hand-delivered a headache bean-bag and home-cooked meals to your office, has the capacity of being cold to her own kid?"

"No. She's nurturing like you. Ella doesn't have a cold bone in her body," I whisper, thinking back to one of our conversations.

"I'm sorry you felt unwanted. Your mom loved you with all her heart. Her goal was never to hurt you. She thought she was protecting you."

At the time I found her way of comforting me odd. How would she know what was going through my mother's head? Better yet, why would Mom ever think her suicide would equate to my safety? Now I realize Ella wasn't talking about my mother. She wanted to keep her own kid safe.

"There's always more to the story. As mothers, we think we know best. Only to find out we were wrong. By then it's too late, and we get to spend the rest of our lives regretting those shitty decisions."

We.

She clearly said we, but I missed it. What decision caused her such deep remorse?

Realization throat punches me. "Holy fuck. She gave him up for adoption and regrets doing it. She alluded to something, but at the time, I didn't understand what she meant. That's why she's not part of his life."

"And why might she be afraid to tell you something like that?"

"Because I've expressed a shitload of abandonment issues. She didn't want me to equate her with my mom."

"Bingo." Lena's eyes burn into mine. "And *who* do you think the father could be?"

My mouth drops open, and a sick feeling settles in my gut. Ella told me the only men she's ever willingly slept with are Paolo and me. Paolo is a family man, who's a huge part of her life. If the kid were his, he'd be around. They'd be together as a unit.

That leaves one other person.

"That motherfucker knocked her up. It all makes sense now."

"Doesn't it, though?" She sips her coffee. "We're just speculating here, so we could be totally wrong, *but* I hope you realize how unfair it is to judge her without having all the details."

I knot my fingers in my hair. "Why wouldn't she just fucking tell me? She said she loves me. She called me her soul mate for fuck's sake. She knows my deepest, darkest shit. I laid it all on the table."

"That doesn't mean she owes you her story."

"But I told—"

"You weren't always forthcoming, right? Think of all the therapy you've gone through and everything you've learned to get you where you are. Just because you're ready, willing, and able to give her your whole truth, that doesn't mean she's on the same page. Is she in therapy?"

"No."

"Okay, so this woman was abused as a child, endured it for four years, and may or may not have given birth to her rapist's baby, and you're telling me she's *not* in therapy? Are you fucking kidding me? No wonder she can't talk about it. She's been in survival mode her whole life."

"So have I."

Lena grips my arm. "You've done a lot more than survive, Garrett."

She's right. I've fucking thrived despite it all.

"People heal from trauma at different speeds. You don't have a right to demand that she be in the same place as you."

"I'm not trying to make demands. I only want her honesty, Leens. I wanna know her as well as she knows me."

"I know you do, but you need to look at the big picture. She's a rape survivor. Her body, her power, was taken from her. Her voice didn't matter to the man who hurt her. She's used to not being heard. Why should she talk?"

Another light bulb goes off in my head. "What if Ella's mother knew she was being abused and did nothing?"

"Exactly. Think about how Wendy acted when you went to her for help. How did it feel to be dismissed?"

"Like my pain didn't matter."

"Right. You were made to feel like your voice wasn't worth hearing. So, not only was Ella repeatedly raped, but the circumstances were bad enough for her to claim her mom was dead. Maybe the woman was dead to her. Is it a lie? Technically. But do technicalities really matter when someone has endured what she went through? Think about your coping methods. Are they all squeaky clean?"

"Definitely not."

"You don't have a right to vilify her without knowing all the details. Just because she withheld them, that doesn't mean she did it in bad faith. Maybe she can't go there. I think you can attest that willingness to talk about one's trauma is a big part of healing."

"The healing started when I met you."

I picture that night at the cabin when we sat in front of the fire. The haunted look in her eyes when she told me her rape wasn't a one-time deal. How her reason for being a quiet lover felt like a punch to the stomach.

"I lost my virginity with a knife to my throat. Making noise was never an option for me."

I'll never forget the way she cried and clung to me after my nightmare. My pain was her pain. We were one soul in two bodies. Mirror images of each other. Soul mates.

"Tu sei la mia anima gemelli."

How the fuck could I walk away?

"When did she first tell you she's a survivor?" Lena's question jolts me out of my thoughts.

"At the hospital as an explanation for why she walked out on me after

Burlesquerade. Apparently, I said something her rapist had said, and she freaked the fuck out." I meet her eyes. "I just wanted to hold her. She told me she doesn't snuggle, and I said, 'It can be our little secret. No one has to know what we do.' I triggered her in a big way. That's why she took off."

"Makes sense. I doubt she was ready to disclose something so personal that early in the game, which means she felt bad about hurting you." She cups my jaw like she does when she really wants to drive her point home. "Bottom line, Ella needs to heal at her own pace. Her story is hers to share, if and when she's ready to. If you love her, you need to accept that it may never happen." She releases me and sits taller. "Is that something you can live with?"

"Yes."

Unequivocally yes. I will accept the truths she offers me.

If she allows me back into her life.

I rub my hands over my face. "I fucked up big time. I was such a dick. I wouldn't let her talk." My eyes start to burn, remembering how she cried when she begged me to listen. "I ruined her Christmas. I told her that her words didn't matter to me anymore."

She winces and holds a hand over her heart. "Oof to the tenth power."

"How the fuck do I come back from that?"

"Acknowledge your fuckup and apologize. Give her your trust. Prove how sorry you are." She points to my injured hand. "You can do all that after I fix *this* fuckup."

"I'm coming with you to get my Jeep. I need to see her."

"I was hoping you'd say that."

Fifty-Three

Fear, faith, and a mother's love

Ella

Sometimes friendship looks like lunch dates and gossip. Other times it involves tissues and a shoulder to cry on. Today, it boils down to a sponge and spray bleach.

Paolo stands over my stove, scrubbing the ravioli water residue off the burner and nearby counter. "This shit's all over the place. Fresh ravioli cook in minutes. Did you leave the room?"

"No, I lay there and watched it boil over."

He narrows his eyes. "Are you being sarcastic?"

"No."

The burner sizzled and spit when water bubbled over like a subdued geyser. It flowed down the front of the stove, bringing along bits of disintegrated ravioli. I watched the growing puddle approach me with the same level of care someone would show drying paint. I didn't move off the floor until tendrils of smoke rose from the pot.

"Jesus, bella." His expression softens when he realizes I'm dead serious. He stoops to wipe the oven door, then scrapes at the pot's interior with a spatula. "You could've started a fire."

"But I didn't." I pick at some hardened ravioli dough on the island, digging my nails into it.

"Where did you sleep?"

I point to the spot in front of my fridge, then turn my attention to the stuff under my nails. It will be a long time before I make homemade pasta again.

Paolo approaches with a heavy sigh. "Go take a shower. I'll clean everything up. Then we'll go somewhere."

We have a standing date on the day after Christmas because he knows how much I hate being alone on my son's birthday. He does his best to keep me distracted from the hollow ache that throbs deeper with each passing year.

Today, numbness replaces that ache.

"Where are we going?"

"Any place you want." He touches my shoulder. "I can't have you crying in your apartment all day."

He knew something was up when I answered the door wearing last night's clothes with mascara all over my face. It didn't make sense to pretend everything was fine after my world crashed down around me. Why waste energy I don't have?

To Paolo's credit, he didn't bash or threaten Garrett like I thought he would when I filled him in on everything that happened. He simply listened.

A courtesy Garrett lacked in spades.

I'll never forget how he demanded my explanation but wouldn't allow me to give one. Or the disgust on his face when he called me a liar. "*Save your stories for the next asshole who's stupid enough to believe them.*"

Those words broke my heart.

Garrett broke *me*.

The band around my chest tightens. "I won't cry, caro, I don't have any tears left."

"Either way, you need a change of scenery." He points to the envelope on the counter. "Are you going to open it?"

I shrug instead of answering.

"I can read it for you, if you want."

I nod. "Go for it."

Sliding his finger under the seal, he opens the envelope and withdraws some folded papers.

Oh, good. She wrote me a novel.

Paolo unfolds the pages and leans on the counter, silently turning them over as he reads. Some appear handwritten. Others are typed. I could make out the words if I wanted to, but I'm more interested in his reaction to what he's reading.

Paolo is an expressive man. I always warn him to never play poker because his face is an emotional barometer. Now, the knot in my stomach grows, watching his forehead creases deepen and his dark brows come together. He refolds and tucks the letter back into the envelope after he finishes, then turns to face me. His deep brown eyes meet mine, and what I see inside them stops my heart.

Fear.

I clutch his arm. "Tell me."

He takes a few slow, deep breaths, like he knows his next words will hurt me. "Your mother has metastatic breast cancer. She's in New York for treatment at Sloan Kettering. It doesn't look good. She qualified for participation in an experimental drug trial."

My mother has been dead to me for a long time. The news of her failing health stirs up feelings I'm not sure what to do with. Sadness and guilt infuse the anger I've clung to, disrupting the balance I've created for myself.

"What else?" I whisper, knowing the worst part is yet to come.

"Her illness is called BRCA2 breast cancer. It's caused by a genetic mutation. Given its hereditary nature, you are considered high risk. She wants to make sure you get checked for mutations in the BRCA gene."

"And if I do have those mutations?"

"Your chances of developing breast and ovarian cancer are significantly higher. Your grandmother died from BRCA2 breast cancer. Now, your mother has it, meaning the link in your family is strong. The mutations can be passed along to males, so your son may also be at higher risk of developing breast or aggressive prostate cancer. That is, *if* he inherited a mutation from you."

I cover my mouth to stifle a sob. The tears I thought had dried up start flowing in rivers down my cheeks. I gave my child up to protect him and give him a better life, only to find out I may have endangered him anyway.

Paolo wraps his arms around me. I cling to him, burying my face in his chest as I fall apart.

He strokes my hair. "I know this is a lot to process, but we don't know anything for sure. You may be perfectly fine."

My body feels foreign, my own skin and bones suspicious. The bra cutting into my sides might be supporting flesh that could kill me. My blood isn't safe. My fucking DNA could be a ticking time bomb.

I've lost control of my safety again.

Paolo knocks on my bedroom door. "Are you almost ready to go?"

We're heading to his parents' place for a late lunch because I don't have the energy for a real outing. Besides, Paolo needs to be at La Bussola by four, and I've already wasted most of the day crying.

The Benicasa home is a haven. I've always found comfort there, and his mom gives the best hugs. God knows I need some warm embraces to ease the chill that has been clinging to me since I learned of my mother's illness.

My scalding hot shower didn't help soothe me. Nor did the lavender bodywash I doused myself in. Calming serenity, my ass.

I've been standing in front of my mirror for twenty minutes, naked from the waist up, probing my breasts for lumps. Droplets from my wet hair cascade down my back, soaking into the waistband of my yoga pants. My breasts always hurt like a bitch around my period. But now, I'm questioning the tender lumpiness I get every month. Have I been missing my body's clues for years? My eyes trace the curves for the hundredth time. They look normal enough. Right?

I march across my room and fling the door open. "Are they normal?"

"Whoa." Paolo blinks rapidly and takes a step back, then clears his throat and looks away. "Uh, why aren't you dressed yet?"

"Look at me, caro." I wait until his eyes meet mine. "Do they look like there's anything wrong with them? Is anything off with their coloring? Size? Shape? What about my nipples? Are they weird?"

He stares at my breasts for a long moment before speaking. "No. They look fine."

"Fine, as in, *good* fine? Or are they weird and you're just saying that because you're afraid to hurt my feelings? Do they look okay compared with other boobs you've seen?"

He grips the doorframe. "They're perfect, Ella."

I cup them, prodding the flesh once more. "Did you ever notice any lumps?"

"You never let me touch them, so I really can't answer that."

Right. Garrett was the only one I allowed. I certainly won't be calling him for a breast health update.

"Do you think I have cancer?"

Paolo releases a heavy sigh. "I think you're scared, and rightfully so. But you can't diagnose yourself. You've got to wait for more information. You may not even have the gene mutation. Try to push this out of your mind until you know more."

"I feel like I can't trust my own body," I whisper, my eyes welling up again.

"Then put your faith in something else."

Maria Benicasa settles beside me on the couch in her living room. "What's wrong?"

I give her a weak smile and sip the tea Paolo made for me. "Nothing."

She tips my chin up and meets my gaze, her warm brown eyes searching mine. "I have eight kids. I know when someone's lying to me." When I don't answer right away, she adds, "You were smiling from ear to ear at Midnight Mass. Now you look as miserable as Massimo. What changed since Christmas Eve?"

I glance at her son through the archway to their kitchen. He's still scowling into a glass of whiskey. His longtime girlfriend broke things off yesterday, making his Christmas equally as shitty as mine.

I meet Maria's gaze again. "Massimo and I are in the same boat. I also had a breakup last night."

Her eyes widen. "Oh? Paolo never mentioned that you were seeing someone."

My heart cracks down the center with the reminder that I hurt him too. "That's because Paolo doesn't like him."

She sighs. "I don't think that's the reason he kept quiet about it." She nods toward the kitchen, where Paolo is attempting to console his brother. "He's always been the kind of man to chase the unattainable."

"I'm sorry," I whisper, unsure of how much she knows. The look in her eyes tells me it's a lot more than I hoped. "I never meant to hurt him." My ragged voice cracks beneath the suffocating weight of my guilt.

Maria wraps her arm around my shoulders. "You have nothing to apologize for. He is responsible for his own feelings."

"I care for him deeply. I just—"

"Dolcezza, I understand. You can't force that kind of love." She touches my cheek. "He's happy to have you in his life in whatever capacity you allow. We all are."

How can she possibly call me "sweetness" when I've been anything but to her son? A tear rolls down my cheek. "I don't deserve him. Or any of you."

"Nonsense. Everyone deserves a family's love." She grips my shoulders. "Your last name isn't Benicasa, but you're one of us. You're family, Ella. We all love you."

"Thank you. I love you too."

She pulls me into a tight hug and strokes my hair. "Now tell me about the foolish man who broke your heart."

Fifty – Four

Snowbanks, perseverance, and a vow

Garrett

Snow ordinances can eat a bag of dicks.

After cruising up and down the streets near Ella's apartment for a half hour, Lena and I finally realized my Jeep was, in fact, missing. We located the pizza place I'd seen and walked the entire block. Then we noticed the "no parking" sign. The fucker was ten feet away, but I missed it in my haste to see Ella. Now I have to shell out four hundred bucks to have my vehicle released from the impound lot.

Lena purses her lips. "At least you know why you couldn't find it last night. I was beginning to worry about your sense of direction. It wouldn't be the first time I wanted someone to put a tracking chip in you."

"Why the fuck would they tow someone's ride on Christmas?"

She points to the wallet I'm holding. "Cash money. Duh."

I motion to the dirty snowbanks lining the one-way street. "I hope the city is happy with itself. They did a shitty job plowing."

"Probably because your car was in the way?"

I narrow my eyes at her. "Thanks. I didn't put two and two together."

We trudge back to her Subaru, and Lena drives toward the impound lot. I stare out the passenger window and pick at the Velcro on my finger immobilizer.

"Stop picking."

My eyes dart over to her. "The edge is sharp."

"I'll trim it when we get home." She juts her chin at my hand. "It's kinda funny you hurt your middle finger. Now it's gonna stick up all the time until you can stop wearing the brace."

"It makes sense since the past twenty-four hours have been one big 'fuck you' to me."

"Do you have a game plan?"

"Well, she's not taking my calls, so I'll have to grovel in person. I'm gonna head back over to her place once we get my Jeep."

"And if she's not home?"

"I'll wait for her."

"What if she's not receptive to your groveling tactics?"

"I don't know what I'll do." The possibility of Ella truly being done with me feels like a cleaver to the chest. "If she won't take me back, I guess I'll leave her alone."

"Really?" We stop at a red light and her eyes meet mine. "The Garrett Casey I know doesn't quit."

"You have an absurdly high opinion of me then."

"Gar, you're the most persistent guy I know. Don't you dare tuck your tail and run. If you love this woman, you fucking persevere until you earn her forgiveness."

I approach the doorman for Ella's apartment building, forcing myself to stay calm. "Hey, how's it going? I'm here to see Ella Sammons. Would you mind buzzing me in?"

He shakes his head. "She's not here."

"Damn. Do you have any idea where she went?"

"She left around two with that guy she hangs out with. Paul or whatever."

Paolo.

The pain in the pit of my stomach grows. My stupidity pushed her back into the arms of her haven. I hope I'm not too late.

"Can you please tell her Garrett came by?"

"Sure, man."

"Thanks," I mutter, trudging back to my Jeep. This time I paid attention to the signs and put a fuckload of money into the meter before parking.

I slide into the driver's seat and check my phone. Ella still hasn't responded to any of my texts, and her number goes straight to voice mail. I can't blame her for shutting me out. I was an asshole. My behavior erased all the progress we made together.

My planning skills fail me, and I have no idea how to proceed. It's not like I can march into La Bussola and throw myself at her feet.

Or can I?

La Bussola is packed for a Monday, making me wonder if I stumbled into a private holiday party. Waitstaff carrying trays laden with food and drinks hustle through the dining area. It's easy to distinguish the employees from the patrons because they're wearing crisp, white shirts paired with black pants.

Ella is nowhere to be seen, but that doesn't mean she's not here. As part of the Benicasa inner circle, I'm sure she has access to the kitchen and staff-only areas.

I approach the hostess, an attractive middle-aged woman wearing a red sweater dress. Peering through a pair of tortoiseshell reading glasses, she scrawls something in her notebook, then places a stack of menus beneath her mahogany podium.

"Welcome to La Bussola. Do you have a reservation?" Her thick Italian accent gives away her identity before she makes eye contact.

"No. I'm looking for . . . a friend."

Paolo's mother studies my face, her dark eyes focusing on mine. Her expression's intensity mirrors what I've seen from her son. She steps out from behind the podium and props her hand on her hip. "Hello, Garrett."

I blink a few times instead of answering.

She must find my deer-in-the-headlights imitation amusing because she chuckles. "You're surprised I know who you are."

"Um, yeah."

She stares up at me. "If someone in my family is upset, I know about it. The same goes for my restaurant. If something happens here, you can bet your ass it will be on my radar."

Great. I'm already on her shit list. The woman can't be taller than five foot four, but her formidable presence makes my insides shrivel.

I stuff my hands into my pockets. "I assume you're about to ask me to leave."

"It depends on why you're here." She tilts her head to the side. "If it's to stir up trouble, you know where the door is."

"I'm not here to cause drama. I just need to see her."

"For what reason?"

It doesn't serve me to play coy. I'm not sure how much she knows, but this lady clearly doesn't fuck around.

"To beg for forgiveness."

"Good answer. Come with me." She turns on her heel and heads behind the bar.

I follow without a word. No one with half a brain cell would challenge a woman like this. Most days I have at least two brain cells. Except for yesterday, obviously. There were zero synapses firing when I fucked up the best thing that ever happened to me.

She motions to the glass bottles shelved nearby. "Would you like something to drink?"

Yes. "No, thank you. I don't drink."

Resting her elbows on the gleaming bar, she watches my face for an eternity before speaking. "Unfortunately, you're a little too late. Ella left twenty minutes ago."

"Okay. I'll try her at home."

"She wasn't headed home."

I wait, unsure whether I should ask about Ella's whereabouts or let her continue staring me down in silence. It's not my place to interrogate the woman in her own restaurant, but I didn't come here to leave without answers.

"Do you know where she went?"

"No." She points toward the door to the kitchen. "But I'm sure my son does. You can ask him."

"With all due respect, Mrs. Benicasa, I doubt your son will entertain any questions from me."

"He might surprise you." She turns toward a man seated at the opposite end of the bar, sipping a tumbler of whiskey. "Massimo."

If I recall correctly from Ella's story, he's the DEA agent. The guy's a younger, bigger version of Paolo, and if his broody glower is any indication, he's in a piss-poor mood.

He looks up from his glass. "Yeah, Ma?"

"Stop wallowing and go get your brother."

He slams his tumbler down with a scowl. "For the last time, I'm *not* wallowing."

"It's Christmas. Everyone's doing their part, and you're crying into your booze. Tell your brother to come out here."

"Christmas was yesterday," he mutters, rising. His stool scrapes the floor as he shoves it aside. "Which one?"

"Paolo. This man needs to speak to him."

Massimo's dark gaze lands on me and narrows. "Name?"

"Garrett Casey."

Something registers in his head, and his expression intensifies. He gives me a brief once-over, then stalks to the kitchen.

Mrs. Benicasa shakes her head and sighs. "Don't mind him. Massimo has a lot on his plate."

"I get it."

The bell on the door jingles, and more patrons enter the restaurant, bringing a gust of frigid air. Massimo returns a moment later with Paolo, whose scowl is even deeper than his own.

Here we go.

Paolo ducks behind the bar and makes his way over, drying his hands on the black apron he's wearing. Mrs. Benicasa leaves to greet the new arrivals, but Massimo settles on a closer stool, peering at us over the top of his glass like he's ready for a brawl.

Paolo stops directly in front of me and crosses his arms over his chest. "What do you want?"

"I think you know the answer to that."

He narrows his eyes. "She has bigger problems to deal with than you."

"Like what?"

"None of your business."

I can already tell this isn't going to be a productive conversation. Why not get right to the point? Maybe I can rile him up enough to get some answers.

"Where is she?"

"Also, none of your business."

"Fair enough. Answer me this. Is the kid's father the same guy—"

"Don't say another word." Fire flashes in his eyes with the growled command. He points to the kitchen door. "Let's go."

Even though it's against my better judgment, and every rule in my playbook, I follow him. We pass the kitchen and veer down a long hallway. It's darker and much quieter in this part of the restaurant, the perfect setting for a murder. Hopefully, I don't wind up at the bottom of the Hudson.

He points to a small office. "In here." We head inside, and he closes the door behind us before turning to face me. He crosses his arms over his chest once more. "My brothers don't know about what happened to her. And it needs to stay that way."

I nod in understanding. I respect him for safeguarding Ella's privacy.

He settles on the edge of his desk and stares at me in silence.

Paolo stands between Ella and me. I've been in his position, and I know the power he holds as gatekeeper. Thanks to Wes, I'm well acquainted with the role. But this is my first time on the receiving end.

Bottom line, Ella cares for him. It doesn't serve me to be a dick. I need to swallow my pride and accept the fact that he's got me by the balls.

"I didn't come here to start shit." I wait for him to respond. He doesn't, of course. "I know I fucked up."

"You hurt her."

"I know. She blindsided me, and I reacted without thinking. She told me her mother was dead."

"Her mother's been dead to her a long time."

"Why?"

"None of your business."

I release a heavy sigh and rub the back of my neck. "Okay, then what *is* my business? The son she failed to mention? Is his father the man who raped her?"

Pain and fury glow in his eyes, but he doesn't answer. His clenched jaw and flaring nostrils tell me everything I need to know.

I tilt my head to the side. "That's why she gave him up, isn't it? And if my estimations are correct, he's what? Eleven? Twelve?" I ask, even though I don't expect him to answer.

That's fine. He doesn't need to speak. He's expressive enough that I'll figure it out by watching his reaction.

He stares at my face in silence, like he's trying to gauge how much I know. "Thirteen." The word leaves his lips on a defeated sigh. Then he shocks me by adding, "Today's his birthday. She had him five days before she turned seventeen."

I've got him talking now. Good. Emboldened by my success, I chance another question. "Why didn't she tell me about him?"

"Are you fucking stupid?"

"Depends on who you ask," I say with a shrug. "I'm assuming it has something to do with my history."

"Given your reaction to the news, I'd say she had good reason to keep her mouth shut."

"Why? Because I can relate to him? This may be a surprise to you, but abandonment hurts."

He lurches to his feet and grabs me by the collar. It's a move that would send my fist into anyone else's face, but I force myself to keep my cool.

"Let me tell you something. If you think for one second that woman didn't agonize over her decision, you don't know her at all."

"I don't know her as well as I thought I did."

"Yeah? Guess what? *I* do." He grips my shirt tighter. "I was there. I brought her home from the hospital. I heard her crying herself to sleep for months, knowing she had made the wrong choice. I've been there every year when she falls apart on his birthday. You don't get to crucify her for doing what she thought was best." He releases me and steps back. "She's done enough of that herself."

I shift gears. "What did you mean when you said she has bigger problems than me?"

"None of your business."

"Pick a new answer. That one's getting old. What health-related issue did her mother want to tell her about? Is Ella okay?"

He clenches his jaw and stares over my shoulder at the ivory crucifix hanging on the wall. The pain twisting his expression makes my stomach bottom out.

"Tell me," I growl, clamping my hands on his shoulders. "I need to know if she's all right."

"That remains to be seen."

"Where is she?" Releasing him, I repeat my earlier question. "I want to apologize for the way I reacted. I know I was a dick. She didn't deserve any of it. I love her."

His eyes snap to mine. "You don't deserve her."

"You think I don't know that?"

"What do you have that I don't?" His hollow tone mirrors his expression. "How can *you* be the one she loves?"

"I can't answer that, Paolo."

"Neither can I." He slowly shakes his head. "You see, I don't give a fuck about you, Garrett Casey. I don't care about your past. Your wounds. Any of it." I'm about to tell him the feeling's mutual when he adds, "But her happiness means *everything* to me."

"Her happiness matters to me too."

He grips my shirt once more, his fury returning with a vengeance. "If you ever hurt her again, it'll be the last time you hurt anyone. They will *never* find your body." His eyes glow with enough hatred to burn down the city. "I'll be watching you closely, Casey. The next time you fuck up, I'll be there to pick up the pieces. I'll *always* be there. Don't think for a second I'll push her away when she reaches for me."

How does one respond to a statement like that?

I can't blame him for his ferocity. If anything, I admire him. It takes balls to threaten me. Very few people get away with it. His threats don't scare me, even if they do hold truth. I won't give her a reason to reach for him. If Ella gives me another chance, I'll make damn sure I never let her go.

"I'll die before I hurt her again."

A sinister smile curves his lips. "Is that a promise?"

"Yeah." I hold my uninjured hand over my heart to placate him.

"You'll find her at Saint Jude's Cathedral. Now get the fuck out of my restaurant."

Fifty-Five

A secret meeting, an apparition, and solid ground

Ella

I hustle down the sidewalk toward Saint Jude's Cathedral, eager to get out of the wind. My phone buzzes inside my purse, so I pull it out and glance at the screen. Unknown number. Deciding I've already lost all I can lose, I answer it. "Hello?"

"Ella. It's Harvey." My boss's hushed voice reaches my ears. "Do you have a minute?"

"Um, I'm about to go to church. Why? What's up?"

"Listen, I know you're off the next couple of days, but I need to talk to you about something important."

I duck inside a bank's doorway and lean against the ATM. "I have time right now. I'm already late for Mass. What's a few minutes more?"

"No. I need to speak with you in person." His voice drops even lower. "Off the record."

A chill races down my spine. "Is everything okay?"

"Can you meet me for coffee tomorrow morning?"

"Uh, sure. Where? What time?"

"How about Compass Roasters at ten?"

"That works for me. Is everything okay, Harvey?" I repeat the question, growing more uneasy by the second. "Is this about Elias Hawke? I know I told you I couldn't do the interview, but I was overwhelmed when you first said it. I swear I'm trying to track him down." Rather, I *will* be once I get my shit together.

"We'll talk." He coughs loudly. "Gotta go. Bye." The line goes dead.

I stare at my phone in stunned silence. The blinking "missed call" icon catches my attention, but I'm too rattled to deal with it. My boss's behavior has my stomach twisting into knots. What could possibly be so important that we need to have a secret meeting tomorrow? Did my initial refusal to interview Hawke put my job in jeopardy?

A gust of wind sends me scurrying toward the church once more, eager to find some warmth.

Father Angelo rests his hand on my shoulder. "I will take care of it this week. Try to push those thoughts out of your mind."

"Thank you. I'll try."

Mass ended a few minutes ago. I waited for everyone to file out of the cathedral before approaching him about my potential health fiasco, and the plan I formulated with Paolo after we spent the afternoon on the phone.

We called my insurance company and every in-network breast doctor in the city. Of the six covered physicians, only two are accepting new patients. The soonest appointment is eight weeks from now, meaning I get to live with this uncertainty for two fucking months.

"I appreciate your help, Father."

He smiles. "That's why I'm here. I'll let you know when I've spoken to them."

While it would make more sense to reach out to my son's adoptive parents *after* I have more information, I can't handle waiting that long. If he's at risk, I want them to know as soon as possible. I have no clue about their insurance, but I assume a child would be given higher scheduling priority. Either way, being proactive helps me feel more in control of the situation.

Today's his birthday. The least I can give him is the gift of knowledge.

The unopened presents beneath my Christmas tree come to mind, and a wave of pain slams me at the thought of returning to my empty apartment. Alone. Just like always.

Paolo said I was welcome to stay with him, but I don't feel right sapping up his comfort and giving him nothing in return. I could've hung out at La Bussola for longer, but I didn't want my clouds to darken my favorite family's place of business. Although, Massimo's sour mood rivaled even mine.

"Would it be okay if I hang out for a while, Father? I don't want to be home right now."

"Take all the time you need."

"Thank you." I give him a weak smile and head over to the candles.

Father Angelo turns his attention to the poinsettias decorating the altar. He hums "Silent Night" while watering his beloved flowers. His songs usually soothe me. Right now, it makes my heart ache.

Tonight *will* be silent without Garrett in my life.

I make the sign of the cross and light a candle for my grandmother, then select one for my son. I watch them flicker for a minute before settling on the worn leather kneeler to pray in front of the Madonna and child statue.

"Put your faith in something else."

Paolo's words echo in my mind. I beat back the surfacing thoughts of my mother and pray for my health. I've been to hell and back, survived something no one should have to endure, and I'm still here. I may not be strong, but I'm far from weak. I'll handle whatever cards I'm dealt.

Alone.

A tear slides down my cheek. Then another. I make no effort to wipe them because I've used up all my energy today. Harvey's mysterious call was the icing on the cake. I don't know what I'll do if my job is at risk. Swallowing tightly, I trace the marble statue's curves with blurry eyes and succumb to the "if onlys" swirling in my head.

I should've been honest with Garrett from the start. He wouldn't have gotten involved with me, but that's better than feeling like half of my soul shattered. With him, I found treasure in a sea of pain. Passion after years of apathy. He was the mirror who reflected the best parts of me and absorbed my darkness. But I ruined our bond by hiding behind a mask. *Tu sei la mia anima gemelli.* My words haunt me, like they've been doing since he slammed the door behind him. I lost the only man I've ever loved because I was afraid.

I lost my baby for the very same reason. My fears about being a shitty mother seem so foolish now. Even though I was a terrified teenager with no money, and probably couldn't have provided for him, the fact that I didn't even *try* kills me. If I feel this much love for a child who I haven't held in thirteen years, I can only imagine how full my heart would've been if I had raised him.

I'm tired of the cycle of fear and loss. How many times do I need to sabotage myself before I finally learn? Now that my health is in question—and quite possibly my career—I feel more lost than ever. When will faith and triumph take over? When is it my turn for happiness? How can I find peace when my life is a raging tempest?

Movement in my periphery draws my attention to the left. "Sorry, Father, I'm almost—" My mouth drops open, and my lungs stop working.

It's not Father Angelo coming to check on me.

Garrett silently kneels beside me like an apparition my broken heart conjured. The kneeler creaks beneath our combined weight, and his woodsy scent fills my nose. Heat radiates from where our shoulders touch, telling me I'm not imagining him.

He's really here. Beside me. I don't move or speak for fear he might vanish. Questions flood my mind. I open and close my mouth, unsure where to begin.

How did he know where to find me?

That's easy enough. The only person who knew I was coming here was Paolo, which means he sent Garrett my way. My dearest friend set aside his own feelings in favor of my happiness. It shouldn't surprise me—he's always been selfless—but my heart aches, knowing how painful it was for him.

Garrett rests his elbows on the marble banister in front of us, swiveling his head to meet my gaze. Regret glows in his golden eyes, a feeling I'm all too familiar with. Even with dark circles beneath them, they still have the same soul-stealing effect.

He doesn't have to tell me he's sorry. I already know. It's written on his features. Everything from the muscle pulsing in his jaw, to his slumped shoulders begs for my forgiveness. For God's sake, the man is on his knees. In church.

As if on cue, the church bells echo through the cathedral, telling us it's seven o'clock. It's been almost twenty-four hours since we imploded.

He slides his hand toward mine but doesn't touch me, lingering mere inches away. His upturned palm is an invitation I'm not sure I should accept. I stare at his hand in silence, aching to hold it, but terrified he'll let go of me again.

Is he capable of trusting a woman who lied to him? Will he understand

and respect my motives, even if he doesn't agree with them? Can he accept there will always be a part of me in hiding?

Are we worth the risk to each other?

The answer is yes. We're at much greater risk to ourselves alone. Sometimes need surpasses risk, and hope outweighs caution. The very ideals we're afraid to hold on to are what finally save us. Healing and forgiveness aren't solitary. My redemption swims in a sea of molten gold.

I slide my hand into his waiting palm and interlace our fingers. His warmth seeps into me. His strong grip is my anchor.

"Ella, I'm so sorry." The emotion in his whispered apology takes my breath away. "I reacted out of anger. I was hurt and confused. You didn't deserve to be treated that way."

"I'm sorry I wasn't completely honest. I'll give you a full explanation if you're still interested in hearing it."

"I don't need an explanation. You don't owe me a damn thing." He grips my hand tighter. "Just tell me our connection is real. I need to know there's truth behind what I'm feeling." He blinks rapidly and draws a few slow, deep breaths. "I love you, Ella." A tear slides down his cheek. "Please tell me it's real."

Our love is not a masquerade. It's an irrefutable verity.

"Every second we spent together was real, Garrett. *Tu sei la mia anima gemelli. Ti amo.*" I cup his face with my free hand. "It *is* real. You're the only man I've ever loved. The only person I've allowed close enough to see my darkness. I love you so much more than you realize, tesoro."

He wraps me in his arms, and I melt into his embrace, my tears dampening his shirt. We cling to each other with the desperation of star-crossed lovers secretly meeting in a forest. Like we've spent our lives reaching for something that's finally tangible, and we'll be damned if we let it go. Dangers lurk all around us, but we're safe because we have each other.

Our days of floating in the ether are over. We're on solid ground now. Together. And I know to the depth of my soul, that's where we'll stay.

This must be what faith feels like.

Fifty–Six

Holy water, a keepsake box, and answers

Garrett

The questions haven't gone away, but Ella is in my arms. She's warm. Soft. And real. Those are the only answers I need.

I hold her tighter. The Velcro on my finger immobilizer rubs against her hair, reminding me of last night's stupidity. I can't believe I broke my fucking knuckle. It throbs like a bitch, but the pain is tolerable.

Because she's here.

Ella's wearing a college hoodie and yoga pants. Snow boots replace her trademark stilettos. Her hair is tied back in a messy bun. She's makeup-free, and her eyes are bloodshot with dark circles beneath them, but she's never been more beautiful.

"Did it catch fire?" she whispers.

I pull back to look at her face. "Huh?"

"The holy water. You said it would burst into flames if you walked into a church."

A laugh rumbles in my chest. "No. But I didn't dip my finger in it. So, I really can't be sure."

"We should test it on the way out."

I cup her face in my hands. "What are the rules?"

"I'm not sure." Her wide turquoise eyes meet mine. "We probably need new ones."

It makes sense she's wary of me and my intentions. I was a dick last night. I yelled in her face and told her I didn't trust her. I made demands and pushed boundaries I had no right to encroach on. I silenced her when she needed to be heard. She cowered from me in fear.

All because I used moves from her rapist's playbook.

The reality of that disgusts me, and I regret my behavior with every fiber of my existence. She should never have reason to make those correlations about me. Ever.

And I'll do everything in my power to prove that to her.

"Can we please start over? I need a clean slate, El. I've gotta show you last night isn't who I am."

"I know that, Garrett."

"Do you?"

"Yes."

Part of me worries she's saying it to appease me, but I need to trust her if I'm ever going to redeem myself. I need to listen *and* hear her. Without judgment or doubt.

I brush my thumb over her lower lip. "So, can we start over?"

She narrows her eyes in confusion. "Start over, how?"

"From the beginning." I climb to my feet and help her up, then hold out my hand to her. She clasps it, still unsure, but that doesn't deter me. "Hi, I'm Garrett Casey. I'm an only child from Lancaster, Pennsylvania. My parents both killed themselves and left me feeling unwanted and abandoned. I resent my mother for putting me in a shitty situation, and I'll forever be a broken little boy with mommy issues. I struggle with depression, anxiety, and a constant feeling of loss. I'm a recovering alcoholic with an addictive personality and a long history of self-destructive behavior. I tend to bite off more than I can chew. I need to excel at everything, so it feels like I'm in control. I love graphic design and theater. I hate clowns. I have a voracious appetite for sex. I have no concept of romantic normalcy, but I know my heart beats for you."

"I'm Ella—" She snatches my other hand and gently caresses it. "Oh my God. What happened?"

"Boxing accident. I, uh, had a rough night. Broke a knuckle."

"Are you all right? Does it hurt?"

"It's fine. I'll live."

She nods, studying my bruises. "I remember you saying you turn to boxing when the cravings are bad." She stiffens, and her gaze snaps to mine. "Please tell me you didn't call Anya."

"No. I didn't. I wouldn't do that to you." Sex never once came to mind during my devastation.

She chews her lip. "Did you . . . have a drink?"

"No." I stare into her eyes and slowly shake my head. "I bought a bottle and carried it home. Opened it. Held it to my lips. I came so close I could taste it. Then I looked at the clock."

"What time was it?" she whispers, peering into my soul.

"Eleven minutes after eleven." I gesture to the crucifix behind the altar and press a hand to my heart. "I swear."

I'm not a religious man. But for her, I'll swear on the Madonna and child statue in front of us, every pane of stained glass in this cathedral, the priest himself, and the God she believes in. I'll do whatever it takes for her to understand my sincerity.

"I love you, Ella. *Tu sei la mia anima gemelli.*"

Tears fill her eyes once more, and she throws her arms around my neck. "Let's go home. I want to show you something."

We head down the aisle toward the cathedral's rear, walking hand in hand. The church is empty, save for Ella's priest, who's fixing the hymn books in the last pew.

He greets us with a smile. "All set, Ella?"

"Yes, Father Angelo. Thank you." She gestures to me. "This is Garrett Casey, the man I told you about."

His white robes swish with his approach, the gold embroidery glinting in the cathedral's dim lights. "Hello, Garrett. Nice to put a face with the name."

We shake. "Nice to meet you, sir."

"I trust you two have worked everything out?" He has kind eyes—unlike the judgy priest at Jim and Wendy's church.

"We have, sir."

He wrinkles his nose. "Sir is too formal. If Father isn't your style, Ang is cool too."

I smile because I've never heard a priest use the word cool. This one is clearly way cooler than any clergy I've met.

"I'll keep that in mind. Thank you."

He smiles and touches mine and Ella's shoulders. "Peace be with you."

"And also with you," she murmurs on our behalf. "Good night, Father. Buon Natale."

Peace is something I never imagined finding, but I feel it right now. From my toes to the top of my head.

Ella leads us into the vestibule, buttoning her peacoat as she walks. She stops by the marble font containing holy water and smiles up at me. "Wanna give it a try?"

"Sure. Why not?" I make a show of lowering my finger to the water, then abruptly dunk my entire hand. Yelping, I jump back like it burns me. "Aargh! It hurts!" I clutch my faux scalded hand to my chest, but the priceless look on her face makes me burst out laughing. "Gotcha."

"Not funny." She pouts for a split second before joining in my laughter. "I can't believe you fell for it."

"Um, it was a convincing yelp. That was a jerky thing to do, by the way."

"Guess what, Cupcake?" I stage-whisper, flicking droplets of holy water at her. "I'm a dick sometimes."

"You can't say dick in church." She grabs my sleeve and tugs me outside.

We descend the front steps to the sidewalk and stand in a streetlight's glow. It's snowing again, the cold white powder dusting our hair and eyelashes.

Ella stands on her tiptoes and kisses me slow and deep. I pull her close, losing myself in a heaven I thought I'd lost. It's a kiss that erases time and dries our tears. It heals the wounds we've inflicted on each other, and the ones that came before. It's a kiss of forgiveness. Redemption.

The wind gusts around us, but we don't feel the cold.

Only peace.

I examine the ornaments on Ella's Christmas tree. They're all hand-painted pieces of art, but the most intriguing ones have a tiny number written in permanent marker on the bottom.

She enters the room carrying a wooden box and sets it on the coffee table. "Beautiful, aren't they?"

"They really are. So intricate." I flip a piano ornament over and run my finger over the number thirteen. "What's this about?"

"The numbered ones are for my son. Every Christmas I pick out a special ornament just for him. I bought the piano in Bryant Park on my way to visit you at the hospital." She brushes her finger along the tiny keys and releases a wistful sigh. "Today is his birthday. He just celebrated his thirteenth Christmas. I'm not part of his life—I'm not even sure he knows I exist—but not a day goes by when I don't miss him." She looks up at me with damp eyes. "Giving him up was the biggest mistake of my life."

Her pain slices through me. I want to say something, but I don't know how to ease that ache for her, so I wrap her in my arms and hold her tightly.

"Thank you," she whispers. "I needed a hug."

We settle on the sofa and sip the hot cocoa she made for us. She retrieves the wooden box and lifts the lid.

"Is this your treasure chest?"

"Something like that." She withdraws an envelope. "I'm going to tell you a story. It's all true, but if I pretend it's not about me, it'll be easier to tell you."

I take her hands in mine. "Ella, you don't need to tell me anything you're not ready to share. Your story is yours. You don't owe it to me."

"I want you to understand why I am the way I am." She pulls a sheet of paper from the envelope and hands it to me. "Read it if you can."

I unfold what looks like a birth certificate, but I'm not sure because it's in Italian.

"Once upon a time, a baby girl was born in Rome. Her name was Rosella Battista, and she was the daughter of Raffaele and Concetta." She hands me a newspaper clipping. The woman in the picture is wearing a white dress.

"Your parents' wedding announcement?"

She nods. "They were very much in love. Raffaele was killed in a car crash when Rosella was two." She unfolds an Italian newspaper article depicting a mangled sedan. Then another scrap with her father's obituary. "His death destroyed Concetta, and she swore she'd never love another man. After a few years, she moved to America with Rosella, hoping for a fresh start. Rosella was eleven at the time. They lived in an apartment on Garrett Street in Queens. Unfortunately, the building sold after six months, and they had to move. Concetta relocated them to Manhattan. Housing was very expensive there, much like it is now, so they lived in a slum."

I listen intently, terrified she'll stop talking.

"Concetta got a job at a nearby diner. She worked long hours, so Rosella was often left alone. Americans call them latchkey kids." She stares at her hands for a moment like she's afraid they may bite.

I hold out my upturned palm like always. She grips me and squeezes like I'm the lifeline she needs. I squeeze back to let her know I'm here, but I stay silent.

"Concetta was a beautiful woman, and she garnered the attention of many men. One day she met a wealthy man at the diner. He was a frequent patron. This man was incredibly handsome and charismatic." Bitterness laces her tone, and she takes a few deep breaths before continuing, "He treated Concetta to fancy dinners and expensive gifts, and it wasn't long before she fell in love with him. She and Rosella moved into his apartment, which was like a palace compared to where they'd been living. He was kind to Rosella and quickly earned her trust." Tears well in her eyes, spilling over as she blinks.

A sick feeling pools in my gut, already knowing where the story leads.

"And then, one night when Rosella was thirteen . . ."

I touch her cheek. "You don't have to continue, El. Everything makes sense now."

"No, I need to." She wipes her face on her hoodie's sleeve. "I need you to know." She straightens, rolling her shoulders back so she sits taller. "Rosella was thirteen the first time her mother's boyfriend raped her. He held a knife to her throat and threatened her with eviction, physical harm, even death. Since she didn't want to ruin her mother's fairy tale or wind up on the streets, she kept her mouth shut.

"When she was old enough to get a job, Rosella started working at a classmate's family restaurant. She washed dishes and bused tables, saving every cent she earned. Her classmate's older brother found her crying in the supply closet one afternoon. He made her a bowl of soup and asked if she was okay. She lied to him, but he saw right through it. And so it became their routine. Every shift he'd feed her a bowl of pasta fagioli and ask if she was safe. And she'd lie every time." She squeezes her eyes shut. "But he knew she wasn't okay."

My respect for Paolo grows, imagining myself in his position. How would I handle it if one of my employees was in danger? Would I trust my gut? Would I keep asking questions?

Absolutely.

Ella meets my gaze. "One afternoon, Rosella realized her period was two weeks late. On the way to work, she bought herself a pregnancy test at the pharmacy near her job. She peed on the stick in the women's bathroom at work and fell apart when the pink plus sign appeared. She was only sixteen." She squeezes my hand tighter. "She was too upset to leave the bathroom. A patron told an older server there was a young woman crying in the far stall. The coworker finally coaxed Rosella out. Her friend was waiting in the hallway with soup. He led her down the hall to the office, closed the door behind him, and sat on the edge of his desk." She stares at our entwined hands as the memories hit her.

I envision him seated on the desk, just like he did with me, and can't fathom how helpless he felt. Now I truly understand where his ferocity stems from.

Ella snags a tissue and blows her nose. "He said, 'Rosella, I know you've been lying to me. I'm not mad, and you aren't in trouble, but I want you to listen to me very closely. There's a room waiting for you at my parents' house if you ever need a safe place to stay.' Rosella was moved by his kindness, so when he asked what was going on, she showed him the pregnancy test. He handed her a tissue and wrote something on a take-out menu." She reaches into the wooden box and withdraws a tri-folded page, placing it in my hand.

Scrawled on the back of La Bussola's menu is a Manhattan address, a phone number, and a note:

> Our door is open. Any time of the day or night. No questions asked.
>
> ~P

"Rosella tucked the menu in her purse and went home. The *landlord* was there, and he'd been drinking, so he was particularly rough with her that night. Something changed while he was on top of her. It was like he could sense her growing defiance before she could. He became violent and squeezed her neck while repeating the same threats as always."

Bile rises in my throat when she demonstrates the sick bastard's hold on her neck. I've never wanted retribution more than I do right now.

"Rosella skipped school the next day and went to the diner where her mother worked. It was the only way she knew she could speak to her privately. She showed Concetta the marks on her neck and told her what happened, even revealing her pregnancy news." Ella's haunted eyes meet mine. "But Concetta didn't believe her."

"What the fuck did she think happened to your neck?" I sputter, knotting my hands in my hair. "Did she think you did it to yourself?"

"No one but Concetta can say what she thought, but I can tell you what she said." Tears stream down her cheeks. She doesn't bother to brush them away. "She called me a slut. Said I was an ungrateful drama queen who should've kept my legs closed. Instead of trying to ruin her life with lies, I should just admit one of the Benicasa boys knocked me up. You see, I was obviously *jealous* of her happiness." She makes air quotes around the last part and releases a humorless laugh. "Rape's every girl's dream, right?"

I'm so twisted up by her story, I can hardly breathe, let alone speak. I remember how it felt when Wendy blew me off. I understand the devastation of betrayal at the hands of a family member. A piece of me dies inside, recalling the words I used last night. I called Ella a liar. I'm no better than her piece-of-shit mother. My eyes fill with tears, but I blink them away. This isn't about me.

"Two things happened that day." Ella's voice halts my inner monologue. "I cut my mother out of my life, and the girl that was Rosella Battista ceased to exist. I haven't used my given name since. Especially, since he liked to whisper it while he fucked me."

Every muscle in my body tenses with the urge to rip the motherfucker's throat out. "I'm sorry I—"

"Most people already called me Ella, so that part was easy enough. I picked up Sammons when I was old enough to legally change my name. Mrs. Sammons was my neighbor when I got my first apartment on my own. She reminded me of my grandmother."

"What happened when you left the diner?"

"La Bussola wasn't open yet—they open late on Mondays—so I went to the address Paolo gave me. His younger siblings were in school, and his parents were buying supplies for the restaurant. He was the only one home. I will never forget the look on his face when he saw my neck."

"I'm surprised he didn't go after your . . . landlord. He made a point to threaten my life earlier."

"He doesn't know who hurt me. I never told him that part because I *know* he'd kill him."

"He couldn't figure it out?"

"He hasn't yet, and I'd like to keep it that way. All he knows is that some guy raped, impregnated, and assaulted me. He knows my mother not believing me was the reason I cut her off. I never told him my relationship to the bastard who hurt me. Or that it went on for four years. You're the only one who knows that part."

"Did he ask?"

"He still does once in a while, but I'll take it to the grave."

"Why?"

"Because Paolo was there during the darkest time in my life."

"I understand and respect that, but your silence protects the fucker who raped you."

"It does, yes. But it also preserves my peace. More importantly, my silence protects Paolo."

"He seems like he can handle himself."

"You don't know him like I do. When I say he'd kill the landlord, I mean it." Her expression darkens. "And he'd get a lot of joy in doing so."

That makes two of us.

I nod, remembering the look in his eyes when he threatened me. "He's pretty fierce about you."

Just like I am with Lena.

"That's because he was there every step of the way. He drove me to the clinic for the abortion I'd scheduled, braved the protesters outside and sat in the waiting room with me, pretending to be my partner so I wouldn't be alone." She stares at her fish tank for a moment, like the pair of angelfish swimming around are also part of our conversation. "It's an impossible choice to have to make. I don't envy any woman put into that position, no matter the circumstances. For me, with my Roman Catholic upbringing, and all the societal stigmas surrounding it, the guilt became suffocating. I tried to dissociate from all that, you know, remind myself of the reason I was there, but I couldn't. Some small, terrified part of me believed I was at fault for my rape."

"No. Absofuckinglutely not. I told myself the same thing, but it was only through years of therapy that I finally accepted I was the victim. It's really fucking hard for a man to call himself that. And for a long time, I felt weak and pathetic for *allowing* myself to be victimized. But you know what? I wasn't the coward who preyed upon a child. I was an innocent. The same goes for you. We are not responsible for the crimes committed against us."

"I know." She wipes her cheeks. "But at the time I couldn't get past the idea that maybe the pregnancy was God's way of punishing me. I was afraid of what might happen if I terminated it."

I clench my jaw, wishing I could go back in time and wipe those notions from her head. "*That*, right there, is why I have no use for religion."

"I get it. But you need to understand the way I was raised. I couldn't separate myself from what I'd learned. The guilt took over, and I decided at the last minute I couldn't go through with it."

I squeeze her hand and brush my thumb over her knuckles. "What happened next?"

"Paolo brought me home, fed me, and held me while I cried. He—and his family—supported me throughout the entire pregnancy. He comforted me for months afterward when I dealt with horrible postpartum depression. He's always been there, Garrett. After everything he's done for me, the *last* thing I want is to see him thrown behind bars for murder. The same goes for you. Don't bother asking for the piece of shit's name. Or any clues about him."

"So, you're saying justifiable homicide is out of the question then?" I press the issue because there's a primitive part of me that craves vengeance for her. And while my tone says the statement is only in jest, the opposite is true.

I am dead fucking serious.

Ella grips my arm. "*Yes.* You both mean too much to me to lose."

"Do you think Paolo assumed the guy was your boyfriend?"

"Probably."

"What about your mother? Did she ever realize you were telling the truth?"

She shrugs. "Who knows? She became as good as dead to me, which is why I told you she *was* dead. She tried to contact me a few times before I changed my phone number, but I haven't spoken to her since that day. As far as I know, she lives in Philadelphia. I'm so sorry I lied to you."

"Baby, please don't apologize. I understand."

"I tell most people I'm from California because it makes it easier to explain my solitude. My lack of family and friends makes more sense when they think I'm a West Coast transplant. Even Jake thinks I'm from Santa Barbara. Paolo is the only one who knows otherwise. And now you."

"He told me his brothers don't know about what happened to you."

"That's because he's a man of his word. He promised he'd keep my rape a secret from his family."

"Which one was your classmate?"

"Massimo."

"I kinda met him tonight."

"He's going through a breakup. We had a commiserative drink together."

"You said we need new rules, and I'm fine with that, but I think you should know we are *not* broken up."

"I know that, tesoro." She kisses my cheek. "But we were at the time."

"Semantics and technicalities."

She's silent for a moment, then reaches for her wooden box again. "I'm sorry I didn't mention my son. I didn't want you to judge my decision or equate it to what you went through." She hands me a black-and-white photo. Her name and the date stamp on top tell me the nebulous image is an ultrasound picture. Not that I have any experience with those.

I squint at the fetus's silhouette, and what appears to be his boy parts. "Holy shit. Is that his wiener?"

"You and your word choices," she says with a snort. "Yes. That image was captured the day I found out I was carrying a boy."

"Huh. That's gotta be weird."

Sadness floods her expression. "You have no idea what it's like to simultaneously love and hate the child growing inside you. I hated him for his father's actions, but part of me loved him because he was mine. I felt it every time I puked in the morning, with every flutter and kick in my belly. Even when the labor pains started, I couldn't escape the mixture of love and hate. It wasn't until they laid him on my chest, that love took over. I knew I loved him when I looked into his eyes. But I still couldn't keep him."

"Because you were afraid you wouldn't be a good mom?" My voice is as ragged as I feel.

"Yeah. I couldn't protect myself from what happened, so how could I take care of an innocent child? How could I trust myself not to resent him for what his father did? Or worse, what if his father tried to claim him? I was still a minor. I was terrified he'd be taken away by the state and potentially placed with an abusive family. Father Angelo helped arrange a private adoption with parishioners from Sacred Heart, one of Saint Jude's sister churches. He vouched for the couple and promised that my baby would be in good hands. I've never met them. I don't even know who they are. It's better that way."

"Why?"

"I would've found a way to keep tabs on him. Maybe even tried to be part of his life. He deserved a clean break, and I truly believed the separation was the healthiest option for me. I wouldn't be able to move past my trauma if I had to stare into his eyes each day. I did what I thought best for my child—and me—but it wasn't until after the nurses brought him to his new parents, that I realized how fucking wrong I was. I'll never move beyond what happened to me. And I'll never stop aching for the little boy I gave up." She holds her hand over her mouth to stifle a sob. "I was so stupid, Garrett."

I pull her into my lap, and she buries her face in my chest. Her body shakes with her sobs, each one stronger than the last. I tighten my arms around her, wishing I could take her pain away. How could I have compared her to my mother?

"You're a good mom, Ella. You're selfless, strong, and courageous. I love you, and I'm proud of the woman you are." I kiss the top of her head and run my fingers through her hair.

I didn't think it was possible to feel any more connected to her than I did yesterday. Until she laid herself bare for me tonight. Now I know why the universe brought us together.

Eventually, her tears slow. Her shuddered breaths even out, and she finally looks up at me with swollen red eyes.

I cup her face and use my thumbs to brush her tears away. "Thank you for telling me."

"I'm sorry I didn't tell you sooner."

"It's okay. Everything makes sense, and I understand why you made the choices you did. I will never be able to apologize enough for how I reacted last night, but I hope you know how sorry I am."

"I do."

"Good." I smooth the hair back from her forehead. "I'm curious why the uterus that housed you during your formative months found it necessary to show up last night."

She hands me another batch of folded papers. "To give me this."

Fifty-Seven

A startled rooster, a coincidence, and an affirmation

Ella

Garrett's reaction to my mother's letter is even stronger than Paolo's. He drops the pages and crushes me to his chest like his embrace can change my potentially faulty genetics.

"I can't believe this." His tortured whisper breaks my heart. "I won't lose you, Ella. I don't give a fuck who or what thinks otherwise."

I rub my hands up and down his back. "I don't know anything for sure. And even if I *do* have the mutated gene, it's *not* necessarily a death sentence. Cancer would be a risk, not a guarantee. I may have the mutation and still be perfectly fine."

That's the narrative Paolo repeated while we did our research. It's the mantra I've recited in my head all day. I'm still not sure I believe it, but it's helpful to cling to hope in a sea of uncertainty.

"When will you know?"

"Paolo and I made a ton of phone calls today. We figured out my insurance coverage and reached out to all the covered breast doctors. The earliest appointment we could snag is eight weeks from now."

"Eight fucking weeks?" He knots his hands in his hair. "Are you kidding me?"

"I wish I were, but I'm not. I won't have any answers until after Valentine's Day."

"Why the fuck aren't there any appointments sooner than that?"

"I don't know."

"Lena has connections at New York General. She knows tons of people. I'm sure she can call in some favors." He yanks his phone from his pocket and sends her a text.

I cup his jaw. "Listen, I don't want this to stress you out."

He blinks rapidly, cocking his head to the side like a startled rooster. "What makes you think I'm stressed?"

"Call it a hunch." I walk over to the Christmas tree and retrieve his unopened gift, placing it in his lap. "Take a deep breath and open your present."

"You want me to think about wrapping paper when the woman I love is at risk?"

"No. I want you to be strong for me. I need you to hold me together when I feel like falling apart. Steady me when my mind spins out of control. I can't spend the next eight weeks curled up beneath my blankets dreading a lab test that could change my life. I need to *live*. Right now. And I need you to help me."

"How?"

"Occupy me. Tell me everything will be okay. Kiss me senseless. Make me laugh. Make love to me." I wrap my arms around myself, forcing a calm I don't feel. "I need you to be my spine, Garrett. Keep me on my feet when I feel like crumbling."

"I can do that." He presses his hand to his chest. "I *will* do that for you. And no matter what the outcome is, I won't leave your side."

"Thank you." I point to his gift. "Open it before I start crying again."

He slides his finger beneath the paper's edge and unwraps it, his eyes widening when he realizes what he's holding. "You made this for me?"

"Yes. It's like a combination of a fancy scrapbook and a coffee-table book, but you can put it wherever you want. All the pictures are ones I took on our upstate adventure. There are a few of yours in there too."

Some photographs are in black and white, others in vivid color. Each one has a caption describing the picture and how I felt the moment it was taken.

"I absolutely love it, Ella. It's perfect. Thank you so much." He leans in and kisses me, his touch so tender I could weep. He stares into my eyes after he breaks the kiss. "I'm about to blow your mind, Cupcake. Seriously. Wait until you understand what I'm talking about." He releases me and rushes over to snag the other gift. His smile stretches ear to ear as he places it in my lap. "Open it and get ready for some freaky-deaky soul mate stuff."

I peel back the paper and gasp. "Oh my God."

"Right?"

Our gifts are identical in theme, except this coffee-table book consists of his artwork instead of photographs.

I turn the pages, awestruck by his talent. He cataloged our adventure in charcoal and rich, colored pencil. Pastels and oil paints. He presented everything with the sophistication only a graphic designer is capable of. The cover boasts a cupcake so realistic I could lick it. His captions are a compilation of funny quotes, suggestive comments, and anecdotes about our time together.

"This is beautiful. I love it so much, tesoro. I can't believe we gave each other the same gift."

Garrett tilts my chin up, pinning me with his golden gaze. "I can. After all the little coincidences, it doesn't surprise me one bit. What does shock me though, is the depth of my feelings for you. I didn't know I could love someone like this."

"Like what?" I ask because my heart needs the affirmation.

He rests his forehead against mine. "Like you were made to save me from myself."

THE END

~Stay tuned for more Garrett and Ella in *Prodigy*~

Playlist for Masquerade

"Mysterious Ways" by U2

"Come Here Boy" by Imogen Heap

"The Warmth" by Incubus

"Eyes on Fire" by Blue Foundation

"Tunnel Vision" by Justin Timberlake

"Secret" by Maroon 5

"Oh My God" by Adele

"I Want You" by Third Eye Blind

"Toxic Pony" by ALTÉGO, Britney Spears, & Ginuwine

"S&M" by Rihanna

"Sacrifice" by Black Atlass (feat. Jessie Reyez)

"God is a Woman" by Ariana Grande

"There's Nothing Holding Me Back" by Shawn Mendes

"Nasty Naughty Boy" by Christina Aguilera

"Gorilla" by Bruno Mars

"High" by Whethan & Dua Lipa

"Lion Eyes" by Beth // James

"Mercy" (acoustic version) by Shawn Mendes

"Mercy on Me" by Christina Aguilera

"No Light, No Light" by Florence + The Machine

"Ocean Eyes" by Billie Eilish

"Dive" by Ed Sheeran

"Crucify" by Tori Amos

"Bad Reputation" by Shawn Mendes

"Let You Love Me" by Rita Ora

"Why Should I Worry" by Billy Joel

"Hunger" by Florence + The Machine

"Wild Love" (acoustic version) by James Bay

"Love So Soft" by Kelly Clarkson

"Power Over Me" by Dermot Kennedy

"Peer Pressure" by James Bay (feat. Julia Michaels)

"Easy On Me" by Adele

"Outgrown" by Dermot Kennedy

"Wicked Game" by Grace Carter

"Train Wreck" by James Arthur

"St. Jude" by Florence + The Machine

"Power" by Isak Danielson

"Us" by James Bay & Alicia Keys

"Redemption" by Dermot Kennedy

"Remedy" by Adele

"Wild Love" by James Bay

Other Books

Compass Series

True North

North Star

Horizon

Symphony (forthcoming)

Title TBD (forthcoming)

Prodigy Series

Masquerade

Prodigy (forthcoming)

Supernova (forthcoming)

Standalone

Afterglow

Devil in the Details

Thanks so much for reading! It means the world to me. If you enjoyed *Masquerade*, please leave me a review.

Stay tuned for *Prodigy*, book 2 in the Prodigy Series.

Keep watch for *Symphony*, book 4 in the Compass Series.

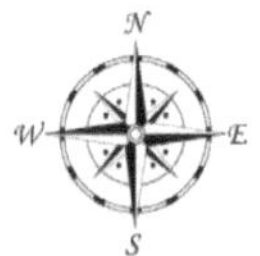

Please visit my website and subscribe to my newsletter for updates and new releases.

Join my readers' group on Facebook: Aria Wyatt's Speakeasy
www.facebook.com/groups/ariawyattsspeakeasy

About the Author

Aria Wyatt is a pharmacist mom who spends the inhumane predawn hours with a cup of coffee and her laptop, gleefully indulging in her passion for romance. Her novels range in heat from steamy to scorching, and she doesn't shy away from writing flawed characters with real life issues.

She resides with her husband and two children in New York's picturesque Hudson Valley, near the Catskills and iconic Woodstock. The avid reader balances marriage, motherhood, her pharmacist career, and her romance author dream. When not writing, she dabbles in photography, using the natural beauty of the region to her advantage. She's a self-proclaimed cat lady who cannot live without coffee, chocolate, music, and books.

Author of *True North* and the Compass Series, Aria has a soft spot for those who are searching, yearning, and ultimately, finding. Whether on a mission to find themselves, find love, find forgiveness or solace, she believes the answer is out there somewhere.

"Journey to Love."

Author's Note

Garrett's character first came to me while I was writing *True North* back in 2018. His voice was *screaming* to be heard. So much so, I included his point of view in Wes and Lena's story. I saw him almost as clearly as if it were his book, and I had to *force* myself to rein in my enthusiasm. I knew he'd get his moment to shine, but I had to wait. I HATE waiting. <Insert foot-stomping> I wanted to write his story right then and there. Naturally, I made him an integral part of *North Star* because I couldn't help myself. I was thrilled to discover his heroine's identity at the end of that book, but I never expected Ella to be as mysterious to me as she was to Garrett. No joke, she was a fucking challenge. The most difficult character I've written to date.

I knew and loved Garrett, but Ella didn't want me to know her. Like, at all. She hid behind a mask, and no matter what I did, I couldn't connect with her. That disconnect bled into the words I wrote, and everything about this book felt off.

Character development is a fundamental part of my writing process. I like to consider it one of my strengths. Imagine my frustration when I couldn't decode the heroine *I* created. My productivity came to a screeching halt. My enthusiasm for this story, these characters, dried up. When I tried to force it, Ella retreated deeper into herself, and I began to doubt my story-telling abilities. As I'm sure my writer friends will attest, self-doubt is a nasty bitch.

Masquerade taught me that forcing my creativity is a surefire way to shut it down. It was only when I stepped back for a hefty chunk of time that I was able to refill my creative well and reignite my passion for Garrett and Ella's story. I do my best thinking in the shower—weird, I know—and one morning I had such an incredible Ella epiphany, I got shampoo in my eyes. While they stung like a bitch, I was all smiles on my way out the door because I finally felt a spark. I was *excited* to write—something that hadn't happened in far too long. I listened to a random Spotify playlist on my way to work that day. There was one song that made me pull over and just . . . *vibe*. It was the acoustic version of "Wild Love" by James Bay. I listened to it on repeat all the way to the pharmacy. And again, on my way home, ten hours later.

That day was a turning point for me. All of the missing puzzle pieces seemed to magically appear and fit themselves together. Best of all, "Ella the Enigma" finally removed her cloak. Imagery danced in my mind. Cupcakes.

Castles. Mirrors and clocks. I got up at 3 a.m. the following morning to write. The words flowed out of me. I was at work later that day, sipping my coffee in between checking prescriptions, when another plot bunny bounced through my brain. (I keep scrap paper nearby for those moments.) When I picked up my phone—which I was using as a paperweight—to grab a piece of paper, I glanced at the screen to discover it was 11:11. Something clicked in my head. It felt momentous, so I treated it as such. Listen, I'm a sucker for serendipity and happenstance. I adore those freaky coincidences that raise the hairs on my arms. I honestly cannot tell you how many times I've peeked at the time to discover it's 11:11. It's weird, and sometimes feels impossible, but IT HAPPENS ALL THE TIME. I like to think of it as a sign of encouragement from the universe. A little "atta girl" kick in the ass to keep me writing.

As I mentioned above, I hate waiting. I'm sure my readers aren't fond of waiting either. I realize it's been over a year since my last release, and I'm truly sorry for the delay. The thing is, I refuse to rush a book. I simply won't do it. I owe it to my readers, my characters, and myself to give each story the time it deserves. As I discovered with this one, some books—and characters—need more time to percolate. Thank you for your patience.

Acknowledgements

I always panic when it comes time to write this section because I worry about accidentally forgetting someone. There are so many people who've had an impact on my author journey. It's difficult to narrow down the list, but I'm going to try to keep it specific to this book. Here goes:

Jen Liese, you are an angel. I'm blessed to have you in my life with your megaphone and pom-poms. Your friendship, support, and endless encouragement mean the world to me. I love YOU more.

Thank you to my beta reader author friends who always give me constructive feedback and encouragement. You're all amazing and I adore you. (Not everyone got to read this one ahead of time because I was riddled with self-doubt, but I'll do better next time.) **Liz Schille** and **Cassandra Cripps**, I appreciate you more than you know! Thank you for your helpful suggestions and the much-needed confidence boost.

A huge thanks goes out to my friend **Krystal Dixon**, who's been salivating for Garrett's story since reading *True North*. Your feedback was invaluable, and the tweaks you suggested are *chef's kiss* perfect. Thank you for your enthusiastic support.

Claudia Fosca Stahl, I'm so grateful to have *met* you through Sarina. I truly appreciate you taking the time to read *Masquerade* (and all my other books). Your opinion means a lot to me, and I was beyond thrilled when you loved this one.

To my editor, **Eve Arroyo**, thank you for everything. Your feedback and comments in my manuscripts always make me smile. When you said this was my "best book yet," I knew my months of thinking (and rethinking) weren't in vain.

To my proofreaders, **Virginia Tesi Carey**, and **Rosa Sharon** of **My Brother's Editor**, thank you for catching the small stuff.

To **Stacey Blake** of **Champagne Book Design**, as always, thank you for the beautiful book innards and your endless patience.

To my cover designer, **Lori Jackson**, you deserve a medal for putting up with all of my tweaks. Thank you for bringing my vision to life.

To **Jean Woodfin** of **JW Photography**, thank you for all your help with image selection. **Dan Rengering**, thanks for letting me use your face. I hope you don't mind that we gave you freaky eyes.

A huge thank you to my publicist, **Linda Russell** of **Foreword PR & Marketing**. You always know when to check in on me and give me those virtual kicks in the ass I so desperately need now and then. I appreciate the handholding too. Your support and encouragement help heal the self-doubt boo-boos.

To the bloggers and bookish peeps of Romancelandia, thank you for going out of your way to spread the word. Self-promotion makes my skin crawl, so I truly appreciate every one of you. I see you, **Kelly B.**, **Mikayla S.**, **Katie P.**, **Stacy C.**, **Krystal D.**, and the countless others who have taken a chance on me.

To all of **my amazing author friends**, you inspire me. Keep writing.

To my author bestie, **Kristie Wolf**, I've said it before, and I'll say it again: We've got this. I love you and I'm so happy to have you in my life!

Thank you to **my husband and children** for being supportive and patient with me. I love you so much.

Lastly, thank you to **my readers** for connecting with my words and characters. (And for your patience while I take for-fucking-ever to write my books.) I couldn't do this without you!

Much love,